Maraakus felt a sudden chill as the hair on his neck lifted. The sight of the big dog fleeing in terror seemed unnatural.

He backed slowly against the trunk of a thick oak tree and heard a heavy body moving through the bushes. With the tree protecting his back, he fixed his eyes on the thicket and saw a slight movement to his left—a pale, vaporous shadow drifting low across the ground. Then he saw Lannon lying on his back, his legs under a small bush, a gaping hole in his chest. The strange shadow was steam rising from the man's opened body.

Maraakus leaned against the tree and breathed deeply; his heart pounded and his legs trembled—more from anger than fear. Then something moved closer, breaking branches and snapping dead limbs underfoot, circling to his left. The sound of slow, heavy breathing came from the thicket, accompanied by a low, hissing sound.

Maraakus gripped his sword tightly. What little visibility he had left was reduced by a cold, stinging sweat that ran from his forehead into his eyes. Then he saw movement behind the thicket and stepped forward. "Let's see how you like the taste of cold steal!" he shouted. "Come on! You won't find me as easy as the others!"

Larry Elmore
and
Robert Elmore

RUNES OF AUTUMN

First Printing: July 1996
Printed in the United States of America.
Library of Congress Catalog Card Number: 95-62241

9 8 7 6 5 4 3 2 1

ISBN: 0-7869-0504-2
8256XXX1501

TSR, Inc.
201 Sheridan Springs Road
Lake Geneva, WI 53147
U.S.A.

TSR Ltd.
120 Church End, Cherry Hinton
Cambridge CB1 3LB
United Kingdom

To our families, both immediate and extended,
for their unfailing support and encouragement during the
writing of this book.

To our many friends, for the patient reading and valuable
suggestions. You know who you are. Thank you.
We are deeply grateful.

To Jo Gregory and Kevin Clark, for their special assistance
during the early stages of this book.

To my wife, Tennis.
To my granddaughters, Kirstin and Jennifer, for whom this
world is new and each day is filled with true magic.
—Robert Elmore

To Betty, my wife.
To my daughter, Jennifer, and my son, Jeremy.
Thanks for loving and understanding a husband and father
who spends so many hours in the worlds of art and fantasy.
—Larry Elmore

AND TO YOU, OUR READERS,
WE SINCERELY HOPE YOU ENJOY OUR STORY.
—Larry & Robert Elmore

PROLOGUE

After a quick, apprehensive look behind him, Andor dropped to his hands and knees and plunged headfirst into the bearbriar thickets, ignoring the sharp thorns that pierced his arms and face, and the small rocks that sliced his hands and knees.

A limb snagged his rucksack. He lunged forward, digging his toes into the moist earth, grimacing as the thin strap cut painfully into his shoulder. A second vicious jerk parted the worn leather and he scrambled forward, leaving the old pouch behind. Moments later, he emerged on the hunting trail beyond the dense tangle of brush.

Jumping to his feet, Andor wiped his eyes with the tail of his tunic and looked south across the old planting fields. The new bridge over the Dove was still visible in the last dim light of evening. Beyond was the village—and help . . .

"Run!" Keam had shouted. *"Get help! Don't look back!"*

Andor had obeyed Keam's order. Only now his brother's anguished screams seemed to echo in his ears as he fled down the narrow mountain path, flinching from trees that seemed to reach out with crooked fingers, cringing past familiar boulders that now loomed up to enfold him in some horrible darkness—a limitless, ghastly black void that only an eleven-year-old boy can imagine when he is terrified and utterly alone.

A rock turned under foot. He staggered, tripped over a root and sprawled facedown on a clump of arrowgrass. Then he was back on his feet, stumbling, fighting to maintain his balance, only vaguely aware of the slender, black-tipped arrowgrass cane buried in his side. He ignored it like he ignored the burning in his lungs and the leafless branches lashing him across the face. These things did not matter; his world had turned upside down when Keam slid backward into that dark hole. And worse yet, Andor blamed himself.

"Keeeaam!" he shouted, then increased his pace. "I'll get help, Keam! Can you hear me? It's not supposed to be like this! It was me that followed the wounded rabbit into the thicket! It's all my fault! *Keam!"*

Suddenly the footpath ended and he ran out into an overgrown planting field bordering the river. Once more he paused to call his brother's name, but there was no answer, only the continuous moaning of the wind in spindly trees and the harsh rattle of arrowgrass canes. He began to laugh, unaware that the sounds coming from his throat were shrill, hysterical.

"You're not dead, Keam!" he shouted, between bouts of laughter. "This is just one of your jokes! You're trying to scare me!"

He leaned against a tree to catch his breath and his mood changed to anger. "Damn it!" he shouted. "I've had enough! Cut it out!"

There was no answer.

"You win, Keam! I was really scared. Come on out! I can beat you to the bridge."

Only the wind answered, soughing softly in the trees and thickets. Still, Andor refused to admit that his brother might be dead.

"I know what you're doing, Keam!" Andor called. "You're standing out there in the dark, watching me. Are you trying hard not to laugh out loud? Answer me, Keam!"

Andor shivered in the cold evening air. Tomorrow we'll be hunting, camping, and working together, he told himself. Nothing can separate us for long. Not that dark hole in the mountain or the small bag of coins in our rucksack. And certainly not some pretty trinket like this old amulet.

Now, realizing he still clutched the amulet tightly in his right fist, he opened his hand. In his disturbed state of mind, perhaps he only imagined that the pink stone sparkled at the end of its golden chain, but he was suddenly consumed by rage and revulsion. Somehow the amulet was to blame for every misfortune that had befallen them that day. It was the amulet that had separated him from Keam.

"I begged you not to take this damned thing, Keam!" he screamed. Then he raised his arm over his head and flung the amulet into the darkness.

At the same time he heard something in the undergrowth off to his left. He listened carefully, waiting as the sound moved in his direction.

"Keam? Thank the gods!" he shouted, unable to contain his joy and relief. "That is you, isn't it?"

He was answered with the sounds of splintering brush, loud snorts, and heavy breathing. Something much larger and heavier than Keam advanced through the dense undergrowth with ponderous, deliberate footsteps.

Like some exhausted, terrified animal pursued by ravenous

hounds, Andor wheeled on tired legs and set off in a staggering run toward the new bridge. A hard blow on his left shoulder knocked him off his feet and a heavy body that reeked with a foul, evil-smelling odor crushed him into the damp earth.

The boy's hoarse screams were silenced by a sharp, momentary pain on his forehead and a deeper, ripping pain in his chest. Then, as the pain stopped and his terror faded, Andor felt himself sliding into a warm and peaceful place . . .

CHAPTER ONE

Fergus tossed the last few sticks of split oak on the pile, then measured the stack of firewood with a critical eye. Barely enough to last through tomorrow, he decided. Keam knows it's the height of the killing season, that the rendering fires burn day and night. Frustrated and angry, Fergus walked out to the Northern Road and looked toward the village, fully expecting to see Keam's loaded cart bouncing over the rutted road with young Andor seated at his side. The road was empty.

Perhaps one of them is ill, he thought. Still, the other boy would surely have sent word, or talked a friend into helping with the delivery. At any rate, Fergus thought, I'll have to make arrangements for firewood no later than noon tomorrow. With or without Keam.

"Very strange," Fergus muttered to himself. "Very strange, indeed."

Outside his sleeping space in the storage shed, Fergus kept a basin for bathing. As usual, he found it filled with warm water, and a cup of soap had been placed beside it. A large linen cloth hung from a wooden peg near the door. Through the open doorway of the smoke-filled rendering house, he could see the huge, iron caldrons of bubbling fat suspended over the cooking fires. He could not see Zandria, the old woman who tended the rendering pots, but his supper sat on a rough board shelf outside the rendering house door. It was wrapped with a white cloth and his dented, copper mug stood beside it.

Zandria had married late in life but soon found herself with a son and a daughter, both of whom died in infancy. Her husband was a soldier, and he died on the frozen plains of the Tarbisu Steppes during the infamous Fourteenth Campaign. When the wars ended, Fergus stayed on in Stridgenfel, and like Zandria, found work at the slaughterhouse, tending the iron kettles of boiling fat and stoking the hickory smoking fires. The hard labor and long days hardly mattered to Fergus, but they had aged Zandria beyond her fifty-four years.

Fergus and Zandria had a sort of bantering relationship that provided them both with some slight relief from the bone-wearying dullness of their work. Hearing the way they talked to each other, few guessed they shared not only a mutual respect, but a genuine friendship. In fact, Fergus had long suspected that Zandria would have welcomed a different kind of attention, but at nearly sixty-three he considered himself too old to shoulder the weight of such a responsibility. So he cared for her like a younger sister and she returned his mild affections as best she knew how.

After carrying the old linen cloth, the cup of soap, and basin of water inside the shed, Fergus stripped off his clothes. He was thin to the point of emaciation with long, sinewy arms and legs. An angry red scar started low on his left side and ran to the center of his back—a memento from a sword thrust—and he was missing the little finger on his right hand. His hair was full and white, falling long to his shoulders, and he carried himself with a pronounced stoop. Only his sharp, dark, penetrating eyes hinted at the vigor of his youth.

When he'd finished bathing, Fergus dried his body with the linen cloth and dressed. Carrying his worn woolen cloak, he pulled the door shut behind him, walked to the rendering house, and took down his supper. He could see Zandria sitting on a low stool, resting her head in her left hand and staring into the flickering flames. Firelight reflected from beads of sweat on her forehead and tinged her graying hair with traces of red.

"Good night, Old Woman," he said softly. "Thank you." As usual, she gave no reply but he knew she heard him. Carrying his supper in one hand, and his mug of ale in the other, he set off toward the market square.

He entered the village through the north gate and walked slowly past the homes of the more prosperous merchants and property owners. His destination was Stridgenfel Tower, a tall stone edifice that had served as a lookout post during the many years of war. The tower had been his last posting as a soldier before finally being mustered out of the king's army just over three years ago.

At the market square he turned left, walked past the village inn and continued south to the tower, where he sat down in his usual spot with his back resting against the foundation stones. There he unwrapped his supper of bread and sausages.

Stridgenfel was surrounded by a strong, high wall. At its center stood the tower, capped with a delicately arched colonnade. The village was a convenient stopover for the king's border patrols, used as a place to rest and gather fresh provisions. It was also a favored place to get mindlessly drunk and brawl with the younger townsmen over the real or imagined affections of the local tavern tarts. Even a small village like Stridgenfel had solicitous young women who labored diligently to separate soldiers from their meager wages.

Situated directly astride the Northern Road, the village of Stridgenfel was strategically located four days' ride south of the ancient road known as the Serpent's Way, one mile on foot up a small tributary of the Opal River known as the River of the Dove. Local residents—of which there were fewer than three hundred—simply called it the Dove.

To the north, beyond the Serpent's Way, the lofty peaks of the snow-capped Guardian Mountains formed the northern border of Luwynn. Their cold, melted waters collected drop by drop into small rivulets and cascading creeks that flowed east and west from the summits. These collected streams flowed south, forming the two branches of the mighty Opal River that divided the Kingdom into three roughly triangular sections of forested mountains and fertile valleys.

Stridgenfel Valley lay in the northern triangle, bordered on the east by the Opal, and a series of towering sandstone bluffs. To the west, there was only the deep, primal wilderness of the Great Shadow Forest. At the southern end of the valley, nearly five miles from the village, rose the forested slopes of the Sleeping Sisters, a range of mountains deceptively benign in appearance, but exceedingly dangerous for the unwary traveler. The city of Koeinstadt was six days south on horseback, and it was another two days to Luwynnvale, the great capital city of the kingdom of Luwynn. Beyond Luwynnvale, somewhere in the searing sands of the Barrens—where only serpents and lizards could survive for long—lay the southern borders of the kingdom.

From his position at the base of the tower, Fergus ate his supper and rested while he observed the last of the day's market activities. Strangers traveling the Northern Road brought news from the outside world and he listened, absorbing it all without comment, until finally, as evening wore on, the merchants closed their stalls and wandered off to their homes or to the inn.

At sunset, when the night torch was placed in a bracket at the tower's base, the young boys of the village began to gather. Arriving individually, or in twos and threes, they formed a half circle on the ground in front of Fergus. For more than two years, weather permitting, he had entertained them on Fifth Day evening with old stories heard in his youth.

This was the time of evening Fergus liked best, a time between daylight and darkness when the torch made dancing reflections in the windows of the houses, and in the eyes of the boys who gathered close around him. But most of all, he knew it was a time when the eye could be tricked by strange night shadows. It was a time made for telling tales.

And as the shadows deepened and the red glow faded from the western sky, he would lean back against the base of the tower, sip his ale, and tell them stories from times long past, before the Mighty Wars, when elves, dwarves, dragons, and other exotic creatures lived side by side with humans. Stories of powerful wizards, spells of magic, and heroic quests to the far corners of the world.

As the stragglers arrived, he searched their ranks for Keam and Andor. If they fail to come, he decided, one of them is surely ill, and if they do come to hear the stories, then Keam will get a stern reminder of his duty. He's doing a man's job, and if he wishes to be treated like a man, he'll have to learn to act like a man. He took a long swallow from his mug and sat it on the ground.

"What story shall I tell this evening?" he asked, then clapped both hands over his ears and laughed. As expected, the children began to shout and argue, rather loudly, among themselves. By the time it was completely dark, Fergus had finished most of his ale, and the last few stragglers had arrived.

He waited patiently until the latecomers settled down, then asked, "Where are Keam and Andor?"

"Haven't seen them all day," a younger boy said.

"They're probably at home," one of the older boys guessed. "Maybe their mother won't let them out after dark." He snickered and a smattering of laughter ran through the group.

"Come on, Fergus," another said. "Tell us the one about Jodac and the Pinnacle."

Some of the children began to clap and chant, "Jodac! Jodac! Jodac!" But when Fergus raised both hands for silence, they settled quietly around him.

"Very well," he said. "The story tonight will be about Jodac and the Pinnacle." Then he leaned back against the tower and waited for the murmuring to stop.

A woman standing in the street looked in their direction. "Crazy old man," she muttered, shaking her head.

"And a fine evening on you, milady," Fergus replied. "Have you come to hear the stories, too? You're certainly welcome." He tilted his mug to his lips, then placed it back on the ground.

"Old drunk!" she sniffed. Shaking her head and muttering to herself as she walked away.

Fergus smiled and took another sip of ale from his battered copper mug. Then he began his tale, gesturing and speaking with a soft, animated voice. "A long time ago," he said, "before the Mighty Wars, when humans lived side by side with the ancient races, powerful wizards and terrible dragons were common in Stridgenfel Valley, and humans were . . ."

Slowly, with the skill of a born storyteller, old Fergus spun out the tale of Jodac, the evil wizard of Stridgenfel. And Rafin, the village catchpole, passing by on his evening security rounds, paused at the corner of the stables to listen.

"At last," Fergus was saying, "in despair at the cruelty of Jodac, the forest elves sent for the leaders of the valley dwarves. Together, they formed an alliance with the men of this village and sent word to Jodac, demanding the release of all his captives. But Jodac simply laughed, so hardened was his heart. 'This is my answer,' the evil wizard shouted. 'I hereby order that one hundred humans, two hundred forest elves, and three hundred valley dwarves be thrown to their deaths from the top of the Pinnacle! And may you forever remember this day!' And it was done."

An excited murmur rippled through the crowd of children.

Fergus pursed his lip and put on his best grim expression. "It must have taken them several days. I can hardly bear to think about it."

"What happened to the rest of the elves and dwarves?" asked one of the younger boys. "If there were so many of them, why don't we ever see any?"

"Oh, they're around, young man," Fergus declared quietly. "You never know if one is watching or not. But soon after Jodac's evil deed, they tore down their homes in the forest and destroyed their planting fields in the river valleys. They packed up all their possessions and moved far, far away. Some say into the Sleeping Sisters, or beyond the Guardian Mountains. Others say they went west, deep into the Great Shadow Forest, where they live to this very day."

"I don't believe in elves and dwarves," an older boy declared. "My father said they exist only in old legends. I don't know a single person who's ever seen one."

"Just shut up, Tarl," another boy shouted. "Listen to the story."

"But they did return, at least one time," a young boy named Palen argued. "Didn't they, Fergus?"

"Yes," Fergus replied. "One day, about a year after they moved away, thousands of forest elves and valley dwarves gathered in the fields north of the Dove and swarmed over the Pinnacle like angry hornets. They threw Jodac to his death, just as he had done to their people, and pulled down his stone keep and destroyed the only path up the Pinnacle. Not one trace of it has ever been found."

"Ha!" an older youth scoffed. "My father says you're a crazy old man, telling crazy old tales."

Fergus smiled. "Perhaps he's right." He picked up his cup and drained the last few drops onto his tongue. "But you'll recall my words," he admonished gently, "the next time you're alone, outside the village walls, and it starts to grow dark. You'll see that flicker of movement from the corner of your eye, just the smallest shifting of a shadow.

"Perhaps it's only the clouds playing tricks with the moonlight. Of course, it might well be something else. There's no way one can be absolutely certain unless. . . ."

His voice was soft, almost a whisper. "Well, we won't talk about that," he continued, "but we've all seen them, haven't we? Strange, ominous shapes that appear only when the moon is hidden behind strings of black clouds, and even the most familiar path seems forbidding and fraught with danger.

"And we've all heard those voices, haven't we? Those voices that call us by name from the gloom of the bearbriar thickets, or those soft, moaning sounds that you can sometimes hear out in the planting fields.

"Oh, people will tell you it's only the night wind blowing through the trees. Maybe they're right. And maybe not. Personally, I believe it's the angry, restless ghosts of Jodac's victims . . . all those poor humans, elves, and dwarves thrown to their deaths from the Pinnacle."

"Maybe even Jodac's ghost?" Palen asked.

"I never thought about that," Fergus said softly. "But I don't mind telling all of you that I shudder to think what might be lurking out there when the sun goes down and the fields are swallowed up in the cold blackness of night. Of course, there's one way to find out for sure . . . though I certainly don't recommend it."

"How?" Palen asked.

"By taking a walk around the Pinnacle," Fergus said. "A man could go alone on some cold, moonless night when the voices are whispering through the trees. I think all his questions might be answered. But I'll leave that up to one of you. I certainly won't be going."

He paused and there was only silence from the boys. Each was lost in his own thoughts. Fergus smiled, reluctant to break their reflective mood. "Anyway," he said loudly, "it's getting late. Run along home and take care not to encounter any evil mountain elves on your way."

The boys got slowly to their feet, laughing and talking about the old story. They milled about for a few moments, then formed into small groups and wandered off in different directions.

"Walk in the middle of the street!" Fergus called after them. "And stay clear of deep shadows. . . ."

Hearing soft laughter, Fergus turned to see Rafin leaning against the stable wall nearby, arms folded across his chest.

"That sounds like good advice," Rafin declared. "I may do the same. There's a strange scent on the wind tonight. . . ."

"No question about it," Fergus agreed. "Damned spooky. No telling what's out there in the darkness, watching for the unwary, waiting with sharp claws and bared teeth."

Rafin grinned and arched his brows. "Right you are," he agreed. "It's enough to make a man's hair stand on end."

He reached out to rattle the shutters on a merchant's stall, then kicked at the closed door. Satisfied that both were secured for the night, he clapped Fergus on the shoulder and walked away, chuckling to himself.

When Rafin was out of sight, Fergus picked up his supper dish and wrapping cloth. With his dented, copper mug dangling from one finger, he walked off toward the village inn, then stopped. There was still time for a measure of mulled wine before bed, but he decided to pay a visit to Keam and Andor's mother first. Perhaps she could shed some light on why the boys hadn't delivered his firewood.

At a small house not far from the Temple of Judbal, he knocked lightly on the door and heard the locking bolt as it was pulled back. A woman in a long brown robe opened the door.

"Fergus! What are you doing here?" she said, obviously surprised to see him standing on her doorstep. "I'm sorry. Won't you come in?"

"Best evening, Marrtee," Fergus replied. "I just stopped by to speak with Keam—the firewood, you know."

"He's not here. Neither is Andor. When I heard you knocking, I thought my sons had finally decided to come home."

"Then they . . . the boys haven't returned?" Fergus asked, aware of how lame his question must have sounded in light of what she had just told him; however, his attention was focused on the woman's face. She was obviously worried about her sons.

"They were supposed to be home by dark," she said. "If they're not home by morning, I was going to ask Rafin to go look for them."

"Oh, I wouldn't worry too much," he said, patting her on the shoulder, "You know how boys are when you turn them loose in the woodlands. Besides, they've stayed overnight in the beech groves many times."

"Yes, but not without telling me beforehand." She frowned and wiped at her eyes.

"Keam's a capable young man and a good woodsman—and he always watches out for his younger brother. I'll make you a promise, Marrtee. If my firewood is not being unloaded by sunrise, I'll go out there myself. You know I'll find them."

She smiled and nodded. "I'd be most grateful."

"Maybe I'll swat their backsides, too," he added. "Just a gentle reminder not to do this again. Now you get some rest and try not to worry."

After she closed the door, Fergus walked quickly back to the market square. The night sky was clear, the air was growing colder, and the thought of his warm cot in the storage shed was comforting. He pulled his cloak tighter around his thin body, then glanced up at the glittering stars and located the Bow-of-the-Hunter. He estimated the time of evening from its position in the sky, and quickened his steps toward the village inn.

Chapter Two

Like a drifting wisp of early morning fog, a figure emerged from the morning-damp woodlands of the Great Shadow Forest and walked slowly into a grassy clearing. He wore a hooded cloak of rough-spun woolen yarns, artfully dyed to blend with the sun-dappled shade of the thick woodlands. His body was lean and his shoulder length hair was thick and gray. He moved like a long-limbed man in his middle years.

In the center of the clearing, Grommdum climbed up onto a slab of dark granite known as the Weeping Stone. No one knew why it was so named, nor could anyone interpret the ancient symbols carved on its surface. Such knowledge was lost in the dim reaches of the past. Now the Weeping Stone was simply a place where one could find solitude, a place for quiet meditation.

Following a path worn by countless feet, Grommdum walked quickly up the slanting rock and seated himself on its very tip, some thirty feet above the grassy clearing. For a time he sat motionless, watching the morning breeze stir the bright autumn foliage. But at last, as if reluctant to begin some arduous task, he heaved a long sigh, then reached into a side pocket on his jerkin and took out two small cloth bags.

The first bag contained a chip of chalk-stone, which he used to draw a circle around himself. Then, while chanting softly, he opened the second bag and poured out four small piles of blue powder, one for each of the four winds. After blowing them away with a single puff of breath, he closed his eyes and waited, confident that the spell just cast would bring understanding of the worrisome sight observed for two consecutive days: a dark circle around the sun.

The air grew warmer. Morning dew dried on the Weeping Stone as the autumn sunlight heated the dark granite. Still Grommdum sat with closed eyes, motionless, drifting in a state of restful meditation, gradually absorbing the ebb and flow of the life-forces around him.

Suddenly, flinging up his hands, he recoiled as if from the threatening flash of a lightning bolt. But his fear was immediately replaced by a deep sense of warmth and well-being when a woman with silver hair stepped out of a swirling mist and fixed him with piercing blue eyes.

Grommdum, she said gently. *Like thy father before thee, I have need of thy services.*

Grommdum's eyes moved behind closed lids, following the image of his vision. He murmured softly, "Am I allowed to know your name?"

The shaggy brows above his closed eyes lifted. She did not speak, but he heard her voice within his mind. He lowered his head and raised one hand to his forehead in a traditional gesture of respect.

"The valley called Stridgenfel?" he said. "Yes. I know the place, but it is many leagues to the east."

The words sounded strangely flat to his ears and echoed back at him from different directions; he scarcely recognized the voice as his own.

Again he listened carefully as she spoke in his mind. When she finished, he heaved a deep sigh and shook his head.

"Many years have passed since I was a teaching Multan. Still, I will do as you have asked. But how shall I find this one who is to become my student?"

The woman in his vision smiled and a sign appeared before her, floating in the air.

Grommdum nodded. "No. I'll not forget," he promised. "There will be no delay."

The words "no delay" echoed on and on, becoming fainter and fainter in his ears, yet their meaning became deeply impressed on his mind. After a time, he was surprised to find himself watching a brightly colored caterpillar crawling resolutely up his arm. The creature paused for a moment, perhaps to decide if the climb was worth the effort, then dropped off. It landed on the Weeping Stone and marched steadily away, a small, undulating coil of black and yellow bristles.

Looking up, he noticed that the black circle surrounding the sun was no longer visible and wondered how long his vision had lasted. After stretching out his legs, he rubbed the stiffness from his wiry thighs, then proceeded to his calves, massaging them through the leather of his boots.

"I'm getting too old to sit like this," he told himself. "Surely, how one sits could not alter the results of a spell to any appreciable degree. I must remember to bring this up in Council."

That said, he shifted his traveling pouch to his left shoulder, stood, and retraced his steps down to the base of the Weeping Stone. With a last look westward, toward his simple home in the forest, he stepped down on the grass and set off at a brisk pace. Before him was the morning sun and the eastern horizon.

❧ ❧ ❧

"We don't need the entire village out here," Rafin said to the tallest woodcutter. "Take some men to the bridge and turn those people back. Don't let any more get across."

As the man hurried away, Rafin knelt beside the body of young Andor and tried desperately to ignore the pain in his stiff right leg. It had been badly broken nearly five years ago, and when it finally healed, it was some two inches shorter than his left, causing him to walk with a curious side to side movement. But he could move with surprising agility if necessary and wield a broadsword with astonishing speed and power.

Reaching out, he gently turned Andor onto his back. A woman clutched at her stomach, staggered backward, then sank slowly to her knees. Rafin closed his eyes and clenched his fists. As a hardened veteran, a survivor of more than thirty-five years of bitter campaigning in the Mighty Wars, he knew well what soldiers sometimes did to their enemies on the field of battle. Such actions had always troubled him; he considered them barbaric, unnecessary, and unprofessional. Moreover, this was not a field of battle, and the body before him was not that of a soldier or even a man. This was the mutilated body of a small, eleven-year-old boy.

As village catchpole, it was Rafin's sworn duty to maintain law and order. Until now, that consisted of little more than breaking up brawls at the village inn and minimizing theft by young boys who filched apples from the market stalls. There had never been such a senseless act of violence in Stridgenfel.

He looked up at the crowd gathered around him. Women cried on the shoulders of their husbands. Men stood with grim, frozen faces. The dead boy's mother, a tired and work-worn woman, lay weeping in the muddy field, pounding her bosom and tearing at her clothes and hair, while grieving daughters made efforts to comfort her. A few older children pushed their way forward, trying to see Andor's body between the legs of the adults.

Someone handed Rafin a blanket and he spread it near the body. Slipping his arms under Andor's legs and shoulders, Rafin placed him tenderly on the blanket. Hadrax, the village baker, reached down and picked up the boy. "I'll take him to Yettik," Hadrax said quietly.

Rafin nodded. "Tell him not to do anything until I get there. I want to make a closer examination of the . . . of Andor."

Hadrax gave a quick nod and walked away toward the new bridge, followed by Andor's family and nearly all of the villagers. Soon, only Fergus and two other men remained in the field with Rafin and Rafin's young niece, Alyna.

"Keam is missing?" Rafin asked.

Fergus nodded. "Yesterday, when the boys failed to return from a hunting trip, I became worried. They missed their firewood deliveries—"

"That's not like Keam," Rafin interrupted.

Fergus frowned. "It certainly isn't. This morning, I went out to track the boys. I found Andor here, but there's no sign of Keam. You know those boys were nearly inseparable."

"Let's spread out and search this field," Rafin ordered. "Alyna will stay with me. I want you on the north end of the field, Fergus. Kavius and Rohmeth, cover the middle."

The three men began their search through the thick tangles of brush, while Rafin and Alyna made their way to the south side of the field and began walking along the edge, paying particular attention to the area close to the river.

After walking a short distance, Alyna stopped. "Uncle Rafin!" she shouted. "I've found something!"

Rafin hurried down to the river bank and pushed his way through the bushes. Alyna was standing in a flattened circle of broken brush some twelve to fifteen feet wide. He walked carefully around the area but saw nothing that explained what he was seeing. "Very curious," he remarked. "What is it?".

Alyna tilted her head and shielded her eyes from the morning sunlight. Then she turned slowly to her left, walked down to the water's edge and pointed.

"There's something . . . there . . . on that tree limb."

Rafin stared but saw only the smooth surface of the river and a pattern of widening ripples where it flowed around a naked tree limb snagged in the river's shallows.

"I'll get it," Alyna said.

After removing her leather slippers, she gathered her robe about her knees and stepped into cold water that rose just above her ankles. She leaned down and picked something from the limb. As she waded back, the object flashed in the morning sunlight. "Here," she said and dropped it onto his outstretched palm.

Rafin turned the object over in his fingers, studying it carefully. The stone was a clear pink color, surrounded with a mounting of thin, hammered gold. The links of the chain were fashioned from gold wire that had been rolled and flattened, giving the chain a curious, silky texture.

"What is it?" she asked.

The pink stone winked in the morning sunlight and Rafin shrugged. "It must have washed out of the fields during a heavy rain."

He turned the amulet with his fingers. It was quite common for the village children to find old relics left by the valley's early settlers. Some believed they were evidence of ancient races who lived in the valley before the coming of humankind. Usually, old tools and weapons were found, but jewelry had been picked up from time to time.

"I saw it shining in the sunlight," Alyna explained, obviously pleased by her discovery. "Yet I got the strangest feeling when I picked it up . . . and when I looked into that pale pink stone . . ." she shook her head. "I'm sure it's just my imagination. But the amulet is beautiful, isn't it?"

"Yes," Rafin agreed, though he actually thought the amulet rather plain. He handed it back to her. "You keep it. Wear it when you feel like dressing up." He smiled as she dropped it into the pocket of her robe and sat to put on her slippers.

Rafin loved his niece dearly, but he'd been forced to admit that she was somehow different from the other young women in Stridgenfel. First, her father had gone off to the wars, and his exact fate was never learned. Then her mother, Kirastin, Rafin's only sister, died from the vomiting sickness when Alyna was only five. And the following year, while he was away fighting the Mighty Wars, Rafin's wife, Jenfirle, succumbed to the same vile plague, leaving only his aged mother, Sheya, to care for young Alyna. Sheya not only reared the child with love and tenderness, but taught her to read and gave her instructions in some of the ancient healing arts. Sheya died four years ago, less than a year after Rafin returned from the wars, just before Alyna turned seventeen.

With the death of his mother, Rafin had expected Alyna to marry within a year. The young men of Stridgenfel came in droves to her door, bearing gifts and whispering sweet promises. But Alyna turned inward, contenting herself with caring for their home, reading her books and practicing the healing arts for the villagers. She had become a beautiful young woman with a maturity far beyond her years, possessed of a self-confidence that emanated from some deep, inner strength even Rafin couldn't fathom.

Fergus and his companions were approaching from their left. Rafin waited until they were within earshot and called out to them. "Did you find anything?"

"Nothing," Fergus shouted back. "Some broken bushes at the end of the field, but no sign of Keam."

"I found the younger boy's tracks in the western end of the field," one man shouted. "Looks like he came running down from the slope below the Pinnacle."

Taking Alyna by the hand, Rafin helped her up the riverbank

and onto level ground. "Well, we didn't find any trace of Keam, either," he told them.

"Maybe he's still alive," Kavius said hopefully. He glanced at Fergus, but the old hunter didn't speak.

"After I take a closer look at Andor's body," Rafin said, "we'll organize a real search party."

Fergus led the small group through the field. They crossed over the bridge and began following the road back to the village. Alyna and Rafin followed some distance behind.

"Do you think he's really alive?" Alyna asked.

"If he's alive, we'll find him," he said. "Did you notice anything strange about the marks on Andor's forehead?"

"Marks?"

"Yes. Deep cuts, in an oval pattern?"

"They weren't just scratches?"

"Maybe," Rafin said quietly. "But if they're not, I may have to send for Maraakus. Andor may have been killed by an Ammak scouting party."

"Ammaks!"

"*Shhh!*" Rafin told her. "Not so loud. I know it sounds crazy, but I saw marks like this on the Tarbisu Steppes."

"Then send for Maraakus. Even if you're wrong, he'll understand."

Rafin smiled. "No," he said, shaking his head. "He'd not appreciate me raising a false alarm. But if I'm right, I can't fight a pack of crazed Ammaks alone. That's why I want a closer look at Andor's body. I have to be absolutely certain about this."

They stopped at the north gate and she stretched up on her toes to kiss him on his bearded cheek. "You'll make the right decision," she assured him.

"Don't mention any of this, Alyna. I could be wrong."

"I won't," she promised.

At the home of Yettik, Rafin found Andor's body, untouched, on a table in the back room. He unfolded the blanket and began a closer inspection of the body. A portion of the boy's right thigh was missing, and what appeared to be bite marks were plainly visible on the left hip. But what arrested Rafin's attention was the gaping hole in the boy's chest. He had been slit from neck to navel; his organs had been jerked from his body and now hung over his right side in a mass of dirt, dead leaves, and dried blood.

Rafin stepped back and nodded, then watched as Yettik carefully replaced the organs in the boy's body cavity. Looking up from his work, Yettik frowned. "What kind of animal tears open its prey and eats only the heart?"

"By all the gods. . . ." Rafin muttered, rubbing his eyes with the tips of his fingers. "Are you certain it was an animal?"

"No question about it," Yettik declared. He pointed to a gaping wound on Andor's right leg. "But I've never seen bites like this before. This animal is *big*."

Rafin pointed to the boy's forehead. "Clean away that blood. Let's see what's under it."

Yettik fetched a pan of water and sponged away the blood, revealing a series of cuts above the dead boy's brows.

The pattern is certainly oval-shaped, Rafin thought. Then again, they might be only deep scratches. It's hard to tell.

"How long has the boy been dead?"

Yettik shrugged. "Hard to say."

"Your best guess?"

"A day. Not more than two. May I prepare him for the funeral pyre?" Yettik asked.

"Yes. If the family can't pay you, I'll bear the cost."

"There'll be no cost, Rafin. This boy could have been one of my own. I have two nearly the same age."

"I'm certain the family will be grateful," Rafin said. "Now, old friend, I must ask you to do something else for me. I want you to say nothing about a missing heart, or these marks on his forehead. Such information will only add to the family's grief."

Yettik gave him a puzzled look. "Very well," he replied.

He clapped Yettik on the shoulder and walked out of the house, leaving the old undertaker to his work.

At the village slaughterhouse, Rafin found Fergus sitting on the steps of the deserted killing platform, patiently whetting the steel points on his arrows. The old man's left thumb was bleeding from testing the razor-sharp edges. Rafin picked up an arrow and inspected the newly sharpened point. "What are you doing?" he asked quietly.

Fergus paused but did not look at him. "I'm going hunting," he said, resuming his task.

Rafin sighed. "Yettik thinks an animal killed that boy," he said. "Is that what you think?"

The sharpening stone made soft, rasping sounds against the steel point. "That's exactly what I think," Fergus replied. "Andor was partially . . . eaten." The soft scraping sounds stopped for just a moment, then they resumed, slow and deliberate. "You know that."

"Something fed on the boy," Rafin admitted. "Judging from the bites, it was certainly large. But there's nothing around here that big. I just don't know."

"Ever seen a northern bear? Well, I have. They stand three times taller than a man. I once saw the body of an Ammak— what was left of it—who'd been half-eaten by one. Andor's body looked the same."

Rafin arched his brows. "Doesn't sound like something an intelligent man would hunt alone."

Fergus smiled. "We both know I'm the one to go out there first," he said. "And if we're going to find that animal, we must act immediately. One good rainstorm and we'll lose its tracks. I may look like a creaking old man, but my sight is keen, my limbs are strong, and I'm the best hunter and tracker in this valley. That's why you're here. You want me to lead the search party."

"And you won't?"

"Fifty men stumbling through the woods and tearing up the

trails is the last thing we need," he said. "Give me until morning. If I find no sign of the boy, or the bear, then we'll all go out there and turn over every damned rock in the valley."

Rafin stared at the old man. "And what if Keam's alive? He could be lying out there in the cold with—"

"Keam is dead." Fergus said flatly. "And if he isn't, I'll still find him quicker than all of you put together."

"I'll go with you." Rafin insisted.

Fergus fixed Rafin with a glittering stare. "You're a good man, Rafin—the best catchpole this village has ever had, and my closest friend—so I'll speak plainly. You're a damned poor woodsman."

"I'm not a squirrel chaser!" Rafin growled. "I'm a soldier!"

Fergus smiled. "I mean you no insult, Rafin, but you move through the woods like a cow. Mountain trails are difficult enough with two good legs. You'd only slow me down."

"I have a horse. . . ." Rafin muttered.

"Horses can't go everywhere."

"You certainly are a stubborn old goat!"

"True," Fergus admitted. "But I'm right. I'll start at the old field where Andor was found." He picked up the arrows and stuffed them into his quiver. "It should drink after feeding. I expect there'll be tracks somewhere along the river. Its lair won't be far away. Maybe in the mountains to the west of the Pinnacle."

"What if it isn't an animal, Fergus? What if it's a man?"

Fergus looked up and studied him carefully.

"I think Andor was killed by an Ammak patrol," Rafin said quietly. "You served on the Tarbisu Steppes."

"You know I did," Fergus replied.

"Did you ever see one of our sentries after the Ammak shamans finished with him?" Rafin asked.

"Ammaks? Shamans?" Fergus shook his head. "I know what you're getting at, but you're wrong. Andor had an arrowgrass cane in his side and cuts all over his body, not just on his forehead. And if you chase a man through enough bearbriar thickets, his mother won't recognize him."

"I know," Rafin admitted. "Whatever it is, just don't try to kill it alone."

"We'll see," Fergus said. He picked up his bow, put an old hat on his head and slung the quiver of sharpened arrows over his right shoulder. "At any rate, I'll see you this evening—after dark." He paused to look up at the gathering clouds. Reaching into his tunic, he slipped a leather thong over his head.

"Hold onto this, Rafin," he said. "There's more buried under my sleeping cot. If anything should happen to me, see that I get a decent funeral. Whatever's left, give a third to Zandria and the rest to Marrtee. Without Keam and Andor, the family will need money."

Fergus walked quickly away toward the new bridge. A light mist began to fall and it was getting colder. Rafin watched as Fergus crossed the bridge and walked slowly along the river's overgrown banks. Near the edge of the forested slopes below the Pinnacle he waved. Rafin returned the signal with a wave of his own; then Fergus moved into the woods and vanished from sight.

Rafin sighed, picked up the sharpening stone and placed it on a small table, then started off for the north gate. The slow, steady drizzle changed to light rain, and the wind strengthened, flapping the hem of his cloak about his knees. He thought of old Fergus making his way through the damp woods.

"Take care, old man."

❧ ⬥ ☙

Rafin went back to the slaughterhouse at dark, but Fergus did not return. When he failed to come in by morning, and was absent from the funeral services, Rafin became more than a little concerned for his old friend's safety. Accompanied by Hadrax, the woodcutter Rohmeth, and Danis—son of Relius the

Armorer—Rafin rode out to search for his old friend. They found him sprawled in a small clearing on the northern bank of the Dove, about four miles upstream of the village. His old bow lay broken at his side. Like Andor, he had been savagely mutilated and partially eaten.

Rafin was filled with silent rage as he placed the old hunter's body across his own horse and picked up the broken bow. They returned to the village with heavy hearts and made their way to the home of Yettik. After placing Fergus on a table in the back room, Rafin motioned for Danis to sit and sent the other men home.

Danis was a sturdy youth who had impressed Rafin with an even disposition, inquiring mind, and sober maturity far beyond his seventeen years. Alyna treated him like her little brother and sometimes Danis seemed like a nephew—even a son—to Rafin. He had made the young man's acquaintance soon after assuming his position of village catchpole. The occasion was a free-wheeling brawl behind the village inn, where Rafin had found himself surrounded by four drunken travelers with drawn short swords, and his back pressed against the cold stones of a house.

"You need some help?" a voice had asked, and he had turned to see a tall youth with a drawn bow.

When the four travelers laughed and pressed forward, Danis shot the biggest man in the leg. Before the others could react, he had notched another arrow and shot a second man in the arm. Rafin slapped the hilt of his heavy broadsword against the third man's head, dropping him in an addled heap on the wet paving stones. Whereupon, in view of the rapid shift in numerical advantage, the fourth man had spun on his heels and disappeared. His partners were snatched from the ground, marched to the village gates, and unceremoniously thrown out. Then, grinning like boys stealing apples, he and Danis had retreated to the inn.

Since that time, Danis had become Rafin's unofficial assistant. And though he never mentioned it, Rafin fully intended to recommend to the village governors that they retain Danis as their next catchpole. Next to old Fergus, Danis was the best bowman in the village, having been taught by the master archer himself.

A close examination of Fergus's body revealed wounds nearly identical to those of the young boy. The heart was missing. There were deep cuts on his forehead. The oval pattern was crudely made, but clearly visible.

Or is it? Rafin asked himself. Is this the same mark I saw on the Tarbisu Steppes? The wars are over—the Ammaks defeated. They would not dare cross Luwynn's borders.

Sinking heavily into a chair, Rafin stared angrily at the mutilated body of Fergus. Make a decision, he told himself. Which is worse? Sending the message and being wrong, or failing to send a message and being right?

Looking up, he saw that Danis and Yettik were watching him, waiting for him to speak. "I very well might be . . . mistaken. The evidence is certainly inconclusive" he told them, "but those deep scratches on his forehead could indicate more than just a . . . local problem."

"What do you mean?" Danis asked.

Rafin gave him a grim smile. "What I'm about to tell you is to go no farther than this room. Is that clearly understood?" He paused, receiving a nod from both of them.

"I saw similar marks on the foreheads of men some time ago," he continued. "It was on the Tarbisu Steppes, at the end of the wars. Of all the armies that comprised the Triad forces, the Ammaks were the most savage, and the last to be defeated. They were fanatical fighters, seemingly immune to pain, and showed little fear in battle. You see, the Ammaks believe they own the eternal spirit of an enemy killed in combat. These become their servants for all eternity. Therefore, the more people they kill, the more servants they will have . . . and that will make them very powerful and respected in their afterworld.

"There was a man among us who had an uncanny ability to understand these savages. I believe he was the only man they truly feared. The Ammaks called him *Maraakus Oti-Makidon*. In their tongue, that means 'death's shadow'—or something similar—and he took the name as his own. He never lost an engagement with the Ammaks. He learned to speak their language, he learned their customs, and he pursued them with cold, dedicated hatred. After old General Havaloc's debacle—the Fourteenth Campaign—the king made Maraakus a general. I was his executive officer.

"We came to a point where only the Ammaks offered any true resistance to our armies. King Marllof decided that we had only one hope of securing a lasting peace. The Ammaks would have to be driven far to the northeast—back to their homelands in the frozen wastes of the Tarbisu Steppes—and so thoroughly decimated that they could never again become a threat to Luwynn. He chose Maraakus to accomplish this task.

"In the third year of the Tarbisu campaign, we established a rather weak fortification on the banks of a wide river that remained frozen for most of the year. Thanks to the brilliant leadership of Maraakus, our casualties had been extremely light, and we believed the Ammaks had been reduced to perhaps no more than fifty thousand in all the steppes. We set about strengthening our position, and by late summer we had obtained fresh supplies but we were unable to move forward until additional troops arrived. The Ammaks dug in on the opposite bank of the river and the war grew strangely quiet."

He paused and cleared his throat before continuing. "Then," Rafin said softly, "what passes for summer in that gods-forsaken place was gone. The weather grew intensely cold and we began to lose our sentries, and men from scouting parties, one-by-one. A day or two later, we'd find the missing man stretched out on a boulder near our fort. He'd be dead, all right, but the only sign of injury would be a strange mark on his forehead. A mark shaped like an eye, with a hole in the center.

"Of course," Rafin continued, "our surgeon investigated the wound and found the dead men's brains cooked within their skulls, probably with a hot iron. We never knew for certain how this was done, but it spread great fear among our soldiers. Some said it was done by the Ammak shamans, that they possessed the secrets of magic. Others said the Ammaks had been joined by some . . . monster . . . dragon. . . .

"There were all sorts of wild stories going around and desertions increased by the day. Sometimes deserters were caught and hanged but it did little good. Men reported seeing patrols of ghosts and evil spirits riding across the barren landscape on horses whose hooves never touched the ground . . . huge horses that breathed fire. Morale and discipline began to deteriorate; desertions increased steadily. The men feared the magic of the Ammaks more than the hangman's rope.

"To this day I'm not entirely convinced they were wrong. I was as frightened as any of them. Of course, Maraakus refused to accept such an idea, insisting that such beliefs were nothing but ignorance and superstition. In fact, he gave me a generous tongue lashing for entertaining such thoughts. And no man has experienced a tongue lashing until he's had one from Maraakus.

"At any rate, we struggled along in that eerie, hellish place. The nights grew very cold and we knew that winter came quickly to the Tarbisu Steppes. Then our patrols reported that the Ammaks were gathering several miles upstream on the far side of the river. Their strength was estimated at perhaps seventy thousand. Our entire garrison numbered less than forty thousand men. Desertions increased and we were nearly powerless to prevent them.

"Maraakus became exceedingly frustrated. He thought the entire Ammak army would fall on us as soon as the weather turned cold enough to completely freeze the river. He was right. The cold Tarbisu winds began to blow out of the north and we knew winter was upon us.

"Maraakus moved our army back to a wide valley and we took up a position behind some low hills. He said the Ammaks, thinking we had fled in panic, would attack us at the first opportunity. Less than a week later, the river froze and the Ammaks started breaking camp.

"Bear in mind that Maraakus believes in *this*," Rafin said, slapping the broadsword strapped to his waist. "He has no patience with those who believe in magic. But to my utter astonishment, he sent for Balzarr—a magician who traveled with our garrison—and commanded him to cast a spell, one insuring victory over the Ammaks. Then he ordered individual spells of protection for every member of our garrison. Every carter, cook, stable groom, and camp-following harlot.

"Balzarr worked steadily for three days and two nights without rest. But it was done. We made our preparations and waited. Two days later, in the early morning, the Ammaks swarmed across the river. By noon they were defeated. You cannot begin to imagine the extent of the slaughter. I think no more than several hundred of them escaped back across the frozen river. And so ended the Mighty Wars. And that's where I first saw this mark."

Old Yettik stood up slowly and walked to the window. For a long time he stared out into the street. Danis sat silently, head bowed, his hands folded in his lap.

"You're certain it's the same mark?" Danis asked, without looking up.

"Close enough," Rafin sighed. "Only the hole is missing. It takes no great imagination to see how this could set off a wave of panic that would sweep over this land in a matter of days. That's why I must insist that neither of you repeat what I have told you. I could be badly mistaken. But if I'm right, and these marks were made by Ammaks, I must get word to Maraakus. I pray that I'm wrong, but can I afford not to send the message?"

"That's a question only you can answer," Yettik replied. "I'm thankful the decision is not mine to make."

"I need more time to think," Rafin told them.

"May I prepare Fergus for his funeral?"

"Yes," Rafin replied simply.

"I'll see to it," Yettik said. "Fergus talked to me several times about this eventuality. It will be just as he wished."

Rafin murmured his thanks, motioned to Danis, and they left. "Now what?" Danis asked when they were outside.

"We go to the slaughterhouse," Rafin replied. "To Fergus's sleeping quarters in the storage shed. I promised him I'd see that some things were done—the settling of his affairs—and it's time I kept that promise."

CHAPTER THREE

Fergus's funeral pyre, like Andor's, was constructed with pitch pine logs to burn fast and hot. A short old man in frayed robes—the priest from the Temple of Judbal—stepped forward, mumbled a few words that Rafin couldn't hear, then flung a small bag into the fire. There was a brilliant flash of white light and the fire roared. A dense column of vermillion smoke rolled across the shallow waters of the Dove and diffused into the wet forest. The raging inferno reduced itself to a circle of white ashes and glimmering coals in a surprisingly short time.

Rafin stood silently, watching as mourners started back for

the village. Most gave him a nod or a grim smile. He nodded to each in turn, acknowledging their expressions of shared grief, yet he was deeply troubled. Could he have prevented the old archer's death? Should he have used his authority as catchpole to insist that Fergus either join an organized search party or stay in the village? He felt a hand on his arm and turned to see Zandria standing at his side.

"I overheard you asking him not to go out there alone," she told him. "Fergus was a stubborn old man. Don't allow yourself to assume responsibility for his death."

Rafin could only stare at the woman.

"Even if you'd locked him in the bilboes," Zandria continued, "he'd have gone out the moment you set him free."

She turned and started up the footpath toward the village, then paused to look back over her shoulder. "The entire village knows you've asked people not to go out unless they're in groups of three or more," she informed him. "They're not listening. Go see Gaimal at the weaving shop. Her husband left early this morning to run his traps. He went alone and she's very concerned."

Rafin nodded, silently cursing Gaimal's husband, a trapper by the name of Nanak. He watched until Zandria disappeared around a bend in the footpath before turning to Danis.

"When we get back," he said, unable to conceal his anger, "I want a dozen armed men on horseback assembled in the market square with provisions and water for a full day. I'll talk to Nanak's wife to see which way he went. We'll leave no later than midmorning. Saddle my horse and bring my sword."

Danis set off up the footpath at a fast walk. Rafin took Alyna by the arm and followed. He shot a quick look at the sky. Dark clouds promised rain, probably by early evening.

Leaving Alyna at the market square, he went straight to the weaving shop, a small, wooden structure located behind the village inn. He found Gaimal and spoke briefly with her, learning only that Nanak had established three lines of traps and that she had no idea which line he had intended to work. He attempted to allay her fears, and by the time he returned to the market square it was nearly noon.

"Very well," Rafin said loudly, after settling into his saddle. "Nanak left before dawn. Fortunately, he's on foot. Unfortunately, he has three lines of traps and we don't know which one he's working. One goes north along the western banks of the Opal and turns west into the mountains. A second line runs up the Dove, then turns north toward the old ruins—you all know where they are—that's probably the longest line."

"It's ten miles or more to the ruins," one of the men said. "That's more line than a man can work and still return in a day."

Rafin nodded. "The third line runs south, following the Opal down to the end of the valley, then it turns west and follows the base of the Sleeping Sisters back to the Northern Road. That's a long line, too, but it can be worked in one day. We have to split into three groups, but within your groups, stay together. Don't get separated. Danis, take four men with you and get started on the south line. Let's all keep a sharp eye out for any trace of young Keam, too."

He looked to his left and saw Hadrax, the village baker. An unspoken message passed between them. Rafin nodded and said, "Hadrax will go north with four men. The rest will go up the Dove with me. I hope you all brought oiled cloaks. We'll probably have rain this afternoon.

"My group will be the last to get back," he continued. "When you find Nanak, tie him across a horse if necessary, but bring that idiot in!"

This last remark brought a wave of laughter from the group.

"I'm very serious," Rafin admonished. "If we don't find Nanak, or he hasn't returned by morning, we'll try again tomorrow. Any questions?"

The men looked at each other and shook their heads. "No?" Rafin asked. "Then let's get at it."

Danis reined his horse out of the group, four men joined him, and the young man led his search party toward the south. The rest of the men followed Rafin and Hadrax to the north gate and onto the Northern Road.

After crossing the new bridge, they split into two groups. Rafin took five men with him and they turned west into the abandoned planting fields. At the edge of the forest, they dismounted and pressed forward on foot, leading their horses and walking slowly upstream. They paused frequently to call for Nanak but received no answer.

The first of Nanak's traps, a simple deadfall, was found a mile beyond the spot where Fergus had been killed and a heavy rawhide snare was found a few hundred yards farther along. Both traps had been freshly baited and set. They found footprints that went north from the river, following a small mountain stream that flowed from the general direction of the old ruins, which were still several miles to the north.

Several more traps were found by midafternoon and then it began to rain—a slow drizzle that soon changed to a steady, chilling downpour. By early evening they lost the trapper's tracks. The small creek became a rushing, muddy torrent, and they could no longer see the forest footpaths through the rain and growing darkness. Miles from where he knew the ruins to be located, Rafin called a halt. Cold, wet, and nearly exhausted, they turned back toward the village.

It was long after dark when Rafin led his group across the new bridge and discovered that none of the men had gone home. But from the way they all sat silently on their horses, he suspected that Nanak had not been found. This suspicion was quickly confirmed by Danis.

"We checked as we came through the village," Danis told him, "but he hasn't come back in. My line had no catches. All the baits were old—at least a week."

Hadrax wiped the rain from his face and turned the collar of his cloak up about his neck. "We found our line, too," he said. "The baits were maybe three days old. No catches."

Rafin nodded. "We found all fresh baits and no sprung traps. For a while, we followed tracks toward the ruins but lost them in the rain."

"What next?" Hadrax asked.

Rafin looked up into the dark sky and slashing rain. He wiped his face with his right hand and hesitated for a moment.

"Well," he said, "it's pointless to try tracking in this weather. If the rain doesn't stop, we'll just have to wait. Then we'll all go up to the ruins together."

"Maybe he'll come in tonight," a man suggested.

"Yeah," said another. "If not, maybe in the morning."

"I hope so," Rafin said, shaking his head. "I want to thank each of you. I know it's been a miserable day. Go home and get some rest. We'll try again tomorrow, if the rain stops."

There was little conversation between them as the men rode to the village.

❦ ❦ ❦

It rained steadily the following day and the dark skies gave no hope of relief from the constant downpour. After going three times to the home of Nanak only to learn that he'd not returned, Rafin decided that another day of searching would be pointless. If Nanak had sheltered in the ruins, it was unlikely he'd stay out more than two days. And if he'd met a fate similar to Andor and Fergus, then all that could be gained was the retrieval of his body.

Convinced of this, Rafin made his decision and penned a short message on a small piece of paper. After tucking it into his pocket, he took down a small box from a shelf beside the fireplace and counted out twelve golden ravens.

Danis watched, shaking his head. "Pretty damned expensive!"

"But the only certain way of getting a message to someone in a hurry," Rafin told him.

They walked past the inn, then turned left and stopped before a wooden shed butted up against a stone building. A plank fence extended from the back of the shed; a blue sign with two interlocking gold circles hung over the doorway. Near the entrance was a second sign bearing words painted in red block letters. Danis stopped to read it.

> *TO KILL A CRESTED COURIER FALCON*
> *OR INTERFERE WITH ONE IN ANY MANNER*
> *IS PUNISHABLE BY DEATH!*

Rafin pushed open the door and they entered. Both sides of the shed were lined with widely separated perches made from rough-cut oak; eight perches were occupied by tall, fierce-eyed, crested courier falcons. A brightly colored jess was attached to a brass ring nailed firmly to supporting posts under each perch. The birds' ragged white crests had been dyed various colors, denoting the flight path each bird had been trained to follow.

Trained crested courier falcons flew only between two roosts, and responded to only two signals. They flew only by day and ate nothing during a flight. This training was instilled while a bird was young by allowing it to obtain small amounts of slightly poisoned food. This produced a mild sickness—from which the bird quickly recovered—and within a few weeks a bird would accept food only from a handler it recognized. This eliminated any possibility of it eating a poisoned bait or hunting on its own during a flight.

Apparently Rafin and Danis had arrived at feeding time; the birds clutched large pieces of raw meat in their long talons. When the two men entered, the birds ignored the meat and stared back with unblinking, pale red eyes. Their sharp, hooked beaks were slightly open and they displayed not the slightest indication of alarm at the appearance of two strange beings in their midst.

Danis approached a large, dark falcon with a green crest. Whistling softly, he extended his right hand.

"I would not advise that, Danis!" a voice said.

They turned to see Dax, a thin, sharp-nosed young man. He was wearing a bright red jerkin with yellow sleeves, the distinctive dress of an apprentice falconer. Dax held up his right hand. He was missing half of one finger.

"I was careless," the young man said casually. "I'm lucky. Mika has lost two. Do you wish to speak with my master?"

"We do," Rafin replied.

"Please wait," Dax told them. "He's releasing a bird. I'll tell him you're here." He pointed to a pair of thin, red cords. "Please stay between the red markers. The birds are fond of going for the eyes. Oh, they wouldn't eat them, of course, but they'll take them anyway." He turned and went out the back door of the shed.

Danis whistled softly and eyed the birds with new respect. "And to think I once wanted to apprentice as a crested falconer," he muttered, wiggling the fingers of his left hand.

Rafin laughed as Danis stepped carefully to the center of the marked aisle, then the back door opened and a short, portly man entered, followed closely by his young apprentice.

"Rafin!" Lumoss shouted. His booming voice belied his short stature. The falcons fluttered nervously. "Any news on Nanak?"

"Not yet," Rafin replied. "That's why we're here. I need to send a message to Koeinstadt." He handed the master falconer the note he had written.

Lumoss removed a wooden tube from his pocket, rolled the note in a tight stick, inserted it into the cylinder and replaced the cap. "Bring me Love Charm," he said to Dax.

The apprentice nodded and put on a heavy leather glove that reached to his shoulder. He picked up a leather hood, walked to the end of the shed, and stopped before a large bird with a blue crest. After the hood was placed over the bird's head, Dax untied the jess and Love Charm stepped up on his left wrist. As her talons gripped the leather glove, Dax winced with pain. but he walked back to them and stood patiently while Lumoss attached two bells to the bird's left leg. The wooden cylinder was attached just above the bells. "Uncover," Lumoss said.

Dax removed the bird's hood. Love Charm shrieked and slashed at him with her hooked beak.

"And you named that thing Love Charm?" Danis asked.

Lumoss smiled. "Yes, indeed. A more gentle, loving creature never lived. She's a real sweetheart—and very fast, too. If only she weren't so affectionate. That's her only flaw, you know?" He grinned and Rafin chuckled softly.

Love Charm fluttered, then spread her wings. Their span was well over four feet. Danis eyed the bird suspiciously and Love Charm glared back with her clear, steady red eyes. Suddenly she opened her beak and slashed repeatedly at the leather glove while emitting a series of piercing cries.

"When do you think it will arrive?" Rafin asked.

"By midday tomorrow at the very latest. Love Charm will stop just before dark, but she'll be well on her way by then. This is the best bird I have."

"Will she fly through this rain?" Danis asked.

Lumoss laughed and stroked the falcon's back with a bare hand. "They don't mind the rain. Only darkness will force them down. They'll even fly through a lightning storm. These birds are absolutely fearless. Even a mountain eagle flees in panic at the sight of a crested falcon."

Rafin counted out the twelve coins he'd brought with him and Lumoss dropped them into a box on the table.

"You may watch the release, if you wish," Lumoss said to Danis.

They followed Dax and Lumoss out the rear door and into a courtyard surrounded with a high, board fence. The rain continued to fall in cold, wind-driven curtains. Lumoss held out his arm and Love Charm stepped up onto his wrist. He spoke to the bird and shook the bells several times. The falcon rubbed its head under the man's chin, its talons gripped just tight enough to maintain its balance. Lumoss raised his arm and the bird sprang into the air.

With strong, rapid strokes of its broad wings, the crested falcon climbed nearly straight up into the sky and began flying in a series of tight circles. Lumoss placed a silver whistle to his lips and blew a single, penetrating blast. The falcon answered with a shrill cry of its own, wheeled sharply, and flew rapidly to the south. It disappeared almost immediately in the rain and low-lying clouds.

Lumoss turned to them with a smile. "As I said, best bird I have," he beamed. "She'll get your message there in record time."

Rafin thanked Lumoss and they left. "Some love charm," Danis muttered when they were on the street outside. "What now?"

"Maraakus could be on his way to Stridgenfel by this time tomorrow. If there is an Ammak patrol about, I don't want him riding into the valley alone. You and I will leave tomorrow morning in time to make it through the Sleeping Sisters before dark. We'll camp at the Traveler's Spring and wait for him."

"He could ride right past us."

Rafin laughed. "Not if we camp close to the road. He'll check out any camp he sees. Maraakus is not one to let strangers get behind his back."

❧ ❧ ❧

Maraakus spoke softly to the black horse and patted the animal firmly on the neck with a gloved hand. "Soon, big one," he said soothingly. "Have a little patience."

Hearing the familiar voice of its master, the animal's ears moved and it tossed its head, rattling the buckles of its bridle. Maraakus smiled, then leaned forward and drew his sword from the scabbard attached to his saddle and looked slowly around. His eyes met Rafin's. His oldest friend and most trusted field commander, Rafin was mounted on his big gray horse, the reins wound tightly around his left hand in the manner of a seasoned warrior. In his gloved right hand, Rafin carried the big double-edged heading sword, his preferred weapon for field combat. A yellow signal streamer was tied around the blade, close under the hilt.

Perhaps a dozen paces behind Rafin, facing in the opposite direction, old Fergus, the king's master archer, waited for his orders with his long bow hanging loosely in his right hand. In his left hand was an arrow. Its tip was wrapped with a strip of cloth soaked in pine pitch. Near his left foot was a flaming torch; the butt end of its handle had been pushed into the ground. Now the old man nodded. No hint of fear was visible on his weather-beaten face, but his lips were compressed in a thin, bloodless line.

By turning in his saddle, Maraakus could see the lines of his army: ten full divisions, more than forty thousand men. Yet for the sounds of clanking weapons and the stamping of nervous horses, a strange and apprehensive silence lay over them all.

Rafin closed his eyes, tilted back his head and breathed deeply of the damp, pine-scented mountain air. "A good day to be alive," he observed, tapping his helmet firmly onto his head. "May the gods protect you this day, my general."

"And you, my old friend," Maraakus replied. He brought his weapon to his lips and kissed the cold metal blade. Then he addressed Rafin with the time-honored salute of professional soldiers. "Honor to us all," he said.

"And to our cause," Rafin answered. The old soldier's face was grim, but he raised the sword with a steady arm and the yellow signal streamer fluttered gently in the early morning wind.

At Rafin's signal, Fergus touched the arrow to the torch. He notched it on the bowstring and pulled the heavy bow to a full draw. As the arrow streaked into the morning sky, Maraakus heard the slow, measured cadence of the horsehide drums as they pounded out the order to advance. And with a quavering moan, like that of some dreadful beast being shaken from a deep slumber, a sea of men stepped forward on a rising tide of sound. The ground trembled with their steps and the air was filled with the sounds of shouting men, clanking metal, marching feet, and the pulsing rhythms of the war drums.

Maraakus touched the horse with his heels and the animal jumped forward in a prancing walk. He reined it to a slow, steady pace, tightened his grip on his sword, and fixed his eyes on a group of low hills with tree-covered crests. As they neared the lower portions of the slopes, the Ammaks advanced to meet them. In ragged groups, they streamed from the trees and quickly formed up by the tens of thousands into a single, massive wall. Then, screaming their pagan war chants, the Ammak savages poured down the hillsides like spreading pools of black blood.

While most were naked to the waist, some were dressed in animal hide armor with brightly feathered, leather helmets. Their faces were painted white and their eyes were circled in black.

An arrow whistled past his right ear and Maraakus urged his black horse forward at a quick gallop. A collective roar filled the valley as the front lines of the two armies met and flowed together on the rocky slopes. He fought in a strange, unemotional trance, unmindful of the noise and general confusion that was typical of hand-to-hand confrontations. His sword moved with a will of its own, slashing, thrusting, and parrying blows from all directions, while the superbly trained black horse responded quickly to signals given by its rider's feet and the bit in its mouth.

Despite their obvious lack of leadership, the savages fought hard and well, but the army Maraakus had brought to the field of battle was well trained, disciplined, and ably led. Slowly, foot by foot, they forced the Ammaks back up the slopes, but it was apparent that both armies were taking heavy losses and the battlefield was soon covered with the dead and dying from both sides. Sharp cries of anguish could be heard from the dying and curses from the wounded as they struggled to regain their footing. A standing soldier had a chance to defend himself, but a man on the ground would be trampled to death under the advancing waves of soldiers and the steel-shod hooves of horses.

A glancing blow, struck from behind, knocked the metal helmet from his head and Maraakus swayed in his saddle. Falling forward, he wrapped his arms around the lathered neck of the black horse as the animal reared and pivoted.

To his right, he saw an Ammak soldier lifting a heavy spear. As the man set his feet firmly and raised the spear to the throwing position, Maraakus kicked the black horse forward and thrust his sword into the man's body. It entered through the left armpit, just above his rawhide armor, and the man's eyes went wide from shock and fear. Maraakus jerked the sword free and watched as the mortally wounded Ammak turned to his right, threw back his head and fell forward across the body of a fellow soldier.

Now the black horse staggered across the ground and carried him to a small clearing at the top of a hill where he saw a circle of tall, upright stones. As the big animal stumbled between the stones and into the circle, Maraakus was filled with an eerie sense of foreboding. The clashing of weapons, the hoarse screams of the wounded, and the incessant throbbing of war drums became strangely muted.

I've gone too far, he thought. I must return to my men.

He jerked the reins, attempting to turn the horse back to the battle on the slopes behind him, kicking the animal repeatedly with his heels. The horse ignored both the kicks and the bit in its mouth. It stood head down, lathered sides heaving with exhaustion, while blood flowed freely from a deep wound on its left shoulder.

As he leaned forward, attempting to staunch the flow of blood with his left hand, he saw the giant Ammak chieftain standing just inside the circle of stones. The huge savage was naked to the waist and wore a red fur loincloth that reached to his knees. His feet and legs were encased in leather wrappings held in place with thong lacings. His long arms and broad shoulders were covered with strange swirls of blue, red, and black tattoos; heavily greased hair hung in stiff, plaited ropes to his waist. The face above his thick yellow beard was painted white. His eyes and mouth were outlined in black and surrounded with clusters of red dots that resembled the dried scabs of an odious pox. In his huge, bloodied hands, the Ammak carried the largest battle-axe Maraakus had ever seen.

The giant smiled, raised his axe in a mocking salute, and walked ponderously into the circle of stones. Sunlight glinted from the long, sharp cutting edge of the axe.

Maraakus straightened quickly in his saddle and raised his sword. His right arm felt numb and curiously leaden. Looking to his right, he saw several of his own soldiers standing shoulder to shoulder with a group of Ammak warriors. They were laughing and jostling each other as they tossed gold and silver coins to the ground. They appeared to be placing wagers on some type of sporting contest. Maraakus smiled and waved to them, pleased to see that they were enjoying themselves.

One by one, the soldiers fell silent. Then, as if in response to some unseen command, they began clapping their hands in a slow, steady rhythm, like the sound of marching feet on the surface of a cobbled street.

The Ammak chieftain swung his weapon in a menacing, pendulum motion. As the clapping increased in speed and intensity, Maraakus realized that the noise was timed perfectly to the movement of the huge battle-axe. Then, without warning, the Ammak chieftain charged across the circle. His lips were pulled back, exposing teeth filed to sharp points, and he snarled like a rabid wolf.

Maraakus leaned to his left and swung his sword. He felt a dull shock in his arm as the blade bit deeply into the giant's left shoulder. He heard the Ammak roar with pain, but the giant did not go down. Maraakus thrust the sword into the Ammak's protruding stomach and saw the blade penetrate to half its length.

Still the giant stood upright and Maraakus was overcome with a paralyzing sense of fear. He knew the blows had been well struck, but the man gave no indication that he was wounded. Not even the thrust to the stomach had brought forth blood, and Maraakus wondered what sort of man could withstand such wounds.

The stone circle shimmered before his eyes and Maraakus saw the small village of his birth. He was fourteen years old and standing before an Ammak warrior in the street near his home. At his feet lay the body of his mother. The body of his father was nearby, a sword still clasped in his dead hand.

Every house in the village was burning. It seemed like the world had been painted in red, undulating in the heat of the raging fires, while a thick, choking smoke swirled through the village and rose into the glowing sky. Black shadows darted through the streets as villagers fled in panic, tripping over the bodies of their friends and kinsmen, while the shrill screams of women and the hoarse curses of men filled the air.

Ammak soldiers shouted loudly to each other in harsh, grating voices as they dragged the helpless villagers from their homes. And the savages laughed, encouraged by their victim's shrieks of terror and by their futile attempts to escape or cover their nakedness with their hands.

Maraakus heard his sister calling his name in a shrill, terrified voice. He turned to see her being dragged down the street with her wrists tied behind her. Their eyes met; she screamed his name and urged him to run. He wrenched loose a paving stone from the street. Holding it overhead with both hands, he rushed at his sister's assailant, but a tall Ammak with filed teeth stepped in front of him and swatted the stone from his hand with a bloodied axe.

Again the scene shifted. He was back in the strange stone circle and the giant Ammak's figure shimmered before him. The savage was smiling as he swung his axe and Maraakus felt it bite into his left leg, just above the knee, then watched with fascinated horror as the severed limb went spinning through the air, landing at the far side of the stone circle.

The axe continued on, into the left side of the black horse, striking it just behind the shoulder. The animal screamed; its front legs collapsed, pitching Maraakus to the ground in an agonized heap. The Ammak soldiers at the edge of the circle were cheering and throwing coins at their giant chieftain. Maraakus heard his own men shouting at him, pleading for him to get up from the ground. Their voices were shrill, like the voices of terrified women.

His life's blood spurted from the stump of his severed leg into the green grass of the clearing; the steady, painful ringing in his ears became nearly unbearable. Looking up, he saw the Ammak standing over him, raising the axe overhead with both hands. Then, after looking once toward the men standing at the edge of the circle, the giant threw back his head and howled at the darkening sky.

Maraakus tried to get up. All his instincts as a soldier and a man were urging him to move, to avoid that last, fatal blow; but he was far too weak. The curious ringing in his ears was subsiding and now he could hear the violent pounding of his own heart.

With the last of his remaining strength, he pushed his face deep into the sweet-smelling grass. He heard the giant singing his pagan war chant and the sound of the war axe whistling through the air. Then his body jerked violently; the muscles in his back convulsed and he awoke.

He was alone in his sleeping quarters, drenched with sweat, the damp bedclothes pushed down to his waist. For a long time he lay motionless, shivering and staring into the darkness of his sleeping chamber. The night fire had burned out long ago and the cold, damp air from the stone walls of the room felt good on his feverish body.

The old dream had returned, bringing with it all the sorrow and anger that he had carried for so many years. As with some old battle wound or a stiffening knee that ached with changes in the weather, he had learned to live with it, but the memory of his earlier years remained vivid and sharply focused in his mind.

He recognized the components of the dream, the burning of his home village, the cruel and violent deaths of his family. He remembered the morning after the Ammak raid when he had stood in the street, covered with his own blood, staring down at the body of Karrla, his sister. Her hands were still tied and she had been mutilated with a knife.

Bruised and bloodied, he had wandered the smoldering village for a time, moving silently past other survivors—young men like himself and old men with frozen, vacant stares. Women stumbled past with expressionless, tear-stained faces, bearing the bodies of young children in their arms.

It was midday before he found a small handbarrow and pushed it back to the place where his family lay dead in the street. One at a time, through sheer determination or strength born from grief, he managed to drag their bodies onto the handbarrow and push it out of the village to a small clearing in the woods. Using only his hands, he scooped out a shallow grave and gently rolled the bodies of his family into it. Then he covered them with the dark, damp soil. He shed no tears. All he felt was anger and a cold, merciless hatred.

For a time—exactly how long he did not know—his life was a confusing jumble of days and nights, then weeks and months, spent pursuing the Ammaks with weapons taken from the village streets. And, against all odds, he survived, killing the Ammaks' stragglers and night sentries with the stealthy skill of a forest predator. He knew his luck would not last, of course. In time, the Ammaks would surely kill him. And his death would be most unpleasant.

Some five or six months later, he made his first contact with Luwynn's First Division—Rafin's division. He had been following them for many weeks, still conducting his own private war. Rafin's scouts knew what he was doing, of course, and had tried repeatedly to coax him into their camp by leaving small amounts of food and water, the occasional quiver of arrows, or keen dagger.

At first he accepted only the weapons. By then he had become nearly an animal, furtive, trusting only in his own abilities. But finally, as winter came on and game became scarce, he began to accept their food.

Maraakus recalled standing on a small hill above their camp, watching smoke from their fires rise into the evening sky and savoring the smell of roasting meat. A tall, bearded officer with a heavy broadsword belted to his waist had waved, motioning him down, inviting him to enter the camp. Maraakus stared back at him without moving. The bearded soldier picked up a metal plate, filled it with food, and walked boldly out of his camp. He placed the food on a rock at the base of the hill and went quickly back to the fire.

After dark, the food was still sitting on the rock, well beyond the glow of their campfires. Maraakus picked it up and went quickly back to the safety of the trees. After eating every scrap and licking the cold, greasy plate, he stood on the top of the hill and sent the plate sailing smoothly into the center of their camp. It landed with a clatter at the feet of the bearded officer, but the man hardly bothered to look up.

Three days later, he walked into their camp. He came to trust the bearded man—Rafin—and before long, Maraakus was following the Ammaks and gathering information on their movements, estimating the strength of their forces, noting the direction of their marching, and reporting back to Rafin.

The Ammaks came to know this mysterious scout well. No one knew his name, but they called him *Maraakus Oti-Makidon*. In the Ammak tongue, this meant "death's own shadow," a spirit who came at night and killed soundlessly, then melted back into the forests and mountains.

In time, he ceased to use the name his mother had given him at birth. He became Maraakus Oti-Makidon and by the time he was twenty-eight, he was a general, with three divisions in his command, and Rafin as his executive officer. Three years later, he was Supreme General of the Legions of Luwynn. Together, he and Rafin led the army that drove the Ammaks from Luwynn and into the Tarbisu Steppes. And with their defeat, all his disturbing dreams had ended. Until last night. His old friend's words came readily to mind.

Fergus is dead.
He and a small boy have been brutally murdered.
Two others are missing—presumed dead.
Marks on foreheads of victims match those from Tarbisu Steppes.
I need your help.
—Rafin.

❧ 🦋 ☙

After looking south along the narrow road, Rafin turned his horse left into a small clearing where the pines and dense undergrowth offered a screen from the cold wind.

"This is a good spot," he said. "We'll camp here for the night. If Maraakus left the day after he received my message, he'll be along no later than tomorrow morning. Tonight, young Danis, we build a fire and eat hot food!"

"The gods are truly merciful," Danis declared. "I don't think I can swallow another bite of cold dried meat, stale bread, or hard cheese."

Rafin laughed. "Excellent rations, my young friend. Excellent rations, indeed. On the other hand," he added, "I'll not object to a warm meal."

Danis grinned and removed his bow from his shoulder. "I'll show you excellent rations," he declared. "You make camp and build a fire. I'll take care of our supper." He turned his horse and rode quickly back to the Northern Road.

When he returned, Rafin had cut evergreen branches for their shelter and built a fire. "Here's a supper for traveling men!" Danis announced and dropped three rabbits beside the fire.

Rafin grinned and while Danis tended the horses, Rafin dressed the small animals and impaled them on sharpened green sticks. Before long, the smell of roasting meat was drifting through the woodlands. Satisfied that supper was cooking properly, Danis slipped off his boots, placed them next to the fire, then rolled himself in his cloak and stretched out on the ground. The next thing he knew, something was nudging him gently in the ribs. He opened his eyes to see Rafin standing over him. It was not yet dark.

"Hungry?" He held out his knife. A steaming leg from a rabbit dangled from the point.

Danis nodded and threw off his cloak. He slipped his feet into his boots and found that while they were not completely dry, they were warm. He took the meat from Rafin and began to eat.

Danis chewed the meat and stared into the fire. The rabbit was cooked without salt but he thought he had never tasted anything as delicious. He took his knife from his belt and cut off a back leg. "I shouldn't have fallen asleep," he said.

"We've pushed the horses hard—and ourselves—but we're here a day early," Rafin told him. He held out the last piece of rabbit. "I'll take you for a traveling companion any time." Suddenly he turned to his right and cocked his head to listen.

"What's wrong?" Danis asked.

"Did you hear anything?"

"No."

Rafin's horse lifted its head and looked toward the Northern Road. Both ears tilted forward. Then Danis's young gelding, untrained as a warhorse, lifted its head and nickered softly.

Danis stared into the gloom of the forest but heard no sound and saw no movement. After a while he turned to Rafin and arched his brows.

"Look at my horse," Rafin whispered. "See how he moves his head? Something's making a wide circle around our campsite."

"An animal?"

"I don't know," Rafin whispered. "But man or beast, our horses know something's out there."

"What do you want to do?"

"Nothing, yet," Rafin answered. He whistled softly to his horse. The big gray looked at him over the campfire, eyes glowing luminous yellow, then swung its head back toward the Northern Road.

"Whatever's out there just changed direction," Rafin whispered. "Now it's headed back toward the road."

"Then it knows there's only two of us," Danis whispered.

"Perhaps," Rafin agreed. "Then again, maybe it simply found the woods too thick to permit quiet movements. You stay here by the fire."

Reaching down, Rafin picked up his sword. "I'll be right over there, in that stand of pines. It probably won't attack before getting closer—particularly if it doesn't know how many are in our party—and the woods are dry, so you'll hear it coming. There'll be plenty of time to pick a target, so don't miss. Meanwhile, try not to look in my direction. Get your arrows ready." Leading his horse by the reins, Rafin moved into the thick pines and disappeared from view.

Danis immediately picked up his bow and fitted an arrow on the taut string, then stuck four more into the ground beside his left leg. His mouth was dry and his heart was pounding in his chest.

Before long, just as Rafin had expected, there were sounds of movement in the forest to his right, followed by a sharp rustle of dry leaves behind him. Then, as he was easing himself up on both feet, a tall shadow suddenly appeared, standing just outside the glow of their campfire. Firelight reflected from the blade of a drawn sword. Danis's heart froze.

"Will you come out to meet me, traveler?" the figure called. "I intend you no harm, but I'll not be forced to watch my back for the next few days. And you can tell your friend in the woods to step out where I can see him."

Danis heard Rafin suck in his breath. The stranger raised his sword and jumped quickly to one side.

Rafin moved out into the clearing. "By all the gods!" he shouted. "I'd know that voice anywhere. I'll bet it has an ugly face to go with it!" He stepped over the fire and stood facing the man.

The stranger lifted his face. "Rafin? Well, I'll be damned for a false cleric! What are you doing out here? I'm on my way to find you!" The stranger sheathed his sword and the two men embraced in the middle of the clearing.

Rafin stepped back and waved. "It's all right, Danis. Come! Meet my old friend, General Maraakus!"

Relieved, Danis lowered his bow, walked up to Maraakus, and extended his hand. It was taken with a firm grip, but the man before him was not what he had expected. Maraakus stood several inches shorter than Rafin—though his shoulders were nearly as wide—but his movements had the grace and restrained animal quickness that made one think of a mountain cat. When he threw back the hood of his traveling cloak, that impression was reinforced by deep-set, green eyes that studied him with just a hint of amusement. Or was it curiosity? At any rate, one could tell they missed very little.

A small scar was visible on his right cheek and the ends of his drooping mustache reached nearly to his square jawline. His stance was relaxed, but there was an overall impression of confidence and strength. Only a fool would fail to recognize that Maraakus could be an extremely dangerous man.

"This," Rafin said, "is Danis, son of Relius the Armorer. He's a brave young man, and good traveling companion."

"A pleasure to meet you, Danis," Maraakus said. "From personal experience, I know how difficult it is to travel with this old scoundrel. You have my deepest sympathy."

"The pleasure is mine," Danis replied. "I've heard much about you, sir."

"Bah! He rode to glory holding the hem of my cloak," Rafin declared. "I taught him everything I know about soldiering. Fortunately, he was bright enough to remember most of it."

Maraakus smiled and winked at Danis. "He speaks the truth. Unfortunately, what Rafin knows can be taught in a day's time."

They all laughed and Rafin placed his arms around them both. "Come," he said. "Tonight, we camp together. We've much to tell you, Maraakus."

CHAPTER FOUR

The annual blanket of fallen leaves was accumulating on the forest floor and across the Northern Road. The cool wind blew through them in multi-colored drifts of flaming reds, dusky browns and brilliant yellows. The horses swished noisily through the dry leaves and not even a deer could move silently through the woods. Bearbriars drooped with their dark purple clusters of sour berries and the arrowgrass canes were drying and turning pale yellow. Only the evergreens seemed untouched by autumn's hand.

It was midday when Rafin stopped in a wide clearing and dismounted. There, under the spreading branches of ancient oaks, a small spring trickled from a fissure in the mountain. Unknown travelers had trapped the clear waters behind a dam of rocks, creating a pool some five feet across and nearly a foot deep. He took down their waterskins and dropped them at the edge of the pool.

"We'll rest the horses here," he said. "The hardest part of the climb is still ahead."

High above them, two pairs of almost identical peaks rose steeply from the valley floor. Halfway up their sides, the trees thinned and disappeared, leaving only occasional clumps of brush clinging to dangerous slopes of loose rock. The tops of the mountains were hidden in the midday clouds and the pass between them was shrouded in deep shadow.

"Beyond this point there's no water until we cross the mountains," Rafin was saying. "We must rest and eat."

While young Danis replenished their water supply, Rafin fed a measure of grain to each of the horses. After the animals had eaten, he led them to the pool and let them drink.

Maraakus ate the cheese and bread that Danis brought him and washed it down with water. Then he stretched out on the ground with his head on his rolled cloak. Sheltered from the wind by tall trees, he rested in the autumn sun and was soon sleeping, but at a touch on his shoulder he was instantly awake. Rafin was leaning over him, frowning, holding a finger to his lips in a gesture of silence; his unsheathed sword was in his right hand. Maraakus got quickly to his feet and Rafin leaned toward him.

"We have company," he whispered. "They're in the trees above us—higher up the road."

Maraakus buckled on his sword, then pulled a dagger from his boot and stuck it in his belt. With his fingers, he signaled to Rafin in the familiar language of the battlefield. Twice, he rolled his hand into a tight fist and made another sign with his thumb and index finger. He pointed to Danis, then at a pile of broken rocks to the left of the spring,

Rafin nodded and whispered his instructions to Danis. The young man went quietly to his horse and took down his bow and a quiver of arrows. Then, with barely a sound, he disappeared into the rocks that Maraakus had indicated.

Rafin slipped a narrow-headed fighting axe into his belt. Sword in hand, he moved silently across the clearing and melted into a bearbriar thicket.

Maraakus stood motionless in the middle of the road, waiting to hear any unusual sound from the trees above them. Somewhere down the slope of the mountain, a woodpecker drummed away on a dead tree; small birds chattered all around him; acorns dropped into the dry leaves with their familiar popping sound and he could hear the occasional rustle of a squirrel or other small animal. All normal sounds of the forest. Still, he had absolute confidence in Rafin. If his old comrade-in-arms said they had visitors. . . .

Then came that peculiar silence that only man can cause in a woodland. Small birds hushed their chattering in the undergrowth; squirrels stopped their rustling on the forest floor and climbed quickly to safety in the trees. All around him, the normal sounds of the forest ceased.

Maraakus looked north, where the old road curved gently around the mountain. Now he heard men talking and the swish of their feet through the dry leaves as they approached the bend in the road. Soon they would be in sight of the spring.

He counted them as they walked into view. There were seven of them, all heavily armed. Two men carried swords in sheaths buckled to their waists. A third man was tall and thin, with the face of a hunting hound; he carried a battle-axe, a sword in his belt, and a rusty pike with a bent tip.

The fourth man, perhaps the leader of the party, was short and very fat. He was dressed in a filthy brown tunic and his head was covered with a green hood. At first glance he appeared to be the more harmless of them all, except for the cocked and loaded crossbow carried in his left hand.

But it was the last three who arrested his attention; two large and powerfully built men in dented, rusty war helmets, wearing short swords and animal skin boots, carried a makeshift, canvas litter between them. The seventh man rode on the litter and appeared to be a great deal smaller than his companions. He was dressed in dirty white fur garments. His arms were folded across his chest with his hands concealed in the sleeves of his clothing. A soiled hood covered his head and face so that not even his eyes were visible.

Maraakus continued to study them as they approached the spring. When they were some thirty feet away they stopped, lowered the litter to the ground and lined up in front of it. The fat man with the crossbow walked a few steps closer to the spring and looked carefully around. His eyes took in the three horses standing on the far side of the clearing and the man with his hand on the hilt of his sword standing in the middle of the road. Then he looked quickly to his left and right before turning his attention back to Maraakus.

"Best evening on you, stranger," the fat one said. He spoke slowly, and the tone of his voice had an unpleasant rasp, like the scrape of a dagger on a sharpening stone.

"And on you, good traveler," Maraakus replied cheerfully.

"Where are your companions, good stranger?" the fat one asked. "Surely, one man does not ride three horses." The others laughed roughly and bumped each other in the ribs with their elbows.

"I ride with my two young sons," Maraakus answered. "They shall return before long—with a few squirrels for our supper, I hope."

The fat one studied the horses carefully. "It would appear that one of your sons is quite tall, judging from the set of his stirrups." He pointed toward Rafin's horse with his crossbow.

Maraakus' eyes never left the fat one. Very observant, Maraakus thought to himself. The fat one is certainly not stupid.

"Well seen, good traveler," Maraakus said pleasantly. "Indeed, sir, I am blessed with a tall, strong son. One needs such to care for him in his old age."

"Yes," the fat one agreed. "Those of us who are fortunate enough to reach old age." He grinned, showing a mouth full of rotting teeth. "In your case, good stranger, it would appear that you're overly blessed. Fine sons and even better horses."

Maraakus smiled and tightened his grip on the hilt of his sword. "I wish that were so. The boys are a blessing, but the horses are ill-tempered and lazy. That is why we travel so slowly."

"From where I'm standing," said the tall man with the hound's face, "they look to be fine animals. But I seldom see horses close up . . . unless I'm eating one."

This remark struck the others as particularly amusing and they began pushing and shoving each other with a good deal of rancorous laughter. The fat one turned and looked in their direction. Instantly, the group fell silent.

The fat one walked back toward the litter and bent down close to the white hood. Maraakus saw the man on the litter nod slightly. Then the fat one turned and retraced his steps. He stopped about twenty paces in front of Maraakus.

"Lazy and ill-tempered your horses may be," he said to Maraakus, "but we find them most suitable. I've no doubt they'll be of greater value to us than they apparently are to you. At any rate, we intend to have them, and your valuables."

With a speed that belied his girth of body and slowness of speech, the man lifted the crossbow to his shoulder and triggered the weapon in a single fluid motion.

As the crossbow lifted, Maraakus threw himself to the left, the direction he hoped would be the most difficult for the man to track. The deadly bolt buzzed past his right ear, then he heard Rafin shouting curses from the bearbriar thicket and the soft twang of a bowstring. Rolling quickly to his feet, Maraakus snatched his sword from its scabbard.

When the man in the green hood triggered the crossbow,

Danis had released his arrow. The slender shaft sped true to the mark, catching the fat man squarely in the throat. The sharp hunting point extended a full six inches from the side of the man's neck and the fat man stood in the middle of the road with gaping mouth and bulging eyes. He tried to scream, but the effort only produced a gush of blood that flowed over the front of his dirty tunic and into the dust of the road. Then he fell backward in a sitting position, his hands hanging loosely at his sides, his body held erect by his bloated stomach.

The rest of the fat man's party drew weapons and pressed forward. There was no screaming or wasted motion, just the steady, confident advance of professional thieves—murderers who knew their business.

Rafin burst from the bearbriar thicket with a deafening bellow. His great broadsword cut down the hound-faced man with a single stroke. A big man with a dented helmet rushed him from the right and Rafin parried the thrust, then tripped and fell heavily to his knees. The bandit raised his sword with both hands and slashed downward. Rafin balanced his huge sword in the palms of his hands and took the blow in the middle of his blade. The thief's sword broke in two pieces upon contact with the heavier weapon. For a fraction of an instant the man with the dented helmet hesitated. That was all the old soldier needed. Using both hands, Rafin swung the heavy broadsword in a deadly arc, cutting the man nearly in half.

Maraakus saw the two men armed with smaller swords rushing across the clearing, heading for the rocks where Danis had been hiding. He shouted and saw Danis raise his bow and send an arrow toward the front man. It passed between the first man's body and his left arm, burying itself in the left side of the man behind him. The second man clutched at the arrow with a feeble hand, sank slowly to his knees and fell forward, driving the arrow completely through his body.

The first man reached the rocks and raised his sword over his head. Maraakus snatched the dagger from his belt and threw it at the back of the man standing over Danis. The slender blade entered between his shoulders and the man fell soundlessly across Danis, pinning him to the ground.

Danis pushed the thief off his chest and ran toward Maraakus. "Behind you, General!" he shouted.

Maraakus turned and saw the sun reflecting from the helmet of the second litter-bearer. He countered the thrust of the man's knife and smashed the hilt of his sword against the bandit's head with a sweeping, backhand motion. The blow glanced off the old war helmet, but still knocked him to one side. As he went down, he slashed at Maraakus with the short-bladed knife. Maraakus delivered a hard kick to the side of the old war helmet, but the man rolled over once and sprang to his feet. He swung his knife wildly, missing Maraakus by a fraction of an inch. Then he raised the rusty blade over his head and rushed forward.

Maraakus stepped quickly to one side. The man tried to check the downward motion of his arm, but his speed, and the momentum of his rush caused him to momentarily lose his balance. Before the man could recover, Maraakus drove the point of his sword through the man's chest.

When he pulled the weapon from the man's body, the thief fell face down in the road. He coughed and pulled one leg up to his side, as if making an attempt to regain his footing. The leg straightened; the fingers of his left hand twitched and scraped at the dusty road. Then he gave a deep, rattling sigh. His head rolled to one side and he lay perfectly still, his eyes wide open.

Maraakus heard Rafin and Danis shouting and he turned to see the man in white fur running quickly away. Without so much as a backward glance at his dead companions, the escaping thief suddenly left the road and vanished into the trees. After a while, they caught sight of him on the far side of the valley, still running south at the edge of the forest.

A cursory search of the dead men quickly convinced both Rafin and Maraakus that the thieves were not responsible for the murders in Stridgenfel. The three men tossed the bodies into a deep ravine. By midafternoon they entered the pass between the Sleeping Sisters and wound their way between walls of rock and around fallen boulders. At last they emerged from a narrow canyon and found themselves on a rocky, treeless slope. Here the Northern Road descended through high forests of pine, red gum, hickory, and oak.

Shortly after entering these high woodlands, Rafin turned off on what appeared to be a hunting path. Maraakus and Danis followed and they rode into a small clearing on the very rim of a high cliff.

"I thought you'd like to see where we're going," Rafin said, as he dismounted. "It's quite a sight from up here."

Maraakus tossed his horse's reins over it's head and, too, dismounted. Then he and Danis followed Rafin out onto the rim of a sheer cliff.

"That's Stridgenfel in the distance," Rafin said, "and down there is where we come out of the forest."

Maraakus looked where Rafin was pointing. Far below them, the Northern Road emerged from the thick forest and curled down to the valley floor. There it passed through neatly tended fields before sweeping on toward the village.

Maraakus shivered. He was tired. It was cold at this altitude and he could smell the promise of winter in the wind that whipped his riding cloak around his legs and sent dead leaves whirling into space over the edge of the cliff.

"Tell me, Rafin," Maraakus said. "Where was the first body found—that of the young boy?"

"There," Rafin said, pointing with his gloved hand. "In that abandoned field north of the Dove, just left of the bridge."

Maraakus looked past the village to the overgrown fields on the north side of the river. "Abandoned?" he asked. "Why?"

Rafin shrugged. "I was born in Stridgenfel and I've never known them to be planted."

"Farmers say they're cursed." Danis offered.

"Cursed?"

"According to old legends, it happened long before the beginning of the wars," Rafin explained, "when the evil wizard Jodac built a stone keep on top of the Pinnacle—that tall, oddly shaped mountain just north of the village."

"And doesn't every valley have its own wizard?" Maraakus asked, shaking his head. "These lands are filled with tales of evil wizards, elves, and dwarves." He looked carefully at the mountain. "I see no stone keep up there."

"According to the old legends," Rafin said, "it was pulled down by an army of elves after his death. But his magic was very powerful. With his dying breath, he cursed the fields and promised death by starvation to all inhabitants of Stridgenfel."

"Which never happened, obviously."

"Cattle that grazed on grasses from those fields soon sickened and died. Grain grew tall and heavy with seed, but before it could be harvested, it was consumed by a strange gray rot—a result of the curse."

Maraakus smiled. "Or perhaps too much wet weather. There could be any number of logical explanations."

"That's possible," Rafin agreed. "Still, the villagers were afraid, so they cleared new fields on the south side of the river. Since then, no farmer has tried to plant the northern fields."

Maraakus grinned. "Land is land, Rafin. It does not grow lush crops if it's poisoned."

"But if the poison is magic. . . ." Rafin insisted. "Even you have used magic. When it suited your purpose."

"Magic? I believe you're referring to the time we engaged the Ammaks on the Tarbisu Steppes. Do you recall the attitude of our troops prior to that battle?"

"I remember. You commanded Balzarr to cast spells for us—that we might defeat the Ammaks. It was done, and we were victorious."

"Ah, yes," Maraakus agreed. "We destroyed the Ammaks, but no credit should be given to that dolt of a magician."

"But you commanded him to—"

"I demanded spells for my armies," Maraakus said, "because they needed something to make them forget their weariness from days and nights of forced marching with little rest, poor rations, the fear of battle, and the stench of death. So I gave them what they needed: a little confidence, and a little courage. And for those who needed something different. . . .?" He smiled and slapped Rafin on the shoulder. "Well, old friend—for those that needed it—I gave them a little magic."

"But we all believed," Rafin said.

"Not all," Maraakus said. "But most. Oh, there was magic that day, but it came from confident soldiers and strong sword arms. Not from some pompous ass in flowing robes and a head full of meaningless jabbering. Do you remember what happened to our marvelous Balzarr?"

"As I recall," Rafin replied, "he was killed by Ammaks, early in the day."

"Not so," Maraakus said. "Balzarr died of a snakebite. He was bitten by his little pet—that brown viper he carried in the pocket of his robe."

Rafin shook his head, but Maraakus could see that he was not convinced.

"And Fergus?" Maraakus asked, turning back toward the valley. "Show me where he was found."

Rafin pointed to the neatly cultivated fields to the left of the village. "There," he said. "West of the planting fields, in the distant forest to your left. He was on the north bank of the Dove, a few miles upstream from the village. Fergus and Andor died approximately three, maybe four days apart. Both were mutilated and disemboweled."

"And we have two missing people. Again, a boy and a man. Very strange." Maraakus said. "How old are they?"

Rafin considered the question. "I'm not certain," he said. "But I'd guess Nanak to be about fifty-five. Keam was no older than fourteen."

"Of all the boys in the village," Danis said. "Keam and Andor were Fergus' favorites. He liked to gather a group of boys around the stone tower and tell them stories and old legends. He had no children of his own."

"Fergus was the best hunter and tracker I've ever known, Maraakus." Rafin said. "You know what kind of archer he was. There is nothing in these forests—no animal, anyway—that could possibly kill him."

"Considering the alternative, Rafin," Maraakus sighed, "I hope you're wrong."

"I hope so, too," Rafin replied.

❧ ❧ ❧

By late afternoon they were descending slowly toward the valley floor, allowing the horses to set their own pace down a steep section of road. Suddenly Danis pulled his horse to a stop and pointed. "Look!" he shouted. "There's smoke coming from the village!"

Rafin had been telling Maraakus—perhaps for the tenth time—about finding Andor's body, the death of Fergus, and their failure to find Keam and Nanak. With each telling, Maraakus elicited some small detail that Rafin had previously omitted. Now they looked toward Stridgenfel and saw a thin column of black smoke rising into the sky.

"A house is burning!" Danis said. "We must hurry!"

"There's no point in running these tired horses," Rafin said quietly, squinting into the distance. "Funeral pyres are made with pitch pine logs. By the time we arrive, there'll be nothing but ashes."

"Funeral?" Danis whispered.

"Perhaps it's not another murder," Maraakus suggested. "People do die from natural causes."

Rafin stood in his stirrups and shielded his eyes from the morning sun. "No," he said. "See the color of the smoke?"

Maraakus saw that the smoke was now rising in a bright, scarlet plume, drifting eastward on the wind. "The klersep casts a powder into the flames and turns the smoke red." Rafin explained. "This so the gods might grant special consideration during the judging of the eternal spirit of a murder victim. Taken before your allotted time, you might be unable to repent your mistakes. If you happened to die a man of poor character."

Maraakus gave his old friend a curious look. "Klersep? Isn't that what they used to call a priest of Judbal? I thought that religion died out . . . two hundred years ago."

"In these mountains, many people still believe in the old ways. Stridgenfel has one of the few surviving temples of the Judbal religion. The old klersep manages to exist on the charity of his followers. A crazy old man, but harmless."

Maraakus exhaled through his pursed lips, making a low whistling sound. "Let's see, now. A valley once controlled by an evil wizard who was killed by an army of elves. A place where the superstitious rites of the Judbal religion survives, where people are murdered by animals—maybe Ammaks—is that all, Rafin?"

Rafin did not reply and Maraakus noticed his stoic expression and the firm set of his jaw. Maraakus reached out and placed his hand on the old soldier's arm.

"I spoke not to offend you, Rafin," he explained. "I've lived all my life believing only in things that I can see, touch, ignore, or kill with a sword. That's all I know. It's difficult for me to reason in terms of mythological beings, giant animals, magic, and ancient religions."

Rafin gave him a thin smile. "Tonight," he said, "you'll meet my niece, Alyna. Although she seldom speaks of it, Alyna knows much about the . . . ancient ways. It was from her that I've learned to accept some things that I don't fully understand. Unlike you, I've always believed that old legends and superstitions contain a kernel of truth. While I'm no fanatical believer, I've come to understand that there are . . . possibilities . . . beyond that which I can see, touch . . ."

"Ignore."

"Ignore . . . and kill with a sword. I'm asking you to keep an open mind."

❧   ☙   ❧

By early evening they were out of the mountains and onto the valley floor. They continued to follow the Northern Road through a section of planting fields and entered a thick stand of beech, then passed through into another field bordered on the north by the tangled line of a hedgerow. Here the road made a sweeping curve to the right and approached the village walls.

They entered Stridgenfel from the south by passing through an open gate. Rafin drew his horse close to a woman carrying a bucket of yellow pears. "Lerac!" he shouted.

She stopped and turned in their direction with a look of surprise on her face. "Rafin! They said you went to Koeinstadt."

"Not quite," Rafin replied, offering no other explanation for his rapid return. "As we came down out of the mountains, we saw the red smoke."

The woman's face grew sad and she wiped a tear from the corner of her eye. "Little Milari," she said, shaking her head. "Just like Andor and Fergus."

"By the very gods!" Rafin exclaimed, turning to Maraakus. "Now, we've lost a little girl! Did they find Keam or Nanak?"

"No." the woman replied. "They're still missing. When is this all going to end, Rafin?" Without waiting for an answer, she turned and walked away.

"Soon," Rafin muttered to himself.

Maraakus shifted his gaze toward the old stone tower. He could see a crowd of people and hear their excited shouts. Something was happening at the center of the village.

"More trouble," Rafin warned.

They went quickly toward the crowd and used their horses to clear a path. The crowd closed behind them as they went forward to the base of the tall stone tower.

"Witch!" a middle-aged woman shouted, shaking her fist. "You gave her the powder! Do you deny it?" She was directing her anger at a young woman of about twenty who stood next to the old tower with her back pressed firmly against its walls. For a moment Maraakus sat motionless in his saddle, stunned by the young woman's beauty. She was tall—just a few inches shorter than Danis—thin, but with rounded hips and strong, slender legs. Soft, dark brown hair cascaded over both shoulders, framing a perfectly oval face, from which curiously pale blue eyes stared back at him. Her generous yet delicate lips turned up in a slight smile. With a deliberate effort, Maraakus broke his gaze and returned his attention to the villagers gathered around the tower.

"Certainly not!" was the girl's defiant reply. "She asked for the powder and I gave it to her. How was I to know she would use it on your husband? But if you shout at him like this at home, I'll wager she didn't have to use very much!"

The crowd roared with laughter. The older woman's face flushed with anger, but she turned her wrath on an old man standing near the girl.

"There! You see?" she shouted. Spittle flew from her mouth and the old man shrank back, wiping his face with the back of his hand. "You're responsible for this! This is what happens when a klersep encourages the arts of witchcraft!"

"Alyna!" a young man shouted. "Do you have more of that stuff? I'd like to buy a full quarter-weight! I can think of several girls I'd like to try it on!" There was more laughter and a girl stabbed the young man in the ribs with her elbow.

The old man walked between the quarreling women. His head was bald but for a fringe of white hair over each ear. He was dressed in the long robes of a cleric and the eight-pointed star of the Judbal priesthood hung from his neck on a silver chain. In a futile attempt for silence, he raised his hands over his head, waving them for attention.

Most of the crowd ignored him. An egg sailed past his head and another hit him in the chest; the bright yellow yolk ran down his robe and dripped on his foot. The old man wiped at the egg and succeeded only in smearing it over his robe.

"Blasphemy!" the priest shouted. "You have committed blasphemy!" His face flushed with rage and he raised both hands toward the heavens. "Hear me, almighty Judbal!" he intoned. "Send down thy punishment for this grievous insult to your most humble servant. Send fire and ice from thy heavenly abode to—"

"Here comes your fire and ice, you old fake!" yelled a tall youth at the edge of the crowd. He stooped down, picked up a fresh piece of horse dung and flung it at the cleric. It missed the old man's head by a fraction of an inch and stuck to the wall of the tower. The crowd roared with laughter. The old priest eyed the dung and shook his bony fist at them. Then he walked quickly away, shoving a path through the crowd.

Rafin winked. "Not even our exalted klersep commands respect when dealing with quarrels of the heart."

"What's going on?" Maraakus asked.

Rafin shook his head. "It sounds like my niece gave a love powder to some girl and it was used on Finna's husband."

"He's the little man in the blue tunic," Danis said, raising his voice above the laughter of the crowd.

Maraakus looked at the man. He was about fifty, balding, with white hair and squinting eyes. "Him? That man with the skinny legs?"

"That's the one," Rafin declared. He laughed at the expression of doubt on the general's face. "Haven't you heard that love is blind, Maraakus?"

"Aren't you the village catchpole?" Maraakus asked.

Rafin fixed a fierce scowl on his face. "That's me, sir. At your service."

Maraakus smiled. "Well, aren't you going to break this thing up?"

"No," Rafin replied. "Most fun this village has seen in weeks. The gods know there's been little to laugh at recently."

Maraakus sighed and turned his attention back to the crowd. "What about Alyna? Aren't you concerned for her safety?"

"I don't think she's in any real danger," Rafin answered.

The woman, Finna, turned to face the crowd. "Ask her about the killings," she hissed. Her face was red and angry. "This witch knows more than you think! Ask her!"

"What about that, Alyna?" someone asked. "Do you know something we don't?"

"I know what all of you know!" shouted Alyna. "Nothing more!"

"In a pig's eye!" Finna screeched. Her harsh voice carried above the general noise of the crowd. "This is the work of a witch! We all know that!"

"Your uncle might know more than he's telling," the same man suggested. He was tall, with red hair and a hooked nose.

"Damn," Rafin muttered. He reached down and placed his hand on the hilt of his broadsword, then nudged his horse forward, forcing his way to the front of the crowd. A stone sailed over his head and bounced off the tower. That produced angry muttering from the front lines of the crowd and some of the men turned to look over their shoulders, trying to determine who had thrown the stone. A woman pointed at the red-headed man.

Rafin ducked his head and wheeled his horse. "The next man who throws a stone will be ridden down!" he shouted. Then he drew his heavy broadsword and rested the hilt on his knee in the manner of a soldier at the ready position. The crowd fell back slightly and Rafin pointed the sword at the man with red hair.

"Drop it, Ewart," he demanded, "or I'll lop off your damned hand!" The stone fell to the ground, sending up a small puff of dust.

Maraakus pressed his horse into the circle and drew his sword. The sight of the two men with drawn weapons had a quieting effect on the crowd. Several pointed at Maraakus and spoke behind their hands. Danis moved up beside them and the crowd fell back a few more paces and grew still.

Rafin's eyes settled on the man with red hair. "You have until sunset to get out of this village, Ewart," he informed the man. "Take your possessions—if they're really yours—and clear out! We don't want men like you in Stridgenfel. If you ever return, I'll lock you in the bilboes until you rot! Now get out!"

Ewart left quickly, accompanied by whistles and jeers. "Good riddance!" a woman shouted after him. "Maybe we won't have to lock our doors at night . . ."

"Cerlus?" Rafin called, addressing another man by name. "How's your leg? I remember how it looked the night they brought you to Alyna. You still have it, I see." Rafin dismounted, sheathed his sword, and bent down to pick up the stone Ewart had dropped. He walked up to the young man and took him by the wrist. "Here," Rafin said. He slapped the stone in the man's hand. "Throw this at the woman who saved your leg."

Alyna was still standing against the old tower. Her gaze was steady and she appeared unafraid.

Cerlus dropped the stone and smiled at Rafin. "I'd never raise my hand against her," he declared, "and if Ewart had thrown that second rock, I'd have beaten him within an inch of his life."

"Is your mother doing better, Sibar?" Rafin asked a stout woman with tangled hair.

"Much better, thank you," Sibar replied. She smiled at Alyna and winked.

❦ ❦ ❦

"So who's ready to stone this girl?" Rafin asked the crowd, "This girl who's never done anything but help everyone in this village at one time or another."

The crowd shifted nervously, then started to disperse. Several people went to Alyna and touched her on the shoulder before leaving, while others muttered soft apologies before walking away. Soon only a handful of people remained around the tower.

Even old Finna apologized. "It was not your fault, Alyna," she said. "Please forgive me. I was angry at the wrong person." With that, she grabbed the small man Danis had identified as her husband and dragged him off by the ear.

Maraakus watched as Alyna picked up her bag of vegetables and walked slowly across the market square. Pausing briefly, she looked back and flashed him a dazzling smile. He gave her an awkward wave and she headed up the street, hips swaying and dark hair blowing gently in the wind. Only when she as out of sight did he notice Rafin watching him with a curious smile on his face.

"So," Maraakus said awkwardly. He paused to clear his throat. "That's your niece. She's rather . . . ah . . ."

"Yes," Rafin agreed. "She's quite beautiful, isn't she?"

"What?" Maraakus asked. "Oh. Well . . . actually . . . I was going to say *spirited.*"

"That, too," Rafin agreed. "Shall we go?"

"I'm sorry. What did you say?" Maraakus asked.

"I asked if you were ready to go."

"Lead on, Catchpole," Maraakus replied, thinking that his voice sounded strange and distant. He stared intently in the direction where the young woman had vanished.

At a small house near the eastern wall, Rafin introduced Maraakus to Yettik, who took them to a little room at the back of his home. Yettik drew up some chairs and they sat down to talk.

"Her name was Milari," Yettik began. "A beautiful child, not quite nine years old."

"When was she found?" Maraakus asked.

"Yesterday. When she failed to come back from the high pastures by late afternoon, her brothers went after her. They found her dead." He looked helplessly at Rafin. "I did just as you told me and passed word that it was dangerous to go outside the walls alone. I guess the family figured the goats had to eat and it was daytime—early morning, at least—and Milari often took the goats to the pastures alone."

"And the goats?" Maraakus asked.

"Strangely enough, they were unharmed."

"None were missing?"

"No," Yettik replied. "None were missing."

Rafin cleared his throat. "Was she . . . ?"

Yettik nodded slowly. "Worse, Rafin. She was so small, you see, that when she was . . . opened up . . ."

Yettik rose and walked to a bucket, filled a dipper with water and took a long drink. He brushed a shaking hand through his thinning hair and returned to his seat. "This has got to end, Rafin." His anger showed plainly on his lined, weather-beaten face. "I'm getting damned tired of conducting funerals for babies!"

"It will," Rafin assured him. "Maraakus has come to help us. Did you look at her forehead?"

Yettik nodded. "Like Andor and Fergus. But I said nothing about the marks or missing hearts, just as you instructed."

Rafin looked at Maraakus but spoke to Yettik. "We'll leave you now. Maraakus and I have much to discuss."

"Just end it, Rafin." Yettik said.

Outside, Rafin squatted and drew a mark in the dust. "This is the mark found on the victims. It is the Ammak's mark, isn't it?"

Maraakus drew his boot through the dust, erasing the figure Rafin had drawn, then stood staring out into the street with his hands on his hips. "Perhaps we should talk to that old priest," he said to Rafin. "They often know quite a lot about symbols. Maybe he knows something about that mark."

"We can do that tomorrow," Rafin said. "It's late now. He's locked himself in the temple to recite his evening prayers and he won't talk to anyone until morning. Since we can accomplish nothing more today, we should wash off this road dust, eat a good meal, and get some rest."

Maraakus agreed and they mounted their horses. He felt a pleasant sense of anticipation at the thought of seeing Alyna but made no mention of it. He followed Rafin across the village to a small house on the western side, not far from the market square. The ground floor of the house was constructed of stone and had large windows on both sides of the front door. The second floor was whitewashed wattle and daub, framed by wooden beams and pierced by a round window. A tall shed was attached on the left; a smaller shed jutted from the back. The entire structure was topped with a thatched roof. It was typical of many houses that Maraakus had seen in the village, differing from most of the others in that it had a freshly painted front door and window boxes filled with red flowers.

"Welcome to my home, old friend," Rafin said. "Mine and Alyna's."

They carried their saddlebags inside and dropped them on the floor. Alyna was bending over the hearth, placing a small log on the fire. She straightened as they entered the room. "I've moved down here, Uncle," she told Rafin. "Our guest will have the upper room. I've moved you to the loft."

"Good," Rafin replied. "You'll find the room comfortable. Alyna will show you where to put your things and I'll tend the horses. I won't be long."

"Come, General Maraakus," Alyna instructed. "Bring your things and I'll show you to your room."

Maraakus picked up his saddlebag and followed her to the second floor of the house while Rafin went out the back. The room contained a few chairs and a large table. On the back wall, a fire burned in a small fireplace; a big bed was pushed up against the left wall.

Maraakus liked this house. It was a place where people put down roots, lived normal lives, and raised a family. He was drawn to the room, with its unfamiliar yet comforting sense of contentment. The presence of a young woman living in the house was evident. A brass vase stood on the window sill, filled with freshly cut autumn wildflowers.

On the front wall were shelves filled with more books than Maraakus would have expected to find in any house his old friend Rafin lived in. "You have quite a large collection of books," he remarked.

"They belonged to my grandmother," Alyna said. "I suppose they're mine, now."

"Can you read them?" Maraakus asked, aware that she was studying him closely.

"Yes," she said. "Grandmother taught me. Can you?"

Maraakus smiled, but he detected a slight mocking tone in her voice and it was apparent that she was not intimidated by him or by his reputation. He liked that very much.

"Yes," he answered. "But perhaps not as well as you. Most of my reading has been limited to military matters."

He watched as she moved slowly around the big table, trailing her fingers on the smooth surface. Below a delicate waist, rounded hips swayed gently as she walked.

She acknowledged his gaze with a slight smile and proceeded past him to the largest set of bookshelves. She took down a small volume bound in red leather and stood so close that he could smell the fragrance of mint on her body.

"This is a favorite of mine," she said. "It's a collection of poems—silly little things, really—composed by Lania, a traveling singer of ballads. They're love poems, mostly. Tender affairs of the heart. Shall I read you one?" she asked, looking up at him.

He received the full effect of her pale blue eyes. "A pleasant offer," he replied, smiling at her. "Another time, perhaps?"

"Of course," she said. "Another time." Standing on her toes, she reached up to place the book on the highest shelf. "There's heated water for your bath. You'll find a bathing tub in the downstairs shed, soap on the stand, and fresh towels next to the tub. Supper will be ready when you're both finished."

She went quickly down the stairs and Maraakus closed his

eyes and took a deep breath before untying the flaps of the saddlebag. He took out clean clothing and a leather bag containing a razor and small brass mirror, then gathered it all in his hands and went downstairs. Alyna was tending the pot in the fireplace and did not look up as he crossed the room and opened the door to the shed.

He found a large wooden tub, filled it with cold water from a storage cistern near the back wall and added several buckets of hot water from a huge iron kettle mounted permanently over a small fire. Then he undressed and slipped into the tub.

After bathing he dressed, then picked up his dirty traveling clothes and carried them into the house. Rafin was sitting at the table, drinking from a copper mug; Alyna was placing dishes on the table. Seeing the rolled bundle under his arm, she frowned and fixed him with her pale blue gaze.

"No!" she said sternly, pointing to his dirty clothes with a wooden serving spoon. "You may wear those into the house but you may not *carry* them into the house. Put them back in the shed. I'll wash them tomorrow with Uncle Rafin's clothes."

Rafin laughed as Maraakus turned meekly and carried the clothing back to the shed. When he returned, Rafin was staring into his wine, his shoulders shaking with suppressed laughter. "If you could have seen the look on your face . . ." he said. "Well, General, you just had a taste of true domesticity. See what you've been missing?"

"I'm getting a vague idea," Maraakus said.

Still laughing, Rafin placed his mug on the table and went to the shed.

"Here," Alyna said. She pushed a cup of mulled wine into the general's hand, turned him around, and pushed him gently toward the table. "We'll eat when he's finished."

Maraakus laughed and sat down to drink his cup of wine. The smell from the cooking pot was wonderful. The aroma of fresh bread filled the entire room. In his nearly exhausted condition, the wine made him feel mellow and relaxed. He watched the young woman busily preparing supper and studied her movements as she took the bread from the oven. She brushed a wisp of dark hair from her eyes and smiled. Maraakus glued his eyes to the cup of wine.

CHAPTER FIVE

The Temple of Judbal was located east of the stone tower and faced the market square. Maraakus and Rafin found Danis waiting near the front entrance and he approached them with a look of concern on his young face. "The klersep says he's too busy to talk with non-believers. He's locked the temple doors."

Maraakus smiled. "We'll see about that," he said. "Where are his living quarters?"

"In the back," Danis replied. He led them to the rear of the temple and pointed to a heavy wooden door with a small metal shutter built into it.

Rafin placed his hand against the weathered planks. When he pushed, the door creaked. He smiled and looked at Maraakus. "Shall I knock down the old goat's door? It wouldn't take much to push it off its hinges."

Maraakus shook his head. "Let's try being reasonable, civilized men first."

Rafin pushed at the metal shutter with his left hand and it swung open. Then it suddenly slammed shut, pinching his fingers against the lower edge of the opening. Rafin jerked his hand away from the door and grimaced with pain.

"Go away!" a voice from behind the shutter demanded. "You risk invoking the wrath of Judbal!"

"You've already invoked my wrath, you old charlatan!" Rafin growled, shaking his left hand and pounding on the door with his right fist. "Open this door! Come out or I'll come in and get you!"

The shutter swung open and the face of the old klersep appeared. "State your business." he demanded. "You are interrupting my morning prayers."

Maraakus put his arm on Rafin's shoulder and looked through the opening at the old man. Rafin stepped back from the door.

"We apologize for disturbing you, Holy One," Maraakus said, speaking in a quiet, pleasant voice, "but we have need of your wise advice."

The bright eyes stared suspiciously at them through the opening. Then the metal shutter closed and Maraakus heard the sound of a locking bolt sliding back. The wooden door opened slightly and the priest regarded them distrustfully. "What advice could the mighty General Maraakus seek from a lowly servant of Judbal?" he asked.

"We need you to interpret the meaning of a certain symbol, Holy One," Maraakus answered respectfully. "You may be able to help us end the vicious murders of Judbal's followers in this village."

"What is written in Judbal's Book of Days cannot be

changed," the priest said flatly. "All things are of his will and design. Mortal men can change nothing."

"I'm certain that is true," Maraakus agreed, "but perhaps it's his will that brought us to the temple this morning."

The priest eyed him carefully.

"Of course, for your wise advice we are prepared to make a small gift of gratitude . . . to Judbal." Maraakus added.

"How small?" the priest inquired.

Maraakus held up a single golden raven and the old priest looked at the shiny coin with glittering eyes. "A most generous gift," he acknowledged. "It would surely find favor in the eyes of the blessed one. But I may not touch the gift with my unworthy hand. You must place it on the altar."

Rafin rolled his eyes and Danis covered his mouth with one hand to hide his smile.

"I would have done so, Holy One," Maraakus assured him, "but we found the doors to this sacred place bolted and we could not enter."

"Go back to the front of the temple. They shall be opened for you," promised the priest. The door slammed shut and the locking bolt slid back into place.

Maraakus grinned at Rafin. "You see how honey can draw the fly, my friends?" he asked.

Rafin growled. "Honey, or money? It would have been faster and cheaper to snatch him through that little peephole."

"No doubt," Maraakus acknowledged. "But we want his cooperation, Rafin, not just his attention."

They returned to the front of the temple and entered. Inside, they found that rubbish had been swept carelessly into the corners of the room, and the smell of rancid oil permeated the place. At the end of the chapel room, Maraakus could see a dusty, soot-blackened stone altar covered with a tattered red cloth. Behind the altar, the wall was draped with a rotting tapestry hanging from a tarnished brass rod. A brass bowl stood on a small stone pedestal near the altar.

The priest led them to the bowl and pointed with a thin hand. "Place your offering in here," he instructed, "and I shall pray for its acceptance."

"Not likely that it'll be refused," Rafin grumbled as Maraakus dropped the coin into the bowl. It rang with a dull, hollow sound.

The old priest bowed his head and muttered a few words under his breath. After a short pause he turned to face them. "Your gift was accepted by Judbal," he announced. "Now state your business."

"We have much to discuss, Holy One," Maraakus said, keeping his voice soft and respectful. "Is there a place where we can talk privately? The temple is a public place and it might be best if we talked without fear of being overheard."

"As you wish," the priest responded. He led the way through a door behind the altar and they entered a small room with a table and several chairs, a large bookcase, and a washstand. To their right, an unmade bed stood against the far wall, covered with a pile of thin blankets and clothing. The room was dimly lit with four smoking oil lamps, which explained the rancid odor that filled the temple. The priest shoved a pile of books to the middle of the table and they sat down.

"We are troubled by a symbol that we do not understand," Maraakus told him. "I wish to show it to you. May I have paper and pen?"

The old man rose from his chair, walked to a low shelf on the wall and took down a quill pen, a sheet of soiled paper, and a small pot of ink. He placed them before Maraakus and sat down in the same chair. "Show me the symbol," he instructed. "I will help you if I'm able."

Maraakus inked the pen and drew a rough oval on the paper, two opposing lines, crossing each other at the ends. He turned the paper toward the priest and the old man frowned. Maraakus pulled the paper back and drew a large dot inside the oval.

The priest leaned forward with obvious curiosity. "What you

have drawn is an ancient, evil sign," he declared. "It is the eye of an evil god. Where did you see this sign?"

Maraakus looked across the table at Rafin and Danis. They were staring at the priest with open-mouthed astonishment.

"Yes," the priest acknowledged. "I know the mark. Many years ago, long before the Mighty Wars, the Judbal priesthood stood in opposition to the followers of this false religion. Many people were slain and given the mark on their foreheads. I remember reading about this in one of the old record books.

"Why was this done?" Maraakus asked.

"The sign was used as the personal mark—a signature, if you will—of the cult's leader. He was a loathsome magician who sought to make himself a deity. Any who opposed him were subjected to horrible tortures and forced to acknowledge him as a true god. Then they were given his mark on their foreheads and put to death as examples to others. Death prevented them from recanting their evil oath.

"May I assume," the old priest continued, "that this mark was found on the unfortunate victims of our recent troubles?"

Maraakus regarded him with narrowed eyes.

The old man smiled. "I am old, General," he said evenly, "not feebleminded. However, I promised to help you, so I shall pray about this problem and seek Judbal's guidance. In due time, Judbal will reveal to me the name of the man responsible for these foul deeds. When that happens, I shall tell you."

"I'm certain Judbal will do so," Maraakus agreed. "Meanwhile, Holy One, people are dying with disturbing regularity. Even innocent children are being brutally slain. Surely, if it is within your power to assist us, Judbal would wish you to do so immediately."

"Judbal is a god of peace and compassion," the priest informed him, "while you are men of war and violence. What do men such as you know of Judbal's wishes?"

"Very little," Maraakus admitted. "Except that when you have suffered from violence and inflicted it upon others—

because it was your sworn duty to do so—you come to know it intimately. No man hates violence more than a soldier."

The priest eyed Rafin warily. "I find that difficult to believe," he remarked. "I knew this one as a child. He has always been ill-tempered and quarrelsome. As you can plainly see, age has not improved him. But you're correct. Judbal demands that we march forth in righteous anger against the murderer of innocent people. His purpose is suddenly apparent to me. He has sent you to recruit me for this holy crusade. I have a good sword around here, someplace . . . but I'll have to find it."

Danis grinned and Rafin rolled his eyes.

Maraakus gave them a stern look. "No, Holy One," he said, placing a hand on the old priest's arm. "I must not risk losing you in battle." He tapped the side of his head with a forefinger. "Men with brawn are easily replaced. A thinking man—a person such as yourself—is the most valuable asset any general can acquire."

The klersep nodded solemnly. "Now I understand why you are held in such high esteem, General. You are wise beyond your years. I shall be proud to serve with you."

"And I welcome your assistance," Maraakus assured him.

"However," the old cleric continued, "my time is Judbal's time, and quite valuable. Therefore, he has instructed me to request a small offering for the restoration of his temple."

"And has he a specific offering in mind?"

"I think . . . perhaps a two golden raven offering?" the priest asked hopefully.

Danis grinned when Rafin expelled his breath loudly and muttered, "I'll offer to give you a lumpy head, old man!"

Maraakus glanced up sharply and Rafin fell silent. Reaching into his pocket, Maraakus took out two gold coins, placed them on the table, and the klersep covered both coins with his hand.

"Most generous," the priest assured him. "It shall be used wisely for the glory of Judbal. After all, it is Judbal who has made you a wealthy man, General."

"I'm not nearly so wealthy as some think," Maraakus informed him, "but if this continues, I'll certainly be among the poorest in the kingdom. Now, tell me more about this mark."

"It is also a sign of sacrifice," the priest continued. "It signifies forfeiture of one's eternal spirit to the gods of darkness."

"And this religion survives?" Maraakus asked.

"No," the old man answered softly. "It died out hundreds of years ago. So it is written in the records of this temple."

Rafin was staring at the old man with a look of disbelief. "What in the name of—for three golden ravens, all you can tell us is—"

"Wait," Maraakus said, holding up his hand. "What possible significance might this mark have today? Has this evil religion been revived?"

"I think not," the priest asserted. "So much time has passed. . . ."

"Where did this cult—and this mark—originate?" Maraakus asked. "In the east? The Tarbisu Steppes?"

The old priest fixed him with a glittering stare. "If I remember correctly, it was first seen here, in Stridgenfel Valley. If you saw it in the east, it was carried there during the Mighty Wars."

Maraakus remained silent for a moment. Then he nodded and said, "Where eventually, after hundreds of years, it came to be used for purposes unrelated to its origin."

"Was the mark you saw in the steppes even slightly different?" the priest inquired.

"Yes. Out there, the dot in the center was a round hole in a soldier's forehead. And there were other marks on each side of this symbol."

"That's not surprising," the priest said. "I suspect it was used there in association with some ritual. Alone, it's nothing but a name. In time, of course, a word becomes a name, and some names become words. That's how language changes and grows. But not only do meanings change with time, but so can the way a word is written."

"Yet today, when we come back to the valley where this sign

originated," Maraakus said, thinking aloud, "we see it used as it was in the beginning—as a personal mark or signature."

"So it would seem," the priest agreed. "But only a very evil man would put his name to the slaughter of innocent children. Find this person, General, and you will surely find a follower of the dark arts."

"You think these killings could be part of some kind of black magic?" Danis asked the priest.

The old priest stared back at all three of them without blinking. "I have answered your questions, telling you what I believe to be true. That's all I know at this time. Nevertheless, now that we are working together, I will begin searching for additional information in the temple records."

He waved his hand, indicating the large collection of books in the room. "Many are written in the ancient tongue, of which I can read very little. Other volumes were badly damaged by fire, water, and general neglect in earlier times. As you can see, it may take me a few days, but Judbal will assist me." He waggled a finger at Rafin. "You'll find me a most valuable soldier in this crusade against evil, my ill-tempered friend."

Maraakus rose slowly to his feet. "You'll let me know the moment you have any additional information?"

"Of course," the priest assured him. The gold coins disappeared into the pocket of his robe and he walked from the room.

Danis looked at Maraakus with a puzzled expression. "Is any of what he said important?" he asked.

"I don't know," Maraakus answered, tapping his finger on his lips in a gesture of silence, "but we've gained a little information. Let's see if we can put it to use." He picked up the paper and held it in the flame of a lamp. They watched as the paper slowly burned and the ashes dropped into the oil. Then Maraakus walked out of the room and Rafin and Danis followed him back to the street.

"I'm just an old soldier trying to be a good catchpole for a small mountain village," Rafin said, "but I don't see that we learned much of anything. Are we looking for a priest of some ancient religion, or an Ammak from the Tarbisu Steppes?"

"Neither," Maraakus asserted. "The old priest was correct. I think we're looking for something entirely different. The dead soldiers in the steppes were not ripped open; their hearts were not taken, and the sign on their foreheads was different. Sometimes, Rafin, it's helpful to know what you're *not* looking for. That can save a lot of time."

"That's true," Danis agreed, "but how did we learn what we're not looking for?"

"Rafin, what's the most dreadful thing one can do to an Ammak?" Maraakus asked.

"Burn his body, I suppose." Rafin answered.

"Exactly. They believe burning the body—especially the head—destroys the eternal spirit. Believing that the eternal spirit resides in the brain, the Ammak shamans constructed a special branding iron. They heated the iron and drove it into the skulls of our living soldiers, cooking their brains and leaving those marks on their foreheads. It was the most horrible fate they could imagine for themselves, so they did it to their enemies."

"And that wasn't done here," Rafin said.

"Exactly. In the steppes, the murders were simply attempts to demoralize our soldiers."

Rafin nodded. "What about some secret religious cult?"

"I think we can rule that out, too," Maraakus answered. "You can't go about murdering people, putting identifying marks on them, and expect to keep your activities secret. The whole idea is ridiculous."

"Then what are we looking for?" Danis asked, clearly confused.

"A man. The priest told us the mark originated in this valley as the personal mark of an evil man. So we look back to its original use, then try to figure out who would use it today. I think we're looking for a man who imagines himself to be a magician. We could have a crazy Balzarr in our midst."

"For the moment." Rafin said. "Let's allow the villagers to believe it's an animal. That's something they can easily understand. At least they won't fly into a panic, thinking some evil wizard is about to destroy them with dire curses and spells of magic. Meanwhile, we won't be wasting our time chasing nonexistent Ammaks."

❧ ❦ ❧

"This is where Andor was found," Rafin said.

Maraakus looked down at a small circle of trampled brush marked by cartwheels and eroded footprints. They had ridden out into the fields shortly after leaving the Temple of Judbal.

"Any tracks have been erased by the rain, or trampled by careless feet." Danis remarked.

"The last time I saw Fergus alive," Rafin told Maraakus, pointing toward the northern edge of the field, "he signaled that he'd found Andor's tracks, then disappeared into those woods. He was headed toward the Pinnacle."

Maraakus turned and stared up at the oddly-shaped mountain. The morning sun highlighted the sheer, gray walls of the steep cliffs around its base. To search for tracks on those rocky slopes this long after the death of a man would be a waste of time. Still, Maraakus felt some strange, compelling urge to see the mountain close up. "Let's ride to the foot of the Pinnacle," he suggested. "I'd like to see the entire valley from there, if possible."

"There's no road," Danis told him. "You get there by following a path through the woods. I know it well. I've played around that mountain since I was young."

Rafin gave Maraakus a slight smile. "Then you lead the way," the general instructed.

Riding single file, they followed a wandering path through the trees and emerged on a long, rocky hillside near the foot of the Pinnacle. Looking to his left, Maraakus saw a small pile of stones surrounded by clumps of low bushes. The top of the pile formed a shallow depression that had been glazed by extreme heat. The side of the rock pile contained a small round opening. "Was there once a village here?" he asked.

"I don't know," Rafin replied. "If so, it was long ago."

"That's an old forge," Maraakus said, indicating the pile of stones.

"There used to be a well over there," Danis remarked, pointing to his left. "The top has fallen in and it's full of rocks."

Maraakus looked back toward the valley. From this higher position, he could clearly see the village of Stridgenfel with its walls and high stone tower, and anything else that moved on the Northern Road. To his right lay the new planting fields, cut by the old footpath. To the west, the dark wilderness of the Great Shadow Forest extended to the western horizon. Had he been seeking the ideal location for an observation post to monitor the village and its inhabitants, this would be the spot.

He fixed the geography in his mind and turned to look up, allowing his eyes to take in the steep cliffs that formed the base of the vertically-faced mountain. East of the Pinnacle, the mountain slopes were covered by small trees and long, grassy meadows fell gently away toward the Opal River. But it was the strangely shaped mountain, standing like a dark, brooding sentinel that demanded his attention.

"The young girl, Milari, was found in those pastures," Rafin said, indicating the lands east of the Pinnacle.

Maraakus studied the sloping meadows, noting that the grass was rapidly turning brown. And even at this modest altitude, the wind was stronger. He turned up the collar of his cloak and shivered, even though the wind was not that cold. "Let's move on to where Fergus was found," he suggested.

Rafin nodded and led them southwest, down the steep slopes and toward the Dove. Upon reaching the river, they turned right, following the north bank upstream, away from the village. After riding for a while they passed a low bluff of jagged rocks which ended near a small waterfall. Rafin turned right, then led them up the riverbank and dismounted under the spreading limbs of a massive beech tree standing on the edge of an area recently cleared by woodcutters. Behind them, out of sight behind a screen of willows, Maraakus could hear the waters of the Dove tumbling over the falls.

Pointing with his forefinger, Rafin indicated a place where the forest floor had been recently disturbed. "Fergus was found right here," he said.

Using the dagger from his boot, Maraakus knelt on the ground and gently lifted the fallen leaves and small twigs. Two sets of widely spaced footprints were found in the wet, spongy earth. One set, larger and deeper than the other, had been made by Rafin's oversized boots. Parallel to both sets of footprints, he saw a series of large, oblong depressions and traced them back to the big beech tree.

"His bow was next to his body," Rafin said.

Maraakus looked up at Rafin. "You have his bow? Did you find his quiver and arrows?"

Rafin nodded. "Maybe half his arrows were gone. The rest were still in the quiver. I have them at the house along with the bow."

"How many arrows did he carry?"

Rafin scratched at his beard. "I'd say more than a dozen, but fewer than twenty."

Maraakus walked slowly around the area, carefully inspecting the swampy forest floor. Then he walked back to the beech tree, placed his back to the massive trunk, and studied the clearing before him.

" . . . and the bow was old," Rafin was saying. "Fergus drew it once too often. It broke sideways, just above the grip."

Maraakus looked sharply at Rafin. "What did you say?"

"I said the bow was old."

"No, you said something about how it broke."

"Oh," Rafin said. "It broke sideways, above the grip."

Maraakus looked at Danis and saw the young man frowning. "Danis?" he asked. "You were going to say something?"

"I've had bows break in my hands," Danis declared, "but none like that. I should have noticed that when we found Fergus. That bow was struck hard from the side—or stepped on by something heavier than either Fergus or Rafin."

"I found some large depressions and two sets of footprints." Maraakus said. "One set was made by our big-footed friend Rafin, so let's assume the other set was made by Fergus. I don't know what made the deep depressions, but it was certainly quite heavy."

He walked back to the spot where Fergus was found. Danis joined him and Maraakus pointed to the smaller footprints. "These tracks started from behind that beech tree. Suppose Fergus shot his arrows—say, toward that hole in the thicket—then started running? See the length of his stride? But his killer caught the old man here—where Rafin found him—then killed him and broke his bow."

Rafin and Danis considered this while they followed Maraakus across the clearing to a dense thicket of bearbriars that extended into the woods. Except for a wide break in the center, it formed a continuous wall of thick, interwoven branches, armed with dark clusters of long, vicious thorns. He studied the thicket for a few moments, then positioned himself in the center of the break and turned to face the clearing.

"You first, Rafin," he instructed. "Take cover behind that beech tree. Just pretend you're Fergus. Stand with your back to the trunk, while I shake these bushes. When you hear the noise stop, jump out, and line up a shot at me. Imagine you're holding a bow."

After Rafin positioned himself behind the beech tree, Maraakus shook the bushes for a moment. Rafin stepped awkwardly from behind the tree, raised his left hand, then tripped over a root and fell heavily on his right side. Getting quickly to his feet, the big man pointed across the clearing. "I've got you," he shouted to Maraakus. "My short leg didn't see that root."

Maraakus laughed under his breath, but saw a trickle of blood on the back of Rafin's right hand. Danis was leaning against a small tree, arms across his stomach, making a valiant attempt to suppress his laughter. Rafin was glaring darkly at both of them.

Looking up, Danis wiped his eyes with the back of his hand, then broke into a peal of laughter. Finally, he controlled himself and walked over to Rafin. "Are you all right?" he asked.

Rafin grinned foolishly and clapped the young man on the shoulder. "I suppose it did look pretty funny," he admitted.

"Danis?" Maraakus called. "You do the same thing. When I stop shaking the bushes, jump out and take aim at me."

Danis took up a position behind the beech tree, still laughing softly to himself. "Do I have to fall down?" he asked.

"If you fall," Rafin threatened, "I'll put the flat of my sword across your butt."

Maraakus gave the bushes a hard shake and Danis jumped from behind the tree. With a practiced motion, he raised the bow in his right hand; his left hand was tucked tightly under his left ear. "I've got you!" he shouted.

For a moment, Maraakus stood looking at the young archer. Then he took two steps forward and stopped. "If you shot an arrow and missed," he inquired of Danis, "where would a spent arrow go?"

"Toward the Pinnacle. I can see it over the trees behind you."

"No," Maraakus insisted. "Lower. Where would it go if you shot just over my head?"

"Into that stand of pines," Danis replied.

"Where would your arrow have gone, Rafin?"

"Toward that big oak," Rafin replied.

"Was Fergus left-handed or right-handed?" Maraakus asked.

"Left-handed," Danis declared immediately. "Like me. Why do you ask?"

"Because, you smart young whelp," Rafin said, grinning at Danis, "if we go searching for spent arrows, we go toward the pines. That's where left-handed archers would aim. Didn't you notice that we came from behind the tree in opposite directions? We were at least thirty feet apart—and it's a small clearing—so the angle to Maraakus was quite different."

Danis grinned at the big man. Then he started laughing again. "I'm sorry, Rafin," he said, "but it was funny."

"Let's spread out about ten feet apart," Maraakus ordered. "Take your time and go slow. Make a good search. Where I'm standing the thickets have been broken and rolled down to the ground. Something big came through here, but I can't tell much by looking at the tracks. They're just big depressions in the earth. The same depressions as over there where the body was found. Keep a sharp eye on the woods and maintain a good line toward that stand of pines."

They spread out as directed and pushed into the dense underbrush. After a short distance, the brush thinned and they entered a section of the forest where trees had been recently cut. Piles of limbs were stacked between the stumps and the area was crisscrossed with ruts made by heavily loaded carts.

"The woodcutters have worked in here, too," Rafin observed.

About fifty feet farther on, Maraakus saw a glint of yellow near the base of a tall pine. He walked to the tree, reached down and picked up an arrow. The shaft was ringed with two circles of blue paint and coated with a dark, jelly-like substance. He touched it with a finger and found it thick and sticky. "Over here!" he shouted. "I've found one!"

Rafin and Danis made their way over to his position. Rafin took the arrow and Maraakus watched as it was examined.

"The point is a little rusty," Rafin observed, "but the cutting edges are sharp and the blue circles match the arrows I saw him sharpening. It's definitely one of Fergus's arrows."

"What is that substance on the shaft and fletching?" Maraakus asked.

Rafin brought the arrow to his nose and sniffed. "By all the merciful gods! I've never smelled anything so vile."

"What has blood like that—if it is blood?" Maraakus asked.

"Whatever it was," Danis commented, "The arrow probably struck a fleshy part and passed straight through."

Maraakus looked at the sun, noticing that it was getting low in the western sky. "I think we should be starting back. We've learned a few things today."

Chapter Six

Alyna sat quietly at one end of the table, watching carefully as Maraakus dipped a pen into a pot of ink and added a few additional marks to the map he was drawing. Rafin nodded with approval. The map was a close approximation of the valley, showing the village, the fields, both rivers, the bridge, the old footpath, and the Pinnacle.

"Right here," Rafin said, tapping the map with his finger, "is the high pasture where the little girl was found."

Maraakus made a notation on the map "If we assume that the trapper was killed the day he left the village—since he only tended to a few of his traps and would have come back home when the weather started to get bad—we have about the same time span between killings. Three to four days."

"I agree," Rafin said. "There does seem to be a pattern, since we know Nanak was alive the day we tried to find him. And we know the girl was killed one day before we returned. That's another four day separation."

"Which brings up another problem," Maraakus said. "Today is our third day back and four days since the last killing."

Rafin shook his head slowly. "Are you saying we should restrict the people to the village?"

"Unless you can think of a better way to protect them until this murderer is found."

"I can't," Rafin admitted. "But each gate will require two guards. Even if they stand long watches, we'll need more men. Most of the men in town are older than you and me put together—or little more than boys—and there's only a handful of veterans we can depend on."

"That's all we'll need," Maraakus assured him. "Put a veteran at each position and one inexperienced man with him. Can you find me a dozen veterans?"

Rafin scratched in his beard. "I'll find us twelve."

"Good," Maraakus said, smiling across the table. "We'll post guards only at night and rotate the watch positions."

Rafin gave him a wry grin. "You've considered this from the beginning, haven't you?"

"It crossed my mind once or twice," Maraakus admitted. "You know how I hate not having a fall-back position."

"When do you want to lock the place down?"

"Tonight. I want a man on the ground at each gate and a veteran on the wall above him. And make certain there's a torch at the base of the tower."

"I understand," Rafin said. "But if this lock-down lasts beyond a few days. . . ."

"If my plan works," Maraakus told him, "we won't need more

than four days. And bring in that woman from the slaughter-house, too. Not one person is to be outside the gates after sunset."

"Hmmm," Rafin grumbled. "I'd rather wrestle a bull in the slaughterhouse pens than try to bring in that stubborn old woman."

"I'll get Zandria inside," Alyna said. "Either of you would end up in the lard boilers."

Maraakus tapped his finger on the map. "What do the locations where the bodies were found have in common?"

"They're all north of the Dove?" Rafin asked.

"Right. Anything else?"

"They were alone?"

"We'll assume that, at least," Maraakus said, "and count the two brothers as a single incident. The oldest was probably killed first, but we really know very little about him."

"Keam was fourteen years old," Alyna commented softly. "He worked for Mogrin, the woodcutter, delivering firewood to help support his family. Andor was his brother. Milari was a sweet little girl who loved animals. Fergus was a friend to every person in this village. Nanak was a generous man, a good husband and father."

Maraakus put down his pen and turned to look at her. She stared back and there was a trace of anger on her face.

"Well," she said, "you two sit here, calmly discussing the deaths of our friends, our neighbors, and reducing it to nothing but circles and dots on that map you've made. These were people. Or have you forgotten that? They all had names and families."

"I'm sorry," Maraakus said quietly.

Alyna looked down at the table and folded her arms across her breasts. "It's just that I heard you talking about this being the fourth day, and I was wondering what you would do if . . ." She paused, then shrugged. "Never mind," she said. "I know nothing of military matters. I'll keep quiet while you're talking."

"Tell us what you're thinking," Maraakus insisted.

Her pale blue eyes studied him carefully. "What would you do," she asked hesitantly, "if this killer turns out to be neither a man or an animal?"

Maraakus frowned. "And what might that be?"

"It's just a feeling," she said. "I can't explain it, except to say that it's growing stronger every day. I've tried to put it out of my mind, but it continues to grow. There's something evil in this valley. I feel it now, even in this house."

She reached out her hand and placed it on the map. "I don't think the answer to this problem is in this map you're making. You must look to your instincts and intuition. I have a feeling that the solution is not nearly so simple and logical as you two might think."

"That's certainly possible," Maraakus acknowledged.

"We're probably looking for a man," Rafin said.

"No. It's not a man, Uncle Rafin," Alyna insisted. "It's something else."

Maraakus sat back in his chair and rubbed the stubble on his chin. "Obviously, this killer is either an animal or a man. Animals usually kill only when they're hungry. A man also kills for food, but he kills for other reasons as well—for revenge, out of malice, to rob, or gain power. Some of us have killed in times of war. We have killed in times of peace—in self-defense or in defense of those we love."

Rafin nodded. Alyna looked steadily back at him, waiting for him to continue.

"In this particular case," Maraakus said, "we have very little evidence, so we're forced to make some calculated assumptions."

He raised both hands above his shoulders. "And they may be wrong. Still, we must try to determine a motive and predict the killer's next move. A motive might give us an indication of what we're after and plotting the deaths might show us some pattern."

Alyna gave him a slight smile, but there was little warmth in it. "Not everything can be explained by your soldier's logic, General. Haven't you ever reasoned with your heart? That voice within you that says *believe*, even if it doesn't fit your pattern of cold logic? Haven't you ever trusted your instincts?"

Maraakus and Rafin shared a knowing smile.

"Yes, I've been known to live by my . . . instincts. But I've tried to learn to be a man of discipline and logic," Maraakus answered. "It has served me well. Does that make me cold and unfeeling?"

"I did not say that," she replied haughtily. "I was merely suggesting that you open your mind to options that do not necessarily conform to logical thoughts. What will you do if this killer is neither a man or animal."

"Then what, exactly, would it be?" Maraakus asked, sitting back and folding his arms across his chest.

"General Maraakus," she replied stiffly, "there are forces that you know little about. Some of them would certainly threaten the boundaries of that world in which you live. You and Uncle Rafin are used to dealing with familiar, recognizable objects, applying certain forms of action and getting predictable results. That is your training and experience as soldiers."

"Yes, it is," he replied. "In fact—"

"In fact," Rafin interrupted, "this discussion is doing nothing to solve the problem."

Maraakus smiled. "I'm sorry, Alyna," he said. "There's some truth in what you said. I spoke without thinking and I ask your pardon."

"The fault was mine," she replied. "I was rude and I spoke out of anger. My behavior was inexcusable."

"Enough!" Rafin exclaimed. "Let's not have another argument about who's more to blame. We need to make some decisions here. The day will be over soon."

Alyna laughed and gave Maraakus a smile. Then she patted Rafin on the hand. "Uncle Rafin's right," she said, standing up from the table. "Besides, I must go to the market." She leaned over and gave Rafin a kiss on the cheek. "I won't be long," she said.

She picked up their empty mugs and went down the stairs. Almost immediately, they heard the front door closing.

Rafin glanced up at Maraakus. "You have much to learn about arguing with a young woman, my friend."

Maraakus grinned. "Well," he replied. "As you know, I haven't had a hell of a lot of practice. I guess she's angry with me."

Rafin laughed. "See," he said, as he stood and began putting on his cloak, "you're learning already. I'd better start recruiting my guards. I'll get some people started on the torches, too."

"Good," Maraakus replied. "I'll wait here for Danis. I've had him rooting around for more information concerning the murder of Milari. I can't put my finger on it, but there's something odd about where she was found. Have you heard anything other than what Yettik told us?"

"No," Rafin said. "Just that her oldest brother carried her back and two younger ones drove the goats home."

Maraakus tapped the fingers of his right hand on the paper, making a slow drumming sound. His brow was creased in thought and a finger on his left hand stroked the ends of his long mustache. "Yet Milari's death doesn't entirely fit the pattern, Rafin. She was the only one killed above the valley floor. It may mean nothing."

Rafin nodded. "I'd better get started. We'll talk this evening. I'll probably be standing the first late watch with the guards, to set the routine and make sure they all know what's expected of them."

"Good idea," Maraakus replied, making some notations on the map in his small, neat script. He was so absorbed in thought that he hardly noticed when Rafin left. For a long while, he studied the hand-drawn map and recorded his thoughts and impressions in neat lettering down the left side of the paper. Slowly, he reviewed the entire sequence of events, including their visits to the old planting field and the woods upstream from the village. His thoughts kept returning to the area around the Pinnacle. He had a strong feeling that the mountain was central to their problem and stared at the map, concentrating on the area where Milari was killed.

Very curious, he thought. Why should there be that consistent, three or four day interval between killings? The selection of victims appears indiscriminate—the killer takes both young and old, male and female—and all the deaths occurred north of the Dove and west of the Opal, in the general area of the Pinnacle. Now we're locking down the village. What will happen when we force a break in the pattern?

He placed the pen on the table and went out into the front yard. The Pinnacle was clearly visible, dominating the landscape to the north. For a long time, he stared at the dark, vertical column of stone, the tree-covered top, and the steep cliffs surrounding the mountain's base.

What about the old legend Rafin had mentioned? he asked himself. Could the boys have been up there on that mountain? Was the object of their hunting trip the legendary treasure of Jodac and not game, as their friends supposed? If so, where's the connection to Fergus? The old legend, of course. But how does that connect to the little girl and the missing trapper? Is there really a pattern, or am I simply seeing what I want to see?

As he walked back into the yard, he looked up the street to his left and saw Danis approaching. The quiver of arrows bounced on his back and his bow was strung and carried in his left hand. Danis lifted his right hand and waved.

"I went to Milari's home and talked to her brothers," he announced, as he walked into the yard and seated himself on the doorstep. "Two of the younger boys told me something we didn't know. Milari was found on a footpath near the Opal, not in the high pastures with the goats. Is that important?"

"Yes!" Maraakus said. "Now I'm certain we have a pattern. Let me show you something interesting."

Danis followed him into the house and up the stairs. "Show me exactly where she was found," Maraakus instructed, then smiled as Danis made a small mark on the map. "Rafin and I were discussing this earlier. Our killer is a creature of habit and apparently doesn't like hunting on the steeper slopes. He seems to prefer the more level ground along the river. Habits make you predictable, and that makes you vulnerable."

"I've been wondering about something," Danis said. "Why weren't Zandria, or the animals in the holding pens, or Milari's goats harmed?"

"To be safe, Alyna is bringing Zandria inside the village walls. We'll close the gates and post guards for the next few nights and see if any animals are attacked. I believe this killer moves between sunset and sunrise, at three or four day intervals. If my assumptions are correct, it will be hunting within the next two days. In fact, I think it may be hunting this very night."

"And if the livestock is not attacked?"

"Then we're definitely looking for a man." Maraakus said. "If it's an animal, it'll feed—on goats, if it has to."

"If it's not a man *or* animal?" Danis asked.

Maraakus stared at the young man for a moment, startled to hear Danis voicing the same thoughts that Alyna had expressed just a short time ago.

"Then we'd be dealing with something totally outside our experience," Maraakus replied softly. "But first, we'll consider the most logical possibilities. By forcing this killer to break an established behavior pattern, we just might have—"

The door opened downstairs and they heard the sound of heavy footsteps. Rafin hurried up the stairs. He was breathing heavily and there was sweat on his forehead. "We have a young boy missing."

"How long?"

"Since midafternoon. His name is Palen. He's ten years old. He was sent out to fetch his father—a local farmer by the name of Wayde—from the planting fields, but Wayde had returned earlier. He was down at the inn, drinking with a few friends. Wayde went back to the fields, but the boy wasn't there. I sent fifteen or twenty people through the streets looking for him, but we didn't find him."

Maraakus turned to Danis. "Go saddle your horse and meet us at the west gate," he ordered, as he began to buckle on his sword. "Hurry! There's not much daylight left!"

Danis ran from the house and Rafin followed Maraakus out to the stables. Quickly, they saddled their horses and rode down the street toward the west gate. They passed through and saw a group of villagers standing nearby, talking loudly and pointing to the planting fields. Two men on horseback came out of the gate and rode up to Rafin. Rafin spoke to the mounted men and turned to Maraakus.

"This is Gaylor," he said, jerking his thumb at a short, stoutly built man dressed in dusty clothes. "This other man is the boy's father, Wayde. They own four fields beyond the western hedgerows and they work them together. Palen probably followed the old footpath when he left the village."

Maraakus looked at Wayde. He was a thin, angular man and his sunburned face was fixed in a worried frown. Looking over the small crowd, Maraakus saw another man on horseback.

"Get that rider over here," he instructed. "Ask the rest of these people to stay back. Too many will track up the area."

Rafin nodded. "Lannon!" he shouted, calling the third rider by name. After the man on horseback joined them, Rafin rode back to the crowd and said a few words to them. They listened, then began to move slowly toward the west gate where they stopped and milled around, talking among themselves. Danis came through the gate and joined Maraakus and the other mounted men.

Rafin returned and nodded to Maraakus. "They understand," he said. "They'll stay here."

"We'll search in pairs," Maraakus instructed. "Take the boy's father with you, Rafin. Search that hedgerow to the north of the first field and go down to the western end. Danis and Gaylor will search the southern hedgerow. Lannon and I will search the fields beyond the western hedgerow and along the edge of the forest. Lannon, you take the north end. I'll start from the south. We'll meet somewhere in the middle."

They rode off toward the fields, each pair of riders taking a different direction. A few of the village dogs followed the riders into the evening darkness, barking and baying, before giving up and trotting back toward the village. But a rangy, yellow hound with torn ears follow Maraakus out into the fields. Unlike the others, he neither barked or bayed, but just loped along, keeping perfect pace with the big black horse, his tongue hanging from the side of his mouth and his ragged ears flopping against his head.

Lannon and Maraakus rode straight down the old footpath and crossed through the western hedgerow. They parted at the edge of the forest and Lannon rode toward the north end of the four large fields; Maraakus turned south. Halfway down the fields, Maraakus lost sight of Lannon behind a clump of trees. When he reached the southern corner, Maraakus dismounted and drew his sword. The yellow hound flopped down in the dust, panting heavily, watching him attentively.

Maraakus whistled to the dog and moved into the trees some ten or fifteen feet from the edge of the field. The hound jumped up and followed, nosing busily through the dead leaves and around the roots of the trees.

Maraakus stopped frequently to call for the boy as he worked his way through the woods, but his progress was hampered by the rapidly fading light. Occasionally he stepped out to the open field, searching for tracks. He had nearly reached the bulge in the tree line when he heard shouts.

Going quickly to the edge of the woods, he saw a rider coming across the planting fields, moving toward Danis and Gaylor. He watched while Danis and the man talked, then Danis wheeled his horse and rode west across the fields.

The old hound was standing stiffly, tail down, looking toward the woods. It gave a low, throaty growl and the hair on its back bristled.

Danis pulled his horse to a stop. "They found the boy," he announced happily. "He was playing at the home of a friend. Gaylor went to tell Rafin and Wayde."

"Good," Maraakus said. "Let's find Lannon and get back to the village. It's nearly dark." Putting his fingers to his mouth, he whistled sharply and his horse lifted its head and trotted in their direction.

Maraakus stepped to the edge of the woods and called for his searching partner. "Lannon!" he shouted.

There was no answer. He shouted again without results. Looking north, to the far side of the field, he saw the man's horse browsing calmly on some shrubbery. "Bring Lannon's horse down here," he instructed.

Danis nodded and rode off.

The yellow hound growled and ran a few yards into the woods. It came back almost immediately. Snarling through bared teeth, it turned to face the forest and assumed a pointing position, as though waiting for instructions.

Maraakus walked toward the dog, watching carefully for the slightest movement in the trees and thickets. Off to his left, deeper in the woods, he thought he saw movement.

"Lannon! Is that you?"

As Maraakus moved forward, the big hound began to bark. Then it bounded eagerly into the heavy underbrush. Maraakus followed the dog, working his way deeper into the woods on a line that would take him to the southern banks of the Dove. The fading light blended the trees and thickets together, making it difficult to move quickly.

There was a thrashing sound off to the left and the hound returned, growling and walking with a curious, stiff-legged gait.

Maraakus pointed into the forest. "Go get 'em, boy!"

The hound wagged its tail and went back into the bushes.

Maraakus followed with cautious steps, then stopped as a shift in the wind brought a vile, nauseating odor to his nose and the dog began barking. Then it let loose a series of loud, frightened yelps, followed by a single howl of pain.

Maraakus whistled for the dog, but the woods were silent. An image of the hound, dead and bleeding on the forest floor flashed through his mind. Had something killed it? Something very close? Raising his sword to the ready position, he took a hesitant step forward. Again he whistled for the dog but got no response.

Then something pushed into the dark thickets on his left and a scuffling sound came from his right. Maraakus wheeled about, pointing his sword first in one direction, then another, and crouching low in a defensive posture. But it was the yellow hound that burst out of the tangled undergrowth and ran to his side.

He spoke softly to the dog and pointed to the woods with his left hand. "Hunt, boy! Hunt!"

The dog ignored his command. Whining softly, it tried to crawl closer to his legs, so Maraakus reached down and took it by the scruff of its neck. As he pushed it back toward the dark thickets, he felt a warm, sticky wetness on his fingers. Blood! The dog was injured! "Go on, boy!" he whispered hoarsely. "Get him, old dog!"

The big hound gave a single, plaintive howl and tucked its tail between its legs. It ducked quickly around Maraakus and ran blindly through the woods toward the open fields, and the village beyond.

Maraakus felt a sudden chill as the hair on his neck lifted. The sight of the big dog fleeing in terror seemed unnatural.

He backed slowly against the trunk of a thick oak tree and heard a heavy body moving through the bushes. With the tree protecting his back, he fixed his eyes on the thicket and saw a slight movement to his left—a pale, vaporous shadow drifting low across the ground. Then he saw Lannon lying on his back, his legs under a small bush, a gaping hole in his chest. The strange shadow was steam rising from the man's opened body.

Maraakus leaned against the tree and breathed deeply; his heart pounded and his legs trembled—more from anger than fear. Then something moved closer, breaking branches and snapping dead limbs underfoot, circling to his left. The sound of slow, heavy breathing came from the thicket, accompanied by a low, hissing sound.

Maraakus gripped his sword tightly. What little visibility he had left was reduced by a cold, stinging sweat that ran from his forehead into his eyes. Then he saw movement behind the thicket and stepped forward. "Let's see how you like the taste of cold steal!" he shouted. "Come on! You won't find me as easy as the others!"

When there was no answering sound, he took another step forward and shook the heavy sword. "Come on, damn you!" he whispered.

Then he heard Danis shouting to him from the planting fields. "Maraakus! Where are you?"

"Over here, Danis! Get Rafin! *Hurry!*"

"Maraakus!" Rafin shouted. "I'm here! We're coming in!"

He could hear Danis and Rafin pushing through the brush behind him, moving in his direction. In front of him, a massive black shadow moved off to the right and he heard the sound of breaking branches as though something heavy was being dragged through the thickets. Then he heard it moving away, deeper into the forest.

"Maraakus!" Rafin called.

"Over here, Rafin!"

Rafin and Danis burst into the small clearing.

Maraakus let the sword fall and leaned back against the oak tree. "It was here . . . right in front of me." he breathed. He raised his head to look at them.

"Animal?" Rafin asked.

"I think so," Maraakus replied. "All I saw was a black shadow, but it's that thing we're after! I can feel it."

"And I can smell it," Rafin said. "It smells just like the arrow we found."

"It was coming straight at me, and didn't seem afraid until it heard you and Danis coming," Maraakus said, wiping his hand across his face. "Over there," he said, pointing to the left side of the thicket. "Lannon's dead."

They walked to the thicket and looked down at the body. Like the others, Lannon had been killed and opened up; his forehead was covered with a drying, bloody crust; small wisps of steam still rose from his open chest and disappeared in the cold air.

For a time, Maraakus could only stare at the man he had talked with just a short time ago. And he watched silently as Rafin and Danis picked up the man's remains. Rafin slung Lannon's body across his horse and they rode without speaking through the fields to the village.

As they approached the gate, Maraakus turned to look at Rafin. "Alyna was right," he said softly. "There's something evil out there in that forest. I felt it staring at me. It was almost as though it was . . . willing me to . . . like I was paralyzed . . . with fright. Now I know how those Ammak stragglers must have felt."

Rafin listened, but made no reply.

"I don't know what it is," Maraakus continued, "but it isn't a man. Whatever it is, I won't leave this valley until I see it dead."

CHAPTER SEVEN

Maraakus walked Stridgenfel's high stone wall, deep in thought. To his soldier's eye, the village was under siege. No catapults or rams stood outside the walls. No enemy campfires dotted the valley or mountain slopes. But it was a siege just the same, at least during the hours of darkness.

Do we now have four days until that thing comes hunting again? he wondered. If so, how many men will it take to kill it? Is it an animal? It wasn't a man; men might carve marks on their victims, but animals don't. Is Alyna right? Have I encountered something outside my logical world?

He passed the south gate and continued on, walking and thinking. By the time he arrived back at the north gate, a new day was dawning over the eastern cliff beyond the Opal River. He climbed down a long ladder to the ground and found Rafin standing near the gate, watching him, arms folded across his chest.

"I thought you were resting," Maraakus remarked.

"No," Rafin replied. "I've been watching you walk the walls. Now go home and get some sleep."

Maraakus nodded. "Tell Danis to meet me at noon for a ride up to the Pinnacle."

"Shall I come with you?"

"No," Maraakus said wearily. "Half the village is already up. I wouldn't be surprised if Stridgenfel's catchpole had a busy day ahead of him."

Rafin turned and looked behind him. "I know," he said. "Somehow, they know about the marks and the missing hearts. There's even talk of organizing a hunting party."

"Who's the biggest, meanest, most intimidating man in Stridgenfel?" Maraakus asked. "Besides yourself, of course."

Rafin smiled, pleased that Maraakus had not lost his sense of humor. "That would be Hadrax. He makes me look small. Normally, he's gentle as a newborn pup, but we all know he has a nasty temper."

"Just the man you need," Maraakus asserted. "Deputize him and put a big sword in his hands."

Rafin grinned. "A good idea. Now, go on home and get some rest. I'll send Danis to you around noon."

Maraakus nodded and walked away. Upon arriving at the house, Alyna rose quickly to her feet. "I've fixed you something to eat," she said. "Are you all right?"

"I'm fine," he assured her, "and so are Rafin and Danis."

"The water is heated," she said. "The tub will relax you. I'll make a fresh pot of tea."

When he was finished bathing and had changed into clean

clothes, he went back to the kitchen. Alyna had prepared breakfast and he ate slowly, watching as she moved busily around the room. Finally, she seated herself at the table.

"Uncle Rafin told me what happened," she said. "Did you see it?"

Maraakus pushed the empty plate to one side and took a swallow from his mug of tea. "No," he replied. "Just a big, dark, vile-smelling shadow."

"But it was definitely an animal?"

He rubbed his eyes with the back of one hand. "I believe so, though it's larger than any animal I've ever seen. You were right. There is something very odd—something . . . evil—about these murders. What animal hunts on such a regular schedule? And then there's the mark. . . ."

There was a short silence, then Maraakus sighed. "I'm going go back out to the Pinnacle today."

"Looking for what?" she asked. "For this . . . creature?"

"I don't know what I expect to find. Maybe nothing. You said I should trust my intuition and instincts. Remember?"

"I was wrong. I spoke out of anger and—"

"No. You were right. I've had a strong feeling about that chunk of rock since the first time I saw it. There's a pattern in where the bodies were found. The circle of death is growing wider—coming closer to the village—and my intuition tells me that the center of that circle is the Pinnacle."

Fixing him with her pale, blue eyes she said, "Take me with you."

"No." he told her flatly, "I promised Rafin that I'd keep you out of harm's way. And I have personal reasons, as well," he added.

"And I have personal reasons for asking you to take me with you," she said softly.

❧ ❧ ❧

Danis led them in an easterly direction around the base of the Pinnacle. The afternoon was unusually warm, a rare day in late autumn when the wind blew from the south. Such days could change quickly to overcast skies, bitterly cold winds, and soaking rains that turned to winter snows.

But not today. Today was to be savored and enjoyed as one of the last mild days before winter.

Maraakus divided his attention between the slopes of the high cliffs and Alyna. He was, at best, uneasy about even allowing her outside the village—let along dragging her into what might be the center of the whole evil mess. Yet he smiled as her dappled mare stepped over a fallen rock and she lurched forward in her saddle, then looked back to see if he was watching. "Keep up, now," she admonished playfully. "Don't get lost."

After riding down a slight incline, Danis pulled his horse to a stop and dismounted. Here the village was out of sight, screened from view by tall trees and high vertical cliffs footed with moss-covered boulders. Maraakus dismounted and helped Alyna from her horse. She leaned against him briefly, then walked to a rock and sat down.

Maraakus studied the high, overhanging cliffs around the foot of the Pinnacle, then shifted his gaze to the rock shelves above them, then to the Pinnacle's western side where the sloping top was covered with trees and brush. At the edge of this tree line, the mountain fell sharply away, a vertical plunge of several hundred feet. "Any way up these first cliffs?" he asked.

"I don't think so," Danis replied. "I've crawled all over the base of this mountain looking for one. So has every boy in Stridgenfel."

"Well," Maraakus said, "if I wanted to get to the top, I think I'd try from this side."

Danis laughed. "This is where most of us have tried. See how the cliffs hang out over you? Now look at the rock shelves above them. How wide do you think they are?"

"They could be very narrow or several feet wide. I can't tell from down here."

"We've always thought that you could walk them right to the top," Danis said. "On the western side, you can see where they end at the tree line just below the top."

"Any caves?"

"We've never found any," Danis answered, shaking his head. "There are some wide cracks, but they're all dead ends."

"Let's move on," Maraakus suggested. "I want a better view of the rock shelves from the western side. Let's go back to the spot where you took Rafin and me."

Alyna was seated on a rock with her legs stretched out in the warm sun. "Jodac's mountain," she said. "Why should a sensible adult want to climb up there, anyway? It looks dangerous to me."

"I'm sure it is," Maraakus said. "Though I'd be willing to bet there never was a stone keep up there. No wizard named Jodac and no treasure. Just rocks and trees."

Danis shook his head sadly. "And to think of all the time I've wasted looking for his treasure," he remarked.

"You and countless boys and girls for several hundred years, perhaps," Maraakus stated, tapping Danis on the head with his gloves. "Let's move on. We still have a lot of riding to do."

He assisted Alyna to her saddle and they rode west, following the old trail around the Pinnacle. A short ride brought them out near the spot where Danis had taken him a few days before. Here the cliffs were tilted against the mountain, but still provided no visible way to reach their tops.

As they rode down the slopes and through the thick forest toward the Dove, Maraakus decided that he had learned nothing of value by their ride around the Pinnacle. There appeared to be no way to the top of the mountain and he had discovered no place for a large creature to hide. In the bright light of day, the whole idea seemed rather foolish. A waste of time.

He watched Alyna as she deftly reined her horse through a scattering of stones and realized that his involvement here in

Stridgenfel was complicated by his growing attraction to her. It was something he needed to resist. He should concentrate all his energies on finding and destroying a brutal killer.

Under different circumstances, he thought, I could have welcomed a possible relationship with her. Maybe I'll come back to this village after this problem is settled. A man could be quite happy with the love of so beautiful a wife—and some equally beautiful children. Perhaps a little girl that looks like her and a son to ride and hunt with and . . . By all the gods, he asked himself, where are these thoughts coming from?

He kicked his horse and urged it forward into the water and rode quickly up the far bank. Danis followed and they looked back in time to see Alyna's mare stumble. She gave a small cry, then slid from her saddle and landed with a mighty splash in the cold water.

While Danis threw back his head and laughed, Maraakus jumped from his horse and splashed his way to her side. As he picked her up, Alyna's arms went around his neck and her wet body pressed close to him. "Thank you, General Maraakus," she said mischievously, looking down into water that reached barely to her knees. "You've saved me from drowning, but how will you keep me from freezing to death?"

He helped her to the bank, then put her on his horse and wrapped her in his heavy cloak. When he swung up behind her, she settled quietly against his chest.

Danis took the reins of Alyna's horse. Grinning like the village idiot, he led them quickly through the woods to the old footpath and back to the village.

At the market square, Maraakus took the reins of Alyna's horse and they rode to the house alone. When he finished caring for their horses and went inside, it was late afternoon. Alyna had changed into dry clothes and was busy preparing their evening meal. She looked up and smiled as he crossed the room and climbed the stairs.

He put on dry clothes, then sat down to study the map he had drawn. He was adding notations concerning the rock shelf on the back side of the Pinnacle when the downstairs door opened He heard Rafin talking to Alyna, then the sound of boots on the stairs.

"You were right," Rafin announced, crossing the room and pulling out a chair. "The village is plenty upset and there are all kinds of wild rumors floating around. It took both of us— Hadrax and me—to prevent them from going out to find that thing. Hadrax promised to jerk the head off the first man to step through a gate without permission." He chuckled to himself. "I think they believed him, too," he added. "They couldn't decide who would go first."

"The sun will be setting before long," Maraakus observed. "They'll forget about going out when it gets dark."

"Did you find anything at the Pinnacle?" Rafin asked.

"No," Maraakus replied. "I thought I'd find a cave, but we found only narrow cracks in the cliffs. Some were large enough for a man to enter, but none big enough to conceal a large animal."

"Maybe it can climb," Rafin suggested. "Like a rock lizard— or one of those goats we used to see in the Guardian Mountains."

Maraakus shook his head. "Maybe, but it didn't seem very nimble—or very light—it made a lot of noise and didn't move too fast. Actually, I'm more worried about how we're going to kill something that big."

"I guess we'll find out when we get the opportunity," Rafin said. "Anyway, the ride seems to have agreed with Alyna. I have to go back to the inn after supper. The Shopkeeper's Guild called a meeting to discuss the problem. I promised to attend."

Maraakus looked up with a worried frown.

"Don't worry," Rafin assured him. "Nothing will happen. Most of them are long on talk and short on action."

"I'll go with you."

Rafin shook his head. "No need. Danis will be there. If I need you, I'll send him to the house."

"I could use some time to think," Maraakus admitted.

"Good," Rafin declared. "Now, let's go down to supper."

Alyna remained quiet throughout the meal, but from time to time Maraakus noticed her watching him. Rafin noticed, too. He would grin, she would smile, then look down at her plate, her pale blue eyes shrouded behind her long, dark lashes. Finally, Maraakus excused himself and left the table.

Upstairs, he sat down at the map and tried to concentrate his thoughts on the killings. Down in the kitchen, he could hear the low murmur of Rafin and Alyna talking, the occasional sound of Rafin laughing, and the softer laughter of Alyna. After a while, he heard Rafin's footsteps and the closing of the front door, followed by the sounds of Alyna working in the kitchen. Then he heard her go out through the door to the shed and the house grew silent. He sighed and turned his attention back to the map.

The evening sun was sending a brilliant shaft of light through the small window placed high in the front wall of the room. The light moved slowly across the table until it was shining directly on the map and throwing a long shadow behind the dark pot of ink.

Downstairs, the door opened. He heard Alyna singing softly to herself as she came up the stairs. She sat a mug of mulled wine on the table and walked behind him, trailing her now familiar scent.

He followed her with his eyes as she glided into the bright sunlight streaming in through the high window, noticing the outline of her body through the thin material of her tunic and the sparkling amulet hanging from a chain around her neck. She took down a book and turned to face him.

"Perhaps you'd enjoy me reading to you?" she suggested. "I know it sometimes helps my uncle to relax." She stood perfectly still, holding the book in her hands.

"I won't have any problem tonight," he replied, choosing his words with great care. "I'm very tired. I have only a few notations to make and then I'll sleep."

She walked slowly up to the table, smiled and glanced at the map in front of him. As she leaned forward to examine the map, the folds of her tunic fell away, exposing the deep valley between her breasts. The amulet swung slowly on its chain, catching the sunlight with its pink crystal and casting a slow-moving, enlarged reflection on the white paper before him.

He looked up at Alyna and then back at the map, momentarily unable to comprehend what he was seeing. Within the reflection of the amulet's pink crystal was the outline of a bird and the same mark found carved into the foreheads of the murdered villagers.

He stood quickly, overturning his chair. It skidded noisily across the floor and came to rest against the wall behind him. Hearing Alyna gasp, he looked up to see her backing slowly away from the table with her hands over her mouth.

"Wh-what's wrong?" she asked. "Di-did I do something to make you angry?"

Maraakus raised both hands to shoulder height, hands open, palms exposed and fingers spread. "No," he told her. "Don't be frightened. I didn't mean to startle you. What is that crystal you're wearing around your neck?"

"It's just an old amulet," she whispered.

"Where did you get it?" he demanded, not realizing that his voice was cold and harsh.

"I-I f-found it," she stammered, as her eyes filled with tears. "Uncle Rafin said I could keep it."

"Where?" he demanded. "When?"

"In the river," she replied. Her voice was soft and edged with fear. "B-below the old field—next to the bridge. It was the day Andor was . . ." Tears slid from her wind-reddened cheeks and made dark circles on her tunic.

Slowly, he reached out to her but she shrank back, tripped over a small stool, and sat heavily on the floor. Her blue eyes stared up at him with a wounded expression. "Have I done something wrong? Something to offend you?"

"May I see the amulet?" he asked.

She removed the amulet from around her neck and he examined the pink crystal, turning it slowly in his fingers, then knelt in front of her. "I'm sorry, Alyna," he whispered. "Don't be afraid. I didn't mean to scare you."

"I'm not frightened," she said, looking up with a sullen expression. "I'm embarrassed. I was openly flirting with you and . . . well . . ."

Slowly, he reached out to her and she permitted him to draw her close to his chest. He spoke soothingly, stroking her shoulders and hair, kissing her gently on the forehead. "There's no need to be embarrassed. I'm flattered that you would do such a thing."

She lifted her face to him and he kissed her gently on the cheek. She tried to reach his mouth with her lips, but he held her firmly and prevented her from moving too close. After a while, she settled quietly in his arms, her head on his shoulder.

"Don't you want to kiss me, General Maraakus?" she whispered softly. "Am I so undesirable?"

"Shhh," he said tenderly. "Nothing could be farther from the truth. But listen to me. People are dying in this village. We mustn't complicate matters further with our personal feelings for each other. Please . . . tell me how you came by the amulet."

For a long while he held her and they stared into each other's eyes. Finally, she sighed heavily and broke her gaze. He released her, but in that moment Maraakus realized that something significant had occurred between them, some unspoken commitment had been reached.

She smiled as he assisted her from the floor, then she gathered her dark hair in her hands, gave it a twist and dropped it over her right shoulder. "I found the amulet in the river's shallows," she said, "the same day we found Andor. People often find things along the riverbanks and in the planting fields. They get turned up by farmer's plows, or washed out of the ground during hard rains."

"But a piece of jewelry is unusual, isn't it?"

"I suppose. Mostly, people find old pots and rusty weapons. Small things. Never anything of great value, though people say they're very old. Some think they're proof that the ancient races once lived here—before humans."

Maraakus held the amulet up to the sunlight. He could find no lines or engraving on either side. He walked to the table and held it above the map. As before, sunlight penetrated the pink stone and projected an image on the paper's surface. Picking up his pen, he traced it with dark ink. The bird was an eagle, clutching a spiked disc with sharp talons; above its head was the rune he now thought of as a sign of murder.

Alyna studied the drawing for a moment, then placed a finger over the mark above the eagle's head. "I've seen this part before—the eagle holding the spiked disc."

"Where?" Maraakus asked softly.

She closed her eyes. After a brief time, she opened them and shook her head. "I'm sorry. I just can't remember, but I know what parts of this image might mean."

"You can read this?"

"Yes. No! I mean . . . I can tell you the meaning of individual parts, but not what they mean when they're combined."

"Where did you learn this?" he asked.

"From my grandmother." she said. "Think of the parts as letters. The disc with spikes represents light or power, something like that. On a page of writing, the actual meaning would be determined by the letters on either side. It's a complicated form of picture writing."

"And the eagle?" he asked.

"Strength, or majesty, in motion," she replied. "It can mean movement and action, like bringing or carrying, and it can mean ownership or possession. I know that symbol above the eagle because I've seen your drawings and heard you talking to Uncle Rafin."

They heard the door opening downstairs. "I have work to finish," she told him.

Rafin passed Alyna at the head of the stairs. He gave her a curious look, walked to the table and sat down in a chair. Stretching out his shortened leg, he began massaging his shin with both hands.

"I always know when the weather is about to change," he told Maraakus. "Particularly if it's going to turn cold. This leg gives me ample warning."

Maraakus smiled and picked up the amulet. He dropped it on the map, turned the paper to Rafin and pointed to the drawing he had made.

Rafin held the amulet by the gold chain. "This is the trinket Alyna found," he said, "but what is this drawing?"

"That's what you see if you hold the amulet in the sunlight," Maraakus answered. "The amulet projects that image on a piece of paper. You see nothing looking at the stone."

"By the beards of the gods," Rafin muttered, fixing Maraakus with a questioning look. "How did you discover that?"

"I didn't," Maraakus replied. "Alyna did—in a way."

Rafin turned the amulet in his fingers. He examined it carefully, then looked back at the drawing. "You think this old trinket is connected to the murders?" he asked.

Maraakus slid forward in his chair and rested his elbows on the table. "Suppose I stole something from you," Maraakus said, stroking one end of his long mustache with a forefinger. "Let's suppose this object has little monetary worth, but great sentimental value—like a ring that belonged to your wife."

"Very well," Rafin replied, his brow furrowed in thought.

"Let's further suppose," Maraakus continued, "that you saw me take it and I'm running down the street, trying to get away."

"I'd be right on your thieving heels," the big man declared.

"Exactly," Maraakus agreed. "Since I know you're going to rip off my head if you catch me, what could I do to prevent you from continuing the chase?"

Rafin scratched in his beard and stared at Maraakus. "Probably nothing," he stated. "I'd catch up to you, then draw and quarter you with my bare hands."

Maraakus smiled at his old friend. "No doubt," he said. "What if I threw the ring down some side street? Would you continue chasing me or would you go after the ring?"

"Is this a riddle?" Rafin asked, folding his hands behind his head and leaning back in his chair.

"I'm very serious," Maraakus replied.

"Well," Rafin said. "If I saw you throw it, I'd probably go for the ring. If not, I'd catch you and pull off your arms."

"Exactly," Maraakus said, holding up the amulet. "Now, suppose I'm Andor and I have this amulet in my hand—"

"Where did you get it?" Rafin asked.

"I don't know, Rafin," Maraakus answered patiently. "Let's just say I have it. I'm running from it's rightful owner and I think he's right behind me. I throw the amulet away, hoping he will go after it and I can escape."

Rafin arched his brows and grinned. "Then this owner, who didn't see you throw the amulet into the river, catches up with you and kills you, only to discover you don't have the thing any more. Now he's really furious, so he kills every person he can find, trying to recover his stolen trinket."

Maraakus sighed. He stood up and dropped the amulet on the map. "Strangely enough, I believe that's what happened. I believe that's how the amulet got into the river, and that's why the boy was killed."

Rafin gave him a skeptical look and stood, placing his weight on his aching leg. "Much better," he said, walking a few steps across the room. He bent over and rubbed the back of his short-ened limb. "The weather is definitely going to change, my friend."

"Better or worse?"

"Worse," Rafin told him. "Winter is upon us. My leg never lies." He clapped Maraakus on the shoulder and walked to the stairs, moving with his odd, side to side motion. He steadied himself as he went down the stairs by leaning against the wall.

"Damned stairs are giving me trouble, too," he grumbled.

"You're falling to pieces," Maraakus agreed. "Soon you'll have to hire a boy to lift you to the saddle and pull you up and down stairs."

Rafin grunted. "That'll be the day," he grumbled. "I can still outmaneuver a man half my age!"

Maraakus smiled and followed the old soldier across the kitchen and out to the washroom in the shed.

CHAPTER EIGHT

Maraakus watched the morning service from the rear of the temple. When the antiquated rituals ended and the last worshiper had filed quietly into the street, the klersep went to the brass bowl and scooped out a few coins, counted them, and deposited them in a wooden box under the altar. Though he had not yet acknowledged Maraakus's presence, he looked up and said, "Did you find Judbal's message inspirational, General Maraakus?"

"You have keen sight, Holy One," Maraakus replied.

"Oh, yes. Very little happens in this sacred place that escapes my old eyes. And nothing escapes Judbal's." the old priest said. "I am pleased to see you. In fact, I planned to send word that Judbal has provided information you might find valuable."

Maraakus gave the klersep a wry smile as he walked forward to meet him. Turning to the back wall, the priest pulled on a heavy cord. The rotting tapestry moved to one side, exposing a carved wooden door. He took a slender taper from his pocket, then touched it to the lamp behind the brass bowl.

"Close your eyes, General. Do not open them until I instruct you to do so. I shall act as your guide."

Maraakus allowed himself to be led through the door and into the darkened room. The smell of fresh paint came immediately to his nose.

"Don't look," the priest said. "I must light more lamps."

Maraakus waited patiently, listening as the priest proceeded around the room with shuffling steps. Finally, the old man said, "You may open your eyes."

Maraakus stood in awe, letting his eyes take in the splendor of the room. Brightly colored tapestries hung from stone walls scrubbed free of soot and grime; delicate, painted wooden columns supported a high dome of intricately carved timbers. Behind a gleaming, dark granite altar, he saw an alcove edged with a border of shimmering gold. Inside this small shelter, a white marble statue looked down with a gentle, smiling face. The right hand of the statue held a loaf of bread; his left hand was extended in what Maraakus interpreted to be a gesture of blessing.

"And this," the priest declared, indicating the statue, "is the greatest of all gods—or his earthly representation, at least. No man knows the true form of Judbal. Nevertheless, I have spent years restoring this chapel to its former glory."

"Remarkable," Maraakus assured him.

The old priest smiled. "I show you this for a reason, General, lest you believe I'm motivated by greed. My tastes are simple and I have little personal need for money. The offerings I receive are used to care for needy families in this village; the rest is used to restore the temple. When my restorations are completed—providing Judbal grants me the time—this room will be opened to all."

"I understand," Maraakus said. "You are indeed full of surprises." He watched as the priest walked slowly around the room, extinguishing lamps; then they walked back to the old man's sleeping chamber and sat down at the table.

"Now," Maraakus told him, "I wish to show you something." After withdrawing the amulet and paper from his pocket, he placed them in front of the priest and waited until both were examined before speaking.

"I'd be curious to know what you think the drawing means," Maraakus said, "and what you think of the amulet."

The old man studied both the drawing and the amulet. He sighed and closed his eyes, visibly upset. "That is a plactrogram," he said, tapping the paper with a forefinger.

Maraakus saw the priest's trembling hand. "Plactrogram?" he asked. "I don't believe I've ever heard that word."

"A plactrogram is a symbolic representation of a family surname. Today, we do something very similar, but we call it a coat of arms."

"To what family does it belong?"

The old priest rubbed his eyes and shook his head. "How did you come by this amulet?"

"Alyna found it at the edge of the river. The morning Andor's body was discovered."

The priest sighed and picked up the drawing. "A most curious thing," he muttered, bringing the drawing close to his eyes and tilting it toward the lamp. "There are those who can read and write this language, but the manner of speaking it has been forgotten. This was a language used by the ancient races."

Maraakus smiled. "Are you referring to elves and dwarves—such creatures as that?"

"I am, indeed. You don't believe they once existed?"

Maraakus noticed that the old priest was not smiling. "Are you able to interpret this . . . writing?" Maraakus asked, ignoring the old man's question.

"I am neither a historian nor a scholar," the old man stated. "I am a lowly country klersep of Judbal. I can give you my best interpretation, but if you are seeking the full meaning of these symbols, you need a literate *elf.*"

"I don't need an elf," Maraakus declared. "What I need is a simple interpretation, and the name indicated by this . . . plactrogram. You've obviously seen it before."

"Not exactly," the priest said, "but one containing the eagle and disc was shown to me by a dear friend—a woman named Sheya. It was her family's plactrogram." He sat back and stared at Maraakus, obviously waiting for some response.

"Does this woman live in Stridgenfel?"

"The woman is dead. Sheya was Rafin's mother."

Maraakus caught his breath in a single gasp. A cold numbness flashed through his body and for a while he sat staring at the priest, his mouth hanging open in shock and disbelief.

"No," he managed to say, shaking his head slowly. "I can't believe a member of Rafin's family could be associated with these murders."

"Nor can I," the priest agreed. "Sheya was a kind and gentle person. You've shown this drawing to Alyna and Rafin?"

"Yes. Alyna recognized the eagle and spiked disc, but she can't remember where she saw it."

"Did she recognize this mark?" He leaned forward and indicated the rune above the eagle's head.

"Only as the mark found on the murdered villagers. I don't believe either of them even knows the family *had* a plactrogram. But Alyna knew the meaning of the disc and eagle."

The old priest frowned. "I came to this village when I was a very young man, newly ordained. I was fascinated by the ancient writings that had survived here and I collected every example I could find. I studied them for many years, trying to read and preserve them, but my efforts were largely unsuccessful.

"One day, Sheya came to see me. She had heard of my interest in the ancient language and offered to help interpret the few examples in my collection. On one occasion, she drew her family plactrogram and it closely resembled the drawing on that paper. The eagle and disc were identical, but the mark over the eagle's head was not."

"There was some other mark?" Maraakus asked.

"Yes. As I have told you, this drawing is composed of symbols. To understand them, you must realize that you are looking at a combination of meanings. This one, the disc of the sun, was associated with the practice of magic."

Maraakus remained silent, waiting for the old man to continue. After a brief pause, the priest sighed heavily and sat back in his chair.

"The eagle is a sign of strength and endurance. Sometimes a symbol of authority. The head is turned to the right—toward the future. In its talons, it holds the disc of the sun, indicating that this individual had knowledge and power generally associated with the use of magic. The spikes—the sun's rays—are not all of the same length, which means that other members of this family might have this ability as well. I'm unable to give you a more detailed interpretation, but I believe the common tongue translation of this plactrogram is 'I am bringing knowledge' or 'I am the bearer of enlightenment.' At any rate, it signifies a person or family of great power and unusual ability."

"Such as the ability to practice magic?" Maraakus asked.

The priest smiled. "Despite your skepticism, magic does exist, I assure you."

"Can it be learned?" Maraakus asked.

The priest shrugged. "Probably not. I suspect it is a talent given at birth. And as indicated by this plactrogram, members of Rafin's family are sometimes given this ability in many forms and to varying degrees."

"Then such people must be quite rare," Maraakus commented.

"Once in several generations, perhaps, comes one so truly gifted that human history is altered. Eventually, we recognize these periods in our history. We give them names such as the Dark Time, the Season of Bitterness . . . or the Mighty Wars. Beneficial changes might encompass a time such as the Decades of Great Enlightenment."

He paused to rub his eyes with his thumb and forefinger. "In this case," he continued, "I am quite concerned. The plactrogram shown here contains not only the eagle and disc, but this evil mark, too." He tapped the drawing with his finger. "Please understand that this is not Rafin's or Alyna's plactrogram. It belongs to some other member of their family—a specific individual."

"And you've already told me that you can't pronounce this surname," Maraakus said.

The priest touched him on the shoulder and walked behind him to the head of the table. "Unfortunately, that's true," he said, "but that would be of little use, since you know this symbol belongs to his family. Surnames have all but disappeared from use and have changed greatly over the years. To make things even more difficult, few people even recall that surnames were once quite common. Now they are simply Hadrax the Baker, Bedmam the Smithy, Kalin of the Axe, or . . . Death's Own Shadow."

With that, the old cleric rose and walked to the end of the room. He stood motionless with his back to Maraakus, arms folded across his chest, staring at the stones in the wall. At last, he turned and walked back to the table. He sat down and placed both hands on a leather-bound book. "These are my oldest records. Some of the pages are missing, damaged by water, or in other ways unreadable. But I found one small reference to that evil sign. As I told you, it is a symbol that became the signature of an evil man. A man who wished to become a god. The man's name was Jodac."

"You can't be serious," Maraakus remarked.

"Oh, I'm quite serious, General. And there's more. The image created by the amulet also bears his name. Rafin, Alyna, and Jodac share a common—"

"By the very gods!" Maraakus interrupted loudly. "And you really believe this?"

"It does not matter what I *believe*," the priest asserted. "I am simply reading the image projected by the amulet—which you brought to me. As for the information contained in my temple records, they are written in the common tongue. You may read for yourself." He opened the book, turned back several pages and pushed it across the table. "There is the specific reference to Jodac's signature. When you have finished reading, I will show you some plactrograms used by the ancient races. My collection is small, but every item is authentic."

❧ ✣ ☙

Outside, the sky had darkened to the color of slate and the rain had slowed to a cold, light drizzle. Wood smoke lay heavily in the air, drifting about like a dense, acrid fog. Maraakus turned up the collar of his cloak and stepped out onto the wet street, surprised to find the market stalls closed and shuttered. He thought that strange, until he realized that it was Sixth Day, the day when the markets closed early.

For a time, he stood motionless in the empty street, letting the damp air seep through his clothing and sharpen his senses. When the taste of rancid lamp oil faded from his nostrils, he walked slowly across the market square and stopped at the base of the tower. Taking the amulet from his pocket, he inspected the pale stone and drew the smooth chain through his fingers. Then he slipped the amulet back into his pocket and set off for Rafin's home on the west side of the village.

Upon entering the house, he found the old soldier seated at the kitchen table, eating an early supper before going on watch. Alyna was toasting slices of dark bread on an iron grate before the fire. She smiled as he entered the room and Rafin lifted his hand in greeting.

"Did you speak with the priest?" Rafin asked.

Maraakus nodded and seated himself at the table. Alyna poured him a cup of tea, then sat a plate of meat and a bowl of steaming wheat porridge before him. "You must eat something," she insisted. "There might not be time later."

Maraakus recognized the wisdom of her words and began to eat. "The priest told me some things that might prove helpful. You and I will have to decide if it has any value, of course. Some of it was rather curious."

Rafin grinned. "I'm sure he was delighted to see you," he said. "How much did it cost you this time?"

"Two ravens," Maraakus replied, taking a swallow of tea. "That seems to be the going rate." He smiled at the look of disgust on Rafin's face.

"I still think my method would be quicker," Rafin grumbled. "And more permanent, too!"

Maraakus laughed. "You must learn to exercise patience, my friend. Some things are best accomplished with delicacy."

"Humph," Rafin scoffed. "Delicacy is wasted on that one."

Alyna placed a plate of toasted bread on the table. "You must not mistreat the klersep," she scolded Rafin. "He's a kind man and you should show him a little respect." She fixed her uncle with a stern look.

"He may be kind," Rafin conceded, "but he's also a wily old extortionist."

"He means well," Maraakus said, "and I'm beginning to understand him much better. He said the image from the amulet showed a sort of coat of arms called a plactrogram. It indicates the ancient surname of a family that settled here many generations ago."

Rafin stared at him with a puzzled look. "Did he tell you the surname? They frequently indicate the family's trade or guild, such as Jonn the Smith or Maraakus . . . Priestpayer."

"No," Maraakus answered, laughing, keeping his eyes focused on his food. "He meant the ancient surname. That name common to all members of a family before the coming of the trade guilds and registered professions. Do you know your ancient family surname, Alyna? Have you ever seen it represented by one of these plactrograms?"

She wrinkled her brow in thought. "I seem to remember grandmother speaking of a surname, but I can't recall what it was. And these . . . plactrograms? No, I don't remember seeing or hearing—"

"Our family surname is Porshanneva," Rafin interrupted. "It's one of the oldest names in the valley. My mother told me that when I was just a small boy."

Maraakus took a sip of his tea. "Did she tell you what it meant?" He tried to make his question sound casual.

Rafin laughed. "Of course. She said our family was once very powerful and highly respected in this valley. She always said that it would regain that power and respect in the future. Of course, she never explained exactly what she meant by that. I doubt it meant I'd end up as catchpole."

Maraakus smiled as his old and trusted friend, his strong right arm in battle and steadfast companion during some of his blackest days of despair, sat silently across the table, grinning back at him. And Alyna, the woman who looked at him with such admiration busied herself by stoking the fire.

How shall I tell them that their family is connected to these horrible deaths? he asked himself. Will they believe me? Will I retain Rafin's trust and friendship? Will this delightful and beautiful young woman still look at him with barely disguised affection—even love?

He finished his tea and placed the mug on the table. The fear of losing Rafin's friendship and Alyna's affection settled like a cold stone in his stomach, but he knew he must go forward.

"I don't believe you've ever told me your mother's name, Rafin," he said, in a tone that he hoped sounded normal.

"Her name was Sheya," Alyna answered, picking up her mug of tea and walking to the fireplace.

Maraakus smiled and glanced at her. She was studying him thoughtfully; she was not smiling. The cold stone in his stomach moved. He glanced at Rafin, but the big man was concentrating on his supper. Taking a deep breath, he reached into his pocket, took out the amulet and the drawing, then placed both on the table. Just as he opened his mouth to speak, a loud rapping sound filled the room and they all turned toward the front door. It opened and Danis stepped into the house.

"The evening watch is waiting at the tower," he told Rafin. "You wanted to be notified when they were all there."

"Any final instructions for the guard detail, Maraakus?" Rafin asked. "I told Danis we might want to talk to them before they take their stations."

"Yes," Maraakus replied. "I'll go with you. I want all the guards up on the walls—and I want them heavily armed."

Rafin raised his brows but said nothing. Taking his sword belt off a peg on the wall, he buckled it around his waist and followed Danis and Maraakus from the house.

Alyna stood in the open doorway until they were out of sight, then went to the table and picked up the amulet and drawing. After a quick look out the window, she hurried upstairs to the table where Maraakus had been drawing his map, pulled out a chair, and sat down. Placing the amulet on the table, and with the drawing in her hand, she studied the eagle bearing the disc of the sun in its sharp talons.

I've seen this before, she thought. But where? When? She sighed and closed her eyes, clearing her mind, listening only to the sound of her pulse pounding in her ears. When her heart had slowed to a strong, steady rhythm, a feeling of sadness led her thoughts drifting back to an earlier time and she remembered the day of her grandmother's death. But she also felt some deeper sadness, from beyond that time. Some feeling associated with fire. A hot, red fire. Fire and tears.

The feeling of sadness grew deeper and more oppressive. Now she remembered her mother's funeral pyre. She was a small child, standing in deep snow, shivering in a stinging, cold wind, sheltered only by her grandmother's comforting arm.

And she recalled another occasion, later that day, when she had gone upstairs to her grandmother's room—this room—and found her seated at this very table. Before her was a book and she had a pen in her right hand. Looking up, the old woman had beckoned her close and said, "This is your name, child."

Alyna remembered looking down at the book and seeing only curious markings; but she had accepted her grandmother's statement as fact. "Why, Grandmother?" she had asked. "Why did you write my name in the book?"

Her grandmother smiled and said, "Because someday this book will be yours, Alyna. This is a very special book." She put down the pen and closed the book without further explanation. On the red leather cover was a bird with outstretched wings. It was holding a circle ringed with sharp points.

Alyna opened her eyes and looked at the drawing in her hand. "Where is it, Grandmother?" she asked herself softly. "I know it's not on the shelves. I would have remembered seeing that book."

Her grandmother had always referred to objects as "special" when she'd placed a charm on them. Alyna looked slowly around the room. "It must be in the house," she murmured.

She sat back in the chair and stared up into the darkness of the roof thatching. Then she closed her eyes and cleared her mind, concentrating on the memory of the book. And after a brief time, what her grandmother always called her "talents" flooded her senses, just like when she was a child playing the finding game with her grandmother. The smell of burning logs in the fireplace faded from her nostrils; the soft noises from the street outside were gone from her ears. She drifted, floating in a warm, peaceful state, not unlike that moment when sleep first steals upon a tired body, relieving it of the burden of sight, touch, taste, and hearing.

Then came the mild and familiar stab of pain that her grandmother called "the sacrifice." The pain was gone almost immediately and she slipped into an altered state; her senses sharpened, her mind prepared to detect the presence of a charmed object. Now she focused her mind on the book she wished to find and recited words she had learned when she was very young.

"*Shairmur Aculma*, depart now darkness from my mind. Come forth light to lift the veil of secrecy. *Hurmaltim Imlata,* I am Alyna, thy servant and child. This book I seek, once hidden, is now revealed."

Instantly, she sensed that something was wrong. Terribly wrong.

In her mind, she saw the room illuminated by waves of multicolored light emanating from the amulet that lay on the table before her. She struggled, trying unsuccessfully to open her eyes, seeking assurance that she was seated safely in the room she had known since childhood, trying to break the spell she had cast upon herself.

It's just a game, she thought, isn't it? Grandmother?

Her fear increased as the light was replaced with dark, shifting shadows and she was overcome with a paralyzing sense of terror. The shadows had the substance and weight of living forms, pressing on her, wrapping her in unbreakable bonds of darkness that clung to her, filling her lungs with hot, searing vapors. Her skin burned as if from scalding water and she cried out from the illusionary pain. Her cries became long, wailing moans of anguish, and in her tormented mind, the dark shadows moved closer, shrieking painfully in her ears, until she was suddenly possessed by a sense of evil that was focused on nothing, but was of startling intensity.

Suddenly the air grew thick and unbreathable, sharp and sour like the taste of vinegar. She clapped her left hand to her nose and mouth, choking on the gorge that rose in her throat. With her right hand she seized the amulet and flung it across the room.

Pushing up from the table, she stood on trembling, unwilling legs. In a painful trance, she shuffled to the stairs and started down, guiding herself with a shoulder pressed against the wall. But in her altered vision, the familiar stairs appeared distorted, stretching endlessly before her, steep and narrow, wavering like the undulating body of some vile serpent.

With her last remaining strength, she reached the bottom, stumbled to the front door and clawed at the latch with desperate fingers. Somehow, the door opened and she staggered blindly into the yard, but was immediately overcome by a series of painful convulsions that drove her first to her knees, then full length upon the ground.

Slowly, with considerable effort, she managed to get up on her knees. Again the convulsions struck. Clutching her stomach with both hands, she leaned forward and vomited into the mud. Then she sat back on her heels and began a slow, steady, rocking motion, unable to feel the cold mud, the chilling wind, or the soaking rain.

CHAPTER NINE

"... and nothing comes in or goes out!" Rafin ordered.

He looked carefully at the eight men standing in the yellow circle of torchlight—all recent recruits for what he now called the Stridgenfel Militia. "Any questions? Then set the watch. Two men at each gate—veterans up on the wall."

Maraakus watched as the men marched off with ragged steps and rattling swords, while Hadrax and three other veterans shouted and tried to keep the inexperienced men in line.

Rafin sighed heavily and shook his head. "May the gods protect us," he muttered. "These 'guards' certainly won't!"

Maraakus laughed and clapped the big man on the shoulder. "They're bakers, woodcutters, shopkeepers, and weavers. Isn't that what you told me?"

"If I catch one sleeping, I'll jerk his head off!" Rafin growled. He got four torches from inside the base of the tower and lit them from one burning at the tower's base.

Maraakus took one in his left hand. "Meet me on the north wall after the night torches are set," he said. "I need to discuss something with you."

Rafin nodded. "I won't be long," he promised, then he set off on his inspection round.

At the north gate Maraakus placed his torch in a bracket, then climbed a ladder to the top of the wall. A strong wind was blowing and he could feel a biting chill through his heavy cloak. Straight out of the west, he thought. This could bring the first heavy snow of winter.

After easing himself down on the cold stones, he sat with his legs dangling over the wall. It was dark when Rafin sat down beside him.

"Hadrax will supervise the evening guard detail," Rafin told him. "I'll take the midnight watch and you'll have the first morning watch. What's next?"

"We talk," Maraakus replied. "And after you hear what I have to say, we'll decide how best to tell Alyna."

"You learned something about the image cast by that amulet."

Maraakus sighed, looking down.

"I thought as much," Rafin murmured. "I knew those questions about my family surname were not without reason."

"The old priest recognized part of the image projected by the amulet," Maraakus said. "The eagle and spiked disc are symbols or runes that also appear in your family plactrogram."

"How would he know such a thing?" Rafin asked.

"From your mother," Maraakus replied. "She and the klersep shared a strong interest in plactrograms and ancient—"

"Wait!" Rafin said. "Are you saying that my family—"

"I'm not accusing you or Alyna of anything—you know that. I'm simply saying a link does exist—or seems to. Alyna remembers seeing the eagle and disc, and between the three of us, we must figure out what all of this means."

"That's the craziest thing I've ever heard!" Rafin practically shouted.

"Is it?" Maraakus asked.

"I have no knowledge of these symbols—except what you and Alyna have told me—I don't know how to help. . . ."

Maraakus smiled to himself and shifted his position to face his friend. The big man was volatile, but he had always been reasonable—in his own way. "I know," he assured Rafin. "So that leaves Alyna, doesn't it?"

"I won't have her exposed to danger."

"Of course not. I don't want that, either. But she'll help if you ask her. She might not do it for me."

"Why do you say that?"

"Because," Maraakus said quietly, "she's concerned for . . . what I might think of her."

There was a long silence before Rafin spoke. "That makes sense. Is this concern a mutual thing?"

"Yes."

"I thought as much," Rafin said. "I'm sorry for the way I spoke, but I'm so used to being protective of her. If you're convinced she can help. . . ."

"I've tried to think of another way," Maraakus assured him, "According to the priest, temple records indicate that the rune found on the victims—the same rune that appears over the head of the eagle—is the signature of one your ancestors. A man named Jodac."

Rafin laughed heartily. "So now the legendary Jodac becomes a fully-fledged member of the Porshanneva family? It certainly makes an interesting story—though not one I'd care for people to hear. Can you imagine what this village might think about

Alyna? She already scares some of them."

"According to old temple records, Jodac actually existed. He lived right here in Stridgenfel. Wasn't it you who said old legends often contain grains of truth?"

"I did," the old soldier admitted. "But to believe this story, I'd have to be more demented than that old priest!"

"Maybe not. Remember how the Larrats took the little finger from the right hand of our dead and wounded men? They signed their handiwork—to let you know who was responsible. So did Jodac, by marking his victims with his signature."

"But wasn't that an animal you saw and smelled in the forest? Besides, even if Jodac was a real man he's been dead for generations."

Maraakus nodded. "True, but animals don't drawn runes on their prey. And how many large animals could survive eating only the hearts from a fresh kill?" Maraakus asked. "Lannon's body was whole but for a single bite on his right leg. Only the heart was missing."

"Now that you mention it, eating only the hearts is certainly peculiar. It's hardly enough to sustain an animal as large as you described."

"But the day Lannon was killed—despite its size—it may have been frightened away when it heard you and Danis coming," Maraakus pointed out. "If so, maybe we can turn that to our advantage. And then we may have created another problem. Now that we've locked down the village, we're forcing a break in the four-day pattern."

"Then we no longer have any indication of when it's most likely to return."

"Exactly. We must expect it at any time. Now consider this: Fergus wounded it. It bleeds and might fear two or more people. I believe we can kill it—but for one major problem."

"Finding the damn thing!" Rafin offered.

"We can't kill it until we find it." Maraakus agreed. "Alyna said she could sometimes locate lost objects."

"Looking for a lost bracelet and a vicious wild animal isn't quite the same thing," Rafin replied. "And this creature isn't exactly lost, either."

"But can she do it? Can she tell us where to look?"

"I don't know. My mother said Porshanneva women sometimes had this strange ability and that it was exceptionally strong in Alyna. I thought she was referring to Alyna's skill with the healing arts, of course. But after my mother died, something strange happened. One night, when Alyna was about eighteen, I heard her crying in her sleep. I got up to see what was wrong and she told me she was dreaming about using this . . . ability . . . and wished it would go away."

"Did she tell you why?"

"It frightened her. She was afraid it would come to dominate her life."

"Has she ever attempted real magic?"

Rafin chuckled softly. "Real magic? You, Maraakus, are considering the use of *magic?*"

"I'm willing to try anything that will help us kill that . . . thing."

"Well, what do you mean by real magic?"

"I don't mean healing salves and love powders," Maraakus said. "I mean . . . well . . . *magic*—such as Balzarr claimed he could perform."

Rafin was silent for a moment. "I thought you didn't believe. . . ."

Maraakus laughed. "Perhaps my exposure has been limited to the cheap variety. The obvious tricks and sleight-of-hand practiced by the likes of Balzarr. Let's just say I'm trying to keep an open mind."

"All right," Rafin said hesitantly. "I suppose that would depend on what you call magic. She's able to heal wounds and broken bones quickly. She can sometimes find lost objects, but not always. She's unusually sensitive to things around her, including people. Would you call that magic?"

Maraakus sighed. "I don't know what to call it," he said. "I find it difficult to maintain my objectivity when Alyna is involved."

Rafin smiled and said, "I was curious to see how long you'd go before admitting that. When do you want to talk to her?"

"Tonight," Maraakus replied. "We need answers before that thing comes hunting for its next victim."

Rafin sighed and got to his feet. "I want you to promise me one thing," he said. "If Alyna is the least bit reluctant, you won't insist she do this. Agreed?"

"Of course," Maraakus replied.

"Then I'll ask her to try," Rafin said. "But let's not tell her Jodac was a member of our family. Things are crazy enough without adding that little detail. We'll tell her later."

"Very well," Maraakus replied. "But while we're extracting promises from each other, I'd like to say something about that old klersep. Will you try to be more patient with him? He's a good man and I really believe he's trying to help us."

Rafin grunted in the darkness. "I'll try," he said. "But I can't help wondering what he does with all the money he collects."

Maraakus laughed. "Well, he certainly doesn't spend it on fine clothes and luxurious quarters. On the surface, you're a hard-bitten, crusty old soldier, Rafin. But underneath all that bluster, you're a man of unusual sensibilities. When you have time, go talk to the old priest. Treat him with respect and you may come away with a different opinion."

"Really?" Rafin asked. "Well, if he can help us catch this killer, I'll call him my brother and tote him around the village on my back."

He extended his hand and assisted Maraakus to his feet. After retracing their steps along the wall, they went down the ladder and proceeded slowly through the deserted streets. Soon they turned left into Rafin's front yard. The house was dark and Maraakus thought that strange, considering the time of evening. He opened the door and they stepped inside.

For several moments they both just stood in shocked silence, staring into the cold, darkened kitchen where Alyna sat huddled before the fireplace. Her arms encircled her knees; her head was down and she sat motionless, staring into a glowing bed of dying coals. Her tunic was soaked and muddy, clinging tightly to her shivering body, and streaks of dark mud had dried in her hair and on her leather slippers.

"Alyna!" Rafin called. "Can you hear me?" He called her name several more times but she seemed unaware of their presence.

Rafin muttered a string of oaths, shouldered his way into the room and slammed the door. Alyna flinched, but her gaze remained fixed and unblinking. Then she began a slow, rocking motion and started singing softly to herself as light from the glimmering coals danced in red shadows over her face and body.

Maraakus snatched up the down-filled cover from Alyna's bed and draped it around her shoulders. "Fill the tub with warm water!" he shouted. "She's freezing!"

Rafin hurried out to the shed and Maraakus heard the thumping of a bucket as warm water was transferred from the heating kettle to the tub. He lifted her gently from the floor, then carried her out to the shed. Dropping the bedcover on the floor, he lowered her into the tub. Rafin took off his cloak and placed it over the tub to hold in the warmth. Then he closed the door and stood with his arms folded across his chest. "As the gods are my witness," he vowed. "I'll kill the man who did this!"

"It isn't what you think," Maraakus told him. "Look at her—she's been ill."

"She was well when we left the house," Rafin insisted, "and I've never known her to get sick."

Alyna moaned softly and opened her eyes. She sighed, then looked slowly around the room, obviously confused. "Could I have my warm robe?" she asked. Rafin nodded and went quickly out the shed door.

"Maraakus? Did you bring me in from the yard? You put me

in the tub with my clothes on?"

"We found you huddled in front of the fireplace," he told her. "You were wet and shivering. What happened here after we left you?"

The door opened and Rafin came in carrying her heavy robe. He placed it on the wooden stand, then knelt beside the tub. "Who did this to you, Alyna?" he asked, stroking her forehead with his fingers. "Tell me the name of the man who did this."

"There was no man, Uncle Rafin," she replied. Her voice was soft and weak. "It was the amulet. Please take it out of the house."

Maraakus frowned. "The amulet?" he asked. "How could the amulet—?"

"It's *evil!* Please, Maraakus. Just get it out of this house!"

"Where is it?"

"Upstairs. I threw it away from me."

Maraakus went quickly back into the house, hurried up the stairs and stood for a moment, looking carefully about the room. The fire had burned down to small flames; however, they provided some feeble illumination. The map and other materials from the table lay scattered across the floor; his chair was once again overturned. Then he saw the amulet near the fireplace and snatched it from the floor. Holding it tightly in his right hand, he went quickly down to the stables, where he placed it on a high shelf. When he got back to the storage shed, Rafin was standing next to the tub, staring down at Alyna.

"I've put it in the stables," he told Rafin. "Did she explain what happened?"

"Not exactly," Rafin replied. "She wants us to wait in the kitchen. Let's do as she asks."

Maraakus nodded and followed Rafin into the house. He poured each of them a mug of tea. Rafin tossed another log on the fire and they sat down at the table to wait. After a period of silence, Rafin sighed and looked up with a frown. "She said that old amulet has magical powers," he said, "and I believe her. You also said this affair is more complicated than it appears, and I believe that, too. We've urged each other to keep an open mind, remember? Well, my friend, I think we're about to be put to the test."

The door leading to the shed opened and Alyna walked into the room wearing the long robe that Rafin had brought her. She crossed to the fireplace and sat down before the fire, shook out her wet hair and fluffed it between her fingers. "I'm feeling better, now," she assured them.

Maraakus smiled at her, laced his fingers together and placed his hands on the table. "You gave us quite a scare," he said.

"After Danis came to the house and all of you had gone," she told them, "I took the amulet and your drawing upstairs to the table where you've been working and tried to remember where I had seen that symbol. Finally, I did. It was on the front of a book that belonged to my grandmother."

She paused and looked up at Maraakus. "The eagle is the symbol of my family's ancient surname. Isn't that what the klersep told you this morning? Isn't that why you were asking all those questions after you returned from the temple?"

"Yes," Maraakus answered. "The priest told me that your grandmother showed him this family's plactrogram."

"I thought as much," Alyna sighed. "But the mark found on those poor murdered villagers was not part of our plactrogram. It was not on the cover of Grandmother's book. Of that, I'm certain. Still, I thought the book might give us some information that would help put an end to these killings, so I tried to find it by using a spell she taught me."

Maraakus glanced sharply at Rafin. "A *spell?*" he asked.

"My grandmother called it the finding game."

"And you found the book?"

"No," she answered. "I made a serious mistake. For some time, I have felt an evil presence in this house. When I used the spell—and discovered the amulet to be the source of that evil—it nearly killed me."

"Haven't you used this spell before?" Maraakus asked.

"Not since I found the amulet. When the spell is cast, it clears the mind and makes one receptive to any magical or charmed object, providing the object isn't protected with another spell designed to prevent its detection. I thought that if Grandmother's book was in the house—and if it was charmed—I could find it. When I cleared my mind and made myself receptive, I made myself vulnerable to the amulet's power. It was nearly more than I could bear."

Maraakus got up, walked around the table and placed his hands on her shoulders. "We need to find that book," Maraakus decided. "I won't pretend to understand this. I never expected this affair to lead in this direction—or imagined I would someday be thinking as I am at this moment."

"The proof is in the stables," Alyna assured him. "It's the amulet. This whole thing started with Keam and Andor and that amulet. I don't know how, but I know it to be true."

Rafin looked up and smiled at Maraakus. "I seem to remember hearing that same opinion earlier this evening," he remarked.

"He heard it from me," Maraakus said, speaking to Alyna. "I believe that, too. The amulet is in excellent condition. If it was lost, buried in the planting fields, then washed into the river years later, it would be covered in mud and badly scratched—which it's not—though it's obviously quite old."

"Then where has it been all these years?" Alyna asked.

"If we knew that, we might be able to end this before more people are killed," Maraakus answered. "But there's only one place that we know nothing about. Only one place where Keam and Andor could find that amulet and bring it back to the riverbank in one day. The Pinnacle."

"Except there's no way up," Rafin remarked.

"Not that we know about," Maraakus corrected. "But suppose the boys found a way up and discovered some ruins or even a small cave, then started poking around and found the amulet.

What if they weren't alone on the mountain. Maybe someone—or some*thing*—is living up there and it was his amulet? The boys take it. The owner gives chase. Keam is killed—that's how the boys become separated—but Andor starts running and he's carrying the amulet. Before he's caught by this thing, he throws the amulet in the river."

"I don't know," Rafin said. "It sounds crazy to me. Why kill the boys for a nearly worthless trinket?"

"Because the amulet isn't worthless," Alyna said softly. "Not only is there much evil associated with it, but the amulet has magical powers. It would be priceless—to someone who knew how to use it."

Chapter Ten

Maraakus tapped gently with a small hammer, then pulled on a stone that sounded loosely set. When it refused to move, he sank down on the floor and leaned wearily against the chimney. "Nothing," he said, placing his hammer on the hearth. "They're all tighter than ticks on a hound."

Rafin pulled a small wooden chest from a storage platform under the stairs and put it on the kitchen floor. "You'll have to admit one thing," he said dryly. "My mother certainly knew how to hide a book!"

Alyna knelt beside the chest, raised the lid and began sorting the contents into small piles.

"I'm starting to think that book doesn't exist," Rafin growled, "and I'm tired of looking for it."

"Oh, look!" Alyna said, holding up a pale yellow garment mended with a neatly sewn patch. She gathered the faded cloth in her hands, pressed it to her face, then folded it carefully and put it back in the trunk. "I'll keep this one. It was Grandmother's favorite."

Maraakus let his gaze wander over the room. The entire first floor of the house was strewn with cooking utensils and dishes. Books lay in disorderly stacks, topped with piles of clothing. Cupboards had been pulled away from the walls and placed in the center of the room. Rafin was sitting on the floor under the stairs, face smudged with dirt, cobwebs dangling from his graying black beard.

"Amazing, isn't it?" Rafin growled. "How a house gets filled with things you never use!"

"The trappings of domesticity?" Maraakus asked, giving him a tired smile.

Rafin chuckled softly. "I suppose."

With his head tilted against the wall, Maraakus studied the beams supporting the single layer of boards that formed the upstairs floor. "Well," he commented thoughtfully, dropping his eyes to the underside of the wooden stair treads, "we've checked all the floorboards in this room and I can see the underside of the floor above. Can you think of anything we've missed?"

"Only the roof thatching, and the lining of the well," Rafin answered. He stretched out on his back, his hands behind his head. "I had the entire roof torn off and replaced about two years ago, so I know it's not hidden in the thatching."

"And Grandmother was terrified of the well," Alyna added. "She refused to go near it—" Rafin concurred, "even to draw water."

"Can we put the cupboards back in place?" Alyna asked.

Rafin rolled wearily to his feet. "I don't mind tearing it all out," he muttered, "but I hate putting it back."

The cupboards were moved back against the walls and adjusted first one way, then another, until Alyna was satisfied with their positions. Then she dusted the shelves and began replacing the dishes and cooking utensils in an orderly fashion. "Make sure you dust my books before putting them back," she directed.

"We just did this last spring," Rafin protested. He looked at Maraakus and grinned. "See what you've been missing?"

When the books were on the shelves, the furniture back in position and the household goods put away, Alyna stood in the center of the room with her arms crossed over her breasts and looked around with a critical eye. Apparently satisfied, she nodded and rubbed her upper arms. "Now," she declared, "all we need is a fire. It's cold in here."

While Rafin started a fire downstairs, Maraakus went upstairs to the fireplace on the second floor. When the fire was burning steadily, he returned to the kitchen, put the flint and steel on the mantle, then pulled a chair up to the hearth and sat down next to Rafin.

"Where in Heltum's name could she have put that book?" Rafin muttered.

Alyna put the cover on a small pot, hung it over the fire, then took down a basket of vegetables and dropped them into a bucket of water. Maraakus watched as she washed, rinsed, and placed them on a small, heavy table. She looked up, her gaze making a full circle of the room. Seeing that Maraakus was watching her, she frowned.

"That book is in this house," she declared emphatically, before returning her attention to the food she was preparing. Picking up a big kitchen knife, she split a turnip and reduced it to small chunks. Two large onions, four carrots, and a small slab of salted pork met the same fate. She swept it all into a bowl, walked between Maraakus and Rafin, lifted the lid on the pot, and put in the meat and vegetables. The lid rang sharply as she set it back in place.

"Right now," she told them, "I'm just as frustrated as either of you, but I still believe it's here."

Maraakus nodded, Rafin smiled, and Alyna walked back to the table and set the bowl down with a loud thump. She went to the storage shed and closed the door behind her.

Rafin looked up at Maraakus and grinned. "She's wrong, of course," he said. "We've ripped this place apart. It's not here."

Maraakus frowned. "She may be right," he said. "I doubt your mother would discard a book she promised to Alyna. We'll just have to find it." He rubbed a hand over the stubble on his chin.

"You and Alyna make a good pair," Rafin grumbled. "Both of you are as stubborn as oak stumps. Where can it be?"

Maraakus shrugged and shook his head and for a while they sat without talking, watching the flames in the fireplace. Finally, Rafin looked up at the window to his right and realized that it was growing dark. "It will soon be time to set the watch," he said. "Unless you have some objection, we'll all take the same rotations we had last night."

"No objection," Maraakus replied. "Alternate the guards halfway through their watches. It'll be very cold before morning."

The door opened and Alyna walked in carrying a length of white cord. She knelt and wrapped it tightly around a pile of clothing stacked on the floor near her bed.

"I'm taking these to Marrtee," she told them. "The soup is nearly ready and there's bread in the cupboard. I'll be back soon." She bent and kissed Rafin on the cheek, fastened her cloak around her shoulders, picked up the bundle of clothing and went out through the front door. Before the door closed, wind rushed into the house. The lamps flickered and a puff of smoke swirled out of the fireplace.

"Just like her mother," Rafin remarked. "Shall we eat?" He went to the cupboard, reached up to the top shelf and brought down a brown clay jug. He pulled the stopper and sniffed. "Ah," he said. "Exactly what we need."

"What is it?" Maraakus asked.

"The best apple wine for five hundred miles," Rafin announced. "Been saving it for a special occasion. I hereby declare this to be one."

They ate their supper and talked, pausing only to pour out additional measures of the amber-colored liquid. Maraakus drained his third cup and Rafin split the last of the wine between them and sat the empty jug on the floor.

Maraakus smiled as he studied the older man seated across from him. Theirs was a long-standing friendship, forged during years of battle with Triad forces, tempered in the blazing heat and withering thirst of the Barrens, sharpened by months of marching through the deep snows of the Tarbisu Steppes, and polished by the annihilation of the Ammaks.

And Maraakus would never forget why the old soldier's right leg was noticeably shorter than his left. For in defense of his friend, Rafin had accepted a blow from an Ammak battle-hammer. It was this moment that Maraakus relived again and again in the altered and twisted logic of his dreams.

He watched Rafin draining his cup of apple wine. A man was fortunate—even once in a lifetime—to have such a loyal friend.

Rafin sat his cup on the table and smiled. "Is something wrong with the wine?" he asked.

"No. I was just thinking that when things are settled here, you and Alyna must come to Koeinstadt for an extended visit."

Rafin smiled and gave Maraakus a sidelong glance. "Is your old housekeeper still running a constant stream of nieces and cousins under your nose?"

Maraakus laughed. "Not too many, now," he replied. "I think old Bethle has just about run out of candidates. I never imagined one woman could have so many female relatives between the ages of eighteen and fifty. But that has nothing to do with my invitation. You've always enjoyed yourself at the villa. I think Alyna would enjoy it, too."

"And I'll wager Bethle would enjoy it more than any of us," Rafin commented.

"I'm afraid I don't know what you're talking about."

Rafin smiled. "I think you do," he insisted.

Maraakus laughed. "Do you really believe that's the reason I suggested that Alyna come with you? For Bethle's approval?"

"I haven't the slightest doubt," Rafin replied.

Maraakus shook his head. "Let's don't rush things, Rafin. I already have one tireless matchmaker in my life. Don't you become the second."

Rafin grinned and rose from the table. "I think there's one more jug of apples around here . . . someplace," he muttered. He walked to the cupboard and began rummaging on the upper shelf.

A loud, insistent pounding filled the room. Rafin walked to the front door and opened it. A short, stocky man with thinning hair stood on the doorstep, holding his cloak together with his hands and breathing white plumes of steam into the cold evening air.

"Danis sent me." the man panted. "Telsia's got two travelers in tow and they're trying to kill each other over her. They were drinking at the inn and Jirvean kicked them out. Telsia went with them. They're out in the street trying to knock each other senseless!"

"By all the gods. . . ." Rafin grumbled. "Tell him I'll be right there."

The man jammed his hat on his head and disappeared into the darkness. Rafin slammed the door and threw his cloak over his shoulders, buckled his sword around his waist, and grabbed a thick oak truncheon from behind the door.

"I'll come with you," Maraakus volunteered.

"No need," Rafin assured him. "I can handle two drunks. It's time for my watch anyway. I'll send a runner to wake you before sunrise. You can have the early morning watch. The mornings are getting too damned cold for me." With a wink, he turned and went out the door.

Maraakus gathered up their supper dishes and dropped them into a bucket of water. But after thinking for a moment, he went to the front door and put on his cloak. Taking down his short fighting sword, he slipped it through his belt, then stepped outside into night air that was cold enough to make him shiver. Holding his cloak together with his left hand, he set off for the village inn.

Upon reaching the market square, he turned left and went quickly toward a noisy crowd of perhaps two dozen men and five or six women. They formed a rough circle outside the inn, blocking the doorway and the street. He saw Rafin standing a few paces from the inn's entrance, talking to Danis; they were watching two men stalk each other with raised fists.

Maraakus walked over and stood next to them. "What's the problem?" he asked, raising his voice above the noise of the crowd.

"The problem is standing over there," Rafin answered. He pointed at a young woman in a red tunic. "That's Telsia."

Maraakus studied the girl. She had breasts like ripe melons; her hair was a lustrous yellow, long and shining, almost white, falling nearly to her slender waist. Full, rounded hips flowed smoothly into long legs. She stood perfectly still, smiling, watching the men in the circle, seemingly unaware of the cold wind that was blowing through the streets. Except for the close spacing of her eyes and slightly projecting teeth, she was quite beautiful.

Maraakus raised his brows and looked at Rafin. "Would it be stupid of me to ask how she makes her living?"

Rafin grinned. "She's not quite twenty," he said, as if that explained everything. He tapped his forehead with his finger. "Up here, she's forty."

The men inside the circle moved warily around each other. The smaller one was the youngest. The older man, taller by three hand spans and forty weights heavier, swung a huge fist at the youth. It caught him a glancing blow under his right ear and the young man went down to his knees in the wet street. A mixture of cheers and groans arose from the crowd.

"Shall we stop them?" Maraakus asked Rafin.

"Not right away." Rafin answered. "They're traveling together—business partners. Obviously, there's some disagreement over the division of certain assets!" He grinned and jerked his thumb toward Telsia. Now the crowd was making so much noise that Maraakus could barely hear his friend.

"The youngster was doing well just before you arrived!" Rafin shouted. "I thought I'd give him a chance to whip the bigger man . . . if he can!"

The younger man circled slowly to his right, staying just outside his opponent's reach. A dark trickle of blood flowed from a split lip. The older man's left eye was closing. His bulbous nose sat at an odd angle on his right cheek and a large swelling was visible on the left side of his face. He was breathing heavily, obviously near exhaustion.

"When morning comes," Rafin shouted, "after they're sober, they'll still be good friends, partners, and—"

Suddenly, with the speed of a striking viper, the younger man stepped forward, planted his feet firmly on the ground and brought his right fist up from his hip. The blow caught the big man squarely on the point of his chin and he staggered backward. His hands fell slowly to his sides and his eyes rolled back in his head. His tired legs collapsed and he sank to his side in the street.

A second wave of cheers and groans exploded from the crowd and Maraakus saw coins changing hands. Rafin turned with a smile on his face. "See what I mean?" he said.

"I thought Stridgenfel was a quiet little village."

"It is," Rafin assured him. "You'd like living here. This was nothing but a friendly misunderstanding. For real excitement, you should be here on feast days!"

He handed the truncheon to Danis and moved quickly across

the circle. Seizing the younger man by the front of his tunic, Rafin lifted him off his feet with one arm. Noise from the crowd faded and was replaced with excited murmuring. The young man's feet were nearly a foot off the ground. Rafin's face was contorted with a menacing scowl.

"Allow me to introduce myself," Rafin growled, giving the young man a hard shaking. "My name is Rafin and I'm the village catchpole. How would you and your friend like to spend a cold night in the bilboes?" He shook the young man again and dropped him on the ground beside his unconscious partner.

"The gates will open at sunrise," Rafin said. "If you two gentlemen fail to depart soon after that, you'll regret ever hearing of Stridgenfel. Now pick up your friend, go to your lodgings, and remain there until morning. Do I make myself clear?"

"You do," the young man replied, nodding his head.

As the traveling companions disappeared through the doorway of the inn, accompanied by considerable laughter, Rafin turned on Telsia. "And I want you off the streets, young woman," he declared. "If I see you again tonight, it's a night in the bilboes for you, too."

Telsia walked slowly around Rafin, trailing her fingers across his arm and around his waist. "Lock yourself up with me, Rafin, and make it two days," she said. Her voice was soft and sultry. She smiled, moistened her lips, and moved a step away. Then she turned and regarded Rafin over her right shoulder. Her brightly painted mouth opened in a white, toothy smile. She shifted her weight to her right leg and cocked one hip at him.

Rafin raised his brows and smiled. He flicked his wrist and the flat blade of his broadsword landed with a stinging pop on the girl's ample rear. She cried out in pain and surprise. The few remaining members of the crowd roared with laughter while Telsia glared at Rafin and rubbed her stinging backside with both hands. Then she laughed and went off down the street.

"The performance is over!" Rafin shouted. "Go about your business!"

Maraakus watched until the rest of the crowd had gone, some back to the inn, the rest to their homes. In just a short time, only Danis and Rafin stood with him in the street.

Rafin shook his head and laughed. "That didn't take long," he said. "I'll send a runner when it's time for you to relieve me." He clapped Maraakus on the shoulder and Danis followed him down the street toward the south gate.

When Rafin and Danis disappeared into the darkness, Maraakus started back toward the temple, intent on speaking with the klersep about the missing book. As he passed the tower, a figure moved from the shadows of a side street and into the light of a street torch. Maraakus stopped a short distance away and regarded the man for a moment, then said, "Best evening on you, good traveler."

"And on you, sire," the man answered softly.

"May I be of service?" Maraakus asked.

"I judge you to be a person of some authority," the man replied. "I am a stranger to this valley and I have traveled far, seeking a family that once resided here. Despite numerous inquiries, my search has been unsuccessful, for it seems they are no longer remembered in this place. I need shelter until sun-rising, at which time I will resume my search. I would, of course, have preferred to find shelter in the forest, but was prevented from doing so by the guards at your city gates. Have you knowledge of a place where suitable lodging might be found?"

Maraakus studied the man before him; he was slight of build, nearly as tall as Alyna, with long arms and sloping shoulders. His clothing was of leather, as was the small pack he held with his left hand. A cloak of roughly spun yarn hung from his thin shoulders and its generous hood hid the stranger's face in deep shadow. Large hands with long, delicate fingers clutched an oddly twisted walking staff fashioned from some dark wood. His leather boots were worn and covered with mud, telling of many miles of hard traveling.

"You'll be allowed to leave at first light," Maraakus informed him. He pointed with his right hand. "Regrettably, we have only one public house, the Stridgenfel Inn. It's there, where you see the torches burning. You'll find lodging there."

The stranger shook his head. "No, sire," he replied softly. "The inn is filled with boisterous revelry. I am of some age and need my rest."

Maraakus laughed softly. "There may be a more suitable place. I'm going there myself to speak with an acquaintance. If you'd care to accompany me I'll inquire on your behalf."

"I would be indebted, sire," the stranger replied.

Maraakus led the way to the temple and knocked on the back door with a gloved fist. The metal shutter opened.

"It's late!" the old priest declared through the small opening. "Come back in the morning!"

Maraakus raised his hand. Between his fingers he held a single golden raven.

The priest eyed the coin and then pressed his face to the opening, shielding both sides of his head with his hands.

"It's you," he muttered. "Wait!" The shutter slammed shut and the wooden door opened.

"This traveler needs quiet lodgings for the night," Maraakus said. "I suggested he might find them here."

"This is a temple," the old priest replied testily, "not an inn." He looked carefully at the stranger and back to Maraakus. "Oh well," he said. "Since it's you making the request, I'll remind myself that this temple is a charitable institution, with due regard for the needs of weary travelers."

Maraakus held up the coin, but the old priest shook his head. "Never mind," he said, waving his hand. He leaned out of the doorway and inspected the traveler from head to toe. "Well, come inside, man! Don't just stand there!" He swung the door wider. The traveler stepped around Maraakus and over the threshold.

"I have a question to ask, Holy One," Maraakus said. "Did Sheya lend you a book before she died? A book with her family plactrogram on the cover."

"Certainly not. I'd have remembered such a book."

"Then I bid you best evening," Maraakus said pleasantly.

The klersep and the traveler watched until he was swallowed up by the darkness. "Plactrogram?" the old traveler said to the priest. "That is a most unusual word."

"Indeed," the old priest agreed, looking suspiciously in both directions along the narrow back street. "In fact, the word derives from an ancient tongue that is no longer spoken. Plactrograms are symbolic writings—a most fascinating subject." He closed the door and slipped the locking bolt.

"I have long been interested in all things pertaining to the ancient races and their languages," he informed the traveler, "and I am particularly interested in plactrograms. I have several in my collection."

The traveler nodded. "May I be permitted to see them? Like you, I have some small interest in such things."

"Astonishing!" the priest declared. "Are you acquainted with the language of the ancients? Can you speak it?"

"Well, I . . . I know a few words, I suppose."

"Wonderful!" the old priest exclaimed. "How fortunate that you came to me for shelter. Judbal works in mysterious ways, does he not? I have a warm fire burning. Take off your cloak, my good man. Make yourself at home. I've little to offer in the way of food—perhaps some bread and cheese—since I eat very little myself. I have, however, made a pot of strong tea to go with it and there is enough for two. What name shall I call you?"

"I am called Grommdum," the stranger replied.

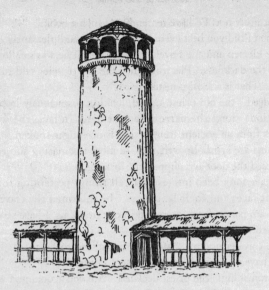

CHAPTER ELEVEN

After easing both feet to the floor, Alyna gathered the bed-covers around her shoulders and walked quickly and silently across the downstairs room. She rubbed the window with her palm and looked out, past the front corner of the house. A dusting of thin snow covered the front yard, but no footprints were visible in the dim light of morning. Yet someone—or something—had stumbled over the firewood stacked outside the kitchen door. Several heavy sticks of split oak were scattered about in the passageway between the house and the storage shed.

Then she heard it again—the sound that had awakened her

from a restless sleep. It was muffled and repetitive, like the hooves of a colt prancing about in a rain-softened field. But this time it was accompanied by low scraping sounds and some heavy object bumped hard against the house.

Suddenly a shadow moved in front of the window, completely blocking her field of view. She shrank back and clapped one hand over her mouth to keep from crying out. When she looked back at the window, the dark shadow had vanished and she saw only the rooftops of nearby houses silhouetted against the early morning sky. Terrified, she turned and rushed up the stairs, bare feet pounding softly on the wooden steps.

"Maraakus?" Alyna called softly. "Maraakus! Are you awake?"

"Yes," he answered. "Why aren't you sleeping?"

"I heard a prowler outside." she whispered. "When I looked out, something . . . big moved across the window."

He rolled out of bed and slipped his feet into his boots. "It was probably a guard going to his watch station," he told her. "But it's nearly time for me to relieve Rafin on the south gate. I'll take a look around."

She followed him down the stairs and watched silently as he buckled on his sword belt and slipped a dagger into his right boot. When he picked up his cloak, she placed a hand on his arm. "Wait," she said. "I've made something for you."

Going quickly to the cupboard near the fireplace, she took down a wooden box and removed a small piece of engraved bone. "I've had this for several days," she told him.

"What is it?"

"A charm—for your protection. I know you don't believe in such things, but please carry it anyway."

Maraakus smiled and touched her cheek. "Very well," he said, tucking the small chunk of bone into his pocket. "Bolt the door after I've gone." He stepped out on the doorstep and the locking bolt clicked behind him.

It had become much colder during the night and flurries of fine snow drifted down from a gray, overcast sky. In the thin dusting of white that covered the frozen ground, Maraakus saw two parallel lines crossing the yard; long scuff marks were visible between them. He followed them out to the street.

Obviously, these tracks were made by a large, horse-drawn cart, he decided. A woodcutter tried to make an early delivery and simply turned into the wrong yard, a mistake easily made in the morning darkness.

As he passed a house with opened shutters, pale yellow light streamed from a window and illuminated a small section of the cobbled street. Bending over, he examined the marks again, noting that the furrows were not always parallel.

Of course, he reasoned, the cart might have a wobbling wheel, but that wouldn't explain why the lines varied in width. And those tracks in the middle don't look like hoof marks, either.

His curiosity aroused, Maraakus followed the wavering furrows down a series of back streets and alleys. Eventually, they led him to the market square. Here the wind had dispersed the light, powdery snow and he paused under a torch mounted on the tower's base to inspect the faint tracks. Nearby was a large metal cylinder hanging from a stubbed-out beam. A wooden club was secured to the tower with a short length of chain. But it was the tower's arched, wooden entrance door that arrested his attention. It stood partially open and he distinctly remembered Rafin pulling it closed.

A loud voice called out from somewhere near the inn. There was an answering shout. A door slammed. A dog barked. Silence returned. He waited for a moment, then picked the torch from its bracket, pushed the tower door open and stepped inside. A pile of unused torches lay on the floor. On his right, a steep, wooden stairway spiraled up into the darkness; it looked old, badly maintained, and had no handrail. The air smelled of decaying wood and rotting straw.

He turned to leave, but stopped suddenly as a soft, eerie moan echoed inside the circular stone tower. Reaching down, he took a dagger from his boot, then raised the torch overhead and looked toward the top of the tower. The soft moaning continued, somewhat louder than before. Wind, he thought, it's just wind echoing through the tower. But. . . .

With the torch in his left hand and his right shoulder pressed against the rough stone walls, he started up the circular stairs holding his dagger before him. The rotting steps creaked loudly under his weight and the soft moaning faded. After a moment it resumed and he continued his climb, moving cautiously, dividing his attention between the sagging stairs and the darkness above.

Where steps were missing, he moved carefully past the gaping holes and made mental notes of their locations. Altogether, he encountered eight missing steps before the stairs ended under a square opening framed by rotting timbers. He lifted the torch and eased himself through the hole.

A sudden fluttering sound filled the air; soft objects struck him in the face, beating him on his shoulders and upraised arms. Falling to his knees, Maraakus ducked his head to shield his eyes and struck wildly with the flaming torch while slashing the air with his dagger. Hundreds of roosting sparrows swirled about him in a terrified, shrieking cloud, before flying hurriedly out into the pre-dawn sky.

As quickly as they appeared, the birds vanished and Maraakus rose slowly to his feet. Standing on trembling legs, he waited until his heart stopped hammering in his chest, then he opened his eyes and looked around. The top of the tower was perhaps twelve feet across. A low stone railing served as a base for wooden columns topped by delicate wooden arches. Overhead, wide ceiling boards had been spiked to the underside of the roof's pegged beams. Now they were warped, blackened and water-stained; faded, peeling paint indicating years of neglect.

Moving to the stone railing, he looked down and saw two torches flaring brightly outside the village inn and one in each corner of the market square. When he looked toward the south gate, a figure passed in front of a torch and moved left into the darkness. A guard walking his post, maybe even Rafin, Maraakus thought. And those shingled roofs are merchant's stalls, and that thatched roof is the public stables.

After replacing the dagger in his boot, Maraakus placed his torch in a bracket secured to one of the columns. The dark, brooding mass of the Pinnacle was clearly discernible, appearing taller than the distant mountains behind it, while the forest where Lannon had died was barely visible, a low, gray smudge at the end of the snow-dusted fields.

In fact, he thought, if the old stairs can be repaired, I'll tell Rafin to put a man up here and—

A sharp, clattering sound came from the merchant stalls near the temple and he immediately raised one hand to shield his eyes from the glow of the torch. Seeing no movement and hearing no additional noise, he took a deep breath and hunched his shoulders, trying to relax his tense muscles.

"You're as jumpy as a weedhopper in a chicken yard," he muttered to himself.

Suddenly he heard another sound from the street below—a dull clattering. It was like the sound made by old charlatan magicians as they rattled animal bones in dry gourds before casting them on the ground and pretending to read the future in the pattern of their falling.

Again he thought he saw movement at the corner of the market square, followed by the soft clattering sound. He stared at a place between two houses and saw long, dark streaks in the light snow—marks not there when he first looked down from the tower's top. Moreover, these new marks crossed each other in front of the temple and again behind the stables.

A door slammed at the village inn and he heard the teasing laughter of a woman and the protesting voice of a man. Then he heard that curious rattling sound as something emerged from behind a line of merchant stalls and ducked into a darkened alley.

Maraakus remained motionless, holding his breath, unable to

identify what he had seen. Suddenly the dark form reappeared. Staying close to the house, it crawled forward on its belly, swinging a massive head from side to side. Then it settled low to the ground, forming a roughly triangular shape, with it's head resting near the corner of the house.

"It's cold out here!" a man's voice shouted.

Looking back toward the inn, Maraakus saw two men and a woman step out into the street. The woman walked backward, leading a man with each hand, laughing, talking to them in a shrill, drunken voice. Her long yellow hair and red tunic was plainly visible in the torchlight. It was Telsia.

"You both have a few coins left," she declared in a loud, slurred voice. "Might just as well spend them here. You'll find nothing to spend them on when you go south on the Northern Road. . . ."

The men voiced reluctance; however, they made only feeble attempts to resist her. She pulled them steadily down the street while they laughed and hung back, making crude jokes about her anatomy. Maraakus could hear their conversations clearly from his position high on the tower.

He shifted his attention back to the dark form as it rose slightly, grew suddenly taller, then settled back to the ground, leaving him with the distinct impression that he was watching a huge bird of prey spreading its wings and loosening its muscles in preparation for flight.

The hair lifted on the back of his neck. Real or imagined, the vile odor of that thing in the woods returned to his nostrils. The muscles in his stomach knotted and his heart began to pound as he watched with mixed feelings of morbid fascination and horror. He knew he was seeing the beast responsible for Lannon's death—the same creature he had encountered in the forest—but he was astonished to see that it was actually nearly three times larger than a horse. It moved about on all fours—with a curious, shuffling motion—and it moved surprisingly fast.

Stepping to his right, Maraakus seized the torch from its

bracket and turned toward the inn. The deep, bone chilling fear that he had felt in the woods seized him, yet he forced himself to move—to warn the people coming up the street.

Drawing back his arm, he flung the torch into the darkness. It sailed through the air like a twisting comet, sputtering, dropping showers of bright sparks in a curving arc. Then it landed in the street with an explosion of bright embers, sputtered briefly, then lay burning with a low, weak flame.

The two men stopped and jerked their hands free of the woman's grasp. They looked quickly about, shouting at each other and pointing drunkenly at the torch, confused and startled by this fiery missile from the dark sky.

"Get that woman back to the inn!" Maraakus shouted. "I'm General Maraakus! Now *move*, damn you!"

The smaller man simply looked around, trying to figure out where the voice had come from, but the bigger man threw Telsia over his shoulder and staggered back toward the inn. She kicked and screamed curses that would have made Rafin blush, but all three of them quickly disappeared from the street.

Maraakus looked back to the corner and saw that the dark form had not moved away. It squatted with its head raised and looked up toward the top of the tower with large red eyes that glowed malevolently in the darkness. The eyes squinted, then narrowed to bright, gleaming slits. Then they widened and fixed on the exact spot where Maraakus was standing.

Quickly, Maraakus stepped behind one of the rotting columns and rested his head against the cold wood, knowing full well that it was too late. The creature had seen him. He heard the soft clattering sound again and he dared another quick look. The creature had moved.

Eyes darting from place to place, Maraakus searched in the dark shadows of the streets. Though he saw nothing, he could hear that curious rattling sound and suddenly realized that it was the sound of heavy claws on paving stones. Immediately, he thought of the metal cylinder and wooden club hanging at the base of the tower—an alarm used to summon help during a crisis, such as a fire in the village. If he could get to that gong . . .

He ran to the opening in the floor and stopped, staring down into the black hole, remembering the missing steps and railing. His only source of light lay burning in the street below. Without light, a descent from the tower on those rotting stairs could kill him. Worse yet, he might survive the fall, but end up injured and unable to defend himself. Screaming in terror, he would then be dragged out through the open doorway. But before he died, that creature would open his chest with a ragged, horny claw and—

Rushing back to the stone railing, he took a quick look down the tower's side and a cold, prickling sensation moved up his back. Some terrifying monstrosity from a feverish nightmare was standing at the base of the tower, glaring up with baleful red eyes, hissing and snorting jets of white vapor into the cold air.

Then, as Maraakus watched in abject horror, the creature reared on thick back legs and reached far up the tower's side, clawing and scratching at the rough surface, while leathery wings battered the tower's base. A forefoot found purchase on the wall and with a hideous snarl, the creature heaved its body off the ground. Then, by hooking the stones with its splintered claws, it began climbing slowly toward the top.

Maraakus stepped back from the railing, suddenly aware of a burning sensation on his right leg. Thrusting his hand into his pocket, he brought out the charm that Alyna had fashioned from a scrap of bone. He could feel the carved markings with the tips of his fingers and the charm felt strangely warm.

Taking another quick look down the side of the tower, he saw the creature drawing steadily closer and felt the charm growing hotter, searing the palm of his right hand.

"For my protection," he muttered. "But I guess I forgot to ask how to use the damned thing."

Motivated by fear and desperation—running purely on instinct—Maraakus stepped up to the low stone railing, raised his hand, and flung the charm at the creature's head. There was a single stroke of blue-white light and Maraakus was momentarily blinded by the brilliant flash. He heard the creature hissing with pain and he looked down to see it clinging tightly to the side of the tower, thrashing its head from side to side. Its red eyes were closed and it clung to the tower with powerful front legs while its back legs scrambled, then locked solidly on the rough stone surface. The massive head lifted. There was a loud, dreadful roar and a great, slobbering mouth opened to reveal double rows of dagger-sized teeth.

Hot, fetid breath reached Maraakus at the tower's top and he reeled back from the stone railing, sickened by the vile odor. Then he heard a series of loud scraping sounds and a dry, leathery foot appeared at the base of a column and hooked the stone railing with long, jagged claws.

Maraakus again reacted instinctively. Snatching the dagger from his boot, he lunged forward and drove the keen blade into the scaly foot. There was a loud croaking sound—just short of a bellow—then the clawed foot retreated and carried the dagger with it.

Stepping back, Maraakus pulled his sword from its sheath and raised it overhead with both hands. The foot reappeared and he leaned his weight into the stroke, trying desperately to sever the creature's foot from its leg. The sword struck cleanly and the shock of the blow traveled up Maraakus's arm. The weapon vibrated as if he had tried to cut through a small oak tree.

The creature bellowed with pain, but reached up to lock a second foot on the stone railing. A scaly head rose slowly up between the clawed feet and red eyes with vertical black pupils fixed him with a malevolent stare.

As Maraakus backed quickly across the tower, the creature swung its left front leg in a wide arc that carried away a column supporting the roof. The backswing tore away a section of the stone railing, showering Maraakus with stone fragments and knocking his sword from his grasp.

Leaping up on the narrow railing, Maraakus swung his body outside the tower, placing one of the wooden columns between them. But when another powerful swing carried away a second column, the rotting roof timbers cracked and groaned, the tower shuddered, and the entire roof sagged to one side, tearing the column from his hands. He tottered briefly, flailing both arms and seeking a new handhold.

Then he was falling, twisting through the air. The roof of the stables rushing up to meet him. The jarring impact knocked the breath from his lungs.

❧ ❧ ❧

Half buried by broken roof timbers and thatching, Maraakus lay on the stable floor, astonished that he was still alive and, as far as he could determine, relatively unhurt. This realization came slowly to his dazed mind, prompted by the nickering of terrified horses kicking the boards of their stalls, a chorus of excited shouts from people outside, and the rapid pounding of his own heart.

A section of heavy timber—one he supposed used to be the ridge pole of the stable roof—lay across his legs; its splintered end rested against the wall of an adjoining stall. Carefully, he pushed the timber from his legs and got slowly to his feet. Satisfied that no bones had been broken, he brushed loose thatching from his eyes and stumbled outside to the base of the tower. Looking up, he saw the creature's massive head and a sharply pointed wing drooping over the edge of the collapsed roof.

Seizing the wooden club in his right hand, Maraakus began pounding on the metal cylinder. Lights appeared in windows; doors opened and slammed; then torches appeared, bobbing and weaving through the darkened streets. Someone shouted his name from across the market square and Maraakus turned to see Danis raising his bow. An arrow streaked toward the top of the tower and the morning air was filled with a horrible screeching.

The arrow had found its mark.

Encouraged by this small success, Maraakus continued to pound the cylinder while Danis sent arrow after arrow toward the creature—each shot followed by bellows of pain. Then he heard Danis shout, "Run Maraakus! *Run!*"

Looking straight up, Maraakus saw long leathery wings lifting. then another shower of broken stone, splintered timbers, and rotting shingles tumbled into the street. With a long, terrifying shriek, the creature launched itself into the air. A wing dipped and the creature wobbled briefly, then its flight steadied as it sailed low over the rooftops, cleared the village wall, and disappeared into the early morning darkness.

CHAPTER TWELVE

Dawn had not yet broken, but the village inn was aswarm with harried serving girls rushing about with loaded platters; men stood two-deep at the long, polished bar, and ale flowed freely from tapped wooden barrels.

Rafin shook his head and grinned at Maraakus. "I guess only an ill wind blows profit for none," he said, raising his voice above the noise of the crowd. He selected a small table in the corner and they sank wearily into their chairs.

Danis leaned forward with his elbows on the table. "I shot that thing a dozen times," he told them, "and it didn't even seem hurt."

"What was it?" Rafin asked. "What can take a dozen hunting arrows and still fly?"

"I can tell you!" a voice declared.

They looked up to see a thin man with a dirty gray beard and long hair standing near one end of the serving bar, surrounded by a small group of men and women.

"I saw it real good!" the man said. "Why, I suppose I was closer than anybody—'cept for the general, of course. I was just standin' there—next to the temple—when the damned thing came right across the market square and went up that tower like a squirrel! Saw it with my own eyes." He took a long swallow from his mug.

"Now I've seen some horrible sights in my time, Jirvean," he said to the stocky innkeeper. "But I ain't never seen nothin' like that before!" He stabbed the hook-nosed man in the chest with a dirty finger to emphasize his point. "Now a man might call me a liar, if he didn't see it with his own eyes. Why, I'd expect that—and right to my face, too—'cept in this case, I wasn't the only person to see the thing! It sat right up, breathin' red and yellow fire, screamin' like all the banshees of hell!"

He paused and took a long swallow from his mug, sloshing a little down the front of his beard. "The blood nearly froze in my veins, friends, when that dragon reached down and squeezed off chunks of that tower—rocks and timbers alike— and started hurlin' 'em at people. One of them columns whipped right by my head. Damned thing missed by this much!" He held up his hand with his forefinger and thumb close together.

"I tell you, Jirvean," he said dramatically, closing his eyes, "it was enough to send a body back to the temple on Seventh Day! And that's for certain!"

"What was it?" a woman asked.

"It was a dragon, mum! No mistakin' it! Dark, dark green it was—with these funny marks around its eyes. And its eyes! I tell you, mum, its eyes had this funny light comin' out in white flashes and I don't mind admittin' that it scared me plenty.

"Now I'm as brave as the next man, I suppose," he suggested modestly, "but to be perfectly truthful—which I always try to be, not bein' able to abide a liar myself, and rememberin' clearly how it happened—that dragon made me stop and think. Now, I figure the way to kill it is to . . ."

Rafin shook his head, snagged a serving girl, and ordered tea and berrycakes. Several villagers pointed at Maraakus and talked in hushed voices. Maraakus noticed Rafin staring toward the entrance and he turned to see the old klersep elbowing his way through the crowd. The old man stopped at their table and reached out to place a hand on Maraakus's shoulder. His face was split with a wide, toothy grin.

"General," he said breathlessly, "I'm delighted that Judbal spared you from serious injury, for I am about to share with you a most fascinating and incredible event."

Maraakus closed his eyes and gave a deep sigh. "I've had my share of incredible events for one morning," he told the priest.

"I'm afraid you must endure another, General," the priest insisted. "The odd stranger you brought to the temple is a most unusual man. I would suggest that you talk with him."

The little cleric paused, looked carefully around, and lowered his voice. "This stranger may be able to help us with our . . . a certain problem that we have discussed," he stated, raising his thick white brows. "He heard you mention plactrograms and he knew the word. After you left us, we had a conversation concerning the ancient races and their writings. Subsequently, I discovered that he reads the ancient tongues quite well."

Maraakus stared at the priest. "You have more than just his word, of course."

"Oh, yes," the priest assured him. "I showed him some examples from my collection—except the one we discussed, naturally—and he could read them all. Moreover, he came here seeking descendants of a certain family. He told me the family surname but I did not recognize it. Then he drew the family's plactrogram. I recognized it instantly, but I lied—may Judbal forgive me—and said it meant nothing to me. Would you care to guess who's family he seeks?"

"Rafin's?" Maraakus guessed.

"Just so."

"By the very gods!" Rafin exclaimed.

"Where is this . . . traveler now?" Maraakus inquired.

"He's locked in my quarters. I left him sitting before the fire, drinking the last of my tea," the priest replied. "He said that if he fails to find Rafin or Alyna today, he will depart for his own country—though he would not say where that is. I know he has come from some far place and must certainly be weary, yet he sat all night before the fire and did not sleep."

Maraakus glanced at Rafin. "You and Danis wait here. I think I should speak with this traveler."

Without waiting for Rafin's reply, he stood and followed the old priest out to the street. They walked quickly across the market square and went to the rear of the temple. The priest twisted a large brass key in the lock and pushed the door open.

Maraakus stepped into the room and the familiar smell of rancid lamp oil greeted him. A single chair sat before the fire and a tall clay mug sat on the hearth. "Where is he?" Maraakus asked.

For a moment, the priest stood motionless in the center of the room; his mouth hung open in obvious disbelief. Lifting a thin hand, he pointed to the chair placed in front of the fire. "I . . . l-left him sitting right there!" he stammered.

Maraakus went to the door leading to the chapel and rattled the latch. It was securely locked. The priest checked the door leading to the room where he had shown Maraakus the statue of Judbal. It too was locked and there were no windows.

"I cannot explain this," the priest said, shaking his head.

"I want that traveler," Maraakus said. "Find him!"

"He is probably out trying to locate Rafin's family," the priest guessed.

"I'll send men to help you search," Maraakus said.

"Keep your men for other duties, General. I'll have a small army of Judbal's followers on the streets before sunrise. If he is still in this village, he will be found," the priest vowed. "I hope I did the right thing in coming to you."

"You did," Maraakus assured him.

A cold gray light was creeping over the village as Maraakus hurried back to the inn. He rejoined Danis and Rafin at their table and told them of the missing stranger.

"I want you to find Hadrax," Maraakus told Danis. "Tell him to see that each guard has a description of this man. He's medium tall and slight of build. His boots and jerkin are leather, but he may be wearing a cloak with a deep hood. He carries a walking staff carved with curious symbols and speaks with a strange accent. They'll have no trouble recognizing him. Tell them to hold this man for questioning. Quickly, then come back here. We don't have long before sunrise."

"I understand," Danis assured him.

Maraakus raised his hand and glanced quickly at Rafin. "One more thing, Danis," he said. "Tell Hadrax to post two of his best men at Rafin's house. Alyna won't like it, but I want it done. If this stranger shows up, take him into custody."

Danis nodded and looked quickly at Rafin, who stood and started to push his way through the crowd.

"By all the gods!" Rafin exclaimed. "I'm going home—"

"Wait," Maraakus cautioned. "He probably doesn't even know Alyna exists."

"The rumors are flying," Danis told them. "I've heard at least six versions of what happened at the tower."

"And not one is anywhere near the truth, no doubt," Maraakus commented, giving the young man a smile. "I have another job for you. When you're done talking to Hadrax, saddle your horse, then get mine and Rafin's. Bring them to the front of the inn. We'll start tracking that animal as soon as you return."

"I'll be back shortly," Danis told them. He drank the last of his tea, stuffed two berrycakes into his pocket and hurried away.

"Don't worry about Alyna," Maraakus said to Rafin, "I'm just being overly protective myself. For now, let's hope we can find enough tracks to locate the lair of this beast. It's big, and very strong, but it doesn't actually fly. It glides—much in the manner of a flying fox—so it needs a high starting place."

"The Pinnacle?" Rafin asked.

The back door of the inn flew open and Hadrax's huge form filled the doorway. He saw Rafin and elbowed his way through the crowd. "Better come quickly, Rafin," he said. He gave Maraakus a quick nod. "There's a white horse at the south gate dragging part of a cart. The damned thing is acting so crazy we can't catch it—but I know this horse."

Maraakus saw that Hadrax's head and broad shoulders were covered with large snowflakes, melting rapidly in the warm room.

"A white horse with two black stockings?" Rafin asked.

"That's the one," Hadrax answered.

"Is it snowing hard?" Maraakus nodded at Hadrax's wet shoulders.

Hadrax gave him a puzzled look. "Yes," he answered, glancing quickly at Rafin. "And it's getting heavier."

"Earlan!" Rafin shouted. "Are your brothers still with you?"

A stocky man with a yellow beard stood up on his chair. The serving room fell silent. "Right here!" Earlan shouted. Two more men stood up in their chairs and looked toward the back of the room.

"Where are your horses?" Rafin asked.

"Out back!"

"You three go to the south gate," Rafin ordered. "Wait for me there. Go!"

Earlan shouted an answer and the three men hurried out the back door.

"Hadrax," Rafin said, turning to the big baker, "keep the gate closed until I get there. Forget the horse. We'll catch it later. I'll be there shortly."

Hadrax turned without answering and rushed from the room.

"By the very gods!" Rafin said, kicking the leg of a table. "I forgot about the old peddler!"

"What peddler?" Maraakus asked.

"A man named Konrin sells metalware and trinkets to the women of the village," Rafin explained. "He travels in a small, two-wheeled cart, drawn by a white mare with two black stockings. Usually, he comes down out of the mountains and makes a night camp in a grove of beech trees beyond the southern planting fields. The next morning, he comes into the village to peddle his wares."

Maraakus turned and went quickly toward the door, leaving Rafin standing at the table. Shouldering his way to the front of the inn, he stepped out to the street. It was daylight. The overcast sky was filled with swirling clouds of snow that the wind was blowing into small drifts along the shallow gutters and against the sides of houses.

"Even nature conspires against us!" Rafin shouted, shuffling quickly up behind Maraakus. "This will cover that creature's tracks in no time. We'll never find it!"

"Perfect!" Maraakus declared. "Just what we need!" He turned to see Rafin staring hard at him. "No," he assured the old soldier, "I haven't lost my senses. This is the first real snow of winter and it'll filter through the trees and cover even the forest floor. You take some men and go look for that peddler. When Danis returns, he and I will track this creature right to its lair. In this snow, we can do that alone."

"You don't want to come with us?" Rafin asked.

"I don't mean to sound callous," Maraakus replied, "but if Konrin is dead, all you can do is take his body to Yettik. That creature was southwest of the village just a short time ago. By now it's heading north toward the Pinnacle, probably on the west side of the valley, through the woods where Lannon was killed. Danis and I will go northwest to the Dove. Sooner or later, it will cross the river and that's where we'll pick up fresh tracks."

He put one hand on Rafin's shoulder. "If you find the old peddler dead, we have three or four days before this thing comes hunting for its next victim. We won't try to kill it alone. If we can find where it lairs, we'll come back for you—and as many men as we can muster!"

Rafin nodded, took in another notch on his sword belt and walked rapidly away. Maraakus watched until he disappeared in the swirling snow. Smiling to himself, he pulled on his gloves and turned his face up toward the gray, overcast sky. "I've got you, now." he said to himself. "Come on down, you cold, wet, beautiful snow!"

Hearing hoofbeats, he turned to see Danis riding up the street, leading Maraakus's huge black war-horse by the reins. When Danis pulled his own horse to a stop, it stood patiently in the street; the high-strung black horse pranced about at the end of the reins, tossing its head and pawing the snow with its front hooves.

Danis jerked his thumb at the snorting animal. "I'm sorry it took so long," he said, "but I don't think your horse likes me. Rafin has a few boards to replace."

Maraakus walked to the big animal and slapped it on the neck. The horse stopped prancing and stuck its nose under the edge of his cloak. "He's spending too much time in the stable," Maraakus said, swinging up to the saddle. "You and I are going to track that animal—or whatever it is—through this snow and find out where it goes. I'm betting it's headed for the Pinnacle." He touched his heels to the horse's sides and they rode off toward the north gate.

From the village, they rode at a quick canter across the frozen fields, then followed the old footpath down to the Dove and dismounted. Leading their horses by the reins, they approached the spot where the funeral pyres of Andor and Fergus had burned, now covered with a blanket of snow.

A strong wind was blowing out of the west, pushing long lines of dark clouds. "The snow is getting heavier," Maraakus declared, studying the sky and turning his face away from the wind. "It'll bury that creature's tracks. We'd better hurry or we'll be wasting our time."

He led the way upstream, then turned right, toward the riverbank. Danis moved out ahead and turned left, working his way through a stand of tall trees and around a dense thicket of bearbriars. "Over here!" He shouted.

Maraakus mounted his horse and rode quickly around the thicket. He found Danis kneeling on the ground next to the now familiar double drag-marks. "That's exactly what I thought we'd find," he told the young man. "The creature drags it's wings when moving about on the ground."

"And it's bleeding," Danis observed, pointing to some dark brown stains in the snow. "Do we follow these marks?"

Maraakus shook his head. "That would take too long," he said, "and they'll be buried under the snow soon enough. We'll head straight for the Pinnacle. It'll stay in the deep woods until it reaches that old planting field west of the high cliffs."

Danis mounted his horse and they rode down to the river. After crossing to the northern bank, they followed a narrow trail through the forest and emerged on the edge of a rocky slope. Danis looked around and said, "I don't see any tracks."

"Take the left side," Maraakus instructed. "I'll go right. Stay out of the trees."

Danis nodded and they separated, moving slowly around the field, working their way toward the base of the Pinnacle. Maraakus picked up the trail where it passed between two boulders and turned straight toward the base of the mountain. He signaled to Danis and the young man rode quickly to his side.

By now, it was snowing heavily and the evergreen trees were drooping under the accumulating weight. Seeing Danis rubbing his hands together and blowing on his fingers, Maraakus pulled off his gloves and held them out to the young man. "Put them on," he ordered. Danis refused them with a shake of his head. "We may need your bow and you'll be of no use with frozen fingers."

Danis stuck his hands into the gloves and Maraakus nodded. "Now we'll find out where it hides."

They approached the base of the Pinnacle and dismounted. Proceeding on foot, they followed the long scrapes up a wind-swept slope and stopped before a snow-covered thicket of bear-briars. A wide, trampled path extended to the far side.

"It made a path through those briars so it could get into that cleft," Danis said.

Maraakus drew his sword. "Stay well behind me," he instructed. "We're not trying to kill it yet. We just want to see where it goes." Then, raising his sword, Maraakus stepped into the trampled thicket; Danis followed with an arrow fitted on his bowstring.

The back of the cleft was narrow and plugged with rubble, no doubt the result of multiple avalanches. Noting a multitude of long scrapes on the wall of the cleft, much lighter in color than the rest of the rock, Maraakus pointed them out to Danis. "This is where it climbs up," he said.

As Danis moved back for a better view, he stepped on something in the snow. Bending down; he dug with a gloved hand and picked up a worn, leather rucksack. "A strange place to leave a hunting pouch," he remarked, handing it to Maraakus.

Using the tip of his sword, Maraakus cut the closing thongs and dumped the contents on the ground. The rucksack contained a thick tallow candle, a fire kit, a ball of string and a waterskin that had frozen and split along one side. There were three shrunken apples, a partial loaf of hard dark bread and the remains of a small block of moldy cheese. The last item was a small leather bag. Maraakus opened the bag and poured the contents into his hand. A small pile of gold and silver coins gleamed in the gray morning light.

He selected one of the coins and held it up for inspection. "This money is very old," he remarked, handing the coin to Danis.

Danis twisted the old leather rucksack in his hands. "It certainly hasn't been up here very long," he agreed.

They bagged the coins and Maraakus dropped them into the rucksack. He tapped the still pliant leather with his right hand. "I'm inclined to think this pouch was lost," he said. "Notice the broken strap?"

"Why wouldn't they look for it?" Danis asked.

Maraakus turned to indicate the freshly made scars on the face of the rock wall. "Because," he said, "I have a feeling this rucksack belonged to Andor—or Keam—and he was being chased. Those boys were up here. Which mean Keam's body is probably up there still."

Maraakus walked to the end of the cleft and looked up between the steep walls of stone, then shifted his gaze to the rockslide, now covered with patches of drifting snow. The top of the slope was out of sight, hidden by the cleft's sharply angled walls.

"Well, those boys certainly didn't climb this vertical wall," Maraakus decided. "Can you squeeze through that crack? See if you can climb up those rocks to your left."

After handing Maraakus his bow and quiver, Danis walked to the back of the cleft and wiggled through the crack. Maraakus retreated to the front of the cleft and waited. He could hear an occasional clattering as Danis dislodged a rock while making his way up the slope.

Suddenly, the cleft reverberated with the sound of tumbling boulders. Maraakus ducked quickly around the side of the opening as small stones and large boulders poured from the narrow split in the mountain, followed by whirling clouds of fine snow. After a time the rumbling stopped and there was silence.

"Danis!" Maraakus shouted. "Can you hear me?"

"I'm all right," Danis called. His voice sounded faint and distant. "There are stairs up here! Shall I go up?"

"No!" Maraakus practically screamed. "Come back! Be careful!"

For a few minutes there was silence in the cleft; then another heavy shower of stones tumbled down the slope.

"I'm all right!" Danis called down to him. "The slide started below me."

After a while he came down the rockslide with both hands spread on the left wall and eased himself through the crack. He jumped down to solid ground and walked out to the entrance where Maraakus was standing. "The whole slope shifted that time," he said. "Luckily, I hadn't started down. Anyway, I think that staircase leads to the ledges on the back side."

"If so," Maraakus said, "the ledges might lead to the top."

"That last rockslide completely filled the back of this cleft," Danis told him. "You can walk right through. The crack gets much wider at the top. Do you want to go in?"

"No," Maraakus answered. "Not right now. This is where the creature goes up to its lair. And I'm almost certain the boys went through this cleft, as well. Let's go back to the village. I may know where to find yet another piece to this puzzle."

Maraakus led the way through the thicket and across the small level area to their horses. They mounted and rode east, around the backside of the Pinnacle, heading for the Northern Road and the new bridge over the Dove. It was past noon before they emerged from the woods and turned south toward the village.

As they approached the new bridge, Maraakus raised his arm and waved when he saw Rafin across the river, approaching quickly on horseback. They crossed the new bridge and pulled up their horses on the side of the road. Rafin soon drew up facing them. "You found the old peddler." Maraakus said.

Rafin brushed the snow from his beard and nodded. "He's dead. Same as the others. We took him to Yettik. All my news is not bad, though," he added. "We found that stranger."

CHAPTER THIRTEEN

As if guarding a prisoner of war, they marched the old traveler to Rafin's house.

"Take this man inside," Maraakus said to Danis and the old priest. "We'll join you in a moment." He motioned to Rafin, who followed him into the passageway between the house and the storage shed. Looking up, Maraakus pointed to the ceiling of the passageway. It was sheathed with whitewashed planking.

"I remember seeing these on the tower," he told them. "Ceiling planks, and only this part of the house has them. I'll bet you the finest horse in my stables that that book we were looking for is under those planks."

"Well I'll be a. . . ."

Maraakus stepped through the stable door, and Rafin, still studying the ceiling planks above him, waited while he reached up to a high shelf, took down the amulet, and dropped it into his pocket. "Say nothing," he told Rafin. "Let's see how our mysterious traveler reacts to Alyna's little trinket."

As the two of them walked into the kitchen, Alyna looked up and frowned. "Maraakus? Are you carrying that . . . that *thing* on your person?" she asked. Maraakus nodded and placed a finger to his lips.

"He has not tried to escape," the priest told Rafin. "I have watched him most carefully."

Rafin and Danis exchanged smirks.

The traveler shook his head. "I choose to be here, you old fool," he growled.

"In any case, you are most welcome," Alyna assured the stranger.

"If you would kindly sit here," Maraakus said, pulling out a chair, "we'll detain you no longer than necessary."

After the traveler was seated between Alyna and the priest, Danis extended his hand. "May I take your walking staff?" he asked.

"You may," the traveler replied, handing it to him and laughing softly as Danis inspected a line of symbols carved into the dark wood.

The old priest shifted restlessly in his chair. His cheeks were flushed and his eyes sparkled mischievously as he rubbed his hands together and cackled softly to himself. The mysterious traveler sat silently, his face hidden in the hood of his cloak.

"As you all know," the priest announced, "I've had several long conversations with this man. His name is Grommdum. He has traveled from a far land to find descendants of the Porshanneva family. He's a most interesting man."

"Wetakian, you dolt," the visitor declared softly. "I am a *wetakian.*"

"I've not heard of such people," Maraakus said.

The priest chuckled. "It's the correct name for members of a very old race of *elves,* General,"

Grommdum glared at the priest and pushed back his hood. Next he removed his helmet-like leather skullcap, tucked it under his belt, then folded his hands and placed them on the table. His fingers were slender and calloused, with long but neatly trimmed nails. He had distinctly pointed ears, an olive-colored complexion, long gray hair, and sharp, black, almond-shaped eyes.

Grommdum smiled and nodded his head in greeting. "Best evening on you, General Maraakus." He chuckled softly to himself.

"Oh, yes," he said. "Even in my homeland we have heard of you. I must admit that I never expected to meet you in this village. And I greet you warmly, young Danis."

Then he turned his gaze to Rafin. "Best evening on you, sire," he said pleasantly. "I hope we will become friends. My father knew your family many years ago."

Finally, he turned to Alyna. "And I'm particularly pleased to meet you, young woman," he said softly, looking directly into her eyes. "Here, give me your hands. Come, young woman. I shall not harm you. It is you that I have come so far to meet."

He held both her hands for a moment, smiled and placed her hands on the table. "Astounding!" he declared. "More raw, untrained potential than I have ever seen before." He leaned back in his chair and smiled at her, obviously satisfied with what he had discovered.

Alyna looked quickly at Maraakus and he gave her a reassuring smile. "Are there others like me?" she asked the traveler. "People with my same . . . ability?"

"Oh, yes," Grommdum assured her. "There are others scattered throughout the lands. Still, it is a relatively rare thing."

Rafin stared curiously at the traveler. "Who are you really?" he asked. "What is your business with Alyna?"

"I have told you—"

"No," Rafin interrupted quietly. "I meant *what* are you?"

"We are what we are," was the wetakian's mysterious reply. "We live on the same land, eat the same food and drink the same water. We seek common goals during out lifetimes—a peaceful existence, the right to raise our children in safety, the love of friends and family. While each of us is a unique creature, our physical differences are merely superficial, as shallow as the color of our skins, as subtle as the shape of our ears or the color of our eyes. We're all creations of the same gods. No matter by which names we call them."

"That's not exactly answering my question."

The old traveler smiled. "I am not a human—if that is what you're asking."

"From where have you come?" Maraakus asked, studying the traveler carefully.

"In your language my home would be called Refuge," Grommdum replied. "It is deep in the woodlands you know as the Great Shadow Forest. My people have lived there for hundreds of years. Before that, we lived here. Not in this village, of course, but in this valley."

"I've heard only savages and strange, magical creatures live in the Great Shadow Forest." Rafin said. "That it's a dangerous, wild place."

"How very odd," the traveler muttered, placing his hand to his mouth and raising his brows. "I must report that to my people when I return. Such news will come as a complete surprise to them." He gave Danis a slow wink.

Danis grinned. "You're an elf?" His eyes sparkled with curiosity.

Grommdum sighed. "That is what you call us, young man, we call ourselves the wetakia."

"Yes, he's an *elf!*" cackled the old priest. "Judbal has sent him to me so that I might meet one of the ancient ones before he takes me to his bosom." He reached out his hand and touched Grommdum on the ear.

"Keep your hands off me, you old fool!" Grommdum growled. "I'll get my staff and beat lumps on your thick skull!"

The priest appeared unconcerned by Grommdum's threat.

Grommdum glared. "I have my own reasons for coming to this place and they have nothing to do with your god."

"Why are you here, old man?" Maraakus asked.

"For the best of reasons, I assure you," Grommdum answered. "As you well know, an old evil has been loosed upon this land. I am here to assist in its destruction."

"And how did you come to know about this . . . old evil, as you call it?" Maraakus asked.

Grommdum gave him a wry smile and arched his brows. "Well," he answered, "that is a bit more difficult to explain."

"But you'll try, won't you?" Maraakus asked coldly.

Grommdum sighed heavily, then sat back in his chair and folded his hands in his lap. "Very well, General Maraakus," he said. "Like Alyna, I have the ability to use what you call magic. There is a meditating spell—one more commonly practiced by members of my own race than yours—which permits the user to place himself in harmony with nature and the forces of life itself.

"Several days ago," he continued, "while in deep meditation—not in a dream, mind you—a sorceress named Ilka instructed me to undertake a long journey. She sent me here to find this young woman," he nodded at Alyna, "and become her Multan."

"I don't know anyone named Ilka," Alyna said.

"She was a wise and gentle sorceress," Grommdum, clearly not surprised, told her, "who freed my people from slavery. She died more than three hundred years ago."

"And you expect us to believe you were sent here by a three hundred year old, dead sorceress?" Maraakus asked.

Grommdum shrugged. "You will believe what you wish," he

replied. "You asked me to explain, and I have done so. My business is not with you, General, it is with Alyna, who is a direct descendant of Ilka herself."

"By Heltum's sacred beard!" Rafin muttered. "It seems Alyna and I are related to just about everybody. First Jodac, and now some dead sorceress."

"What did you say?" Alyna asked. She looked quickly from Maraakus to Rafin. "We are related to *Jodac?*"

"Of course," Grommdum said, before Rafin could answer. "Didn't you know that?"

"I certainly did not!" Alyna emphatically declared.

Rafin shrugged and looked helplessly at Maraakus. "We were going to tell you," he argued in his own defense, "but then we decided—"

"We were simply trying to protect you. To spare you further pain and embarrassment," Maraakus explained. "At the time, our information was largely unconfirmed. Nevertheless, we should have told you. But we knew nothing about this . . . sorceress."

"Ilka," Grommdum said. "Her name was Ilka. She and Jodac were siblings."

For several moments, there was silence around the table. Then Maraakus rose slowly to his feet and stared down at the old traveler seated before him. "Innocent children are dying in this village. My patience is exhausted by tales of visions and fanciful spells of magic. I've encountered many strange people in my life, but none who convinced me he was a true wizard—to say nothing of being an elf. Yet I must admit you're unlike any man I've ever met.

"But any attempt to exploit our misfortune for personal gain is not only foolish," he continued, "but dangerous as well. For your own good, I'll have you escorted to the village gates and released. Don't come back to this valley if you value your life."

Grommdum smiled. "I'm afraid that's impossible, General," he said quietly. "I have business with this young woman."

"Rafin," Maraakus said sharply, without breaking eye contact with Grommdum, "take this man to the village gates. See that he's sent on his way."

"Do not force me to take actions that we'll both regret, General," Grommdum said softly. "I say this not to challenge your authority, or question your motives and sincerity. Even in Refuge, we know you are not a man who takes unconsidered actions." He met Maraakus's stare with his own, equally hard and steady.

Maraakus felt the full intensity of Grommdum's gaze and was impressed by his obvious lack of fear. The man could be telling the truth, he thought. Intentionally or otherwise, he might prove to have valuable knowledge. Still, he decided, just to be absolutely certain, it might be best if—

Maraakus raised one hand as Rafin started to rise and Rafin sank back in his chair. The old priest sat motionless, staring back with a dazed expression, perhaps frightened by the intensity of this verbal exchange, filled with thinly veiled threats.

"Maraakus, what are you saying?" Alyna asked. "I thought you believed—" She fell silent, but her eyes expressed deep anger.

"Please," the old priest offered. "This is my fault. I should have better prepared all of you for this meeting. I have misjudged the situation . . . badly."

Grommdum sighed. "I know how difficult it is for you to accept what I'm saying, General, but what possible motive could I have in deceiving you? Would it not be best if we worked together—toward a common goal? The evil that stalks this valley is very old and very powerful. Unless it is stopped, every person in this village—man, woman, and child—might be killed. Then this evil will move on to another valley, and another village. We must not permit that to happen!"

Alyna placed her hand on Grommdum's shoulder. "This is my home," she said sternly, turning the full force of her pale blue eyes on Maraakus. "I believe him, so I'll decide who stays and who leaves. And I'm not one of your soldiers, General!"

Maraakus suppressed a smile as he sat down. Rafin covered his mouth, but Danis grinned openly.

"Very well," Maraakus said. "I'll listen, old man. But if I find that you're attempting to deceive me. . . ."

Reaching into his pocket, Maraakus took out the amulet and placed it on the table. Grommdum leaned forward, lifted it by the gold chain, and studied it carefully.

"Take care when handling this amulet," he advised. "There is much evil and danger here. The power of this crystal is quite remarkable. Might I ask how this object came into your possession?"

"I found it in the river," Alyna replied. "And I've already had one very bad experience with it."

"Our immediate problem is nothing more than a large animal," Rafin interrupted. "We know where it goes and we know it can be wounded. It's simply a matter of killing it."

"Perhaps," Grommdum agreed. "Still, it's possible that might be more difficult than you imagine."

"Tell us what you think of this," Maraakus said, handing Grommdum a small square of paper.

"Well," Grommdum muttered. "This symbol, the mark that resembles an eye, is the sign for Jodac's name. The eagle is the sign of the Porshanneva family. Therefore, it reads Jodac Porshanneva."

"What does all this mean?" Alyna asked.

Grommdum shook his head. "I do not yet know, my child," he said. "So many questions remain unanswered. Ilka instructed me to come here—to Stridgenfel—and seek out her descendant, a user of magic. Apparently, there is unfinished business between Ilka and Jodac."

For a long time, they sat without speaking. The logs popped in the fireplace and the wind moaned softly under the eaves of the old house. Finally, Maraakus pushed his chair back from the table, walked to the fireplace and stood, chin in hand, thinking and staring into the fire. After a while, he turned back to the table.

"Have you knowledge," Maraakus asked, "of a book with this eagle on the cover?"

The old priest and Grommdum looked at each other. "I have no personal knowledge of such a book," Grommdum replied. "Only what this lout told me after you left us last night."

"I see," Maraakus said dryly. "It seems that our klersep has told you more than I expected. At any rate, we'll soon see if you speak the truth, Grommdum—if that's truly your name."

Grommdum smiled and lowered his eyes to the table. "I have no other, General," he said softly.

"Take Alyna with you," Maraakus said to Rafin, his eyes never leaving Grommdum. "See if the book is hidden under the floor between the house and the shed. If so, let her remove it."

Alyna rose and touched Grommdum on the shoulder, then followed Rafin up the wooden stairs. Maraakus heard their footsteps crossing the floor over their heads, the opening of a door, then the squeaking of the floorboards as Rafin pried at them with his knife. He heard Alyna talking in a soft voice and a slight scuffling sound was followed by a loud thump as a board was seated back in place. Then Rafin came down the stairs, followed by Alyna.

"You were right," Rafin said. "In the rear corner next to the stable. And I don't mind losing my choice of your horses."

Alyna carried a dark brown, ornately carved wooden box and her eyes were brimming with tears. Placing the box on the table, she sat down and wiped her eyes on the sleeve of her robe.

"Well, my child," Grommdum said softly, "The box was made by wetakian hands. Such boxes are designed to hide valuable—or magical—objects and are often protected with spells of concealment."

Maraakus and Rafin exchanged glances, then leaned forward as Alyna put both hands on the box and moved her fingers over the delicate carvings. Placing her thumbs on the lid, she pushed and it came up in her hands. Inside the box was a wine-colored book. On its cover, stitched in gleaming threads of gold, was an eagle with its head turned to the right; its beak was open and it clutched a shining, spiked disc with sharp, hooked talons.

Reaching into the box, Alyna took out the book and placed it on the table. After Rafin put the box on the floor, she opened the book to the first page. It was blank and brown with age. As she carefully turned back the thin parchment, it crackled softly under her fingers.

"Would you like me to read to you, General Maraakus?" Alyna asked. She smiled, but there was a tremor in her voice.

"That is the third time you have asked me that question," he replied. "This time, I would like that, Alyna. I'd like that very much."

Chapter Fourteen

"*Dearly beloved, flesh of my flesh, and blood of my blood, I send thee greetings. Through this book, I now cross the vast emptiness of time and send thee my love and my blessings. I am Ilka, eldest of twins, sister to Jodac, born to the house of Parsid Porshanneva.*"

Alyna looked up suddenly. "Ilka wrote this book with her own hand."

"So Ilka and Jodac weren't simply brother and sister," Rafin said, "But twins."

Alyna glanced at Grommdum and he gave her a smile. "Even

I did not know that little detail," he said. "Go on child. I find this most fascinating. . . ."

She turned back to the book and continued her reading.

"*Above all others in our line, thou hast been chosen to receive this book. It is thine inheritance, preordained by family obligation to the Powers of Enlightenment and Good. It is thy link to the past and to all who have gone before thee. Keep it safe. Study it diligently. Use it wisely, lest the inheritance of this book prove not a privilege, but a heavy burden.*

"*During the period of thy stewardship, this book shall bring thee pleasure and pain, laughter and tears, the blackness of rejection and despair, the ecstasy of love and commitment. Bear it all with courage and humility. They are but warps and wefts in the tapestry of the life thou shalt live. Through thy studies will come strength from weakness, order from chaos, knowledge from ignorance.*

"*In this book is recorded the names of all Keepers before thee and, at the end, thou shalt find thine own name. It was written there by she who gave this book to thee. Name then thy successor and record her name in a like manner before thy death. Take care to pass this book to she with the greatest measure of ability and fear not that you might fail to learn her name. She will become known to thee before such time has expired.*

"*I send thee forth with my blessings, content that thou shalt obey my instructions. Be steadfast in thy studies and remain true to thy responsibility. Be happy. Be good and wise. My love is everlasting. I remain thy loving kinswoman, Ilka Porshanneva.*"

Alyna turned the page and looked up. "My head is spinning. . . ."

The old elf smiled and pointed to the book with a trembling finger. "What you now hold is among the rarest of all objects," he said softly. "That is Ilka's personal spellbook, written in her own hand. To possess such a thing is an awesome responsibility."

"Grandmother taught me very little." Alyna said. "Perhaps I'm not ready—"

"That is why Ilka sent me here," Grommdum interrupted. "I

am to become your Multan—your teacher."

Grommdum gave her a nod, then leaned back in his chair and closed his eyes. Alyna picked up the book, smoothed the page with her hand, and resumed her reading.

"To understand why this book has come into thy life, is to know the history of thy family. In the beginning, our ancestors journeyed forth from a place where life was exceedingly harsh. They found a new land of fertile valleys cut by clean rivers and surrounded by heavily forested mountains.

"Dwelling in this land were races older than humankind—dwarves, elves and other exotic beings. Most numerous were the wetakia, a race of forest elves who lived in small settlements scattered throughout the deep woodlands north of the River of the Doves."

She paused to look up at Grommdum and the old elf smiled.

"I have always suspected that—" the priest began.

"You suspected no such thing!" Grommdum asserted. "Why you have barely enough sense to find your boots each morning!"

"That," the priest insisted, "has nothing to do with what I have thought about—"

"Go on, Alyna" Maraakus interrupted. "Continue reading."

She smiled at the quarreling old men and picked up the book.

"Being by nature both gracious and friendly, the wetakia helped our ancestors construct a small village on the southern banks of the river and clear fertile planting fields on the river's northern side. Unfortunately, our old food seeds grew poorly in this colder land. The first harvest was meager; there was extreme hunger and hardship.

"So that our ancestors would not perish, the wetakia did present them with new seeds from hardy grains and fruits, soft black stone that could be dug from the earth and burned on a hearth, and cloth made from the warm fleece of the mountain animals. Thus, through the wetakia's direct assistance and kind advice, humans prospered and our numbers increased."

"As I've always said," Rafin commented, "legends are often founded on small grains of truth."

"In this case, I say there are more than merely grains," Danis observed.

Alyna pulled the lamp closer and continued to read.

"It was then the wetakia did tell us that a special talent ran strongly in the blood of our family. One female child from each generation—if she possessed a great measure of this talent—did the wetakia tutor in the ancient lore and the customs of their ancestral magicians. The chosen ones were taught to live in harmony with the powers of nature and all living things, and generations would pass before harmony in our family was broken and sorrow descended upon our beautiful land."

Alyna looked up at Rafin and said softly, "I think you'll recognize some of this from Grandmother's stories."

Rafin nodded. He leaned forward and rested both elbows on the table and Alyna turned a page in the book.

"I was born with this talent for magic and, because we were twin-born, so was my brother, Jodac. We were tutored together in the arts of healing and the casting of spells. But as we grew older and our powers increased, the wetakia decided to withdraw from Jodac. My brother's heart was cold and cruel; he sought wealth and dominion over his fellow man. I, however, continued my studies with the gentle wetakia and soon surpassed my brother in power and knowledge, being born with the greatest measure of talent.

"This so angered Jodac that he sought to surpass my abilities by studying the dark arts. In time, his knowledge increased. Jodac became powerful and highly skilled in these arts, but his heart grew ever harder and ever colder.

"Finally, Jodac went up into the snowcapped mountains and sought out the shintanea—those wizards of the mountain elves widely known to practice the dark arts. For seven years Jodac studied with them, learning their evil ways and mastering their darkest spells. He returned to our

village as a man who knew not the meaning of love and compassion.

"I pleaded with Jodac to renounce his evil practices, to use his knowledge to benefit all living things as the gentle wetakia had taught us. But Jodac refused to heed my tearful pleas and brought together a horde of evil followers and did permit them to prey openly on both the human and wetakian inhabitants of the valley, taking many of them into slavery.

"Through their forced labor did he construct his tower atop the dark mountain. Each stone was cut with bleeding hands and each measure of mortar was wetted with their sorrowful tears. Each tree was cut and borne away on aching backs and even the smallest carving was completed under the supervision of his henchmen, and the lash of their cruel whips.

"As my brother's power and wealth increased, his magic grew darker and more evil. Finally, none could stand against him. Wizards from dark places came to seek his advice and favor. From among them he selected two as companions and they formed an evil alliance—the Triad—through which they sought dominion over all lands, and all races."

"Rest a moment," Maraakus said to Alyna. "Rafin? Doesn't that answer a question you and I have debated many times?"

"It certainly does," Rafin agreed.

"All those years we never knew what powers constituted the Triad, or if it actually ever even existed. We certainly never learned the names of its leaders—or founders—but apparently, when its members died in battle, or from old age, their descendants continued to fight wars of aggression against other kingdoms."

"As I said," the old priest remarked, "words, names, and languages change over time."

"This Jodac," Maraakus said, "was responsible for the Mighty Wars, no less."

Rafin nodded and said, "Go on, Alyna. Please continue."

"At last, my brother sought the greatest of all evil powers. He desired to achieve parity with the Forces of Darkness by becoming the absolute

master of evil and in so doing, become a god.

"*To this end he did conjure forth a servant, named it Balsephus, and sent it forth to kill. Each victim did Balsephus consecrate with my brother's sign before carrying their hearts to his master. So deeply possessed was my brother by his evil insanity, that he truly believed he could become a god by consuming the hearts of his innocent victims.*"

"That explains why these murders were committed," Grommdum remarked quietly, "and why Ilka has sent me here to assist Alyna. Balsephus is a kalnath! A conjured beast. He is not eating the hearts. He's still taking them to his dead master."

"What else do you know about these kalnaths?" Maraakus asked.

"Very little," the old elf replied. "My father called them Dark Followers and mentioned them only in hushed tones."

"But this creature is obviously alive," the old priest remarked. "How can that be? Nothing happened for hundreds of years and suddenly it returns, blindly carrying out the instructions Jodac gave it centuries ago?"

"Where has it been?" Danis asked.

"More importantly," Maraakus observed, "why was it inactive for so long? What made it—"

"Balsephus is a horror from the mind of Jodac," Grommdum interrupted. "One can only speculate about the nature of such creatures—or their demented masters. . . ."

"Let's see what else Ilka can tell us," Maraakus said to Alyna. "Please go on." He gave her a grim smile as she again drew the book closer and resumed her reading.

"*Again, I begged Jodac to turn from his evil ways, for though he was gripped by some terrible madness, I loved him still. But when I saw that he would not, or could not repent, I took to my bed, inconsolable in my grief and despair, anguishing over what I knew I must do.*

"*Then, on the anniversary day of our birth, in our forty-sixth year of life, I did fashion a dagger of steel and ivory. I cast upon it a powerful spell and consecrated it with all the force of my will. After concealing this weapon in my clothing, I went up into my brother's stronghold on the dark mountain and sought an audience with him. As his sister, I was allowed passage through his guards and not one dared to touch me.*

"When we were alone, I pleaded with Jodac one last time, begging him to renounce his evil ways. I crawled before him on hands and knees and rent my clothing, beseeching him to return to the village and attend unto our dying mother. But Jodac only laughed. He cursed our family and said, 'What need have I of you—or that weak woman? I take more concern for one of my slaves. At least, a slave has purpose for me.' Then he raised his hands against me and I was caught in a maelstrom of evil forces.

"Realizing that I would soon be consumed by his arcane assault, I used the last of my strength to draw forth my charmed dagger and plunge it strongly into his breast. My brother clutched at the blade with dying fingers and sank down upon the floor as evil swirled about me. And through all this, his conjured servant, Balsephus, did stand as stone and made no attempt to aid his master.

"Suddenly Jodac's chambers were silent and I stood alone, terrified by what I had done. Gathering my clothing about my body, I departed from my brother's private chambers. And though I walked with no outward appearance of fear, I moved past his guards and henchmen with great dread, fearful that they would discover what I had done to their master. Thus did I make my escape, but upon returning to the valley, my hair was white like snow, and I was strangely aged. Thus will I spend my remaining years, bent and disfigured.

"My brother's henchmen soon discovered what I had done, and there was bitter fighting on the dark mountain. When it ended, most of my brother's followers departed from the valley and those who lingered were driven out by an army of wetakian warriors. Then the wetakia destroyed Jodac's tower. With great avalanches did they hide the lower path leading up to my brother's stronghold, forever burying his vile spell-books and ill-gotten treasures within the confines of that cursed mountain."

Alyna stopped reading aloud, scanned the next page and looked up at Maraakus. "That's all she writes about Balsephus. Apparently, this kalnath was sealed inside the mountain along with everything else."

"And quite obviously," Danis commented, "it's found a way out."

Alyna turned to Grommdum. "So Jodac died by Ilka's hand."

"That must have been quite a battle," Grommdum observed quietly. "Between Ilka and Jodac, I mean."

"Still, the ritual killing has resumed," the klersep remarked. "But to what purpose? Jodac is dead. It's all so senseless and . . . brutal!" He closed his eyes and placed his folded hands on the table.

"But one might reasonably expect that of a kalnath," Grommdum argued. "I have heard that they are often designed for specific purposes. Perhaps Jodac didn't think it necessary to make his kalnath highly intelligent—just an efficient killer."

"The mountain was sealed," Maraakus said, "until something happened. Something Keam and Andor did set this thing in motion."

"By all the gods!" Rafin exclaimed. "A stupid, centuries old monster that goes blindly about this valley, murdering people for no purpose—"

"Oh, it has a purpose," Grommdum corrected. "It is doing what it was created to do. Perhaps it knows nothing else, or is unable to realize that its master is dead. In any case, I would not call it stupid. It undoubtedly has a highly developed instinct for survival. That would be a necessary part of its nature. We must not underestimate it, Rafin. I suspect Balsephus is even more dangerous than we first imagined."

"Well," Maraakus declared, "we know it feels pain. It bleeds. Perhaps not normal blood—but it bleeds—and though it seems to heal rapidly, it can be killed."

"When I'm through with it," Rafin growled, "it'll be dead as a paving stone!"

Alyna looked up at her uncle. "What did you say?"

"I said I'm going to kill that—"

"No," Alyna said, looking back at the page she had just read. "You said 'dead as a paving stone' and Ilka said it 'stood as stone and made no attempt to aid his master.' Doesn't that sound strange?"

"Hmmm," Grommdum said. "Balsephus could have been immobilized upon Jodac's death and. . . ."

Maraakus gave the old elf an uneasy squint and tilted his head. This talk of magic and living creatures being immobilized by magical combat disturbed him.

"That would certainly explain why it remained dormant for so long," Rafin said.

"I can't believe I'm sitting here, taking part in such a conversation," Maraakus muttered. "Wizards! Sorceresses! Conjured creatures! These murders have driven us all mad!"

Grommdum smiled. "Bear with us a little longer, General," he said. "Let's continue reading the book. We may yet solve this riddle."

"If I understand correctly," Rafin said, "it seems that most of Jodac's stronghold was underground—inside the mountain."

"That is what my father told me," Grommdum said. "I always pictured it as a series of tunnels and rooms with a single large tower atop the mountain."

"One moment," Maraakus said. "I'm still puzzled by a few things. Jodac conjures up this . . . Balsephus to do his killing. Each victim is marked, and their hearts are removed for Jodac's ritual consumption. And that's what we have been seeing here in the valley. This amulet belonged to Jodac—it bears his name—and was discovered within days of the first murders. Doesn't that indicate a connection between the amulet and Balsephus?"

"I don't know," Grommdum admitted. "But that's a very good question." He rubbed his chin and thought for a moment. "Perhaps the amulet was used as a means of controlling the creature and its removal from the mountain could have once again set the beast in motion."

"If that's so," Maraakus said, "then if we simply destroy the amulet, it might—"

"No!" Grommdum insisted. "That would be most unwise. That amulet could be the only control to which the kalnath responds."

"Is there a way to learn for certain how the amulet was used?" Maraakus asked.

"Not to my knowledge," Grommdum replied. "You see, General, only the creator of such a powerful magical object would know how it works and how to use it. But let us continue, child. What else is in your wonderful book?"

"There's a list of names," Alyna said. "Mine is at the bottom and Grandmother's just before it. There are some interesting comments written beside some of the names." She ran a finger down the page and stopped.

"Subeca, Daughter of Clarrisi. She saved this book from a great fire."

Again, Alyna moved her finger down the page. "And I've heard Grandmother speak of this woman, Helgabath. She stopped the rains and saved the harvest. And here is a woman named Stel who was visited by an elf named Commakk before—"

"May I see that," Grommdum said sharply. His eyes narrowed as he leaned forward in his chair. He took the book from her hands, studied it for a moment, then touched the page with his finger.

"Commakk was my father," Grommdum told them. His finger was touching the list at a point more than halfway down the page. "It is indeed unfortunate that he is not here to help you. Let us hope that his son is up to the task."

Maraakus studied the old elf for several moments. "You don't seem frightened by the prospect of failure, but you must surely realize the danger involved."

"Oh, indeed," Grommdum assured him. "I am not without

some power of my own, General, but it will be Alyna's power that destroys him. I am here merely to assist her. She is largely untrained, but has astonishing potential. When this distasteful business is concluded, she must return with me to Refuge. With proper instruction, Alyna could become the most powerful sorceress of our time."

"No," Alyna declared. "I must remain in Stridgenfel. I'm needed here."

"Our first problem is finding a way to kill Balsephus," Maraakus reminded them. "Until that is done, it's pointless to waste time speculating on plans for the future."

Grommdum smiled. "You are right, of course. One should not number his barnyard fowl by counting unhatched eggs. Please continue your reading, my child."

Alyna turned the page and looked up. "That's all," she said quietly. "The next page is filled with short spells and directions. First is the finding game Grandmother taught me."

"May I?" Grommdum asked as he reached out his hand for the book. She handed it to him and he sat back in his chair and studied a few pages carefully. For several moments he read, moving his finger up and down the fading lines of ink.

"There is much knowledge here," he said, stabbing his finger into the middle of the page. "This is a spell that enables one to repulse heavy objects. A good one to master. And this one," he said, sliding his finger down the page, "will permit one to cast orbs of fire. A little harder to master and control, but certainly worth learning!"

Alyna leaned forward and the old elf smiled. "There is so much knowledge in your book, child," he told her. "you will need help in mastering it. Indeed, there are spells that exceed my own knowledge and experience—and I am considered a competent mage in my own land."

"If Maraakus had not discovered where this book was hidden," Alyna asked, "how would it have eventually come to my hand?"

"I can't answer that," Grommdum admitted, "but it would have happened. Some things have certain powers of their own and it is not for us to understand fully how such events occur. As this old priest might say, the gods often work in mysterious ways."

"Yes," the klersep said. "That is true. And as your uncle might say, we do not thank a friend for the gift of his horse by inspecting its teeth! As for me, I am grateful to Judbal for the privilege he has granted me this day. If you intend to stay for a time in this village, Grommdum," he suggested, "perhaps I might learn to perform some of these spells myself."

The old elf fixed him with a flinty stare and the priest shrugged and sat back in his chair. Grommdum pushed the book over to Alyna. "You would not last long, you old fool," he told the priest. "These spells are not toys, old man!"

He turned his attention back to Alyna. "In this book, we may have the knowledge to successfully do battle with Balsephus. We must confront it on the dark mountain, but to do this, you must be prepared to make great sacrifices. The powers that you will need to call upon are great."

"Perhaps you really were sent here by Ilka," Rafin said, "but I can't permit Alyna to go up there. The four of us—you, Maraakus, Danis, and I—should be more than enough to handle Balsephus."

Alyna stood and walked over to Rafin, leaned over, and kissed him on the cheek. "Dear, dear Uncle Rafin," she said softly. "I have something to say about this, too."

"Rafin is right," Maraakus told her. "It is far too dangerous."

Her eyes flashed and she turned to the old elf. "According to General Maraakus," she said, "Balsephus will not seek another victim for three or four days. Can you teach me some of the higher spells from the last part of this book in such a short time?"

Grommdum looked quickly from Maraakus to Rafin. Then he returned his eyes to Alyna's. He shrugged. "Perhaps," he replied thoughtfully. "First we would have to master the training spells, and that would not be without its own danger. Still, you are human, and human life is short—by wetakian standards. To us, you seem to move with extreme haste, and burn yourselves out like small candles. Your life-forces are strong and concentrated. That is why highly trained humans are capable of becoming more powerful than the most highly trained of the ancient races. This concentration of will—this uniquely human sense of urgency—produces great power. Humans can better withstand the higher inner sacrifices required by this stronger magic.

"On the other hand, the increase in power does magnify the level of danger, not only to the user, but to those around him."

Alyna smiled and walked over to Grommdum. She leaned down and looked him directly in the eye. "Yes or no?" she asked.

Grommdum shrugged and grinned. "Yes," he said.

"We will start tomorrow," Alyna decided. "Meet me here in the morning. We have much work to do."

Rafin and Danis sat in silence. The klersep rubbed his eyes, then blinked rapidly. Alyna picked up her book and after seating herself beside the fire she opened it, and gave Maraakus a defiant stare.

Rafin shrugged. "What now?" he asked.

"We'll go ahead with the plan we discussed," Maraakus said. "Like you, I think only the four of us will go. In the morning, we will make preparations."

Rafin turned and regarded Danis with an appraising eye. "I will ask your father for his consent. If he refuses to give it, I must ask that you stay behind. I want no argument in front of him. Is that understood?"

Danis frowned and nodded his head.

"And I will accompany you, as well," the priest said. "I am still strong and I always thought I would have made a fierce fighter."

"Really?" Grommdum asked. A slight smile played at the corners of his mouth. "A fighter against what? Flies, maybe, if there aren't too many of them."

"No, Holy One" Maraakus said gently. "You are needed here. Judbal's work in this village is not yet finished."

"Perhaps you're right," the old priest agreed reluctantly. I shall seek the guidance of Judbal."

"You will reconsider letting Alyna accompany us?" Grommdum asked. "It is my firm belief that she alone may be able to destroy Balsephus."

"She'll not be going," Maraakus declared. "And if you keep insisting that she accompany us, neither will you."

Grommdum smiled. "And I must remind you, General," he said softly, "that Alyna and I are not under your command."

The wetakian got up from the table, walked to the front door and picked up his staff. As he turned to face them, he placed one end between his feet and gripped the upper section with both hands. Then he began to twist one hand on the brown wood.

A soft light filled the room. Dishes in the cupboards began to rattle on their shelves. The heavy water bucket in the corner of the room jumped from its place on a small wooden stand and settled lightly to the floor. Not a drop of water was spilled. Then the fireplace began to roar; flames leaped high above the burning logs and the room became uncomfortably warm.

After lifting the old walking staff over his head with both hands, Grommdum brought one end to the floor with a resounding thump. The roaring fire diminished to low flames; the bright light faded, and the room grew silent.

Stunned by this display of the elven mage's power, Maraakus watched silently as the old elf raised his hand in a sloppy salute. "Best evening, General," Grommdum said. After walking to the door, he paused with his hand on the latch. "I have a strong desire to leave here as your friend, Maraakus," he said, looking back over his shoulder, "but Ilka has instructed me to aid this young woman in her fight against evil. I intend to carry out those instructions. Do not attempt to interfere with our work." He opened the door and stepped out into the evening darkness.

"Wait!" the klersep shouted after him. "Wait for me!" Then he, too, rushed out, still calling after the elven mage.

Rafin put his head down on the table and groaned. "By the very beards of the gods!" he said loudly. "What have we gotten ourselves into this time?"

Alyna sat silently on the hearth, regarding them with a slight smile.

Rafin walked unsteadily to the front door and put on his cloak. "We drank all my apples," he said sadly. "But the village inn has more than we can afford to drink. Would the two of you like to accompany me?"

"I would," Danis replied.

"I think I'll go, as well," Maraakus said. He coughed to clear his throat, aware that his voice had sounded strangely hoarse. "Apparently, our personal sobriety is one of the few things we still control."

He gave Alyna a weak smile, but she turned her eyes back to her book.

Maraakus sighed and pulled on his cloak. He followed Danis and Rafin out the door and they made their way through ankle-deep snow to the village inn.

CHAPTER FIFTEEN

There was a soft knocking on the door and Alyna opened it. The klersep stepped into the house carrying a large book, a pot of ink and several quill pens.

Grommdum, following close on his heels, pointed at the old cleric and rolled his eyes. "This one insisted on coming," he said, speaking softly from behind his hand. "Today, he fancies himself a scribe. It seems Judbal wants our activities recorded for historical purposes."

As Alyna closed the door, Grommdum whispered to her, "Personally, I have serious doubts about this old fool's sanity."

"I know my duty," the priest declared, eyeing the breakfast Danis was eating. "All must be set down in the Book of Days. It is Judbal's wish. Perhaps I could have some tea—and one of those buttered breads?"

"Of course you may," Alyna replied. "Here, Holy One. Sit next to Danis. May I get you something to eat, Grommdum?"

Grommdum smiled and shook his head. "We've both had morning meals. Not being predisposed to gluttony, mine was quite sufficient."

The old priest selected a large portion of sausage and speared it with a knife. "Mine was sufficient, too," he assured her, popping the sausage into his mouth.

"We can begin when you are ready, child," Grommdum said. "A quiet place will be required where we—"

"You may use the upstairs room," Maraakus said. "Rafin, Danis, and I have our own preparations to make and I expect it will require much of the day. You'll not be disturbed."

Alyna looked at each of them, then fixed her gaze on Maraakus. "Will it be possible for us all to have supper together?"

Grommdum nodded. "An excellent idea. A meal shared among friends. Allies against a common enemy."

"Agreed," Rafin said quietly.

"Very well," Maraakus said. He stood and walked to the door. Taking his sword belt from a peg, he buckled it around his waist, then picked up his cloak. Rafin clapped Grommdum on the shoulder and followed Maraakus and Danis out into the yard.

Grommdum watched as Alyna closed the door behind them, then said, "Let us begin as well. Bring your book; we have much to accomplish."

"Indeed," the priest mumbled. He swallowed the last of Danis's tea and stuffed an apple into the pocket of his robe. "For later," he explained, then gathered his quills and ink, tucked his Book of Days under his arm, and followed Grommdum and

Alyna up the stairs.

The old elf stood in the middle of the upper room and looked slowly around. He grunted with approval, then walked to the table standing before the fireplace. On the table was Maraakus's map, drawings of the runes found on the murdered villagers, and a dry leather pouch with a few coins on top. Grommdum pushed them all to the front edge of the table, then pulled out three chairs and pointed to one of them. "You will sit here and observe quietly," he told the priest. "You will not interrupt. If there is a knock at the door, you will go down and send them away."

"That's my entire assignment?"

"Yes," Grommdum replied. "Three simple instructions that should not prove difficult to follow—even for a dolt such as yourself."

"My, my," the priest responded. "Ill-tempered this morning, aren't we?" He settled into his chair, opened his book to a blank page, arranged his quills and lifted the lid on his inkpot. After inspecting the tips of the quills, he selected one, pushed back his sleeves, inked the quill, and began scratching noisily in his Book of Days.

"What are you doing?" Grommdum asked.

"Recording," the priest replied. "I've started with the instructions—the assignment—you gave me."

Grommdum stared at the priest for a long moment, then sighed deeply. "We have not yet started, you woodenheaded. . . . Must you write down every word?"

Still shaking his head, Grommdum seated Alyna with her back to the fireplace, then took a seat on her left, opposite the priest. "May I hold your book?" he asked.

"Of course," she responded, placing it on the table.

As Grommdum leafed through the book, running his finger slowly down the pages, Alyna shifted restlessly in her chair and chewed gently on her lower lip. She sighed, then folded her hands and put them on the table.

"Patience, child," Grommdum said without looking up. "First, you must relax."

The priest dipped his pen and scratched something in his book.

"It's very important to be calm and receptive to the instructions I will give you," Grommdum added, turning his attention to the klersep. "First, we need to discuss—" He tilted his head and frowned. When the scratching stopped, he leaned over to read what the priest had written.

"Will you stop!" he demanded. "How can I concentrate if you're making that infernal racket with your quill?"

"My sincerest apologies," the priest replied, placing his hand over his heart. "I'm merely trying to keep a complete and accurate record."

"Just observe, man! Later, you may write down what you remember . . . *much* later!"

"Obviously, you have little appreciation for accuracy," the priest grumbled. He placed his pen on the table, folded his arms, and leaned back in his chair.

Despite the acidulous nature of their conversations, Alyna knew the old elf and the klersep were becoming friends. She smiled. The priest struggled to suppress a grin. Then Grommdum leaned forward and fixed her with his sharp, black eyes.

"Listen carefully," he instructed. "Until you understand completely, we cannot proceed.

"There is power within you. Think of it as your . . . eternal spirit, your life-force. From this basic source comes your will and intuition, your sense of morality and justice, your capacity to love, and your ability to feel compassion. Let us simply call this your Power."

"Very well," she replied.

"We are all born with Power; however, very few of us are able to extract even a small portion at will. But if this can be done—and the withdrawn portion then converted to some purpose or effect—the result is magic."

"I see," Alyna murmured. "But as individuals, we surely have varying life-forces. Does this ability to withdraw a portion vary with gifted individuals?"

"Indeed," the old elf replied. "It is this gift—let us call that your Ability—that determines the level of magic one is able to perform. Furthermore, it is Ability that you will improve and refine through practice and study. Thus we have the Power, from which a portion can be consciously withdrawn through Ability. This, when converted, produces Magic."

"And what determines the strength of the magic?"

The old elven mage smiled. "Ah," he said softly. "You have now asked the most important question. That, my child, depends entirely on the quantity of the withdrawn portion of one's Power. Since that is a matter of judgment, it is the most difficult skill to master—certainly the most dangerous—and the primary reason one meets very few powerful—and greatly aged—sorcerers."

"I understand," Alyna assured him.

"Good," Grommdum said. "You see, my child, unlike your life-force, which is fixed at the moment of birth, your Ability can be cultivated and used for either good or evil. Like a garden, it can grow and flourish with the proper care. In your garden you'll grow magical flowers. But just as with any garden, when a blossom is picked, it is used up. And since the effort required to pick that magical flower came from the essence of your being, you will be temporarily weakened. And larger flowers require more effort to pick than smaller ones."

"Yes," Alyna said. "That is what Grandmother referred to as the sacrifice."

"Good! Now if a garden is permitted to do so, it goes to seed—stops producing flowers. So it is with your magical garden. If you pick the flowers with care and tend the garden well, the garden thrives and replenishes itself with even more flowers. These new flowers are larger, brighter, and stronger because they now grow on vigorous, healthy plants in a well-tended garden.

Eventually, your garden is bursting with blossoms—more than you can use."

"So when the user's sacrifice is paid, there is a type of healing or self-renewing growth?" Alyna asked. "Even if the sacrifice is great?"

"Exactly! Let us suppose you are chopping wood and are unaccustomed to the task. At first, you will develop blisters on your hands. They hurt, forcing you to stop. After a few days of rest, they heal and you chop more wood. In time, your hands develop thick callouses and you can chop even more wood. You become stronger with the hard labor and tire less easily. Now, strengthened by practice and labor, you can work longer and harder."

"From where does one's life-force come?"

"From everything, child. From the warmth of the sun and the cold glitter of the stars—the depths of dark thunderstorms, the bountiful earth, the rocks of the mountains, and the rolling waves of the Great Salt Sea. We draw our life-force from all living and non-living things. I think we are but children of some mighty force, stumbling along in our ignorance, yet bound directly to it by the fact of our existence. I do not know how or why this is so, but I know this to be true."

Alyna looked at the old klersep. He was nodding his head in agreement.

"But simply having the Ability to tap into one's Power is not enough," Grommdum continued. "You must be able to choose selectively from all magical influences available. Finally, you must be able to control these selected influences in order to obtain the desired result. Otherwise, the forces will control you. That, my child, can become extremely dangerous—as you have already discovered."

"Yes," Alyna answered. "I have no desire to repeat that mistake. What would happen if I used all my available Power—emptied my garden of blossoms—in a single spell? Would the sacrifice be as unpleasant as what I've already experienced?"

"It would surely kill you."

His reply startled her and she brought her hand to her mouth and stared at him. "Grandmother never told me that—"

"She probably didn't know," Grommdum said. "If she had only a small measure of Ability, she could not have tapped deeply into her own Power. But you, my child, must never expend all your available energies at once. Always maintain enough in reserve to sustain your own life."

"Can someone very powerful tap another's life-force and use it against them?"

"Indeed," Grommdum replied. "That gets quite complicated. We will discuss that later—when you are ready. For now, let us continue with the basics."

The priest stirred in his chair and Grommdum looked in his direction. "You are only discussing *basics?*" the priest asked.

Grommdum gave him a frown.

"Sorry," the priest muttered. "I shall try to remain silent. Judbal protect us all when we move on to higher matters!"

By early afternoon, the fire had burned out and Alyna leaned over the table with her head resting on her arms. "I just can't clear my mind," she said to Grommdum. "I know what I'm trying to do, but—"

"I suppose I'm not the best of tutors," Grommdum admitted. "It's like telling another how to swim. Easy to do, but difficult to describe. Let me see . . . how did the elders teach me when I was younger?"

"You went to the river and they tossed you in with a rope around your waist?" the priest suggested.

"No, you idiot," Grommdum snapped. "I meant how they taught me to recognize my own life-force and tap into it!"

"Sorry," the priest muttered, sinking deeper into his chair and lowering his eyes to his Book of Days.

Grommdum stared at him and rubbed his chin thoughtfully. "But you're right," he said, finally. "She must find the river and she must learn to recognize it, and how to go to it."

He picked up the drawing of the plactrogram and placed it before her, covering the symbol of the eye with his fingers.

"Concentrate on the eagle," he told her. "This is your family plactrogram. Trace it with your eyes. Now trace it with the finger of your right hand. Good."

Alyna stared at the drawing and moved her finger over the symbol. Grommdum's voice trailed off to little more than a whisper. "Close your eyes. Hold the image in your mind. See it growing larger and clearer?"

There was a long silence, then she said, "Yes. Oh, I see it. It's a small light—no larger than the glow of a firefly. No. It's gone. I'm sorry, Grommdum. I'm trying. Really, I am."

After several unsuccessful attempts, Grommdum sat back in his chair. "Just rest for a moment," he suggested.

"I know you're disappointed with me," Alyna said. "But I've never tried anything so difficult in my life."

"Disappointed? Oh, no!" Grommdum assured her. "You are doing very well. Better than expected, in fact. I have even gained a new respect for my own tutors back in Refuge."

"And surely, you must have stretched their patience to the breaking point," the old priest muttered. Then, seeing the frown on Grommdum's face, he lowered his eyes and began scratching busily in his Book of Days.

"Let's try again," Grommdum said to Alyna. "Don't push yourself, child. Just relax and let your mind become totally receptive. Close your eyes and hold the image of the eagle in your thoughts."

Alyna rested her head against the back of her chair and closed her eyes. This time, the tiny pinpoint of light returned, hovering in a vast field of darkness. Then, ever so slowly, it began to grow, becoming brighter and larger, though it remained featureless—an indistinct, slowly revolving yellow ball.

She flexed her fingers, then settled her elbows on the armrests of her chair as a strange, relaxing warmth began at her toes and moved swiftly up her legs. She felt it spreading through her body and out into her fingertips.

"It's back," she murmured sleepily. "The light is back . . . spring sunshine . . . on my shoulders . . . my head."

"The light is merely a beacon, child," Grommdum whispered. "Look past it. Your Power lies beyond the light, Alyna. Follow the beacon to your Power."

"Yes," she whispered. "Somehow, I know that. I can almost touch the light. It's . . . Oh! It's wonderful! So calm . . . so very close."

There was a long silence, then she whispered, "The light is coming from the polished surface of a closed gate. I'm standing directly before it. The gate is made of bronze and set into a smooth wall of polished stone. The wall extends to the horizon on both my left and right. I can hear voices from behind the gate—many voices."

As her hand lifted slowly from the chair as if she meant to knock on the gate, or lift an unseen latch. Grommdum leaned forward and pressed her hand down. "Alyna?" he whispered into her ear. "Listen only to my voice. The wall is a mental barrier. It should disappear when the gate is opened. If it does not, come back to me immediately."

"Grommdum?" she breathed suddenly. "The gate is false! It opened, but there's only stone behind it. What shall I do?"

"Come back to me." The elven mage spoke gently, but now there was an unmistakable urgency in his quiet words. "Alyna? Come back at once!"

She frowned. Then her pale blue eyes opened. When she smiled, Grommdum breathed a sigh of relief. "Don't scare me like that," he admonished. "I was afraid you couldn't hear me."

"I could hear you," she assured him. "Why did I encounter a false gate? What does it mean?"

"It means you're not ready, child," he replied. "The wall is a mental barrier that is protecting you from yourself. The gate is your way through it, but not until you adopt a different frame of mind."

Leaning forward, he frowned and said, "This is serious, dangerous business. You must not go skipping toward your Power like a small child chasing a butterfly through a sunlit pasture."

"I'm sorry," Alyna replied. "You're right. But the feeling of being there is so . . . so—"

"Dangerously seductive?" Grommdum finished for her. "That is why you must exercise extreme caution—even after you are accustomed to going into your Power—and listen closely to my instructions. Now, I want you to go back to the gate. This time, when you knock, it will open and the wall will disappear. Do not pass through the gate. Just tell me what you see."

For a long while, there was only silence in the room. Finally, Alyna opened her eyes. "Nothing," she said. "I can't see the place in my mind."

Grommdum patted her arm. "Because it is not a place, child," he said. "It is a state of mind, and you must learn to achieve this state at will. Now, try again."

"I'm really feeling very tired."

"You are not tired. You are simply not concentrating. But you can do it with just a little more effort. I won't allow you to give up when you are so close to success!"

"Surely, a short rest would not matter," the priest suggested.

Grommdum pointed at him with a long, thin finger. "You will remain silent," he ordered. "I know what I'm doing."

"Bullying the young woman will not help."

Grommdum gave the old priest a puzzled look. "Bullying?" he asked. "I'm not familiar with that term. What does it mean?"

The priest shook his head. "Never mind. I was mistaken."

"Then I trust we'll have no further interruptions?"

"None."

"Thank you. Now, where were we, child?"

"You were bullying me."

Grommdum smiled. "Oh, yes. Very well. Then let us resume this . . . bullying. Close your eyes and feel where you wish to go in your mind. When you see the gate, return immediately."

There was a much shorter period of silence, then she opened her eyes. "Yes," she said. "It is a place in my mind. A thought, really. I can go there anytime I wish."

"Indeed," Grommdum replied. His weathered face wrinkled in a broad grin. "Perhaps I'm a better tutor than I imagined." He sat back in his chair, placed his palms together and gave the priest a self-satisfied smile.

"Shall I do it again?" she asked.

"Patience, Alyna. Patience. We'll soon move on to other matters. Now that you have learned the technique of going to your Power, you will never forget how it's done. Still, you must practice until it can be accomplished with little more than a fleeting though—until it is as natural to you as breathing. Now, tell me about the gate."

"The gate is polished brass and plainly made. There is an eagle on the uppermost portion. That's my plactrogram, isn't it?"

"Indeed, it is," Grommdum answered. "What else did you see?"

She massaged her temples with the tips of her fingers. "The wall was gone. The gate stands alone, atop a small hill in the midst of a dry desert. Yet when I looked through the gate, I saw a white sand beach flooded with bright sunlight."

"And the voices?"

"I was mistaken. There is a footpath from the gate to the beach, and beyond is a golden, rolling sea. I was hearing waves upon the sand." She yawned and said, "I'm feeling very tired."

"Very well," he said. "Let us take a brief rest." He rubbed his palms together and looked up into the roof thatching. "A vast, golden, rolling sea," he mused. "Very interesting. I go to my Power through a thunderstorm. You see, child? Each of us is a unique creature, so we perceive our Power in different ways.

While there are often similarities, no two perceptions are exactly alike."

"Just rest for a moment and listen carefully," he continued. "When I ask you to return to the gate, you must keep my voice in your mind at all times. I shall take you down the footpath to the edge of the sea. Once through the gate, you will feel the force of your Power drawing you down the path. You will feel compelled to follow it. Therein lies grave danger."

He studied her carefully with his sharp black eyes. "Never forget," he said solemnly, "even for an instant, that you are a child of this force and not its master. None can truly master it; we simply use it. Do not allow yourself to be seduced by the lure of this force. If it takes control of your mind and emotions, you might become lost—physically, as well as mentally. When you are within your Power, Alyna, it is a small step from thought to reality."

"I will remember."

"Should you become lost there without the proper training, the basest instincts—those which we all possess—might take control. This can lead to feelings of omnipotence. Nothing you desire can be denied you.

"Hear me well, Alyna," he cautioned. "That feeling of omnipotence is very real, and very seductive. Evil becomes good—if you so will it. Love and hate are the same—if you so will it. Any action, regardless of the pain and suffering it might bring to others may be justified in the attainment of your goals. Many have drowned in their Power, strangled by the failings in their characters. And not one of us is perfect, child."

"That is why one needs a tutor, isn't it?" she asked. "A guide to show them how to use the Power and not be consumed by it?"

Grommdum nodded slowly. "Yes. Lest they suffer the fate of your ancestor, Jodac. Flawed in character and motivated by his evil desires, Jodac went alone or had an ignorant Multan. Either way, he was imprisoned by his baser instincts. Ilka finally accepted this and took the only recourse available.

"Cruel?" he asked. "Perhaps it was. Merciful? Probably. Surely, Jodac must have been among the least happy of men. But you, Alyna, will go to your golden sea with full understanding of its dangers—and avoid the mistakes made by Jodac."

"I understand," she whispered.

"Very well," he said. "This time, when you return to the gate, walk through it, but maintain contact with me at all times. I want to know your thoughts and feelings every step along the way. You may begin."

Once more she closed her eyes. It was a while before she spoke. "Now I'm standing on the footpath," she said. "It seems so . . . familiar somehow . . . as though I've been here before."

"Feelings, child. Tell me what you're feeling. Where are you?"

"Oh, it's wonderful. I'm standing on a hill above the beach. I . . . I'm on the edge of the Great Salt Sea. I've never been to the sea, but I know that's where I am. The waters are moving onto the sand—strong waves. They move so very slowly—thick—flowing like golden honey. I love it here and I wish never to leave. I want to go down the hill and walk across the white sand and step into the—"

"No," Grommdum insisted, keeping his eyes fixed on her face. "Stay where you are. Try to remain calm, but if you feel yourself unable to respond to my instructions, come back immediately. Do not hesitate."

Grommdum leaned forward and touched her on the arm. "Alyna?" There was no response. "Answer me, Alyna! Can you hear me? Describe your feelings, child. Where are you?"

"Here," she replied softly. "On the path." She was smiling, but her eyes remained closed. "May I go down the path, Grommdum? I want to walk on that beautiful sand."

"Yes, but move slowly. Take your time."

"I'm on the beach."

"Excellent. How do you feel?"

"Wonderful," she murmured. "It's so calm and peaceful here."

Grommdum nodded his head and glanced at the klersep. The old cleric was scribbling furiously in his book. Grommdum's eyes searched the table and came to rest on the coins atop the leather bag. He picked up a large silver one and placed it in the center of the table.

"Alyna?" he said softly. "Walk down to the water's edge. Reach into your Power—into the sea—and take up some in the palm of your hand."

"Oh! It's so warm," she murmured. "It flows through my fingers like honey. Such a strange texture. And the colors! It's as though I have been blind and only now can I see the true colors of the sand, the sky, and the clouds. Everything is painted in such strange and vivid colors."

"Pay attention to my voice, Alyna," Grommdum said softly. "Compare that portion held in your hand with the entire volume of the golden sea stretching away to the far horizon."

"What I hold is truly insignificant," she murmured, "if compared to the entire sea. Yet it makes me feel confident and happy. I even feel . . . powerful!"

"But is not the small amount in your hand merely part of the whole?" Grommdum asked. "Is it not identical in every way? If so, then it differs only in volume. Perhaps it is the measure which suits our purpose exactly."

"I don't understand," Alyna said.

Grommdum smiled. "Then we shall use some of it and all will become clear," he said. "Pour most of it back—keeping only a small portion of what you hold—and listen carefully. I have placed a coin on the table before me. Stay within your Power, but open your eyes and look only at the coin."

He saw her eyelids fluttering and watched as she opened her eyes and stared at the silver coin.

"Now, repeat these words after me—exactly as I speak them," he instructed. He glanced quickly at the book in his lap while Alyna sat with an impassive expression on her face and her eyes fixed on the coin.

Grommdum saw the priest shiver in the warm room. The old man was holding his breath. His face was flushed; when he opened his mouth to speak, Grommdum frowned and raised a hand. The klersep exhaled quietly, closed his eyes and sat back in his chair.

Grommdum spoke and Alyna repeated his words perfectly, uttering the strange, musical sounding tones as though she had spoken them since birth. Then he leaned close to her and placed his mouth near her ear.

"The next word I give you will be a release word," he told her. "When you say it, cast a small part—not all—of the withdrawn portion of your Power into the coin. Try to lift it from the table."

The priest was holding his breath again. As Grommdum spoke a single, melodic word, Alyna repeated it. The coin shot up from the table, struck a roof rafter, rebounded and clattered to a rest in the corner of the room. She gasped and slumped forward in her chair and the priest scrambled out of his chair to take shelter against the far wall, holding up his cleric's star in his outstretched hand. Grommdum recoiled in his chair. Startled by the violent, sudden movement of the coin, and the old priest's display of fear, he stared at Alyna with open-mouthed astonishment.

Looking up with tired, lazy eyes, she said, "I did it, Grommdum. It was wonderful—but more difficult than I imagined."

The old elf was still staring at her. "Absolutely astounding," he said softly. "That was . . . well done, Alyna."

"Let's do it again."

"Do you . . . feel all right?" Grommdum managed to ask.

"I feel tired," she said. "My stomach turned over, but I'm fine."

"You must rest for a while," Grommdum said. "That was only a lower spell designed to levitate small objects, but you withdrew more Power than necessary. We must find a way to clearly illustrate a relationship between that which is available, the amount withdrawn, and that portion necessary to accomplish your goal."

He looked carefully around the room and his gaze came to rest on a small wooden box in the corner. He held up a finger, then went to the box and brought back a ball of yarn. Holding it in the palm of his hand, he showed it to her. "This is your Power," he said, tossing the ball of yarn in his left hand. He picked at the ball and found the end of the string. After unrolling a short length, he gathered it in his right hand.

"This," he explained, showing her the portion in his right hand, "represents the amount you withdrew—and it was far larger than necessary. Upon casting your spell, this happened." He snapped the string and dropped the wadded yarn in his right hand onto the table.

"Because you broke the connection with your Power," he continued, holding up the larger ball of yarn, "the sacrifice was paid immediately. But more importantly, the withdrawn portion not consumed by the spell was dissipated through you—the user. It's possible to withdraw so much, and use so little, that the sacrifice—the dissipation of the excess Power—can result in serious injury. Even death. Do you understand?"

Alyna nodded.

"Never break the connection back to your Power." he repeated, pulling another length of string from the larger ball and wadding it in his right hand. "Watch. It's much safer to do this."

After tucking the larger ball of yarn under his arm, he broke off a short piece from the length wadded in his right hand, dropped it on the table, then put the large ball back in his left hand.

"You see?" he asked, holding out both hands. "A small piece from the end of the string has been cast away or used. It's there on the table. But look—the wad of yarn in my right hand is still connected to the large ball in my left.

"Only this," he said, pointing to the short string resting on the table, "was required to accomplish my spell and determines the sacrifice I'll have to pay. The balance of the unused portion—because it's still connected—simply returns to it's source. And that's why you must never break the connection back to your Power. Do you see?"

"Yes," she replied. "I do."

"You described a sea," he said. "Thick and flowing like honey. Power such as that is strong—perhaps the strongest."

"Isn't it the same for all mages?"

"No," Grommdum answered. "For some, their Power is weak and like a large stone. Such persons can only chip off small pieces and use them for simple tasks. For others it may seem like a ball of clay and they pinch off small portions. There is little danger for them, since they never go deeply into their life-forces."

He took another coin from the bag and placed it on the table. "Shall we do it again?" he asked. "Do you feel up to the task?"

"I'm ready," she replied. As she uttered the strange phrases that now seemed locked into her memory, and spoke the release word, the coin rose into the air and floated nearly motionless, less than a foot above the table. Then it drifted the length of the room and hovered over the priest as he sat huddled against the wall. The old man shrank back, holding up his eight-pointed cleric's star, and watching the coin with wide, frightened eyes. It wobbled briefly, then dropped softly into his lap and lay motionless in the folds of his robe. Alyna looked at Grommdum and smiled.

The old elf was grinning like a horse eating leaves from a bearbriar bush. "Absolutely marvelous!" he declared. "I can barely comprehend the things you will someday accomplish, my child."

"I felt it that time," she assured him. "I see how to judge the amount to withdraw and how to release it. It's a matter of feeling. Just knowing, without being told. It's very difficult to explain."

Now we'll move on to the spells I have chosen," Grommdum

told her. "Listen to my instructions at all times and obey them immediately. Do you understand?"

"Yes." Without taking her eyes from Grommdum's, she went almost instantly to the edge of her golden sea. A warm wave washed over her feet and once again she experienced that sense of peace and contentment.

And the wind, she thought. It's blowing gently through my hair, caressing me . . . soft and comforting . . . like the strong fingers of Maraakus. The touch of his hand on my shoulder. Strangely distant, yet intimate and thrilling. A tender, welcomed, seductive feeling.

Suddenly she realized that she had no idea how long she'd been standing there—or how long the voice had been calling her name—but the water was now above her knees and a strong undertow was pulling the sand from under her feet.

Again the voice called—louder this time—telling her it was time to return. But the sea was drawing her with a force that she could not ignore and she dipped her fingers in the water as it swirled about her hips.

"So warm. So comforting. Never have I felt anything so wonderful!"

The water rose above her waist, then up to her shoulders. Now, as if for the first time in her life, she felt an overwhelming sense of herself and the sea around her. The anxious shouts became merely faint, discordant sounds; meaning became lost in the crash of the tumbling surf. Turning toward the beach, she concentrated on the voice and, after a time, heard it clearly. Grommdum was calling her name.

"Alyna! Hear me! You are in danger! Listen to my voice! Return immediately!"

But now, enveloped in a warm, pleasant sense of almost limitless power, she whirled around and around in the water, trailing her arms and hands, splashing sunlit waters high into the air.

"You don't understand, Grommdum! I can accomplish all things!"

Overhead, the red sun sank swiftly toward the horizon and the pale yellow sky darkened to violet. The honey-colored waves tossed her about like the cork from a wine bottle, then rolled onto shore with a noise like distant thunder.

CHAPTER SIXTEEN

The klersep rose slowly to his knees, unable to comprehend the scene before him. Something had gone terribly wrong.

Alyna was sitting on the edge of her chair, body arched and rigid, slender fingers clutching the armrests like delicate claws, lips compressed in a thin, bloodless line. Yet despite all outward appearances of discomfort, her face was strangely serene and her eyes moved behind closed lids, following something only she could see in the deep recesses of her mind.

Suddenly Grommdum seized the young woman by both shoulders and shook her violently. "Hear me, Alyna!" he shouted. "Obey me! Return at once!"

Then, just as suddenly, he dropped her in the chair and stepped back. Holding both hands above her head, the elven mage began making a series of intricate signs, while a torrent of strange, melodious words tumbled from his lips. Fear for the young woman's safety was plainly evident on his lined face.

"Wake her up!" the priest shrieked.

"I can't reach her!" Grommdum shouted back. "She has disobeyed me and gone too deeply into her Power! We're losing her, old man!"

"Well do something!" the priest pleaded, scrambling across the floor on his hands and knees.

"*I can't!*" Grommdum cried, smashing his fist on the table. He sank to his knees beside her chair and looked up with a stricken expression. "Don't you understand? At this moment, her power exceeds my own! She must return on the strength of her own will—or not at all!"

"Is she dying?"

"Not yet. She disobeyed my instructions and went fully into her Power. At this moment, she is vulnerable to all forces—both good and evil. Anything might happen!" He reached up and clasped her wrist with his long fingers. "Hold onto her other arm!" he ordered. "Quickly, man! Move! Perhaps she can still feel our presence!"

The old priest scrambled over the floor and seized her left arm. "Can she hear us?" he asked, aware of the tremor in his voice.

"If she chooses," Grommdum replied angrily.

The priest tilted his head forward on his chest. "Judbal help us," he said softly. "If she dies, we will die as well. Rafin and Maraakus will see to it!"

He closed his eyes and clutched the silver star of the Judbal priesthood in his thin left hand as his lips moved in supplication to his god.

"I am thy old and faithful servant, mighty Judbal," he whispered. "I come before thee to beg for the life of this young woman who . . ."

❧ ❦ ❧

Alyna lifted her eyes to the tops of the waves. Then by her own desire—or perhaps with the help of a vague sense of pressure on both her arms—she rose out of the heaving water and fixed her gaze on the knife-edged horizon. Grommdum's voice whispered in her ear, but she turned, and with deliberate intent, moved farther out to sea where the surface rolled gently in unbroken swells.

Faster and faster, the undulating sea passed beneath her feet, sending up brief reflections of herself silhouetted against a violet sky. Her plain, homespun tunic, molded to her body by the wind, now appeared made of shimmering white silk; the worn slippers on her feet of soft white leather, both stitched with threads of gold and silver. Everywhere she looked, she saw strange and vibrant colors.

A dark, broken line appeared on the horizon, then quickly became a ring of tall mountains enclosing a deep valley. This valley was dominated by a single mountain, a vertical column of stone that cast a looming shadow over a walled village.

The voice of the klersep came as a faint murmuring in her ear. Above it she could hear a second voice, soft and pleading, filled with urgency and sorrow.

"Follow me back," Grommdum was saying. "I am with you. Listen to my voice and obey me, Alyna!"

She felt his presence, but unlike the other times she had sensed him, she was not compelled to obey.

So that is Grommdum's Power? His intentions are good, but he does not understand. How could he? His Power is nothing compared to my golden sea. I am growing stronger and I know where I wish to go.

Her thoughts became her will and as the valley revolved

below her, she saw the fields and mountains. They were covered with a blanket of snow that reflected light from the cool, red sun.

How very strange, she thought. It is winter and the valley is covered with snow, yet I do not feel cold. I feel only the strength and goodness of the people. I feel them in their homes, and in the streets, and I feel the labor that maintains the fields and orchards. I feel all the forces of nature—of life itself. And look! See the Opal River? See it sparkling? Oh! And the Dove is so beautiful, flowing lazily, rippling, pale and pink.

The valley revolved slowly in her field of vision and she saw the new bridge as a narrow blue line across the pink river. The Northern Road appeared as a cream-colored line across a purple forest.

The Pinnacle is so white. No, red! The color of wine. It's changing.

The red sun was setting and the deep violet of the sky subtly changed.

The sun is melting! Flowing and rippling like my sea of Power. Sinking into the ground. See how the Pinnacle is growing dark? Maraakus was right, she thought. There is a strong presence there—an evil presence!

Again, by strength of will, she was rushing toward the Pinnacle, rising higher toward its purple crown of foliage, now brilliantly displayed against the evening's indigo sky. Grommdum's voice became fainter as the valley rushed under her feet in a passing blur and she raced straight toward the mountain, toward its smooth, vertical face. The Pinnacle shimmered before her and she passed through the sunlit stone and into a dark and silent place.

She was standing in a room with a smooth stone floor and rough-hewn walls. The evil presence she had sensed was very near. A shuffling sound came from the darkness. She stepped forward and stopped. The shuffling ceased and for several moments there was only silence. Then the shuffling resumed.

She fixed her eyes straight ahead and a huge, black animal appeared near the end of the room, pacing back and forth in front of a shadowy wall. It moved quickly, its massive head held close to the floor, crossing and re-crossing the room.

She had once seen a forest bear pacing endlessly within a cage; its shaggy fur was matted and peeling away in patches to expose bare skin rubbed to running sores against the walls of its prison. She had felt pity for the bear, but the animal before her elicited no such feelings. It moved quickly and powerfully, like a man preparing to wrestle an opponent on a day of feasting and games, eager for the match to begin.

Now the animal stopped. The great head swung in her direction, then tilted slowly to one side. The red eyes looked down, then up, searching for her among the deep shadows.

Alyna squinted into the darkness, trying to make out the detailed form of the huge creature. It shifted its feet and backed up against the wall, but its head continued that slow, menacing movement. Then it stopped. Only the red eyes moved, searching and probing, and she realized that while it could somehow sense her presence, it could not actually see her.

She, too, stood motionless, staring, lest she signal her position in the darkness like some hapless insect caught in the web of the venomous scarlet spider, a despised creature that spun it's sticky trap between the trees at the edge of the Great Shadow Forest. It was said that a scarlet spider could kill a horse with a single bite.

Suddenly the animal scratched the stone floor with its claws and hissed softly. The mouth opened to reveal it's jagged teeth. It straightened slowly, rising before her like some combined horror made from the formless shadows of her worst childhood nightmares.

She heard its voice, not with her ears, but with her mind. It was rasping, low and guttural; made of many voices, like some poorly rehearsed, discordant madrigal performed by unskilled chanters.

Master?

She shrank back, startled by the intensity of the undisguised loathing and hatred coming from the animal. Suddenly the room seemed very cold.

Cold? She thought, I have not felt cold before. Why am I suddenly aware of it?

She shrugged, willing away the chill, but it remained. A vile stench assaulted her nostrils. She raised one hand and clapped it over her mouth and nose. The animal recoiled behind an upraised arm, seemingly able to sense her emotions as well as her presence.

Master?

Alyna stood motionless and frightened, clearly feeling the malice directed at her by the huge creature. Yet she sensed its confusion, too, as it suddenly looked up and squinted at her. Again, its voice was heard only in her mind.

Command me, Master!

The red eyes flickered; thick ropes of saliva dripped from its lower jaw. It took a step forward, moving with a slow, ponderous motion. Its enormous claws rattled on the stone floor.

Thou art not my master.

It took another step forward, hesitated, then sat back on its haunches. Its eyes widened slightly and for a long while it sat, drooling, breathing deeply with that hollow, rasping sound, the sound of a stone being dragged across a wooden floor.

At last the eyes moved and she knew it had found her in the darkness. She felt its gaze as a probing, physical force and sensed its suspicion and slowly diminishing confusion.

It shuffled closer and its reptilian eyes no longer darted about; they were narrowed to thin slits and focused on the spot where she was standing. The creature breathed a long, rattling sigh; the head lifted and she saw that it was scaled and crusted with filth. Rows of jagged teeth clattered and glinted as the mouth opened and closed. A bony claw lifted from the floor and pointed at her.

Thou art not my master!

Alyna stood transfixed by the intensity of the mindless hatred being directed at her. The feeling was as familiar as it was repugnant—similar to that which she had felt coming from the amulet—cold and malicious, intent on grinding her into soft, pliant prey for the powerful forces that had weakened her and forced her from her own home.

She willed the loathing back at the creature and it recoiled. The red eyes widened slightly but its gaze remained fixed on her. Its voice came in a grating whisper but there was no longer any confusion.

I see thee dimly. Thou art small and weak.

The creature's words inflamed her fear and she stepped back quickly, pressing herself hard against the cold rock wall. The rough surface gouged into the flesh of her shoulders and she felt a rush of pain.

What is happening? Why am I so frightened? I am here only in my mind! But I feel fear! I feel cold and pain! Why am I able to smell the stench of this creature? Where are you, Grommdum? Why have you left me?

She listened carefully, but heard only the ragged breathing of the dark creature mixed with that of her own. Then there was the slow rattling of claws on stone as Balsephus moved forward, swinging its massive head from side to side. Great, leathery wings lifted, encountered the rough walls of the narrow room and dropped back to the floor.

Grommdum! Help me, Grommdum!

❧ ❦ ❧

The old priest's body trembled in his robes; his eyes reflected his anguished fear. Alyna had become little more than a vaporous form floating in the chair, as transparent and insubstantial as summer fog. When his hand moved through her arm and touched the chair, he jerked his hand away and fell forward onto the floor. Grommdum was shouting at him, but he ignored the old elf. Flinging himself flat on the floor, he filled the room with a high keening sound as prayers to Judbal poured continuously from his mouth.

Grommdum grabbed him by his robe and pulled him to the far side of the table. "Stand away!" he commanded. "Stop that wailing! You can't help her!"

"Wh-what is ha-happening?" the priest stuttered.

"She is removing her physical presence from us." Grommdum said. "Touch her now, and you could harm her."

The priest grabbed Grommdum's hand, clutched it to his chest and sobbed hysterically. Grommdum snatched his hand away and after a long moment, and not without considerable effort, the priest managed to control himself.

"Wh-where is she . . . going?" the priest asked softly. He closed his eyes as though he feared the answer to his own question.

"At this very moment, her physical body is merging with her mind and her Power," Grommdum told him. "Wherever she is, we can no longer help her."

"Use your magic, Grommdum," the priest pleaded. "Bring her back."

Grommdum placed his hand on the priest's shoulder. "I am sorry, old man," he said gently. His eyes remained on the ethereal shadow in the chair. "You do not understand. There is nothing I can do. Alyna must help herself. While she is not doing this by deliberate choice, it is the result of not being fully aware of . . . well, many things."

The elf raised a gnarled hand and wiped his eyes. "The blame is surely mine," he told the priest sadly. "I pushed her too hard and too fast. That was a terrible mistake. I am truly sorry. If we had only been permitted more time . . . a year . . . even a few months. . . ." His chin fell to his chest. "I am a stupid, stupid old man!" he declared angrily.

"Elf," the priest corrected gently. His eyes were closed and he leaned heavily against the table.

"Elf? Man?" Grommdum muttered. "What does it matter? Keep thinking of her," he told the priest. "Don't let her out of your thoughts. She may still be able to sense us and that might be all she has to guide her back—if she decides to return."

❧ 🦋 ☙

Alyna watched as Balsephus approached. She shrank back into a shallow depression in the wall, terrified, unable to move as a clawed front foot reached slowly for her. She closed her eyes and pressed harder against the wall and went numb with fear.

After a moment, she opened her eyes and saw Balsephus standing before her with its left foot held up close to its right shoulder. Its red eyes were staring and she sensed . . .

Confusion? Yes! And fear!

The foot moved back in her direction and she watched in horror as it passed right through her body. She felt a slight tugging at her tunic, and the huge claws plowed deep furrows in the rock wall. Looking down, she saw her body plainly, saw her hands clasped across her stomach and her tunic hanging just below her knees, her feet clad in plain leather slippers.

But even in the dim light of the stone chamber, she saw them in their true state and natural colors. The endless variety of strikingly vivid hues had faded.

The creature's foot moved slowly back in the opposite direction and she felt a dragging sensation across her knees. Apparently, Balsephus felt nothing, for the kalnath stepped back and stared at her with narrowed eyes.

What's happening? She thought, I am here, yet this . . . thing can't touch me. Am I really still back in the village?

Balsephus growled in frustration.

Yes! Now I remember what Grommdum said about it being but a small step from thought to reality. The physical body can be joined with the mind. It can happen by accident, when the proper control is not used!

The fear that had gripped her was diminishing and as she organized her thoughts, she felt a new sense of strength and resolve. Focusing her mind on the upstairs room of her home, she called Grommdum's name in a loud voice.

The kalnath reacted instantly. Its massive head dropped nearly to the floor and it moved back a few steps and stopped. When she slipped quickly to her left, its head did not move; its eyes never left the shallow depression where Alyna had been standing. The creature uttered a low, rattling snarl and its reptilian eyes flashed with anger. Again, like a physical force, she sensed its rage and frustration but realized that she was no longer visible to it.

The damp chill of the stone chamber began to fade. Stepping out from the wall, Alyna turned her back on Balsephus and shut out everything but the desire to return home. Slowly, moving with only her will, she passed out of the dark chamber and into the dusk of evening. She moved swiftly toward the valley floor—toward home—but her ability to concentrate began to diminish.

"Grommdum! Help me!"

A roaring sound filled her mind. A numbing fatigue gripped her body and she trembled like an arrowgrass cane in a strong wind. The mountains tilted and the last vestige of control slipped away from her. She began to tumble like an autumn leaf toward the valley floor.

❦   ❦   ❦

Maraakus stopped outside the door, kicked the mud and slush from his boots, and followed Rafin and Danis into the house. The kitchen was quiet, except for the low moaning of the wind in the chimney and the sizzling of a damp log on the hearth.

"Alyna?" Rafin called.

Grommdum answered from the upper room and the three of them trudged up the stairs. The old klersep was kneeling behind the table. He and Grommdum were holding Alyna by her arms and shaking her. She was slumped backwards in her chair, eyes open, staring blindly at the ceiling beams.

Grommdum looked up and put a finger to his lips. "Do not approach her!" he whispered hoarsely. "She will not recognize your touch and may be frightened."

"By all the gods!" Rafin hissed. He took a step forward and Maraakus placed a hand on his arm.

"Wait, Rafin!"

Alyna's head moved in a jerking motion. The rigid arch in her back relaxed. As she settled in the chair, her fingers straightened and she lifted her hands and dropped them in her lap. Her eyelids fluttered briefly; then she opened her eyes and looked slowly around the room. They were shining with tears.

"Grommdum?" she said softly. "Are you here? Am I home? I can't . . . I can't see you clearly. Give me your hand."

The old elf took her hand, curled her fingers in his palm and held them gently in his fist. "I am here, my child," he said softly.

"I was so frightened," she murmured. Then she began to cry softly. "I can't see!"

"Don't be afraid, child," Grommdum said gently. "Your blindness will not be permanent. It is only the result of fatigue. You must rest, and in a short while you will recover."

He turned to Rafin and motioned with his other hand. "Let's help her down the stairs," he said. "She is very weak."

Maraakus stepped behind the table and lifted her in his arms. He gave Grommdum a cold, menacing look, then carried her to the stairs and down into the kitchen. They all followed, their feet thumping noisily on the wooden steps. Rafin set a chair before the fire and Maraakus lowered her gently into it; then threw a fresh log on the fire.

Rafin turned to the old priest, who lowered his eyes to the floor.

"Do not be alarmed, Rafin," Grommdum said, seeing the anger on the old soldier's face.

"What happened here?" Rafin demanded.

"I do not think you would understand," Grommdum replied. "Alyna will recover quickly, and without permanent damage. While she is resting," he said to the nervous priest, "you may wish to catch up on your scribbling. It will be a while before she can continue."

"This has gone far enough!" Rafin declared. "It ends right here—right now!"

Grommdum smiled. "I'm afraid that you and I have very little to say in the matter. Much has changed since you left us this morning. I am merely her Multan. She has discovered how strong she really is. Even I did not suspect this would happen so soon, but it is done. Neither you, nor I, can change anything."

"Then my satisfaction will come from breaking you into little pieces," Rafin growled.

"Stop it!" Alyna said sharply.

They both turned to look down at her. "The fault is mine." she said weakly. "I am to blame for what happened."

"What is she talking about?" Rafin demanded.

"I was inside the Pinnacle," she said softly. "I saw Balsephus and it is an evil, loathsome creature. After a time, it could see me as well. You were right, Grommdum. It *is* a small step from thought to reality."

Grommdum nodded slowly. "I understand, but that was a foolish thing to do, girl," he admonished gently. "Had you remained there any longer, the kalnath could have killed you."

They looked at each other for a long while and an unspoken understanding passed between them. "I know," she said. "I understand much more now. But I also know how much I have yet to learn."

"That, too, is a valuable lesson," Grommdum said. "Perhaps the most useful of all." He smiled, reached out, and patted her on the arm; then turned to look up at Rafin. "She took a journey into her mind, and into her Power. A mistake was made. But a valuable lesson has been learned. Motivated by a desire to learn all she could before we confront Balsephus, she chose to . . . well, let's say she elected to take an accelerated course of instruction. It is not the method I would have chosen for her, but she did not ask for my advice."

Alyna took Rafin's hand. With a visible effort, she smiled and said, "Let's have our supper together, just as planned. I'll tell you what I'm able to remember and what I've learned. But let's have no more talk about fixing blame."

⚓ 🐚 ⚓

It was late evening before they began eating, and throughout the shared supper Alyna tried as best she could to tell them about her golden sea, what it meant, and how she could use it. Grommdum made occasional comments, but except for these rare interjections, they all remained silent.

She told them about the impressions she had brought back from her encounter in the mountain, of her terror, how she recovered the tenuous threads of Grommdum's Power and followed them back with the last of her strength.

"And we have some final work to do this evening," she said, turning to Grommdum, who nodded his head in agreement.

With that, the wetakian smiled and rose from the table. Alyna and the klersep followed him up the stairs. As she passed, she touched Maraakus briefly on the shoulder. He raised his eyes but she went quickly up the stairs.

The early part of the night passed slowly for Maraakus. A routine emerged. He would put wood on the fire, Rafin would stir it with the poker, and Danis would refill their mugs with tea. Then they would resume their places before the fire and stare into the flames, while conversations too quiet to be understood drifted down from the room over their heads.

When he woke, Alyna was touching him on the shoulder and Rafin was smiling down at him. The fire was nearly out. He stood, tossed a small log on the fire, shook Danis, and they all sat down around the table.

"We have prepared ourselves as best we can," Grommdum told them. He picked up the priest's Book of Days and placed it before Maraakus. "I asked the klersep to record the three spells Alyna has learned this evening. You will see that they can serve both offensive and defensive purposes. You, of course, must determine when and how best to use them."

Maraakus picked up the book and read the brief descriptions of the three spells. He quickly memorized their names and their effects; then leaned back and said, "We have a dangerous task before us and no experience with a similar enemy to guide us. Listen well, add what you can, and be ready for anything. . . ."

By midnight the fire had burned down to a shimmering bed of coals. Maraakus had talked throughout the evening in a steady, confident voice, answering questions and discussing suggestions and comments as they were offered. Finally, he said, "Now, we must get as much rest as possible. We'll meet at the north gate, just before sunrise."

"I wish I could go with you," the priest said. "May Judbal guide your steps and strengthen your minds and bodies."

"Indeed," Grommdum added as he stood. The priest followed him, silently, out of the house.

Rafin watched them go; then got slowly to his feet and, without speaking, went out the door leading to the shed. Danis rose, stretched, and placed a hand on Alyna's shoulder. He left through the front door, leaving Maraakus and Alyna alone, seated at the table.

"We'll all be fine, won't we?" she asked.

"Yes," he said, knowing that she was seeking reassurance.

She nodded and gave him that familiar smile and her pale blue eyes sparkled in the lamplight. She stood, and he watched as she bent to blow out the lamp and saw the trembling of her hand when she cupped it around the flame. Then, like Rafin, his mind occupied with thoughts of morning, Maraakus stood, crossed the room, and started slowly up the stairs.

"Good night, Alyna," he said, then paused to look down at her. He was unable to see her face, but her dark silhouette was visible against the red glow from the fireplace. He had not missed the quaver in her voice and he understood the fear she was feeling. Only he and Alyna had stood face to face with Balsephus, absorbing the hate and malice from those cruel, red eyes.

"Good night, General Maraakus," she answered softly. "Sleep well."

CHAPTER SEVENTEEN

As sunlight emerged from behind the eastern cliffs, Maraakus
lifted himself into his saddle and conducted a quick inspection
of the small force he would lead against Balsephus.

His own bow of seasoned yew was tied behind the saddle,
along with a quiver of arrows, all tipped with deep-penetrating
war points, and three torches soaked in a mixture of oil and
melted tallow. A new dagger was in his left boot and his newly
sharpened short sword hung from his belt.

Rafin was carrying his heavy broadsword in a back sheath and
a heavy-bladed dagger had been added to his belt. A sharp war

axe and three torches were lashed to his saddle. He carried Jodac's amulet in the left breast pocket of his leather jerkin.

Danis was equipped with a long dagger, a quiver of arrows and a heavy hunting bow. He stood with his left hand on the bridle of Alyna's horse, listening while Grommdum talked to her in a low voice. She was unarmed, save for a small hunting knife in her waistband, and the old elf had only his walking staff.

Alyna looked up at Maraakus, smiled, and patted her horse's neck. "I know," she said, before he could speak. "Your instructions were perfectly clear. I'm to stay close to Grommdum at all times. I won't forget."

"Are you certain you don't want a horse, old man?" Rafin asked Grommdum. "I can find one that is old and gentle."

"I prefer walking," Grommdum replied. "I trust no creature to bear me on its back."

"Then allow me to get you a proper weapon, at least."

"Totally unnecessary," Grommdum replied, lifting his walking staff in his right hand. "I have a proper weapon, thank you."

Still shaking his head, Rafin swung into his saddle and Danis did the same. After a last look around, Rafin gathered the reins in his big hands. "On your command, General," he said. "Honor to us all."

"And to our cause," Maraakus answered. He closed his eyes and sighed deeply.

I've been driven mad by this affair, he thought to himself. Would any sane man set out to destroy this kalnath—or any beast the size of Balsephus—accompanied only by two armed men, an innocent young woman, and an old man with just a walking staff?

The general lifted his hand and signaled to the guard detail. The north gate swung open and they filed out onto the Northern Road. The gate closed behind them and the heavy, wooden locking bar dropped into place with an ominous finality.

As they proceeded up the Northern Road, holding the horses to a pace Grommdum easily matched with his long strides,

Maraakus silently reviewed the plan they had devised the previous evening. It was a simple plan, Maraakus knew, but one that would give them the best chance for success. Inflict damage, retreat, renew the attack, inflict more damage and retreat. They must blind the animal, then weaken it with an accumulation of wounds until it could be destroyed with minimal risk.

Before midmorning they arrived at the level area near the deep cleft where Danis had found the old rucksack. They dismounted, tied their horses at the edge of the forest and took up their weapons. Maraakus handed Danis two of the torches and stuck one through his belt. After unsheathing his sword, he signaled for them to wait, then walked cautiously through the bearbriar thicket to inspect the ground.

Several inches of snow remained at the entrance to the cleft, nearly concealing the rubble Danis had dislodged while climbing to the top of the rockslide, but there were no tracks to indicate that Balsephus had gone into the cleft since their last visit. Scattered patches of thin ice clung to the vertical walls and he saw no new scratches.

"This is where Balsephus climbs the mountain," Maraakus told Rafin. "By climbing this rockslide, we can reach the cliff tops where Danis found a set of stone steps leading to those high ledges above you. That's where we're going. Balsephus is too large for the steps, so it probably climbs straight up the mountain's face. From the top, it can soar to any spot in the valley."

He paused, waiting for questions. There were none, so he nodded to Danis. The young man slung his bow over his shoulder, walked into the cleft and started up the steep pile of stones. Soon he disappeared behind the curving wall of rock. They waited, listening to the clattering sounds of falling rocks and the soft soughing of the cold, morning wind.

Danis shouted that he had made it and Maraakus stepped carefully onto the face of the rockslide. The others followed, one at a time, and soon they were standing together on the first high cliff, only a dozen paces from the bottom of a crude stone stairway.

Maraakus walked to the cliff's edge and looked east toward the Opal. The distant Guardians were now fully covered with snow and the river sparkled in the morning sunlight. Alyna and Danis were looking west, listening carefully to the old elf as he talked and pointed toward the Great Shadow Forest with his staff. Rafin leaned against the mountain and breathed heavily; a line of sweat stood out on his forehead and his face was flushed.

"Are you well?" Maraakus asked his old friend.

"I'm fine," Rafin replied. He stepped forward a few paces and looked first toward the top of the mountain, then at the open stone steps clinging precariously to the vertical face of the Pinnacle, providing a long, narrow bridge to a ledge some six feet wide. The ledge ran level for a short distance, then rose and disappeared around the side of the mountain.

Maraakus pointed to the patches of ice and snow on the steps, already melting in the strong sunlight. "Stay close to the mountain," he said. "Take your time. Stay off the ice."

Slowly and carefully, Maraakus led them up the ancient steps, testing his footing and kicking loose rocks over the side. These stones fell in slow, tumbling arcs, then clattered faintly on the jagged rubble nearly three hundred feet below. When Rafin—last in line—finally reached the top, they all moved forward along the ledge.

"These vines and roots look recently cut," Danis observed.

"Yes," Maraakus agreed. "Probably by Andor and Keam."

Higher up, on the mountain's eastern side, the ice had melted. The footing was easier, but the wind was stronger, blowing in cold gusts, snapping their clothing about their legs. Now Alyna stayed close to Danis, holding her cloak under her chin with both hands and keeping her eyes on the narrow ledges that switched back and forth across the mountain's face.

Approximately halfway to the summit, Maraakus pointed to a shallow niche that was exposed to the direct rays of morning sunshine. They followed him inside, out of the bitter wind, and sat down with their faces turned to the warming light. Taking

Alyna's hands in his own, he rubbed them briskly until they were warmer, then stuck them under her cloak next to her body. She smiled weakly and shivered. "Where is Uncle Rafin?" she asked.

Startled by her question, Maraakus looked around and saw that Rafin was missing. Rafin!" he shouted. There was no reply. Again he shouted, and again there was no reply. "Stay here," he ordered. "I'll get him."

Less than four hundred feet back along the ledges, he found Rafin sitting with his back against the mountain. Despite the strong, cold wind, the old soldier's forehead was beaded with sweat; his big hands were trembling and his eyes were glazed.

"Rafin? What's wrong?"

Rafin shook his head, took a deep breath, and sat up on his knees. "Nothing. I'll be fine," he said. "I just . . . had to rest for a moment. My short leg, you know? Go on . . . I'm right behind you."

Maraakus studied his old friend for a few moments, then said, "You're not going any higher. You're going back to the bottom before you get yourself killed."

Rafin scowled and shook his head. "Not likely," he said adamantly, rubbing his shortened leg with both hands, "I'm going to the top of this damned mountain!"

"It's the narrow ledges and extreme altitude," Maraakus said quietly. "You're dizzy, aren't you?"

"I said I'm fine!" Rafin growled. "I just needed a rest."

"I'm afraid it's not quite that simple," Maraakus said. "Fear of high places is not easily overcome—at least not right away. There's no shame in being afraid of heights, but you must go back."

Rafin shook his head. "Once we get off these damned narrow ledges, I'll be fine," he growled. "I'll go the whole distance!"

"Listen to me," Maraakus demanded sharply. "This is not a matter of heart. None of us doubts your courage. We have a long way to climb and with each turn the ledges are getting steeper.

Your leg is troubling you, too, and you'll get farther behind as the going gets harder. If you don't turn back, you could fall. Will killing yourself help us destroy Balsephus?"

The old soldier stared back with a defiant expression, arms folded across his chest, head resting against the mountain.

"Be sensible, Rafin," Maraakus argued. "This is not a test of courage—some contest between you and this mountain. We're here to kill the kalnath."

Rafin stared at his old friend for a moment; then nodded. His shoulders sagged. "You're right," he said. "I'd never make it to the top. Twice now I've nearly walked right off the ledge. I don't understand, old friend. I've been on places much higher than this and never felt this dizziness before. Do you remember the cliff top where we camped in the Sleeping Sisters?"

"But that campsite wasn't six feet wide and straight down for several hundred feet to nothing but rocks," Maraakus pointed out quietly. "There were trees and hills to give you a sense of reference. I'll send Danis to help you to the bottom."

"I'll take my time and make it down alone," Rafin promised, "but I won't leave until you're all safely off this mountain!" With that, he reached into his pocket, withdrew the amulet and handed it to Maraakus. He chuckled softly. "I'd give you my broadsword, too, but you never learned to use it well."

Maraakus smiled and clapped him on the shoulder. "I've always suspected you thought as much," he said. "But you're right. The short sword is better for me."

Rafin smiled, then clasped Maraakus's hand. "Luck to all," he said. "Take good care of Alyna. She's all I've got."

"You know I'll do my best," Maraakus assured him. "And we'll be off this mountain before dark, old friend." He dropped the amulet into the breast pocket of his tunic, clapped Rafin on the shoulder and started back up the ledges. By the time he reached the small niche where the others waited, he was deeply troubled. He had lost the strongest, most experienced member of his party, and the top of the Pinnacle was yet to be reached.

"And so," Maraakus told them, after explaining Rafin's absence, "he finally agreed to go back and wait for us at the base of the mountain."

"I still feel the presence of the amulet." Alyna said.

Maraakus reached into his pocket and took out the amulet. "Carry this up front," he said to Danis, "but make certain you don't lose it."

Danis nodded and took the amulet from Maraakus. After wrapping the silky gold chain around the pink stone, he dropped it into the breast pocket of his jerkin and Maraakus, Alyna, and Grommdum followed him out of the warmth of the small shelter.

The ledges ended by late morning and they entered an area covered by trees and tangled undergrowth. Here they picked up a trail that skirted the mountain's sheer western face. Before long, Maraakus saw the ashes of a campfire under an outcropping of rock. Stooping down, he made his way into the low shelter, knelt beside the dead ashes and stirred them with the point of his dagger. There was new soot on the underside of the rock, a pile of dry firewood against the back wall, and two sets of footprints.

"Keam and Andor," Danis said, bending down to inspect the tracks. "We keep finding traces of them."

"Yes," Maraakus agreed. "But I'm surprised they made camp this high on the mountain."

Danis straightened up and bumped his head against the low ceiling of the shelter. He rubbed the back of his head and grimaced with pain. "I'll bet it was because of the storm," he said through his clenched teeth.

"What storm?" Maraakus asked.

"About the time they disappeared, we had a bad rainstorm during the day. I remember because it put out the fire in our forge and we had to drag the entire fire bed. It rained for most of the afternoon."

Maraakus stared hard at Danis. "Think carefully," he said

softly. "After the rain, how many days passed before Andor was found.

Danis dropped back to his knees, still rubbing his head. His brow wrinkled in thought. "Two days," he said. "It was midafternoon when we pulled the fire bed and relit the forge. I ordered firewood that night, but it wasn't delivered until the next day—by Mogrin himself. The following morning, two woodcutters found Andor."

They crawled from under the overhanging rock and Maraakus looked up at the mountain's summit. "It can't be far to the top," he observed. "So when the rain ended, the boys still had time to go up before dark. That explains the new ashes and the dry firewood, too."

He led the way up the path, carefully avoiding the melting patches of snow and ice. The trail suddenly switched back to the north and they found their way blocked by a large, fallen tree. The trunk lay parallel with the edge of the mountain, but the bushy top blocked the path with a tangled nest of broken limbs and dead foliage.

Through branches stripped of leaves by the cold wind, Maraakus saw a large hole—one much too big to have been made by the roots of the fallen tree. Moreover, no avalanche had deposited those piles of stone before the dark opening. This hole had been deliberately enlarged, but far more than necessary for two young boys to gain entrance.

"Is that a cave?" Danis asked.

"Perhaps," Maraakus said, "but the opening has been recently dug out." Looking up toward the top of the Pinnacle, he pointed with a gloved hand. "And that, my friends, is how Keam and Andor gained the summit."

"By all the gods!" Danis shouted. "Those stairs go right to the top!"

"Go take a quick look," Maraakus suggested. "See if there's another opening on top."

Danis went quickly up the ancient steps. After a brief time, he returned, his face flushed with excitement. "The top is no more than two hundred feet across," he told them. "There's a lot of small trees and bushes, scattered piles of rubble—probably from old stone walls—and another set of stairs leading down into the ground. They've been filled in with heavy boulders, but somebody had tried to dig them out—and recently, too—there are piles of sticks and leaves, and some rocks, around the opening."

"Keam and Andor," Maraakus declared. "The boys tried to dig out that stairway, but they reached those huge boulders and found they couldn't move them."

"Then they never got inside?" Danis asked.

"I think they did," Maraakus said. "When this tree fell, it opened a small hole into the mountain or, perhaps, pulled out the wall of a cave. That's where the boys went in. Where else could they have gotten the amulet and those old coins? The top of this mountain was surely picked clean hundreds of years ago."

"But Balsephus enlarged the hole in order to get in and out of the mountain," Alyna said. She turned and stared into the dark opening. "I saw Balsephus *inside* the mountain, not on top. This is his lair. . . ."

"Well," Grommdum said. He rubbed his hands together and smiled nervously at Maraakus. "Suspicion is not proof. For that, I suppose we must go into that hole, too. But I must confess something, General. Like my distrust of horses, I have long been wary of dark holes leading into the bowels of the earth."

"I'm not fond of them, either," Maraakus said, looking at each of them in turn. "And I have no desire to confront Balsephus in some narrow, underground tunnel. But you're right. We need proof. I'm going in, but only to confirm that fact. All of you will wait outside."

"I'm going in with you," Danis said.

"Most unwise," Grommdum told Maraakus, shaking his head. "Our greatest strength lies in our combined talents. We are most grateful for your desire to protect us by assuming the greater risk, but we have already been weakened by the loss of Rafin's strong arm. Will further division of our strength gain us some advantage? And what shall we do if you are killed inside this lair? If Balsephus decides to come after us, we would be without an experienced leader."

"In that case, we might all die," Danis pointed out.

Maraakus exhaled his breath in a long sigh. "You'd have made an excellent field commander, Grommdum."

The old elf looked back with a slightly amused expression. "Even I can see that we have only two real choices."

"Two choices?" Danis asked.

"We can wait for Balsephus to come out," Maraakus explained, "and accept the risk that another villager might be murdered—which will certainly happen if we're watching the wrong hole—or we can go in now, confirm this is where he hides, return to the village, get several dozen men, and draw Balsephus out on our own terms."

"I favor the last option," Danis said.

Grommdum nodded. "As do I."

"And I," Alyna said. "But only if we stay together."

"Then our primary objective has changed," Maraakus declared. "We won't attempt to kill the kalnath; we'll simply find it before it finds us, then get off this mountain as quickly as possible."

Kneeling before the hole, Maraakus placed his sword on the ground and pulled the torch from his belt. After taking a fire kit from a small rucksack, he struck sparks into a ball of tinder, but each time he succeeded in obtaining a flame, the gusting wind blew it out.

"Allow me," Grommdum said. He placed his hand near the torch and snapped his fingers. The torch burst into flames.

Danis grinned at the old elf, then picked up the torch and handed it to Maraakus. "I'd like to learn that one," the young archer said.

Maraakus stared at the elf for a moment, then raised the torch in his left hand. "Let's get it over with," he said.

Danis took an arrow from his quiver and set it on his bow-string. Moving in single file, they followed Maraakus into the dark hole and down a short slope of small stones and gravel to the floor of an underground chamber.

Here, to his great astonishment, Maraakus saw a floor littered with stone rubble, broken furniture, aging parchments and pages from old books. Looking up, he judged the ceiling to be not less than sixteen feet above their heads; the width of the chamber he estimated at about thirty feet. The chamber's length could not immediately be determined, since the far wall was lost in the darkness beyond the glow of his torch.

Danis, pointing to a stone staircase blocked with massive boulders said, "That probably leads to the top of the mountain—where Keam and Andor were digging."

"Is there any doubt that we've entered Jodac's chambers?" Grommdum asked. His voice was soft, but it sounded hollow and reverberated from the cold stone walls.

"Shhh!" Maraakus hissed, raising his sword. "I heard something!" He fixed his eyes straight ahead, looking deeper into the mountain. The only sound was their own ragged breathing and the only movement came from shadows cast by the flickering torch.

Alyna gave a soft cry of fright and Danis touched Maraakus on the shoulder. The general wheeled about and his sword flashed in the torchlight as it rose to the ready position.

Danis eyed the sharp blade that had halted in midair, just inches from his nose. He sank slowly to his knees, knowing full well that he'd come within a hairsbreadth of dying. "My mistake," he whispered. "You didn't know I was behind you."

"This place is already getting to us." Alyna said quietly.

Maraakus nodded and exhaled his breath in a long sigh. "And we must not allow that to continue," he said.

Lifting the torch over his head, he looked carefully around the room, still trying to determine the length of the chamber.

"I can give you additional light, General," Grommdum offered.

"No. We might need the other torches later."

"A most wise decision," Grommdum agreed, "but I was not speaking of torches." He stepped a few paces away and raised his walking staff. Speaking in a low, soft voice, he shook the staff with his right hand and the room was instantly filled with a glaring white brilliance that emanated from a ball of light suspended less than a foot above the top of his staff.

Danis shielded his eyes and Grommdum appeared slightly embarrassed. "My sincerest apologies to all of you," he muttered. "Apparently, my control is not what it used to be."

"Oh, no!" Alyna said softly. She gave another frightened cry and fell on her knees.

Maraakus whirled about, sword raised to defend her, but saw that she was pointing to the remains of a young man pushed against the wall below a rotting tapestry. His body had been partially eaten; his chest had been opened and his forehead was covered with a thick crust of blood. The cold, dry air inside the mountain was already at work, slowly turning the young man's body into a dry, brown mummy.

"It's Keam," she whispered.

For a long while, Maraakus stared down at the body; then turned and looked toward the end of the room, now visible in the light from Grommdum's staff. A large door stood open. Through it he could see a floor paved with black and white stone that continued on into the darkness.

"Another question answered," Maraakus said bitterly.

He jerked an ancient tapestry from its tarnished brass rod and draped it over Keam's body; then walked through the open door into the next room.

For a moment he stood rigidly at attention. He was in a hallway nearly the width of the king's banquet hall in the royal castle at Luwynnvale, and half again as high, with soaring arches that rose from the floor and met in sharp points far overhead, creating a series of vast, interlocking vaults of stone. The arches were deeply carved with figures of strange animals and the walls were set with dark, stone mirrors.

Unlike the floor of the first chamber, this hallway was paved with stones that had been carefully cut, polished and set in strange, swirling patterns that gave the illusion of motion and induced a mild sense of discomfort in all four of them. The patterns were clearly visible, even under the thick layer of dust which revealed a bewildering trail of furrows and huge, oblong tracks made by large, clawed feet.

"Balsephus is in here," Maraakus told Grommdum quietly.

Holding his torch overhead, Maraakus moved slowly down the great hallway, past a smaller corridor on his right. Here too he saw a profusion of tracks coming and going from the tunnel, all belonging to Balsephus.

"Watch the side tunnels," Maraakus whispered. "The creature could be hiding in one of them. And look for tracks made by Keam and Andor, too."

For perhaps sixty paces, they followed the left wall of the gently curving hallway, then moved quickly past the dark mouth of a tunnel framed by a cut stone arch. Just beyond this dark opening, the cavernous hallway ended before a set of gigantic double doors. One door stood open.

"By the great bearded gods!" Danis whispered, obviously impressed by the huge doors. "What kind of room needs an entrance that big?"

"We'll soon find out," Maraakus whispered back.

As he led them through the double doors, Maraakus noted that they were made from thick timbers and reinforced with wide bands of heavy iron strapping. The sturdy doors were fitted with massive iron brackets on their backsides. Heavy wooden beams could be placed across them, preventing entrance when the doors were closed.

Grommdum muttered something to himself and the light from his staff grew brighter, filling the room in a harsh, white glare. They all turned slowly and looked about, astounded by what the light revealed.

The room was enormous, fully sixty feet wide, not less than ninety feet long and forty feet high. Opposite from where they were standing, another set of doors stood partially open, identical to the ones through which they had entered the room. Balsephus's crisscrossing tracks formed a broad path across the dusty floor toward the other set of doors. Maraakus brought his sword arm closer to his body to stop it from trembling.

"A throne room," Grommdum whispered. "Here ruled an evil man—who dared to become a god."

Maraakus walked slowly down the center of the great throne room and Grommdum followed, holding his staff high above his head. Not even the dust of centuries could hide the detailed beauty of the carved walls, the delicate arches and smooth ceilings that sparkled with tiny nuggets and flecks of gold.

Tall alabaster columns capped by intricately carved spheres of polished green marble stood in gleaming rows on both sides of the room. Each column supported a massive lamp cut from translucent, pale green jade and chased with gleaming gold.

In front of the columns, on three sides of the room, white marble benches rose halfway up the walls. The benches were fronted by a low marble railing that defined a large open area paved with veined slabs of green and white marble arranged in a simple pattern of unusual beauty.

At the far end of the room, on a platform raised three steps above the floor, a wall of carved ivory panels stood behind a massive throne hewn from a single block of black marble. And not even the accumulated grime of nearly half a millennia could obscure the smooth surfaces that had been polished to a high luster.

Alyna touched Danis on the shoulder and he jumped, startled by her touch, but he took a deep breath and gave her a smile.

"Surely," Alyna said, "Jodac must have lived in greater splendor than even the king of Luwynn."

"Indeed," Maraakus agreed. "Until now, I thought the king's throne room in Luwynnvale was most awe inspiring. But it's a hovel compared to this room. I wonder how long it took to build this place?"

"Many years—and many lives—no doubt," Grommdum said. "You are looking at the handiwork of Jodac's slaves. Imagine how many humans, wetakia and valley dwarves it must have taken to build just this single room. And despite its awesome beauty, it is an evil place, a loathsome monument to an evil man."

He turned and stepped up onto the raised platform. After walking behind the dark marble throne, he reached out to touch the yellowing wall of ivory panels.

"These were carved by wetakian hands," he said; then stepped back and stood motionless, carefully studying the intricate details.

"What is it?" Maraakus asked. He cocked his head and tightened his grip on his sword. "Is something wrong?"

Grommdum stepped closer to the wall, pressed on one panel, then another. He pushed again at the middle panel, then turned to Maraakus. "There's a small doorway in this wall," he said.

"A secret door?" Alyna asked.

"Yes," Grommdum answered. "I thought there might be one. See the tiny crack that reveals its outline? Ancient kings often had secret ways in and out of their throne rooms. Many did not think it proper to rub shoulders with ordinary mortals. And Jodac fancied himself a god."

"I wonder where it goes," Danis said. "Maybe it leads to his treasure room. Can you open it?"

Grommdum studied the wall carefully. "Perhaps," he said. "Of course. It would take some time, but I believe I could manage to get it open."

"Time is what we don't have," Maraakus reminded them. "Let's remember our objective. We're here to determine where Balsephus sleeps."

"Yes," Grommdum agreed, "we must do that first. We know he is in here, but there is no way for us to know the extent of the tunnels and rooms still open in this place. It is not only dangerous, but highly impractical for just four people to search this . . . this rabbit warren! In fact, now might be a good time to retreat from here. Or at least start back toward the entrance."

"You may be right," Maraakus conceded. "Let's go back to the main corridor. We'll check those smaller tunnels on our way out. Like you, Grommdum, I'm reluctant to go any deeper into this cursed mountain."

He led them back to the main hallway and they turned right, into the tunnel outside the throne room. Almost immediately, they entered a chamber with rough-hewn walls—hardly more than a crude cave—where piles of filthy clothing, clay bottles, and broken furniture littered the floor.

"A barracks room," Maraakus told them. "Probably for his personal guards. Couldn't have been more than twenty."

Danis looked down at his own tracks in the thick dust. "Keam and Andor didn't come this way," he said. "See? Only our tracks and those of Balsephus. Its tracks were in the throne room, too."

"It appears to be wandering through the tunnels." Grommdum observed. "We must be very careful."

Beyond the barracks room, they found an even smaller chamber that contained two wooden racks. One held a few rusting pikes, daggers and swords. Unstrung bows and loose arrows—most of them broken—littered the floor. The second rack held three rows of small clay pots sealed with wax.

"Well, well," Maraakus said softly to himself. "I think the gods just smiled on us, my friends." He handed Danis the torch, stepped up to the rack, pushed just the tip of his sword through one of the wax seals, then sniffed the blade. "Yes, indeed," he said. "Just as I expected."

"What is it?" Danis asked, taking a step closer.

"Fire oil," Maraakus replied. "A very dangerous substance, so don't come too close with that torch. This room was obviously an armory and—"

"Listen!" Grommdum said suddenly. "I heard something."

"I heard it, too." Alyna whispered, moving closer to Danis.

Then Maraakus heard it clearly; it was a low, hissing sound accompanied by a soft rattling like that made by pebbles in a dry gourd. He felt the hair rise on the back of his neck.

"Out!" he ordered. "This area is a dead end!"

They went quickly through the barracks room and back to the main hallway. Maraakus stood at the end of the short tunnel and listened. The hissing grew louder and Maraakus raised his sword and risked a quick look down the main hallway. Against the dim light filtering in through the hole in the mountain, a large, black shape moved slowly in their direction and a powerful stench filled the air. Baleful red eyes snapped open and stared at them from the darkness.

As the great head lifted, Danis stepped out with the torch. Maraakus saw the glint of huge teeth and the dark shape stopped with its mouth hanging open. Then the red eyes narrowed to slits and Balsephus lumbered forward, its claws rattling on the stone floor.

"Danis! Stand beside me!" Maraakus shouted as he slipped his bow from his shoulder. "Light, Grommdum! More light!"

The old elf stepped forward and raised his staff. A blinding white light flashed in the tunnel and Balsephus stood fully revealed. Its advance had stopped and it was crouching low on the floor, obviously startled by the sudden appearance of the bright light.

Danis dropped his torch and raised his bow. With a deliberate, practiced motion, he notched an arrow and pulled the bow to full draw.

"Try for the eyes," Maraakus said, deliberately keeping his voice soft and calm. He sheathed his sword and took his own bow from his shoulder. Now that the initial contact with Balsephus had been made, Maraakus felt better. The fear was still present, but the battle was finally joined; his soldier's instincts and training returned.

Danis's bowstring thrummed and the sound was almost immediately repeated. Maraakus released his own arrow and it slammed deep into the chest of the kalnath.

Danis's arrows had struck Balsephus on the right side of the head, one under the eye, the second in the forehead. "Its head's swinging! I can't hit the eyes!" Danis hissed.

Balsephus snarled, but the sound changed to an angry gurgle as Danis released a third arrow and it embedded itself in the creature's throat. Rearing up on its hind legs, the kalnath growled and scratched at the slender arrows with it's forelegs, breaking the shafts but leaving the sharp points embedded in its face, chest, and throat. Then its eyes opened and the beast dropped back to the floor and scrambled forward on four legs, trailing blood from the wound in its throat.

Danis moved quickly to one side of the hallway. He raised the bow slowly and steadied his aim, leading the swinging head as he would a running rabbit. The bow string twanged softly and the arrow buried itself in the center of Balsephus's left eye.

The beast staggered against the wall; then reared up with a loud bellow of pain. Its forefoot scratched at its face and the arrow broke, leaving much of the shaft sticking out of its blinded eye.

Suddenly the light from Grommdum's staff grew painfully bright and the old elf shouted, "Maraakus! Danis! Get down! *Get down!*"

Danis rolled to his left and came to rest with his face buried in his arms. Maraakus dropped flat on the floor. When he looked back at Grommdum and Alyna, he saw the old elf standing at her side with one hand resting on her shoulder.

Alyna stood tall and erect, seemingly unafraid, and slowly raised both hands over her head. Her blue eyes were fixed with a piercing stare, seeing only the dark form of Balsephus lumbering up the brightly illuminated corridor, mouth agape to expose those double rows of dagger-length teeth, blood streaming from its blinded eye.

"Now, girl!" Grommdum shouted. "Do it now!"

A strong wind began to blow through the hallway, whipping Alyna's clothing around her body and lifting her dark hair in fluttering streamers that extended forward around her face. A soft white glow obscured her pale blue eyes and she closed both hands; then lowered them to shoulder level.

A series of quick words tumbled from her lips in a strange, deepened voice, like that of a much older woman, rising almost to a shout, louder even than the coarse bellows of Balsephus and the moaning of the mysterious wind. Grommdum stepped back and lifted his arm to shield his eyes.

"Release, girl!" Grommdum screamed. *"Release!"*

Alyna opened her hands. Thrusting them forward, she shouted a single word in a commanding voice and a horrible roaring sound filled the hallway. Maraakus pressed his face to the cold stone floor as a prolonged blast to searing heat washed over him. Lifting his head, he saw the massive form of Balsephus— heavy as a boulder—easily picked up and hurled, sprawling, down the corridor; totally engulfed in a seething ball of flame.

CHAPTER EIGHTEEN

As the fireball subsided, Balsephus wallowed about in convulsive agony, clawing the air with club-like feet and fanning the odor of burning flesh with pointed, leathery wings. But its efforts proved futile; it was unable to escape the crackling blue fire that moved in probing, shifting patterns over its tortured body.

Then, as quickly as it appeared, the power of Alyna's spell vanished—as did the kalnath's howling cries—and a deep, eerie silence descended on the great hallway.

"It's dead!" Danis whispered.

"Stay down!" Maraakus ordered. "We must be certain."

With his eyes fixed on the still smoldering carcass, Maraakus got to his feet and raised his sword. He took one cautious step forward, then two more. But Balsephus remained motionless on the floor. Tendrils of black smoke rose from the creature's burned body and drifted slowly toward the vaulted ceiling.

Then, as Maraakus watched in shocked disbelief, a wing lifted and dropped back to the floor. A red eye opened and blinked. A long, shuddering groan escaped from the kalnath's gaping mouth and Balsephus suddenly rolled from its side to a crouching position.

"Alyna!" Danis shouted. "You can finish it now!"

"She can't!" Grommdum shouted back. "She needs time to recover."

Maraakus took a quick look over his shoulder. Danis was crouched against the opposite wall and his expression was one of utter confusion. Alyna had slumped down on her knees and elbows; her eyes were glazed and her body trembled violently. Grommdum stood behind her, holding his walking staff aloft with his right hand and trying to lift the young woman to her feet with his left.

Balsephus uttered a loud, rasping hiss and snapped its massive jaws together with a terrible clacking of dagger-length teeth. A heavy forefoot reached out to scrape at the smooth marble floor with broken claws. Its massive head lifted and the creature raised itself to its full height. It was a terrifying, fire-blackened, one-eyed beast—but a beast that still lived.

Danis jumped up from the floor and ran to the center of the hallway. The hair on the right side of his head was singed almost to his scalp. The searing heat had damaged his bow by parting the braided bowstring and melting the fletching on his arrows. He dropped his useless weapon to the floor and stuck out his arm. "Give me your bow!" he shouted. "I'll kill it while it's just standing there!"

Maraakus looked quickly at the smoldering kalnath. The

charred beast stood motionless near the curve in the hallway, watching them intently with an unblinking red eye. Its horny scales were scorched and curled, but its hissing was growing louder and more ominous. The fire had injured it—and it feared a second taste of the magical flame—but the creature was far from finished.

Maraakus grabbed Danis by the shoulder and turned him around. "We can't attack it directly until we get its remaining eye!" he said sternly. "Pick up your torch!"

After Danis snatched the torch from the floor, Maraakus took another from his belt and touched it to the one in Danis's hand. "Go back to the barracks room!" he ordered. "Drag out those straw mattresses—anything that'll burn. Go!"

Danis disappeared into the tunnel and Maraakus whirled around to face Alyna and Grommdum. "Take her back to the throne room," he told the old elf. "Danis and I will buy us some time!"

Grommdum pulled Alyna to her feet. Slipping an arm around her waist, he half carried her toward the double doors of the throne room.

Danis backed into the corridor dragging two mattresses with his left hand. Maraakus slashed the rotting cloth covers with his short sword, then kicked the straw stuffing over the floor. Danis returned with an armload of broken furniture and tossed it onto the pile.

"Light it!" Maraakus ordered, jamming his torch into the dry straw.

Danis swept his torch through the scattered bedding and the fire spread quickly.

"This won't stop him for long!" Danis shouted.

"We're not finished." Maraakus replied. "Bring out those fire oil pots."

Balsephus lifted its head. Back arched; it backed up a short distance, but its head began that slow swinging from side to side. It hissed and shuffled cautiously forward.

"Hurry, Danis!" Maraakus shouted. "It's coming!"

Danis ran from the barracks tunnel with three clay pots cradled in one arm. Maraakus seized one and threw it across the main hallway. It shattered and the pungent smell of the volatile fluid spread in a choking fog.

"In the middle!" Maraakus shouted, then dashed a second pot against the wall to his right.

Danis threw the remaining pot in a high arc. It landed perhaps fifty feet down the corridor and erupted in a geyser of oily spray. Maraakus immediately seized the young archer by the arm and hurried him toward the throne room.

The fire oil ignited. A stark red light flashed in the corridor, followed immediately by a sharp cracking sound, and a hot wind rushed past. Maraakus looked back through waves of shimmering heat to see a wall of boiling flames rising toward the vaulted ceiling.

After pulling Danis into the throne room, Maraakus threw his weight against the heavy door; it creaked but refused to move. Danis put his back against it too. Through their combined efforts, the door swung shut with a prolonged groaning of rusted hinges and bumped solidly against its stone frame.

"Get the locking bar down!" Maraakus shouted, pointing to a vertical wooden beam held aloft by a huge iron rod. Above the beam, a corroded iron pulley was recessed into the wall and a thick, broken hawser lay rotting on the rusting drum of a heavy windlass secured to the floor with iron pins.

They threw their shoulders against the huge timber. With a loud scraping sound, the oak beam moved slowly from its vertical position, then dropped quickly toward the floor and slammed to a stop in the great iron brackets. The ancient doors groaned under the impact and a thick cloud of dust whirled into the room.

Maraakus stepped back to inspect the doors. Light from burning fire oil flickered through wide cracks in the shrunken planks, but an oak beam nearly thirty inches square barred entrance to the room.

"When the fire oil burns out, we can expect it to attack the doors," Maraakus told Danis. "It knows we can't get out"

"Where was it hiding?" Danis asked.

"In the first tunnel," Alyna said. "The one just inside the hallway entrance. It's the only opening we didn't go into."

Maraakus and Danis turned to look at her.

"She's recovering quickly," Grommdum assured them. He wedged his walking staff into a wide crack in the stone railing. The ball of light above the staff diminished, becoming only as bright as one of their torches. He sat down on the floor and Alyna dropped down beside him.

Danis stuck his torch in a stone urn. Maraakus placed his beside it, then handed Danis the undamaged bow and quiver of arrows. "Well, you got one eye," he told Danis. "Next time, we'll blind it completely. Make every arrow count."

"Oh, I will," Danis promised. "But aren't you afraid it could circle around behind us? Shouldn't we close and bar those other doors?"

"Not until we see what's beyond them. Once the locking bar is down, we won't be able to lift it."

"Maybe not," Grommdum replied. "There's that small hidden door behind the throne. It will take some time, but this certainly seems like the proper time to open it."

"Indeed, it does." Maraakus agreed. "Alyna, stay close to Grommdum. Danis, keep watch through the cracks in the doors and let us know when Balsephus comes up the hallway. I'll see what's beyond this room. I'll be right back."

He picked up a torch and walked quickly through the open doors on the far side of the room. A short flight of steps led down to a small landing. On his left was an arched opening without a door; on his right the steps continued down, leading deeper into the mountain.

With the torch held overhead, he stepped through the arched opening. The room was some twenty feet square and contained four large wooden tables. Fire-blackened ovens and cooking hearths occupied the right-hand wall; another small door indicated a room off to his right. He gave the door a hard kick. To his surprise the flimsy boards splintered and the door fell into the room with a loud clatter.

It was a dead end. Two walls were covered by empty shelves. The center of the room was occupied by the stone casing of an old well topped by a wooden winding-drum with a rusty handle. Behind the well stood a row of enormous clay pots, obviously used in the past for storing water.

He hurried back to the landing and looked down at the flight of steps leading deeper into the Pinnacle. The thought of descending those steps was more than a little disturbing. They might well lead to a labyrinth of rooms and tunnels requiring days to explore. Balsephus no doubt knew them well. Then again, they might lead to another dead-end room.

Suddenly he became aware of a loud, repetitive pounding. Alyna screamed, then Danis shouted, "Maraakus! The fire oil has burned out! *He's coming!*"

Maraakus rushed back up the short flight of steps and slipped through the open door. Alyna stood in the center of the throne room with Danis's sword in her hand, clearly prepared to fight. Danis had backed up to a spot near her. His bow was drawn and pointed at the barred doors. Grommdum was on his knees behind the black throne, slowly and deliberately passing his hands over the carved ivory panels, seemingly unaware that the monstrous kalnath was throwing itself against the barricaded doors.

"The wall brackets are coming loose!" Danis shouted. "They won't hold much longer!"

Even as he spoke, part of a bracket snapped off and clattered out onto the floor. There was a loud, cracking sound and the barricade beam flexed. Several jagged splinters shot across the room. A plank splintered in the center of one of the doors and a huge claw poked through the hole, scraped at the wooden beam, and withdrew.

For a brief moment there was an ominous silence. A large, red eye appeared, stared into the room for a moment, then vanished. Then Balsephus suddenly renewed its assault on the barricaded doors. The ancient timbers groaned and shook, throwing out showers of dangerous splinters and clouds of suffocating dust.

"This way!" Grommdum shouted. He was standing at one side of the black marble throne, waving his staff overhead with both hands. "Hurry!"

Maraakus reached out and turned Alyna around. Holding her with one arm around her waist, he hurried her toward the old elf. "Come on, Danis! Let's get out of here!"

The left door splintered and Balsephus shoved its head through the opening. Danis loosed an arrow, but it struck the door a hand's width from the red eye. Then Balsephus forced a shoulder through the shattered planks and Danis spun on his heels, snatched his torch from the stone urn, and sprinted down the throne room.

Grommdum ducked through a small opening less than four feet wide and Maraakus shoved Alyna inside. Danis took the steps of the raised platform in a single bound and threw himself in after her.

A horrible splintering sound came from the other end of the room. Maraakus looked back in time to see the great wooden bar break in half. And when the battered doors opened wide, thrown apart by the kalnath's considerable weight, Balsephus tumbled into the room and rolled nearly halfway across the floor. But with a speed that belied its immense size, the great beast scrambled quickly to its feet and came charging down the center of the throne room.

Maraakus ducked into the small opening and yielded the battlefield to his enemy—temporarily, at least. Balsephus, unable to reach them inside the narrow passageway, rammed its head inside and bellowed with rage and frustration.

For a moment, Maraakus watched the twisting head and snapping jaws, then he lifted his sword and slashed hard at the squinting red eye. He missed, but succeeded in delivering a deep cut to the creature's upper lip. Balsephus bellowed and withdrew its head. Maraakus smiled with satisfaction and looked up to see Grommdum regarding him with a wry grin.

"That should teach it a good lesson," the elf declared.

"I doubt it," Maraakus replied, "but I certainly feel much better. I also like this narrow passageway. It's too small for Balsephus to get into and carved from solid rock—maybe the only safe place in this tangle of rooms and tunnels."

"It might even be our way out of this mountain." Grommdum agreed.

"Where are Alyna and Danis?"

"I told them to wait just ahead," Grommdum replied.

"How's Alyna doing?"

"Still recovering," Grommdum answered. "After casting a strong spell, some degree of weakness is quite normal, so don't be alarmed. I'm more concerned about what I've observed of the kalnath. Apparently, Jodac endowed it with an uncanny ability to recover from injuries."

"So we're unlikely to kill it with a sword or bow?"

Grommdum shook his head slowly. "Indeed, it may take something more than fire and steel," he replied. "Did you notice how it hesitated to attack after Alyna's spell dissipated?"

"Yes." Maraakus replied. "It was most certainly injured, but not that badly. Why didn't it attack us?"

"It was momentarily confused . . . and frightened," Grommdum answered. "Until now, only Jodac could control or castigate the beast with magic. Suddenly another human appears —one who looks nothing like Jodac—and punishes it with a powerful spell. It wonders how this is possible—who this human might be."

"By Heltum's sacred beard! Are you saying Balsephus thought Alyna was a . . . a person of authority?"

"How do you suppose Jodac managed to control a viscous creature like Balsephus?"

"With magic, of course," Maraakus answered.

"Indeed," the old elf said. "But don't count on getting that same reaction again. Next time, we should expect him to attack immediately and plan accordingly."

"I understand," Maraakus said. "Let's give Alyna a brief rest, then see where this passageway leads us."

Stooping slightly due to the low ceiling, Maraakus followed Grommdum along the narrow tunnel. As they rounded a sharp curve a flickering torch appeared and they saw Danis and Alyna sitting on the floor.

"An excellent place to rest," Maraakus declared. "One couldn't ask for a cozier spot." He shrugged a small waterskin from his shoulder and passed it around.

"How are you feeling?" Maraakus asked Alyna.

"Better," she said. "Much better."

"Good, from now on, this is our safety tunnel. We'll come back in here at the first sign of danger."

After a brief period of rest, they followed Maraakus along the narrow passageway. It continued its curving path and if Maraakus's sense of direction proved reliable, they were now on the eastern side of the Pinnacle.

"We're moving south," Maraakus told them, as they turned a sharp corner. "We might come out in that larger tunnel off the main corridor. The Pinnacle is no more than a couple hundred feet across at the top, so we have to be somewhere near the entrance hole."

"Maraakus?" Grommdum said. He was pointing ahead, to a small door with an ordinary latch. They had reached the end of the narrow passageway.

Maraakus set his hand on the latch and pulled. The door opened and he saw a wall of thick fabric—the back of a hanging tapestry. He shoved it aside and thrust his torch forward.

The room was small and on his right was a chair padded with

rotting fabric, a tall brass oil lamp, and a small table carved from ebony and inlaid with yellowing ivory. Two dust-covered books rested on the table. To his left was a bed with a carved wooden canopy. Faded tapestries hung behind it. Two large brass lamps attached to tall spindles lay on the floor.

The south wall, directly opposite where he was standing, was little more than a flimsy partition of small stones and mortar with an arched opening—a doorway to a second room.

"A sleeping chamber," Grommdum said, looking past Maraakus's shoulder. "Perhaps we've discovered Jodac's private quarters."

Maraakus stepped out of the narrow passageway and they followed him to the center of the room. "Listen!" Grommdum said, raising his hand.

Maraakus cocked his head but heard nothing. Then the distant sound of angry bellowing filtered into the room.

"Balsephus," Danis said. "Why is it suddenly making so much noise?"

Grommdum crossed the sleeping chamber and stopped before the arched doorway. "Maybe it thinks we've gotten away," he suggested. "At any rate, its bellowing sounds much louder from over here."

"Then we're not far from the main hallway, or the entrance hole," Maraakus assured them. He started through the arched doorway but Grommdum put a hand on his shoulder.

"Wait!" the old elf said. "We're not the first visitors to enter this next chamber."

Maraakus thrust his torch through the doorway and saw two sets of footprints on the dusty floor. Each set was accompanied by a trail of irregular, gleaming spots.

"Keam and Andor. . . ." Alyna said. "They came out of that big tunnel in the corner."

Maraakus nodded. "See where they stopped, turned around, then separated? Keam—the larger footprints are his—went to that old storage chest sitting against the south wall. See all those little shiny spots on the floor?"

"Drippings from wax candles! There were candle stubs in that old rucksack." Danis said.

"Exactly. Candles don't give much light, so Keam simply dumped the contents of the storage chest on the floor."

"And found the amulet." Alyna whispered.

"The coins, perhaps," Grommdum said. "But not the amulet. Powerful magical objects are kept close at hand—not stored away in old trunks. But it could have been found in this room, which was obviously a work place . . . perhaps a study."

"The boys' tracks weren't in the throne room—" Maraakus said, "or the barracks room or the armory where we found the fire oil—and we can plainly see that they never passed through the doorway to Jodac's sleeping chamber."

Holding the torch overhead, Maraakus stepped cautiously into the next room and looked around. Danis followed, but Alyna and Grommdum remained in the doorway.

On the left, perhaps four feet off the east wall of the room, Maraakus saw a large stone desk nearly covered with old books and fading parchments. Behind the desk was a wall covered with dark, carved wooden panels and a large opening without a door.

To his right, standing almost against the west wall, was a long stone table. Like the desk, it was piled high with old books and rolled parchments. The top, a thin slab of white marble, was supported on both ends by wooden pedestals. The front was covered by a rotting curtain of red fabric.

"While Keam rummaged through the storage chest," Maraakus said, "Andor went to that desk, then turned and walked to this spot." He pointed to the floor in front of Alyna and Grommdum.

"Where Keam joined him," Danis added.

"Yes," Maraakus said. "Then both boys went behind that long table. They emerged at the far end and paused for a few moments, probably taking a last look around. Do you see all the candle drippings? Then the boys went out the same way they came in; through that tunnel in the corner."

Grommdum stuck his head through the doorway and looked to his right. He studied the long stone table for a moment, then shook his head and said, "See those tall lamps shaped like serpents? Now look at those symbols carved on the wooden pedestals. That's an altar, my friend—though I shudder to think what gods Jodac might have worshipped."

"What made that?" Alyna asked, pointing to a broad swath of oblong impressions and crisscrossing furrows on the dusty floor.

"Balsephus," Grommdum said simply. "Apparently, the kalnath comes through this study room and goes into that opening behind the stone desk. Perhaps to reach its lair."

After a quick look toward the opening on the east wall, Maraakus cocked his head and raised his hand. "Speaking of Balsephus," he muttered softly, "I don't hear it. And that worries me."

"What do you suppose that foul-smelling, evil-tempered beast is doing?" Grommdum wondered.

"We could follow that big tunnel out to the main hallway," Danis said. "Like Keam and Andor."

"And only Andor made it to the entrance hole" Alyna reminded him. "What if Balsephus sees us before we get outside? Or follows us down to the ledges?"

"She's right," Maraakus said. "We can't fight it on the ledges. It would pick us off one by one."

"To defeat Balsephus," Grommdum said softly, "we must first have answers to some vital questions. What did the boys do in this room? Why was the kalnath dormant for so many years? What made it active again?"

"And answering those questions will help us destroy the thing?" Maraakus asked.

"Perhaps," Grommdum replied. "Something extraordinary happened in this room, and it must have happened soon after

Keam and Andor found the amulet. If we can discover where the boys found it we might be able to learn how it works. Even if we're unable to use it we might learn why Jodac's kalnath became active again. We might even learn how to destroy the beast—permanently!"

"I agree," Alyna added quietly. "The amulet is very powerful and I believe it exerts a direct influence on Balsephus. Until we determine how that happens, there is very little hope of destroying the kalnath. All our efforts and risks will be for nothing."

"As you can see," Grommdum said, "Alyna is now prepared to face Balsephus again, if necessary."

"And the next time she'll kill it?" Maraakus asked.

The old elf smiled and arched his shaggy white brows. "No," he admitted. "But she can delay it and give us more time to learn how it might be destroyed. And that's our ultimate objective, isn't it? Well, a method to accomplish that task could be nearly at our fingertips. In Jodac's books and personal writings."

"And if we fail to get our answers?" Maraakus asked.

"We'll have lost only a little time," Grommdum assured him. "But we must try."

Maraakus smiled. "Very well. But first, Alyna goes back into the safety tunnel until the present location of Balsephus is determined, and we're aware of every possible access to this room. Danis, take your torch and go out that large tunnel Keam and Andor used. It should take you back to the main corridor. Find Balsephus. Don't confront it! Just see where it is, then get back here immediately and get into the safety tunnel with Alyna."

"I understand," Danis said.

"If Balsephus follows you, this masonry wall between the study and sleeping chamber won't stop it," Maraakus told the young man. "Stay with Alyna until Grommdum and I return. We'll check out that opening behind the stone desk. Balsephus could come at us from that direction, too. When we're sure it's safe, Alyna and Grommdum will start searching. You and I will stand guard."

Danis nodded and gave them a wide grin. "I'll be right back," he promised. Then he crossed the study and started slowly down the large, dark tunnel.

When the glow of Danis's torch faded, Grommdum turned to Maraakus. "Shall we see where Balsephus goes when he comes through here?" he asked.

Maraakus nodded, then handed Alyna his torch. "I'm depending on you to make certain Danis gets into the safety tunnel. If his torch goes out, you'll have the only light. When he returns, don't allow him to follow Grommdum and me."

"I understand," she answered.

When she was some thirty feet into the narrow passageway, she sat down on the floor. Maraakus waved, gave her a smile, then he and Grommdum went behind the stone desk on the east side of the study room and stepped through the large square opening.

Using the light from Grommdum's staff, they went cautiously down a short flight of stone stairs and stopped on a small landing before an arched opening. Maraakus looked inside. The room was small, less than ten feet square. A wooden door had been broken in with considerable force and the shattered planks lay in splinters on the stone floor.

Grommdum stuck his staff through the opening and ducked inside. "Completely empty," he declared. "Storage, perhaps?"

Something sparkled from one corner of the room. Grommdum grinned, scooped up the small object, then opened his hand to reveal a tiny, gleaming gold coin.

"A treasure room?" Maraakus asked. "If so, then so much for Jodac's hoard of ill-gotten wealth."

"Stripped cleaner than a hungry hound's bone," Grommdum agreed. "After Jodac died, his henchmen probably looted every room in this place. Danis will be sorely disappointed, eh?"

They left the room and continued down the steps, following Balsephus's tracks. Almost immediately, they found another small landing. Here the heavy, nauseating stench of the kalnath was nearly overpowering, rising in a choking cloud from deeper in the mountain.

"We can't be far from where Balsephus sleeps," Maraakus said. "Let's see what's—"

He paused, stepped back, and rubbed his eyes. While most of the creature's tracks continued on down the curving stairs, some on the landing formed confusing, crisscrossing paths that appeared to begin and end on the floor at the right-hand wall. He reached out to touch cold, damp stone and heard Grommdum laughing softly to himself.

"My eyes must be playing tricks on me," Maraakus muttered.

This time, he stepped up to the wall and ran his hand over the rough-hewn surface. There were no holes, no handles or hinges, yet several individual tracks were cut in half by the intersection of wall and floor.

"Another hidden door?" he asked.

"There is no hidden door," the old elf said. "But neither is there a wall."

"No wall? Then what is this?" Maraakus asked. He tapped the stone with his bare knuckles.

The old elf shifted the walking staff to his left hand. "Well, General Maraakus, haven't you noticed that things are not always what they seem to be in this place?" he asked. "Then again, they may well be exactly what you expect." He smiled, stepped forward, and vanished—leaving Maraakus in total darkness.

"Grommdum!" Maraakus whispered loudly. "Where are you?"

"I'm still here," the old elf said, stepping out from the glistening, gray stone.

Maraakus put out his hand. As before, the stone felt solid and clammy to his touch.

"You're being deceived by an illusion placed here by Jodac," Grommdum assured him. "Watch." He thrust his staff toward the stone wall and the landing was plunged into darkness. He withdrew his arm and the light from his staff was as bright as before.

Maraakus shook his head slowly and stared at the elven mage. "How did you do that?"

"It's simple really," Grommdum replied. "Just disregard what you see and feel. Granted, this is a task not easily accomplished by even modestly intelligent creatures. On the other hand, as evidenced by these tracks, Balsephus comes and goes quite often. This tells me it's a kalnath that was given a limited ability to reason. As strange as it may seem, the creature's probably so stupid that it can't be fooled by this illusion."

Maraakus gave the old elf a wry smile. "I'm not sure I understand," he said, "but it's nice to know that I really am smarter than an overgrown lizard. . . ."

Reaching out, Maraakus pushed at the wall. "Are you sure about this?"

"Here," Grommdum said. "Take my staff and walk forward. Just remember—it's an illusion. I'll be right behind you."

Maraakus took the staff and looked suspiciously at the wall. Grommdum smiled. Maraakus stepped forward, then swore softly under his breath as he bumped his head hard and painfully against the rough stone. He staggered back, rubbing his forehead with his left hand.

Grommdum chuckled. "No, Maraakus. You must approach the illusion in the proper frame of mind. Have confidence in what I've told you, and yourself as well. Expect to walk through, and you will. It's really that simple. Try it again. This time, just ignore what your eyes and hands are telling you. Walk through as if you're entering your own sleeping chamber."

Maraakus stared for a moment at the wall, then he raised his chin and closed his eyes. Lifting the staff before him, he stepped forward three paces. He opened his eyes and turned to see Grommdum walking through a crudely made opening.

The old elf took back his staff and smiled. "Very good," he said. "This illusion is now broken. It can never deceive you again. But attempt—"

"No, no," Maraakus said, raising his hand. "I don't want to know. It's all much too complicated for a simple soldier."

"But I suspect you've changed some since arriving in Stridgenfel," Grommdum remarked. "Could you have dispelled that illusion just a few weeks ago?" He raised his staff and a brilliant, white light flooded a long, narrow room.

Maraakus stood as though his feet were rooted to the stone floor, awe-stricken by the scene before him. Lining the floor were stacks of tiny gold and silver ingots and small alabaster urns filled to overflowing with precious stones of unusual size and color. A line of shelves against one wall held tarnished silver bowls brimming with perfect pearls nearly as big as grapes. And in the center of one table, resting on a faded square of red silk, light from Grommdum's staff flashed from the facets of a pale blue diamond as big as a large pear.

Finally, his senses saturated by the magnificent store of wealth, Maraakus followed Grommdum to the far end of the room. They stopped before a bare circular platform raised six steps above the floor. Directly in the center was a small altar made from intricately carved red marble.

"Very peculiar indeed," Grommdum whispered. "A private temple tucked away in the cold depths of this mountain."

"Along with a magnificent treasure," Maraakus added. He scooped up a handful of large rubies and let the blood-red stones trickle slowly through his fingers. "Odd, isn't it?" he asked. "When so many are thrown in untidy piles, they seem to be little more than pebbles from a river."

"Such is often the case with material wealth," Grommdum said, "and one of the reasons why wealth accumulated through greed is ultimately unfulfilling. Yet I suspect that even the smallest gemstone in this room is without flaw. Jodac seems to have kept only the finest of everything for his personal treasure. The rest was probably kept in that other storeroom and carried off by his minions."

Maraakus dropped the rubies on the table and picked up the carved jade box. Grommdum stood watching with one hand suspended in mid-air; his dark eyes were wide and staring.

Maraakus lifted the lid and looked inside. In the bottom was a faded red leather pouch, on which rested a pearl of perfect symmetry. It was nearly as large as a chicken's egg, a lustrous gray in color, tending toward black. It shimmered softly in the glow of Grommdum's staff.

"That alone is worth more than all the rest," the old elf said, speaking very softly. "You are holding Madammia's Pearl. It has been missing for more than a thousand years. Once it belonged to an ancient wetakian leader—you would probably call him a king—and was a sacred symbol of my people and our culture. I wonder how it came to be in Jodac's possession. . . ."

Maraakus shook his head. "We may never know," he said. "Take it. This pearl still belongs to the people of Refuge." He held out the box.

The old elf took it with a trembling hand, pushed the pearl into the red leather pouch, closed the lid and slipped the jade box into the pocket of his jerkin. "You are a most unusual man, General Maraakus," he said with a teary smile. "A lesser man would have insisted on keeping such a priceless object. On behalf of the wetakia, I thank you."

Maraakus smiled and looked about the room. "Nothing but the largest, the rarest, the most precious of . . . everything," he said, shaking his head.

"Indeed," Grommdum said. He stepped up on the raised platform and looked down on the altar. "On my dear Father's memory!" he muttered softly. "You'd better look at this!"

Maraakus jumped up on the platform and looked down, then

stepped back and exhaled slowly through his teeth. "May the merciful gods preserve us! Is that what I think it is?"

Grommdum nodded. "Those brown, shriveled masses," he declared, "are human hearts. The servant continues to carry out its unconscionable instructions. . . ."

❧ ❦ ❧

Danis paused at the throne room entrance and peeked cautiously into the dark interior. At the far end of the chamber, dimly illuminated by his torch, he could see Jodac's black marble throne. On the floor behind it lay the broken remains of the carved ivory screens. The entrance to their narrow safety tunnel appeared as a black square against the wall. What he did not see was Balsephus.

"Where are you hiding, my vicious, stinking friend?" Danis muttered softly to himself.

A cold shiver ran up his back. His eyes went immediately to the open double doors on the opposite wall. There can be only two answers to that question, he thought. If Balsephus didn't leave through those double doors, then it's somewhere behind me!

With a deafening roar, Balsephus shouldered its way through the second set of double doors and charged into the chamber. Halfway across it stumbled over a broken timber and skidded headfirst into a stone wall. And before the terrifying beast could scramble back to its feet, Danis turned and fled down the main hallway.

As he passed the armory tunnel, he tossed his torch through the entrance. Then, sprinting for his life—and guided only by light filtering in through the hole in the mountain—he reached the tunnel leading back to Jodac's chambers and ducked inside. Looking back, he saw Balsephus turn into the armory tunnel, chasing the glow of the discarded torch.

Almost immediately, angry bellowing echoed down the hallway and Danis shrank back against the tunnel wall as Balsephus charged past. But when the caverns grew quiet, he peeked out to see the great beast lying half-hidden behind a pile of rubble, red eyes glowing, head pointed toward the hole in the mountain—their only way out.

❦ ❦ ❦

Maraakus followed Grommdum up the stairs to Jodac's study. When he called softly to Alyna, she came out of the narrow passageway and into the study. She smiled, but he noticed that her torch was flickering. Grommdum snapped his fingers and it flared with renewed life.

"I thought it might burn out before you returned," she said, her voice betraying her fear. "Don't leave me alone again."

"Shhh," Maraakus said, gently gathering her in his arms. "Danis hasn't returned?"

"No," she whispered.

Maraakus gave Grommdum a worried look. "You stay with Alyna," he said. "I'll go look for—"

"No need," Grommdum interrupted. "He's coming now."

Danis came out of the tunnel at a quick trot. The torch in his hand was only a small wooden splinter wrapped with rags. He dropped it on the floor and it went out.

"I found it!" Danis breathed. "It saw the light from my torch and started after me. When I threw the torch into the barracks tunnel, the stupid animal went after it."

Maraakus smiled. "Good work, Danis."

"It wasn't fooled for long," Danis continued. "It came out and headed straight for the hole in the mountain—went right past me. It's there now, maybe thirty feet inside the entrance, hiding behind some rubble."

"It doesn't know if we're still inside or not," Maraakus said. "How far are we from the main corridor?"

"Less than two hundred feet," Danis answered. "But it must

be midafternoon or later. The sun is coming through the entrance hole and there's plenty of light where it's sitting."

"Can we sneak past after it gets dark?" Alyna asked.

"Probably not," Danis replied. "That thing's big, but much faster than you might suspect. If it sees us before we get outside, it can probably catch us. I wouldn't want to try it."

Maraakus shook his head. "You're right," he agreed. "It's too risky."

"I agree," the old elf said. "Since we know where the kalnath is, let's give this study a thorough searching. We might learn something about the amulet from these old books and manuscripts."

"A good idea," Maraakus agreed. He pulled the last torch from his belt, touched it to Alyna's, then handed it to Danis. "Go back to the main hallway and keep an eye on Balsephus," he ordered. "If it comes this way, give us a yell, then get back here *quickly.*"

"Oh, I'll let you know, all right!" Danis assured them. "They'll probably hear me back in Stridgenfel!" He flashed them a broad grin, then hurried away.

Maraakus turned to Grommdum and said, "You and Alyna start searching. I'll take her torch and watch the stairs going down to the treasure room. Our old friend Balsephus might come at us from that direction, too."

Grommdum nodded and tapped his staff on the floor. The glowing ball at its tip flared brightly as he and Alyna turned to the long marble altar on the west wall of the room. Suddenly she stopped and clapped both hands over her eyes.

"Maraakus! Grommdum! It's Jodac!"

"Get back, child!" Grommdum shouted. He jumped forward and raised the walking staff before him like a spear. Then he sighed heavily and closed his eyes. The butt of his walking staff sank back to the floor, but the light at its tip winked furiously. "There," he said, pointing with a thin finger.

With his sword still raised, Maraakus stepped past the old elf and looked behind the altar. There on the dusty floor, nearly concealed by deep shadows, lay the desiccated remains of a man dressed in a rotting, embroidered robe. "By Heltum's beard!" he muttered. "It's a mummy. . . ."

"Not just any mummy." Grommdum said solemnly. He snatched the red cloth covering from the front of the altar, scattering dusty books and dry parchments over the floor.

Now the light from his staff revealed the old mummy clearly and the cause of death was immediately apparent; the slender blade of a long dagger had been plunged through his breastbone.

The fingers on his left hand were curled around the dagger's ivory hilt, but the fingers on his right hand were broken off and lay in a dry, crumbled pile on his chest.

"It's just as Ilka recorded it in the book," Alyna said, still holding tightly to Grommdum's arm. "This is the room where it all happened. Where Ilka killed her twin brother."

Grommdum brought his staff closer, then he and Alyna knelt down and looked carefully at the mummy of Jodac. Grommdum reached out and pushed at the dagger. It refused to move.

"Don't," Alyna said, touching him on the wrist. "There is much power still present in the dagger. I can feel it."

"Indeed," Grommdum said, flexing his fingers. "It is very strong."

Maraakus pointed to the dusty floor. "Keam and Andor found Jodac, too." Their footprints were all around the body.

"Fortunately," Maraakus continued, "we have nothing to fear from this pile of bones. I'm going down to the landing to keep watch. Call me if Danis comes back." He spun on his heel and went quickly to the east side of the room, leaving Alyna and Grommdum hovered over Jodac's mummy, talking in excited whispers.

Holding the torch overhead, Maraakus started down the steps, but before he had descended to the first landing, he heard Danis shouting. He turned and rushed back to the study room.

"Get into the passageway!" he ordered.

Grommdum grabbed Alyna's arm and hurried her out of the study and through the sleeping chamber. After thrusting her into the narrow passageway, he ducked in after her. Maraakus stopped at the doorway in the masonry wall and shouted for Danis, watching as light from the young man's torch danced and flickered in the darkness of the large tunnel. Then Danis rounded a curve in the tunnel at a dead run. "It's not far behind me!" he shouted.

"Hurry!" Maraakus shouted back.

Danis responded with an extra burst of speed. But as he came out of the tunnel, his feet slipped in the thick, dry dust. He staggered to his left, then sprawled face down on the floor. His torch exploded in a shower of fiery embers and he slid under the altar and stopped, face-to-face with Jodac's mummy.

A soft, strangled curse escaped the young man's lips and he rolled quickly to his right, jumped to his feet, threw himself through the doorway in the masonry wall, and bolted into their place of safety. Maraakus snatched up the dropped torch and followed. Danis slid down against the wall and closed his eyes.

"Wha-what was . . . ?" the young man stammered. Then he took a deep breath. "What was that . . . that thing on the floor?"

Maraakus gave him a tight smile. "That thing, my swift and nimble-footed friend," he said, "was the infamous wizard, Jodac. What's left of him, anyway."

Danis closed his eyes and shuddered. "I nearly kissed him."

"What about your other love interest?" Maraakus muttered, looking back at the end of the passageway, "Where's Balsephus?"

Danis got to his feet, went to the entrance of their safety tunnel, and looked out. "I don't understand," he said. "It wasn't far behind—"

"Wait!" Grommdum said. "I hear it."

A labored breathing sound soon filled the chamber and the little passageway and Balsephus stumbled noisily out of the wider tunnel.

Danis backed up, but continued to watch the staggering kalnath through the doorway in the masonry wall.

"It's in the study room!" Danis whispered excitedly. "But it's moving very slowly. Maraakus! You'd better take a look at this! It's dragging one leg and stumbling about like a drunken ox!"

Maraakus stepped up behind Danis just as the beast lurched up to the masonry wall, stuck its head through the doorway, and pushed. The wall collapsed and stones tumbled into the sleeping chamber, bouncing and rolling like dry peas tossed on a kitchen floor.

Maraakus grabbed Danis by the shoulder and they retreated deeper into their narrow passageway. A stone rolled into the entrance. Danis picked it up and threw it back at Balsephus. It struck the monster on the shoulder and bounced harmlessly away, but the huge head lifted. Balsephus hissed loudly and fetid, animal breath reached them from across the room. Then Balsephus lurched left and bumped against the stone altar, sending the white slab of marble crashing to the floor.

"Danis," Maraakus said quietly. "Look! It has two eyes!"

"Absolutely fascinating. . . ." Grommdum muttered.

Danis dropped to a shooting position on one knee and notched an arrow. He tracked the creature's swinging head for several moments, then the bowstring thrummed and the arrow slammed into the center of Balsephus's right eye. "And now it has one again," Danis declared.

Balsephus snorted, then stumbled out onto the rubble from the shattered masonry wall and slumped to the floor, seemingly unaffected by the loss of an eye. Maraakus sat down with his back against the wall of the narrow tunnel. Danis sank down beside him.

"Not much of a reaction," Maraakus said to Danis. "Maybe

the thing's lost too much blood or something."

"No," Alyna said softly. "It's the dagger and the amulet."

Maraakus looked up to see her standing erect in the center of the narrow passageway, staring out at Balsephus. She had stood like that just before casting the fire at Balsephus in the main hallway.

"Could it really be that simple, Grommdum?" she asked softly. "What would happen if two powerful magical objects— one very evil, and the other very good—were brought together?"

"I don't really know," the old elf replied. "Much would depend on the nature of the spells placed on them. But it could be a dangerous situation. In fact, if the powers were exceedingly strong, I'd prefer not to be in the immediate vicinity!"

"And could the final results of this . . . joining of objects . . . this bringing together, be described as a stalemate?"

The old elf hesitated for a moment. "I don't know. They might very well cancel each other and . . ."

He paused, studied her carefully, then nodded his head slowly. "What an elegant solution!" he said, as much to himself as to Alyna. "What gave you the idea?"

"Jodac's mummified body," she replied. She tapped a finger against her chest. "Right here. I saw the depression—right here. Even now Balsephus feels the effects, though the distance is many feet."

"Would one of you explain what you're talking about?" Maraakus asked.

The kalnath hissed and growled, but made no attempt to get to its feet. Its sides heaved and the remaining red eye glared at them. Its mouth opened and its teeth flashed in the light from their torches and Grommdum's staff. Its clawed front feet uncurled and its broken, horny claws scratched loudly on the cold stone floor.

"Alyna is saying that Balsephus is being affected by the proximity of the amulet to Ilka's dagger," Grommdum explained, "and I tend to agree. The kalnath was functioning well until we entered Jodac's private chambers. Now it's moving slowly and with great difficulty. It might not be dying, but it's been weakened. Perhaps we can hasten that process—maybe immobilize it completely."

Maraakus sat up a little straighter. "I can't imagine how you intend to do that, but you have my undivided attention."

Grommdum smiled and Alyna knelt before Maraakus and took his right hand in both of hers. She stared into his eyes and spoke in a low voice. "We may yet get out of here alive," she told him.

He saw that her hands were steady and she displayed none of the fear he had seen just a short time before. What he did detect, however, was an air of barely suppressed excitement.

"When I was looking at Jodac's remains," she continued, "I saw a depression in the center of his chest—precisely the size and shape of the amulet. You saw how the fingers of one hand were missing? Broken off? Those fingers were once pressed to his chest, covering the amulet. Keam and Andor took the amulet from Jodac's body." She looked up at Grommdum and the old elf nodded.

"Go on," Maraakus said. "I'm listening."

"Ilka's dagger still has great power. Grommdum and I felt it quite clearly. That's how Ilka was able to penetrate Jodac's defenses. But something else happened when she plunged the dagger into his breast. Do you recall what Ilka said about Balsephus—how the kalnath reacted?"

Maraakus nodded.

"Balsephus stood as stone because he *was* stone!" Alyna declared. "You see? Ilka didn't know about the amulet because Jodac wore it around his neck, concealed beneath his clothing. When she plunged the dagger into his breast, the amulet and the dagger were almost touching. This resulted in a stalemate— a perfect balance between the evil power of Jodac's amulet and the powerful forces of good cast into the dagger by Ilka."

"And that condition existed until Keam and Andor found a way into this mountain," Maraakus said.

"That's right," Alyna declared. "When the boys took the amulet from Jodac's body, they upset a very delicate balance. The stalemate between the forces of good and evil was broken and Balsephus resumed killing in Stridgenfel Valley."

Maraakus looked up at Grommdum and the old elf smiled. "Are you certain of this?" he asked.

Grommdum nodded slowly.

"Then Ilka survived because Jodac was wearing the amulet?" Danis asked. "Otherwise, Balsephus would have killed her."

"Without a doubt," Grommdum said. "As General Maraakus has told us, the outcome of a battle can depend on a simple, minor detail—an unforeseen accident or twist of fate."

Balsephus stirred. It heaved unsteadily to its feet and shuffled across the sleeping chamber. Thrusting its massive head into the narrow entrance, the kalnath stared at them for a long while, then began biting at the solid rock surrounding the passageway entrance, snarling and hissing in frustration. Finally, it gave up and sank down on its belly, watching, waiting with one huge forefoot pushed into the passageway.

"Then all we have to do is put the amulet back?" Maraakus asked.

Grommdum frowned. "I do not know," he admitted. "At best, that might restore whatever conditions existed before Keam and Andor took the amulet from Jodac's body. But that wouldn't destroy Balsephus—it didn't before."

Balsephus finally gave up. It crawled back to its former position and collapsed on a pile of rubble from the demolished masonry wall. Its red eye remained open, but now it was blinking.

"Are you sure Balsephus isn't dying before our eyes?" Maraakus asked. "If so, we could just wait it out."

"No," Alyna said, shaking her head. "The two objects are hurting it, but I don't believe it's dying."

Maraakus sighed. "Then we'll return the amulet to Jodac's body and get out of here. Danis, give me the amulet."

Danis opened the breast pocket of his jerkin and felt around with his fingers. A look of panic crossed his face. He searched the pockets of his breeches, then looked at Maraakus. "By all the gods!" he muttered, feeling again in his breast pocket. "I've lost the amulet! It could be anywhere in this place!"

"No!" Alyna insisted. "It's somewhere close to Jodac—close to the dagger! That's why Balsephus is acting so strangely!"

"Of course," Maraakus muttered. "It's out there in the study—where Danis fell." He stood quickly and went to the entrance of the passageway.

Grommdum jumped up and followed. When he struck his walking staff on the floor, the ball of light above its tip streamed out into the darkness like a beam of sunlight through a forest canopy. He moved it slowly, much as a man might search for a lost coin with a small lantern.

"Well, well," Grommdum muttered. "The gods are truly merciful—as my old friend the klersep would say. Do you see it?"

They all gathered quickly behind Grommdum and he moved the beam of light across the floor. Beyond what remained of the masonry wall, the floor of Jodac's study was strewn with rocks and books and papers. The marble top and one wooden pedestal from the altar lay on the floor, broken in pieces by Balsephus's heavy feet; however, Jodac's mummy lay undisturbed in the corner with the head barely visible from behind the altar's undamaged pedestal.

"And right there is our amulet," Grommdum said. As he moved the light in a small circle on the study floor, the pink crystal flashed brightly and the gold chain sparkled. The amulet was less than two feet from Jodac's head.

Danis moaned.

"I see it," Maraakus said softly. "Unfortunately, Balsephus is closer to the amulet than we are."

"Too bad it didn't bounce up onto Jodac's chest." Danis joked.

"We're not finished yet!" Maraakus vowed. "There's always more than one way to skin an ugly, over-grown lizard!"

CHAPTER NINETEEN

"Shoot it again, Danis," Maraakus said. "I want to see our evil little friend's reaction one more time."

"With pleasure," Danis said.

The bowstring hummed and the arrow embedded itself in the kalnath's right shoulder. Balsephus flinched slightly, then crawled backward to its former position near the base of the ruined masonry wall.

"It may be slowing down," Maraakus observed, "but it can still move fast enough to be dangerous." He watched Balsephus for a bit longer, then he and Danis retreated deeper into the narrow passageway and sat down with Grommdum and Alyna.

"While Balsephus appears to be resting, I think it's attempting to heal itself," Alyna said. "The amulet and the dagger must be brought closer together."

"How can we do that?" Danis asked.

"By drawing that beast out of the room," Maraakus replied. "I want you to create a diversion, Danis. Go out through the other end of this passageway and come up behind it. Take your time aiming and put an arrow in the back of its head. When it goes after you, run to the throne room and get back through the secret door. After you've drawn him out of the room, I'll wrap the amulet's chain around the dagger's hilt."

"It won't take me long to get behind it," Danis assured them. After selecting the smallest torch, he gave them all a wide grin and trotted away toward the throne room.

Alyna frowned and looked at Grommdum. "I should be the one who picks up the amulet," she said.

"What?" Maraakus asked. "I can't let you—"

"One moment," Grommdum said. "Let's hear what she has to say. Go on, child."

"I don't know why," she said, "but I must be the one who brings the amulet and the dagger together."

"Are you convinced of this?" Grommdum asked. "Are you certain enough to risk your life?"

"Yes," she answered, "I've never been so certain of anything in my life. Not only do I feel drawn to that dagger, but I no longer fear the amulet. I can't explain how I know this, but I'm the one who should bring them together. You must believe me!"

"I do believe you, my child," Grommdum replied. "Maraakus and I will give you as much time as possible."

"What are you saying?" Maraakus protested, still shaking his head. "She could be killed!"

Grommdum smiled. "So could you, Maraakus," he said. "And so could Danis. And I'm old, but certainly not immortal.

Yet I trust Alyna's instincts in this particular matter, so I must insist that she be allowed to do as she thinks best."

The old elf's face was expressionless, but his sharp, black eyes glittered. Maraakus knew instantly that it would do no good to argue. Alyna was smiling and her expression was serene and unafraid. In some strange, undetermined way, she seemed changed and he experienced a momentary sense of loss and deep regret. Then, as if to allay his concern and soothe his confused emotions, she leaned forward to kiss him on the cheek.

"I know what to do," she told him. "We could never have gotten this far or be so close to a solution without you and Danis. But now the time has come when you must trust us—Grommdum and me."

Without answering, Maraakus got to his feet and walked back toward the mouth of their safety tunnel. With his sword balanced in his right hand, he stopped less than ten feet from the entrance and waited for Danis to come up behind Balsephus. Grommdum and Alyna eased up behind Maraakus. Several moments passed; then a torch flickered in the southwest corner of the study.

Suddenly Balsephus emitted a series of loud croaking sounds, clambered to its feet and lumbered backward over the crumbled masonry wall and into the study. As the rampaging beast swung ponderously around, Maraakus saw an arrow protruding from the back of its head. Then Danis raised his bow and a second arrow embedded itself in the kalnath's throat.

The torch Danis had carried burned weakly on the tunnel floor, but provided enough light to enable the young man to shoot. He stepped back two paces and loosed a third arrow into the creature's chest, whereupon Balsephus lowered its head and made a staggering charge toward its attacker.

Danis immediately sent a fourth arrow into the creature's neck, snatched up his torch, and fled back toward the main hallway. Balsephus stumbled after him and the tunnel echoed with the monster's bellows of rage and the young man's taunting shouts.

Yet Balsephus might abandon the chase at any moment, Maraakus told himself. Moreover, the great beast was moving much faster than they had anticipated and. . . .

As fear for Alyna's safety mounted, filling him with a cold dread, Maraakus made his decision. "Keep Alyna back!" he shouted. "I'll do this!"

He jumped out of the tunnel, tripped on a loose stone and fell heavily. A stabbing pain raced through his body as his head slammed hard against the stone floor. Slowly, painfully, he drew his knees under his body and sat back on his heels, dazed and unable to regain his footing.

"Hurry, Alyna!" Grommdum shouted.

"No!" Maraakus protested. "Get back! *Get Back!*"

A loud, ominous hissing filled the room and Maraakus struggled to his feet just as Balsephus lumbered back into the room.

"Alyna!" Maraakus managed to shout.

Grommdum raised his staff over his head with both hands and turned to face Balsephus. And as the huge creature reared up and raised its clawed forefeet, a stark white light filled the room, pouring from the ancient walking staff in a series of blinding flashes.

"Stay back, Maraakus!" Grommdum shouted. "She has it!"

Maraakus shielded his eyes and saw Alyna kneeling beside Jodac's mummy. She was holding the amulet in her left palm. She, too, was nearly blinded by the flashing light and her right hand fumbled at the dagger as she attempted to wrap the chain around its hilt. Balsephus stood perhaps ten feet behind her with its heavy, clawed forefeet hanging over her head. But it stood motionless! A low, croaking sound came from its throat. As the kalnath stared down at her, its single red eye was little more than a gleaming slit on the side of its head.

Alyna's fumbling hands struck the dagger's hilt—a glancing blow that had little force—but the dagger that had been plunged so deeply through Jodac's breastbone came loose and clattered to a rest in front of her knees. Her hand darted to the floor and she raised the dagger over the amulet; the two objects were only inches apart.

"It is nearly done!" Grommdum shouted. *"Stay back!"*

The walking staff flickered unsteadily. "I can sustain this level no longer!" Grommdum shouted. Then the flashing light from his staff disappeared, but the chamber was not plunged into the utter darkness Maraakus expected.

Maraakus turned quickly and saw that Alyna's body was surrounded by a brilliant white glow. He watched with increasing anxiety and morbid fascination as the point of Ilka's dagger descended toward the pink crystal.

Then Balsephus's head slumped forward and a curious, whirling blue glow appeared at the creature's feet and moved slowly up its body. When it reached the paralyzed kalnath's head it disappeared with a loud snapping sound. Balsephus shuddered. The red glow from his eye winked out. And when the scaly green skin under the creature's throat darkened and the burned scales on its back and sides faded to a dull gray, Maraakus realized that Alyna and Grommdum had been right. Balsephus had once again become solid stone!

A series of flashing lights stroked the room like silent lightning from a distant thunderstorm. Swirling patterns of vivid reds and yellows pulsated on the stone ceiling, while thrusting spears of blue and white stabbed the darkness. The chamber began to tremble with the sound of thunder.

Again and again, the lights parted and swirled like miniature whirlwinds, darting away, swooping down to the floor and combining with loud cracking and popping sounds, retreating and reforming, separating only to rush quickly together with ever-increasing violence.

He looked back at Alyna and saw that the dagger's point was nearly in contact with the amulet's crystal. Her head was thrown back and she was screaming; her arm trembled with her efforts to force the dagger ever closer to the pink stone.

"*Ilkaaaa!*" she screamed.

Maraakus stepped forward, then slumped to his knees. "By the very gods! She's been driven mad!"

"No!" Grommdum answered. "Alyna has gone into her Power!"

Danis emerged from the narrow passageway and Maraakus seized him by the shoulders and pulled him down to the floor.

"Ilka and Jodac now finish the battle that was joined long ago!" Grommdum shouted.

Maraakus stared, amazed by the darting lights on the chamber's ceiling. They swirled and merged and separated repeatedly, changing in hue until only two colors remained: a dark, luminescent red at one end of the room and a pure, shimmering white at the other.

"As you command!" Alyna shouted. Then a sputtering blue spark jumped from the dagger to the amulet and Alyna's face contorted with obvious pain. The red and white lights snapped and crackled as they flowed together on the ceiling, and great claps of thunder split the air. Fragments of stone flew about them like wind-driven hail, and Maraakus, Danis, and Grommdum flung themselves flat on the floor.

A terrifying cacophony of fiendish shrieks and moans filled their ears and seemed to come from all directions—from the very stone of the mountain—and the floors and walls of the chamber trembled.

Maraakus saw the tip of the dagger make contact with the crystal and he saw Balsephus's right forearm fall from its body. Its right rear leg crumbled. Then the huge, transmogrified figure of Jodac's conjured servant toppled over, scattering small chunks of rubble in all directions.

Alyna gave a hoarse shout. Her arm was shaking, but she pressed the dagger down and its tip pierced the pink crystal. A thin wisp of black smoke drifted up from the amulet and Maraakus watched, stunned and horrified, as the dagger emerged slowly from the back of Alÿna's left hand. A thin rivulet of blood ran down the rusty blade and dripped on the front of her cloak. He started forward but Grommdum's hands restrained him.

"Do not interfere!" the elven mage shouted. *"You cannot help her!"*

A terrifying humming sound caused them to look up, and Maraakus saw the red and white lights merging into a single, pulsating ball that darted back and forth above Alyna, bouncing from wall to wall, rolling about in the dark arches and dodging between the rough-hewn stone beams of the ceiling.

When Ilka's dagger made full penetration into the amulet and came to a stop with the hilt against the surface of the pink crystal, there was a brilliant red flash and Alyna was picked up bodily and flung violently against the wall of the chamber. Her head struck the stone with a dull, cracking sound and she fell in a motionless heap on the floor. Her right arm was twisted behind her back; her eyes were open, staring blindly back at Maraakus.

"Alynaaaa!" Maraakus screamed. He lunged forward but Grommdum and Danis seized him immediately. He struggled to free himself from their hands, but they pressed him hard against the floor and he was suddenly aware that the noise had subsided.

"Stay back!" Grommdum shouted, but Maraakus shoved him away, then twisted out of Danis's grip, scrambled to his feet, and started toward Alyna.

A white ball of light swooped past him and he shrank against the wall. It danced and swirled about the room, then soared up into the darkness of the ceiling and darted about overhead. Then, buzzing like an angry hornet, it moved quickly to the end of the room and hovered directly above Alyna.

It turned slowly at first, then faster and faster. And as the speed of rotation gradually increased, it began to change color. The opaque shimmer dissolved into a silvery sheen, and the rapidly spinning ball of light took on the appearance of a shining, transparent globe.

Then it slowed, barely spinning, and started to expand. As the bottom edge touched Alyna, there was a loud, crackling sound, but it continued to enlarge until it had passed through her and into the stone floor of the chamber. When it stopped, Alyna's broken body lay sheltered under a transparent hemisphere of light.

The globe paused for only a moment. As it began to rise, Alyna rose with it, suspended, floating within the slowly revolving sphere. The trickle of blood at the corner of her mouth faded and disappeared; her right leg straightened; her right arm slowly moved from behind her back.

Halfway to the ceiling, the globe stopped and she began to tilt; her feet settled toward the floor and her head rose toward the ceiling. When she was upright, the transparent globe began another slow descent. It came to a stop just inches above the chamber floor and tendrils of blue light appeared, weaving slow, shifting patterns within the globe and across its shimmering surface.

Suddenly the globe resumed its spinning and became opaque once more, hiding Alyna from view. A loud buzzing filled the chamber and the globe snapped and crackled as it slowly collapsed upon itself. Then a violent clap of thunder shook the room and it vanished.

Alyna stood suspended a few inches above the floor, surrounded by a white aura that duplicated the lines of her body and clothing. The dagger lay on the floor before her, but the ivory handle was only a gray crust of ash, and the bent, blackened blade was inserted through a smoking cinder.

A strong, moaning wind arose to extinguish their guttering torches. With steadily increasing force, it scattered the contents of the chamber in a whirlwind of debris, a confusing mixture of small stones, books, and sheets of parchment that flowed around Alyna like water around a large stone in a river. Then the wind was gone and there was only silence.

Alyna opened her eyes and looked at him. The white aura surrounding her body faded and she stepped down from some invisible support and walked slowly in their direction. The only light in the room—a now greatly weakened light—came from Grommdum's walking staff.

Maraakus got slowly to his feet. He took a step forward and stopped. This simply was not possible, he told himself. He had seen her flung violently across the room and clearly heard the sound of her head hitting the hard stone wall. There had not been the smallest movement of her body, not the faintest flicker of life in her open eyes. Yet she stood silently before him. The same pale blue eyes stared back at him, brimming with tears that sparkled in the light of Grommdum's staff. He wiped his hands over his face, smearing wet streaks of dirt across his cheeks.

As though sensing his relief—and his confusion—she smiled and her lips parted. "I love you, General Maraakus," she said. Her voice was low and soft, barely more than a whisper.

She smiled. He knew she was waiting for him to speak, but he was unable to say the words that formed in his throat. Instead, he reached for her injured hand, but she stepped back quickly and raised both hands before her. He saw no evidence of a wound in her left palm, but a shadow—perhaps a twinge of momentary pain—flickered in her pale blue eyes.

"Do not touch me," she whispered. "The last remnants of Ilka's power are not yet dissipated. You might be harmed."

There was a cold, awkward silence in the room. He turned to see Grommdum and Danis watching them. Danis was kneeling on the floor. His face was pale and he stared back with a puzzled frown. Grommdum leaned heavily on his old walking staff and regarded Alyna with a curious, appraising expression. Then he gave her a knowing smile, nodded, raised a trembling hand, and let it fall back to his side.

Finally, it was Alyna who broke the silence. Her voice was

soft but there was also an unmistakable sound of strength and confidence.

"It is over now," she said to Grommdum. "The last vestige of Jodac's magic is broken. His amulet and his kalnath have both been destroyed."

"Indeed," Grommdum replied. "Yet one task remains. The destruction of these dark chambers."

She gave just the smallest nod of her head.

"What about the treasure?" Danis asked, looking from Grommdum back to Maraakus and Alyna. "Can we keep any of it?"

"You may keep it all—if you can carry it down the mountain," Grommdum answered. "There is enough to make the entire village wealthy. Yet you must remember that the greatest reward comes from an appreciation of the wonders nature can create."

"You're right, of course," Danis agreed, "and if there's as much treasure as you say, a man would have to travel a far distance to find a more appreciative fellow than me."

Grommdum chuckled and threw his arm across the young man's shoulders. "I must spend more time with you, Danis," he said. "You have sadly neglected your philosophical training. Too much emphasis on the martial skills and too little on refining your inner sensibilities." He led them all down the stairs to Jodac's temple room.

They entered through what now appeared to be a simple, open doorway. Grommdum struck his staff on the floor and it blazed up with its customary brilliance. He leaned the staff against the edge of a table and went immediately to the altar and picked up a wand made from ebony and inlaid with gold. This he handed to Alyna. Then he circled the room, stopping only once to take down two small books bound with red leather. He slipped these into a pocket within his outer cloak, closed a large book that was lying on a table and tucked it under his arm.

"And this," he said, handing Alyna the large blue diamond, "Shall be your talisman, the symbol of your authority. It is the custom in Refuge for a tutor to assign a name and a talisman to his student. Henceforth, you shall be known as Alyna, Sorceress of the Blue Diamond. You, my child, shall outshine this magnificent stone."

Alyna smiled and slipped the diamond into her pocket.

"That is all you and I require," Grommdum told her. "The rest of Jodac's magical possessions are evil in nature and should be buried with his remains."

Then he turned to Danis and Maraakus. "Take what you will," he said. "What is not taken shall be sealed forever inside these chambers."

Maraakus took hold of a large wooden trunk, dumped a collection of old robes onto the floor, and tossed in several stacks of gold and silver ingots. The alabaster urns containing precious stones were dumped into the trunk and completely buried under large rubies and emeralds taken from the long wooden tables. Next he emptied the silver bowls filled with grape-sized pearls and poured in a large box of diamonds.

Danis had been standing silently, just inside the room. "Danis!" Maraakus said. The young man looked up, startled from his trance. "Start gathering it up," Maraakus told him.

Once awakened, Danis scurried about, clearing shelves of more gold ingots, which he threw into the trunk along with heavy figurines cast from gold and additional leather bags of pearls and diamonds. The larger gemstones, those resting on display bases, were stuffed into Maraakus's rucksack after he dumped its contents out onto the floor.

Next, Danis raked together a pile of large gold coins and began stuffing them into his pockets. He laughed loudly as a pocket split and a shower of treasure poured out the leg of his breeches.

Maraakus looked up to see the young man standing in a puddle of gleaming gold coins and colored stones.

"You will find that a man can carry only so much heavy gold in his pockets!" Grommdum told him.

"Let's leave this place," Alyna said finally. "I need to get out into the fresh air."

Carrying the heavy trunk between them, Maraakus and Danis stumbled after Grommdum and Alyna. Through sheer determination and considerable effort, they managed to drag it up the stairs, through Jodac's quarters to the larger tunnel, and out to the main hallway.

After a brief rest, they heaved the trunk from the floor and carried it toward the hole in the mountain. No words were spoken until they were passing the body of young Keam, still resting under the tapestry Maraakus had used to cover him.

"Shall we take Keam home?" Danis asked.

"No, Danis," Alyna answered. "We'll not disturb him further, nor tell his family of the horrors we found in Jodac's private temple. That would bring them no comfort. But I want to say a few words for Keam before we leave him."

After drawing back the tapestry, Alyna knelt and placed one hand on the dead boy's chest. A series of soft words flowed from her lips. Then she pulled the tapestry back over the body, looked up and nodded.

"From this day forward," she said, "the Pinnacle will not only be a tomb for Keam, but a memorial to the others as well. I think they would like to be remembered by something as permanent as a mountain." Then she and Grommdum led the way up a rising slope and out into late afternoon sunlight.

❧ ❧ ❧

Maraakus and Danis wrestled the heavy trunk through the fallen tree and dropped it in the middle of the path. They walked back to find Grommdum sitting on a rock before the dark entrance and Alyna standing to one side, looking out over the valley and village of Stridgenfel. A bitter wind whipped her cloak about her legs and blew her dark hair across her face, but she seemed not to notice the cold.

"Give her a moment," Grommdum whispered. "An important decision is being made."

"What kind of decision?" Maraakus inquired.

But even as the old elf put a finger to his lips in a gesture for silence, Alyna turned to face them. "Would you walk with me?" she asked Maraakus.

Taking him by the hand, she led him to a place apart from Grommdum and Danis, to the flight of stairs leading up to the Pinnacle's summit. After seating herself on the lowest step, she brushed back her hair and gave him a wistful smile.

"I love you," she said, her voice was soft and husky, filled with restrained emotion.

"And I love you," he told her.

Reaching down, he caressed her cheek with the backs of his fingers. She covered his hand with her own, pressing it hard against her face.

"This . . . trouble in Stridgenfel is over," he said. "Come with me to Koeinstadt."

"My heart is breaking," she told him. "But we both know it is not completely finished—not yet. And just the thought of being separated from you is nearly more than I can bear. It's as if some cold hand has suddenly seized my heart and I fear that it will stop beating. Yet I must go with Grommdum to Refuge. You must return to Koeinstadt without me."

He started to speak, but she raised her hand and placed a finger on his lips. "Wait," she whispered. "Please let me say this while I have the courage to do so—while traces of Ilka's power still linger in my mind. Otherwise, I shall be blinded by my love for you.

"Grandmother had a home and a husband and a family," she continued. "I want those things too, but. . . ."

A single tear slid down her cheek. He reached out and wiped it away with one finger. "I know," he whispered.

Reaching down, he took both her hands in his own, then turned her left hand up and kissed her palm. This whole trip to Stridgenfel had turned out so very different than he had anticipated. It was truly a strange and complicated clash of duty and jumbled emotions. He could not think of the proper words to express what he knew they both were feeling, so he knelt down before her and kissed her gently on the lips. She leaned forward and buried her face in his shoulder.

After a while, she stood and took him by the hand. "Come," she said, "let us finish our work and go home." Her voice trembled, but her expression conveyed only strength and resolve.

After leading him back to the others, she turned to Grommdum and the old elf nodded slowly before speaking. "Alyna and I will close this mountain," he told Maraakus. "Never again shall there be access to Jodac's chambers. Take Danis with you. Go down past the fallen tree and wait for us there."

Following Grommdum's instructions Maraakus took Danis through the fallen tree and they looked back to see Alyna and Grommdum standing to one side of the dark entrance.

"You must help me," he heard Grommdum say to Alyna.

With her right hand in his left, the elven mage faced the mountain. As he raised his walking staff, Alyna raised her left fist above her head. For a moment they stood motionless. Then the mountain began to tremble.

Maraakus and Danis fell to their knees as a loud rumbling came from deep within the Pinnacle. Wave after wave of wind-driven dust poured from the dark hole and Maraakus realized that Jodac's chambers were being demolished. With every violent belching of the mountain, another section of his evil stronghold was being destroyed.

After what seemed like a very long time, the wind carried the dust away and nothing remained but the enlarged, black hole. Then Alyna waved her hand and Grommdum pointed his staff at the opening. They spoke identical words—soft lilting phrases in some foreign tongue—then Alyna thrust her hand forward and Grommdum shook his old wooden staff.

A steady rumbling was heard, but there was no gushing cloud of dust. A strange, blue light appeared around the edges of the opening and the granite rock shimmered like dross on the surface of melted lead. Then the sides of the opening flowed together; the rumbling stopped and the hole was gone.

"Now it is truly finished," Grommdum said, as he guided Alyna through the fallen tree.

Maraakus took a last look at the mountain. Where moments before he had seen a dark, gaping hole, he now saw only smooth, gray stone. He signaled to Danis and they followed Alyna and Grommdum toward the ledges that would take them to the bottom of the Pinnacle.

Epilogue

Two days later, Maraakus was once again mounted on his black horse as it stood outside the west gate of the village. Rain had moved over the valley during the night, followed by a cold, bitter wind that drove the rain eastward, leaving behind a world glazed with ice—a world that shimmered and sparkled as though it were dipped in liquid diamonds.

Danis was leaning forward in his saddle, talking with Grommdum and the old klersep. Alyna sat on her dappled mare and waited patiently as Rafin adjusted the bridle. She was dressed in leather riding clothes and wearing boots that reached up to her knees. Behind her, secured to her saddle with thongs, lay a rolled bundle of clothing that contained her grandmother's book and the wand Grommdum had taken from Jodac's altar.

At the front of her saddle, under her left leg, she carried a small sword with a silver hilt—a present from Relius the Armorer, Danis's father. A small, thin dagger was stuck through a dark blue sash knotted around her waist to keep her fleece cloak securely closed and under her right arm she carried a small waterskin.

Reaching out, Maraakus touched her on the arm, then took her hand with his hard, calloused fingers and said, "It's too cold to travel."

"Yet you and Danis are riding south," she replied.

"That's different," he grumbled. "We're accustomed to the cold."

"And I'll soon become accustomed to it, too," she assured him. "Please don't be worried. Grommdum said you could come to Refuge in the spring."

He noticed the tremor in her voice. "Yes," he said softly. "I'll come when winter has broken."

"Then I'll await your arrival," she whispered, wiping tears from her eyes.

"I'd feel better if you carried some weapon other than your walking staff," Rafin said to Grommdum. "Would you like a small sword—maybe a long, sharp lance? From personal experience, I know there are still roving bands of deserters wandering about."

Alyna laughed and Rafin turned to look at her. "We'll be perfectly safe," she assured him.

Maraakus looked again at the western sky. "It'll snow today. Can't you wait until this storm has passed?"

"It will be much warmer when we enter the woodlands," Grommdum replied. "And there are shelters along the way. As for the dangers you fear, I have been walking this land for more years than all of you have lived, my friend. My staff is all I have ever needed. Besides, only a witless fool would challenge the combined power of my staff and that of Alyna, Sorceress of The Blue Diamond. And there would be little to fear from one so stupid."

Grommdum was smiling but Maraakus was not convinced. "What direction do you travel?" he asked.

The old elf lifted his staff and pointed west. "We'll follow this footpath down to the Dove, then go directly west into what you call the Great Shadow Forest. By noon today, we will meet the trail to Refuge."

"The trail is marked?"

Grommdum smiled. "Oh, yes," he replied. "But human eyes would not see it. In what direction do you travel?"

"Danis and I will go south through the Sleeping Sisters."

"Then his father has given his permission."

Maraakus grinned. "Relius said Danis works hard and willingly, but has no true love for the forge."

"Ah," Grommdum said. "A man should seek the work he truly loves, I suppose. And you, Rafin?"

"I will remain here," Rafin said. "At my age, I try to avoid winter travel."

Grommdum smiled and stuck out his hand. "Sometimes we get smarter as we get older," he agreed. "Good-bye, Rafin. Alyna will be well cared for." He shook Rafin's big hand with a strong grip.

"You have your pearl?" Maraakus asked.

"Indeed," Grommdum said, patting his pocket. "I will tell my people how it was recovered. Take care that you use your treasure wisely, Maraakus, for the benefit of all your people."

Maraakus nodded. "Rafin and Alyna have turned over a large portion to Hadrax, the village baker. It will be administered by the village fathers to establish lines of trade with other villages. A strong commercial and trading network should be of value to the whole kingdom. Perhaps the wetakia would like to consider a line of trade with Luwynn?"

Grommdum smiled, "Perhaps," he said. "We might be willing to discuss that at some future time."

"Another portion was given so that the temple may be restored," the klersep told Grommdum. "A separate fund is being established to help needy families in Stridgenfel."

"And a generous portion was set aside for the wetakia," Rafin said.

"Give that portion to this old fool, too," Grommdum said, jerking his thumb at the priest. "We have little need of such things in Refuge."

Rafin grinned. "I'll see to it," he promised.

The priest shook Grommdum's hand. "Take care on the road, old man," he said, dabbing at his eyes with his sleeve. Then he hugged Grommdum and walked away toward the west gate.

Grommdum smiled, then lifted his right hand and waved. "I am not a man! I am an elf, you old. . . ." He shook his head wearily. "I will be glad to have a rest from your incessant questioning, Antodais!" he shouted.

The priest lifted his hand and waved, then disappeared through the gate.

Danis laughed. "The priest is named Antodais? I know a Thrackian boy by that name who comes with his father to buy weapons."

"Yes," Grommdum said. "The old priest's mother was a Thrackian. The name means 'furious warrior,' and suits him well, don't you think?" He and Danis grinned at each other.

Grommdum shook hands with Danis, then rubbed his hand over the soft muzzle of Maraakus's horse. "This is the first of these creatures that I have found to be trustworthy," he declared, hiding his face in the horse's mane. Then he lifted his right hand above his head in a gesture of farewell, turned away, and walked quickly down the footpath toward the river.

Rafin patted Alyna's horse on the neck, then handed her the reins. "See that you stay close to Grommdum," he said.

"I will," she promised. Then she leaned down and kissed him

on the cheek. As she wiped her eyes on the sleeve of her cloak, Rafin walked away toward the village gate.

"You will come to me at the proper time," Alyna asked. "I have your promise?"

Maraakus looked down the footpath where Grommdum was striding rapidly away. As though he could still hear their conversation, the old elf lifted his hand. Four fingers were spread and pointed up at the cloudy sky.

"I will meet Grommdum here in four months," he promised. "When the first spring moon is full, I will come to Refuge."

She smiled, leaned forward, and lifted her face. He bent down to kiss her. Then she touched her heels to the dappled mare. It stepped forward and trotted quickly down the footpath. When she caught up with Grommdum, she slowed the horse to a walk, keeping pace beside the old elf.

At the far end of the planting fields, Maraakus saw the old elf turn, look back toward the village, and raise his staff over his head. Alyna waved, then she and Grommdum disappeared into the forest.

Maraakus took a deep breath and expelled it with a long sigh. In less than a month he had seen things that could never be explained with human logic. He had met the woman he loved, witnessed true magic, talked with and fought beside a member of the ancient races, and, finally, he had helped defeat a powerful, evil force. Now he could go home. But in just four months he'd return to Stridgenfel, meet Grommdum, and accompany him to Refuge. Until then. . . .

"Honor to us all!" Rafin shouted.

Looking up, Maraakus saw Rafin standing by the west gate with a big fist raised overhead.

"And to our cause!" Maraakus shouted back.

The old soldier grinned, then turned and disappeared through the gate.

Maraakus looked west, but only bare-limbed trees waved back.

"In the spring, Alyna," he said softly to himself.

"What did you say?" Danis asked.

"It's going to snow," Maraakus answered. "I hope we can make it through the pass before it gets too deep."

The black horse moved out at the touch of a heel and Maraakus turned to take one last look toward the Great Shadow Forest, just as the first snowflakes began to fall.

If you enjoyed *Runes of Autumn,*
look for these other great titles from

The greatest science fiction character of all time returns in

Buck Rogers
A Life in the Future

From the moment of the terrible crash that should have ended everything, the very life of Anthony "Buck" Rogers hung by the thinnest of threads . . .

. . . until he regained consciousness more than four hundred years later!

Here, for the first time, is the true story of Buck Rogers's life in the future . . . as only best-selling author **Martin Caidin** can tell it.

Now available in hardcover from TSR!

Mary H. Herbert's acclaimed saga of the Dark Horse Clans
continues in

Winged Magic

Peace has come at last to the Dark Horse Clans, but when
Kelene and Gabria are kidnapped by a Turic tribesman, the frag-
ile truce is threatened and mother and daughter are forced into
helping the diabolical Fel Karak.

A mysterious tribe from the mountains, Kelene's winged
Hunnuli Demira, and the people of the Clans join forces to
battle a fearsome magic more powerful than any they have ever
seen.

Another evocative tale by **Chrys Cymri**, author of
Dragons Can Only Rust

Dragon Reforged

Sentenced to walk the Changewinds as punishment for his
crimes, Gonard leaves the safety of the Settlement and submits
himself to the irradiated blasts of air that can make even the
most intelligent being go mad.

Seeking shelter from the winds and his own haunted past, the
dragon finds his way to a place where his tortured soul and crip-
pled body might at last be healed.

But such is not to be. For forces even more powerful than the
winds drive Gonard and his companions to an inexorable con-
frontation with the nature of life . . . and the finality of death.

When an Indonesian nation uses itself as collateral against a debt and can't pay up, Fiscal Development, Inc. calls on the F.R.E.E.Lancers for help. The agency soon finds that there is more at stake than money, as ancient inventions team with new technologies to endanger the fate of the world.

F.R.E.E.Fall

In a technological future, ancient artifacts and scrolls have little relevance. But in the country of Malacca, new archeological discoveries lead to incomprehensible leaps in technology. Lee Won Underhill and the F.R.E.E.Lancers enter a desperate race to seize control of Malacca and defeat a rogue SAS officer, who commands a force of deadly metables equal to their own.

Fast paced action by **Mel Odom**, available now from TSR!